Die a Little

A Novel

MEGAN ABBOTT

POCKET
BOOKS

LONDON • SYDNEY • NEW YORK • TORONTO

First published in the USA by Simon & Schuster Inc., 2005
First published in Great Britain by Pocket Books UK, 2008
An imprint of Simon & Schuster UK Ltd
A CBS COMPANY

1 3 5 7 9 10 8 6 4 2

Simon & Schuster UK Ltd
Africa House
64-78 Kingsway
London WC2B 6AH

www.simonsays.co.uk

Simon & Schuster Australia
Sydney

A CIP catalogue record for this book is available from the British Library

ISBN: 978-1-84739-346-3

The author gratefully acknowledges permission to reprint the following
material: 'Shanghai' by Bob Hilliard and Milton DeLugg © Copyright
1951 by Bourne Co. and Amy Dee Music Corp. c/o Milton DeLugg.
Copyright Renewed. All Rights Reserved. International Copyright Secured.

Book design by Ellen R. Sasahara

Printed by CPI Cox and Wyman, Reading, Berkshire RG1 8EX

For Josh.

Acknowledgments

MY WARMEST GRATITUDE to Paul Cirone for all his efforts and conviction, and to Denise Roy for her keen editorial insight and sustaining guidance. To my early and encouraging readers and dear friends, Christine Wilkinson and Alison Levy. To Darcy Lockman, for her friendship and perpetual support. And without whom: Patricia and Philip Abbott, Joshua Abbott, Julie Nichols, Ralph and Janet Nase, and Jeff, Ruth, and Steven Nase. And most of all, to Joshua Gaylord.

Die a Little

LATER, the things I would think about. Things like this: My brother never wore hats. When we were young, he wouldn't wear one even to church and my mother and then grandmother would force one on his head. As soon as he could he would tug it off with soft, furtive little boy fingers. They made his head hot, he would say. And he'd palm the hat and run his fingers through his downy blond hair and that would be the end of the hat.

When he began as a patrolman, he had to wear a cap on duty, but it seemed to him far less hot in California than in the South, and he bore up. After he became a junior investigator for the district attorney, he never wore a hat again. People often commented on it, but I was always glad. Seeing his bristly yellow hair, the same as when he was ten years old, it was a reminder that he still belonged to our family, no matter where we'd move or what new people came into our lives.

I used to cut my brother's hair in our kitchen every week. We would drink cola from the bottle and put on music and lay down newspapers, and I would walk around him in my apron and press my hand to his neck and forehead and trim away as he told me about work, about the cases, about the other junior investigators and their stories. About the power-mad D.A. and his shiny-faced toadies. About the brave cops and the crooked ones. About all the witnesses, all his days spent trailing witnesses who always seemed like so much smoke dissolving into the rafters. His days filled with empty apartments, freshly extinguished cigarettes, radios still warm, curtains blowing through open windows, fire escapes still shuddering . . .

When I finished the cut, I'd hold out the gilt hand mirror from my mother's old vanity set and he would appraise the job. He never said anything but "That's it, Sis," or "You're the best." Sometimes, I would see a missed strand, or an uneven ledge over his ear, but he never would. It was always, "Perfect, Sis. You've got the touch."

Hours afterward, I would find slim, beaten gold bristles on my fingers, my arms, no matter how careful I was. I'd blow them off my fingertips, one by one.

For their honeymoon, just before New Year's 1954, my brother and his new wife went to Cuba for six days. It was Alice's idea. Bill happily agreed, though his first choice had been Niagara Falls, as was recommended by most of the other married couples we knew.

They came back floating on a cloud of their own beauty,

their own gorgeous besottedness. It felt vaguely lewd even to look at them. They seemed to be all body. They seemed to be wearing their insides too close to the surface of their skin.

There is a picture of Alice. The photographer—I'm not sure who it was—was ostensibly taking a picture of our godparents, the Conrans, on their thirtieth wedding anniversary. But the photographer snapped too late, and Uncle Wendell and Aunt Norma are beginning to exit the frame with the embarrassed elation of those unused to such attention and eager to end it, and what you see instead is Alice's back.

She is wearing a demure black silk cocktail dress with a low-cut V in the back, and her alabaster skin is spread across the frame, pillowing out of the silk and curving sharply into her dark hair. The jut of her shoulder blades and the angular tilt of her cocked arm draw the eye irresistibly. So like Alice. She didn't even need to show her face or have a voice to demand complete attention.

It had all begun not six months before.

My chest felt flooded by my own heart. I could hardly speak, hardly breathe the whole way to the hospital, lights flashing over me, my mind careering. They said, "What is your relation to William King?"

"What's wrong?"

"Are you his wife?"

"What's wrong with my brother?"

But he was fine. He was fine. I was running down the hospital corridor, shins aching from my heels hitting the floor so hard. I was running when I heard his voice echoing, laughing, saw his downy, taffy-colored hair, his handsome, stubby-nosed profile, his hand rubbing the back of his head as he sat on a gurney, smeary smile on his face.

"Lora." He turned, speaking firmly to calm me, to strip the tight fear from my face. Hand out to grab my arm and stop me from plowing clear into him, he said, "I'm fine. I just hit my head, got knocked out, but I'm fine."

"Fine," I repeated, as if to fix it.

His jacket over his arm, his collar askew, he had, I noted with a shiver, a break of browning blood on his shirt.

"Someone hit your car?"

"Nah. Nearly did, but I swerved out of the way. The driver kept going off the road and into a telephone pole. I stopped to help her, and while I was trying to get her out of her car, another car rear-ended it and knocked us both down. It was some show."

He laughed when he said it, which was how I knew the driver was young and pretty, and troubling and helpless, all of which seemed, suddenly to me, to be just what he wanted, what he had been waiting for all along. It happened just like that. I realized it about him just like that, without ever having thought it before.

"Is she all right?"

"She had a concussion, but she's okay. She sprained her wrist trying to break her fall." He touched his own wrist as he said it, with great delicacy. This gesture confirmed it all.

"Why did she veer off the road? What was wrong with her?"

"Wrong? I don't know. I never even . . ."

When the sergeant came by to get more details for his report, he told us that the woman, Alice Steele, would be released momentarily. I asked him if she had been drinking, and he said he didn't think so.

"No, definitely not. She was completely coherent," my brother assured us both. The young sergeant respectfully nodded.

Her eyebrows, plucked and curvilinear like a movie star's, danced around as she spoke: My, how embarrassing—not just embarrassing but unforgivable—her actions were. She never should have been driving after taking a sedative even if it was *hours* before and never should have been driving on such a crowded road when she was so upset and crying over some complications in her life and with the rush to get to her friend Patsy's apartment because Patsy's boyfriend had hit her in the face with an ashtray. And, oh God, she wondered, what *had* happened to Patsy since she was never able to get there because of the accident. Would Patsy be all right? If there were scars, her modeling career would end in a heartbeat, and that would mean more trouble for Patsy, who'd had more than her share already.

Watching, listening, I imagined that this would be how this new woman in my brother's life would always talk, would always be. As it turned out, however, she rarely spoke so hazardously, so immoderately.

She had a small wound on her forehead, like a scarlet lip. It was this wound, I calculated, that had flowed onto my brother's shirtfront. A nurse was sewing stitches into it with long, sloping strokes the entire time she spoke to me.

I tried not to watch too closely as the wound transmuted from labial-soft and deep red to a thin, sharp, crosshatched line with only a trace of pucker. The nurse kept murmuring, "Don't move, don't move," as Alice gestured, twisting with every turn of phrase, never wincing, only offering an occasional squint at the inconvenience.

"Lora. Lora King," I answered.

"You're the wife of my knight in shining armor?"

"No. The sister."

"I'm Alice. Alice Steele. You're smiling."

"No. Not at you."

"Where is that heroic brother of yours, anyway? Don't tell me he's left?"

"No. He's here. He's waiting."

A smile appeared quickly and then disappeared, as if she decided it gave away too much. As if she thought I didn't know.

The three of us in my sedan. I drove them to Bill's car, which was unharmed. I knew he would offer to drive her home and he did and they vanished into his sturdy Chevy like circling dangers. Patti Page trilled from the radio of his car as it drove off. I sat and listened until I couldn't hear it any longer. Then I drove home.

At first, it was the pretext of checking on her recovery.

Then, it was his friend Alice, who needed a ride to the studio, where she worked in the costume department as a seamstress's assistant. She lived with a girlfriend named Joan in a rooming house somewhere downtown.

Then, it was Alice, who had bought him the new tie he wore, with the thin periwinkle stripe.

Next, it was Alice, with whom he'd had chop suey because he happened to be by the studio around lunchtime.

At last, it was Alice over for dinner, wearing a gold blouse and heels and bringing a basket of pomegranates spiced with rum.

I prepared ham with pineapple rings and scalloped potatoes and a bowl of green beans with butter. Alice smoked through the whole meal, sipping elegantly from her glass and seeming to eat but never getting any closer to the bottom of her plate. She listened to my brother avidly, eyes shimmering, and complimented me on everything, her shoe dangling from her foot faintly but ceaselessly. It would be true in all the time I knew Alice that she would never, ever stop moving.

She asked many questions about our childhood, the different places we'd lived, our favorite homes, how we'd ended up in California and why we'd stayed. She asked me if I enjoyed teaching high school and how we'd found such a lovely house and if we liked living away from downtown Los Angeles. She asked me where I got my hair done and if I sewed and whether I enjoyed having a yard because she had "*always* lived in apartments and had never had more than a potted plant and no green thumb besides, but who cares about that, tell me instead about how you keep such lovely petunias in this dry weather and does Bill help at all or is he too busy playing cops and robbers," with a wink and blinding smile toward my rapt brother.

Five months to the day after they met, they decided to marry. The night they told me, I remember there had been a tug over my eye all day. A persistent twitch that wouldn't give. Driving to the restaurant to meet them, I feared the twitch would come at the wrong moment and send me headlong into oncoming traffic.

As I walked in, she was facing my freshly shaved and bright-faced brother, who was all shine and smile. I saw her shoulders rise like a blooming heart out of an hourglass puce-colored dress. He was towering over her, and she was adjusting his pocket square with dainty fingers. From the shimmer lining my dear brother's face, from the tightness in his eyes, I knew it was long over.

The day before they were married, we moved Alice's things from the rooming house in which she'd been living for over a year. It was a large place in Bunker Hill, a house that had once been very grand and now had turned shaggy, with a bucket of sand for cigarettes at the foot of its spiraling mahogany staircase.

Apparently, Bill had been trying to get her to move out since he first visited her there. "I know places like this. I spend days knocking down the doors of places like this," he had told her. "It's no place for you."

But, according to him, she only laughed and touched his arm and said that he should have seen her last place, in a bungalow court where, the first night she spent there, a man stabbed his girlfriend in the stomach with her knitting needle, or a fork, she couldn't remember which. "She was all right," Alice had assured him. "It wasn't deep."

When we helped her pack up, I noticed how many clothes Alice had, and how immaculately she kept them, soft sweaters nestled in stacks of plastic sleeves, hatboxes interlocked like puzzle pieces in the top of her closet, shoes in felt bags, heels stroked in cotton tufts to keep them from being scratched by the hanging shoe tree, dresses with pillowy skirts tamed by sweeping curls of tissue paper or shells of crinkly crepe.

Alice smiled warmly as I marveled at each glorious confection. She said she accumulated most of the clothes from her work at the studio. The seamstresses were often allowed to take cast-off garments deemed too damaged or too worn. No clothes or costumes were ever supposed to be given away but used over and over until the fabric dissolved like sugar. At a certain point, however, the clothes were passed to the girls, either because the designers could do nothing more with them, or as a favor or trade for extra or special work.

So after five years of studio work, Alice had accumulated quite an array of repaired clothes, the most glorious being a dress Claudette Colbert had worn, which was nearly impossible to put on or off. It was a delicate black velvet with netting around the neck, and it made Alice's small chest look positively architectural, like cream alabaster jutting up from her wasp waist.

Our godparents hosted the wedding party after the ceremony at City Hall. The other junior investigators from the D.A.'s office and my fellow teachers from Westridge School for Girls filled the small house.

No one came from Alice's family. Her only guests were a few coworkers from the studio, who sat on a corner couch, smoking and straightening their stockings.

At the time, she said that she had no family to invite, that she was orphaned and alone. She was a native Southern Californian, if there was such a thing. She was born in Santa Monica Hospital to a domestic with Hollywood aspirations and a recently discharged chauffeur. That was all we really knew.

At the party, my eyes could barely leave her, this woman who had entered our life and planted herself so firmly at its sharp center.

She buzzed around the party, hovering with large, rain pail eyes, a body compact, pulled taut over every angle, raw-boned, and a few years or a few ounces away from gaunt, ghostly. Her appeal was a kind of thrilling nervous energy, a railrack laugh that split her face in gleaming abandon.

There was a glamour to her, in her unconventional beauty, in her faintly red-rimmed eyes and the bristly, inky lashes sparking out of them, blinking incessantly, anxiously. Her hair was always perfectly coiffed, always shining and engineered, her lips artfully painted magenta. When she'd turn that black-haired head of hers, a collarbone would pop out disturbingly. She had no curves. She was barely a woman at all, and yet she seemed hopelessly feminine, from her airy walk, her muzzy, bobbing gesticulations, her pointy-toed shoes, and the spangly costume jewelry dangling from her delicate wrists.

Even though Bill and Alice repeatedly urged me to live with them, I moved into a small apartment while they honeymooned.

"I can't imagine you two apart. What is Bill without Lora? Lora without Bill?" Alice would say, dark eyes pounding.

"I'll be closer to school. It'll be easier," I assured them, packing up the chocolate-colored figured rug, white and rose chairs, and rough cream drapes of our living room, the heavy dining room table we'd had since children, the blond bedroom set my grandparents had given me upon my graduating teachers' college.

I moved to a one-bedroom on Pasadena's west side, as Bill and Alice prepared to move from our duplex to a pretty new ranch house in tonier South Pasadena. They bought it with Bill's savings, borrowing against his pension.

It was strange at first. Bill and I had lived together for so long, not just as children but always. As I polished the dining room set, wedged uncomfortably in the corner of the living room of my new apartment, I remembered a thousand evenings spent at the round, knotty table, long nights when I was studying for my certification and Bill was at the police academy. He always wanted to work for the district attorney. He wasn't joining the force because it was in the family (it wasn't), like so many of the others, and he wasn't doing it because he wanted to see action, to be a tough guy. He did it out of a larger purpose that he would never say outright but that I could feel in everything he said, every look he gave as we drove through the city, as we saw the things one can see in a city, driving through, watching, watching everything.

Now, rubbing a soft cloth over each knot in the table, I could nearly picture us seated there, books spread out, coffeepot warm. He would rub his eyes, run a finger under his collar, sometimes pass me a grin like "Lora, look at us, look how devoted we are, look how alike we are, we're the same, really."

And we were. Taking notes, furrowing our brows, our necks curled, craned, sore, and aching, and yet exhilarated, our whole lives beginning and everything waiting for us.

Before my brother met Alice, there were always women telling me, "I can't believe your brother's not married" or "How is it no woman has snatched him up yet?" I never really knew how to answer.

He could have married anyone.

And he had girlfriends, but it never really led anywhere. When I first started teaching, he dated Margie Reichert, the sister of his partner. Tiny with fluffy hair and empty eyes, Margie had the vaguely tubercular look of a child-woman. She often ran into minor troubles generally instigated by her shyness, her difficulty in speaking up before it was too late. When Bill discovered Margie was paying for utilities on her small apartment, in violation of her lease, he spoke with the landlord and ensured Margie receive a refund for the months of bills she'd paid. When Margie's boss at Rush's Department Store fired her for stealing, Bill quickly learned the other salesgirls were using Margie to conceal their own shortchanging. Soon enough, Margie had her job back.

Everyone was certain they would marry.

Somehow, they never did. The time came and passed, and they seemed to see each other less, and Margie decided to move with her family to San Diego after all. There seemed no pressing reason to stay.

Besides, Bill was so absorbed in his job, in getting to where he wanted to go. And we were this team, both moving forward, digging our feet in, making roots. A new family, a family born anew.

In this fashion, six years had passed.

And now, it was as it should be. Bill had found someone. It seemed, at some point, I would, too.

Let me say this about my brother. My brother, he was one of those gleaming men, a jaw sharp, color always flushing up his straightedge cheekbones. And, amid all the masculine rigidity, all the razor lines and controlled flesh, lay a pair of plushy, girlish lips, pouty and pink, and a pair of lovely and nearly endless eyelashes—eyelashes so extravagant that as a young boy he had taken our mother's nail scissors to them. But of course they'd grown back, immutable.

With a more moneyed background you could imagine him as one of those glorious, arrogant, seersucker-suited men out of novels. But with his middlebrow roots, he could never be less than earnest, more than provincial in his views, his tastes.

And yet, there was Alice.

While they lounged in a haze of lovesick in Cuba, a honeymoon far beyond my brother's modest income, their new bungalow filled itself happily, riotously—gifts from family and friends, but also things Alice ordered to set up their new home.

A full set of smooth pink and gray Russel Wright everyday dinnerware, my mother's Haviland china in English Rose, a series of copper fish Jell-O molds, a large twelve-slice chrome toaster, a nest of Pyrex mixing bowls, a gleaming bar set, tumblers, old-fashioneds, and martini glasses with gold-leaf diamonds studding the rims, a bedroom set with soft, dove gray silk quilted coverlets, matching lamps with dove gray porcelain gazelles as their bases, a vanity with a round mirror and a silver deco base, a delicate stool of wrought curlicues holding up a pale peach heart seat cushion, a tightly stuffed and sleekly lined sofa, love seat, and leather wing chairs in the living room, with its green trim, jungle-patterned curtains, and a large brass cage in which a parrot named Bluebeard lived.

The only remnants of our old house, aside from the china and a family desk of plantation oak, are a set of rose-hued photographs, one of Bill and me at ages six and nine, and one of us with our parents in front of a fireplace before their last Christmas, before dying in a base-camp fire overseas, my father in plaid robe and Santa hat perched jauntily, Joel McCrea–handsome, and my mother, all ripe grin and tight curls, tugging us close to her lace-trimmed dress.

Bill and I are so unmistakably siblings, both with rough blond hair, popping eyes, and downy faces, round elbows curling out of matching holiday suspenders. While mine attached to a stiff skirt and Bill's to short pants, our seated poses conceal the distinction.

. . .

When I first visit the newlyweds' house, I can't help but notice there are no framed family photos from Alice's side, not even a stray snapshot. When I ask her why, she says she doesn't have any. Thinking about it, however, she remembers one bit of history she can show me. Running to her closet and back, she brings out an old Culver City newspaper article that ran in honor of the fiftieth anniversary of an establishment called Breuer's Chocolates. Accompanying the story is a photo of a shapely young girl in her teens, a blur of black hair and arms with curlicue dimples, sales smock pulled tightly across her chest, a cloud of airy divinity puffs in front of her.

"That's me, believe it or not." Alice smiles. Finger pressed to the round girl in the picture, she talks about how she used to have a soft white belly, sweetly spreading pale thighs, a faint, faint pocket of lush flesh under her chin. It happened when she was working at Breuer's, making a dollar a day.

As Alice tells it, she would come to work so hungry, having eaten only eggs and hash for dinner the night before. How, after all, could she stand it, inhaling that rich, warm smell all day and not sampling it? It was easier to filch a whole box from the wrapping room than to slip them out individually from the case. All day long, she would make trips to the ladies' room or her locker and savor a piece or two, a waxy cream, a brittle honey-eyed toffee, a dissolving coconut spume.

Of course, she eventually tired of chocolate, but not for a long time, and when she did, there were nougats, jellied candies shaped like wedges of lemon or lime, butterscotch coins she could slide under her tongue all day, paper sacks of sharp candy corns. Oh, she wouldn't be hungry until late at night after a full day at the store. And then a smooth hard-boiled egg or a starchy wedge of day-old was all she needed. A dentist later told her she was lucky to have teeth like a hillbilly, impenetrable.

As I look at the woolly image, she explains how, when she left the chocolate shop for a sewing factory, she lost fifteen pounds in a month, both from working hard, long hours and from nights out with her new girlfriends—other factory girls who brought Alice into their circle, spending nights at the army canteen, dancing and drinking gin fizzes instead of eating dinner and sleeping.

Looking at the younger Alice, however, I'm struck by something. It is clearly her in the picture: her thick eyelashes, upturned nose, wide mouth. But there is something in her face that seems utterly foreign, utterly exotic and strange to me. Like someone I've never met, someone who no longer is.

It is one month after the wedding and long past midnight, and I am lying in bed in my brother's new house, wide awake, thinking I should have made the drive home, where I could have nursed my insomnia with some exams I needed to grade, or at least played the radio or turntable to ease my racing mind. Instead, I am holed up in the makeshift sewing room/guest bedroom, staring at the alarming seamstress dummy lurking out of the darkness. I wonder how early in the morning I can leave without being rude.

Somewhere beyond the door, I hear a faint rustling, and I imagine my brother awake. We would have a late-night talk, chamomile tea or even a cold beer, me curled in a chair and him slouched on the floor, rubbing my feet. We would play records, and he would talk through the case that was bothering him, or I would talk about the student who was troubling me, and the night would curl in on itself so comfortably.

I hear what sounds like pages turning. Someone is definitely up, and it must be my brother. Alice's fourth martini has to have put her in a very sound sleep.

I slide my robe on and make my way to the door. Opening it delicately, and walking down the hall, I see one of the living room lights on. As I move closer, I realize it is only Alice after all. Her legs tucked beneath her on a wing chair, she is paging through one of our thick old family photo albums.

I am about to turn around and head back, not wanting to disturb her, but as I do, my eyes play a funny trick.

I stop suddenly at the archway and find myself stifling a tight gasp. Under the harsh lamp, in sharp contrast to the dark room, her eyes look strangely eaten through. The eyes of a death mask, rotting behind the gleaming facade. A trick of the light somehow—

"Lora!" Alice says, surprised, jolting me out of my thoughts. She realizes how loudly she's said my name and covers her mouth with her hand, smiling. "You scared me."

"I'm sorry," I say. "I couldn't sleep."

"Ditto. Sit down."

I move over to the sofa beside her, tightening the belt on my robe and trying to avoid looking her straight in the eyes, which still have that rotting look, set deeper than her doll-like face.

"I was just looking at some of the old King family history," she whispers with a tone of playful conspiracy.

"Really?" I look over at the pages open in her lap. There are my brother and I fishing on the dock of our grandparents' property, he waving a mangy trout in the air. We were probably around four and seven, and both of us tanned and naked to the waist in a way that makes me blush.

"The faces alone—if it weren't for those little braids tucked behind your ears, I couldn't tell you two apart," Alice says, trying to meet my gaze.

"Yes. Same blond curls, until Dad made Bill get regular military-style cuts."

"And you a little tomboy, too."

"We both liked to fish and play outdoors. Cowboys and Indians, I guess. I don't really remember," I say, even as I remember everything, *even in one wave of sharp grass, rowboat creek, feet pounding tag, whispers from top bunk to bottom in the heavy July night.*

"It feels so different, so . . . impossibly different from my childhood." Alice rubs her brow.

"I guess you were a city girl."

"Hmmm," she murmurs. "That, too. And no brothers or sisters and no grandparents I ever met. And no homestead. I mean, I know you moved a lot because of your father's different posts, but it seems like you always had a real home. A house, the same furniture and things. We always lived in furnished places. I remember instead of counting sheep, I used to recite the places I'd lived: five bungalow courts"—she counted them off on her fingers—"Corrington Arms, El Cielo Court, La Alambra Bungalows, La Cienega Arms, Golden Dreams Bungalows. And eight hotels, four rented rooms, two in-house maid's quarters, and one rented house that my mother skipped out on so fast we left everything behind but a laundry bag full of dirty clothes. We never even had the same car for more than a few months."

Alice grins, as if suddenly remembering. "The only thing that was constant was the set of Johnson Brothers china my father had from his mother and her mother. It dated back to the Gold Rush, I think. When I was little it had twelve place settings. Each move, when my father would pack it up carefully in the same old cloth napkins, there would be fewer pieces. I broke a few washing them. Rough moves broke lots of cups, especially the handles. But mostly my mother would throw plates or saucers at my father when they fought. Surest way to get a reaction out of him."

I smile and feel relieved to see Alice's eyes turn gray-brown, like coffee with cream. It is a story filled with dirty ghosts, yet there's a fondness in the way she tells it, a pleasure in its rangy tumult.

"I always used to sweep up the shards afterward. I can picture the little blue flowers now. One night . . .

"One night, she was so mad, so furious, I remember she cracked one over her own head. And I remember laughing, because it was funny, like in a movie. Like Laurel and Hardy or something. But then it didn't seem funny at all when I looked at her face, which looked cracked, too. There was blood, yes, but it wasn't that. Her face was so . . . unhinged . . . that it was as if it had split. As if she had split." Alice touches her face as she says it, the heel of one hand under her chin, the other on her forehead. "It scared me. My pop, too. He kept looking at her. She was standing still, her arm hanging there, holding the broken shard at her side. She was shaking, but she didn't say anything. Like she was shocked by what she'd done. Like she couldn't believe she'd gone that far."

As Alice tells me this, I turn away from her. I stare hard at my hands, wrung around each other. I am afraid to look over at her because I know what I will see. I will see her eyes turning, always turning back to rot.

After the honeymoon period, when real life had to resume for them, Alice was determined to make a home. She had quit her job, had her last day at the studio just before the wedding. She was so relieved, had found herself disgusted by her work, tearing fabric apart and replacing panels because of a variety of stains left by actresses, stains suggesting encounters had while still in costume. She'd throw them in the bin to be laundered, always asking the laundry girls never to bring her costumes that hadn't gone through them first. She wouldn't miss that, she assured me. Not one bit.

Now, hunched over her Singer, she made curtains for every room, bright curtains that hung stiffly or blew languorously; she painted the walls by hand, apple green, buttercup yellow, crème caramel. She planted tomatoes in one corner of the small yard and dug flower bulbs along the perimeter, trimming the grass around every curve of the small footpath to the front door.

Bill insisted I take all our cooking and baking wares, farm-style pieces of cast iron and heavy wood. It was just as well for Alice, who wanted her own things, and she set out to fit her sunny yellow-painted kitchen with all things modern.

Small, well-chosen pieces, of course. She bought a set of casserole dishes with rattan frames made by Gladding, McBean. She asked my brother for, and received, Broil King by the Peerless Electric Company for her birthday. She bargained successfully with the salesmen at McCreary's Department Store in downtown Pasadena for a prime deal on a set of Samson folding chairs by Shwayder Brothers. She bought a Cornwall Thermo Tray with gold finish and wooden handles for serving hot artichoke hors d'oeuvres and tuna squares.

Only a few times would I actually see Alice cleaning, but the immaculate house revealed that cleaning must have been going on all the time. I could picture her on hands and knees, hair covered in a topknot cloth, scrubbing fervently, greedily, so gladly because nothing seemed to make her happier than seeing pure lines, smooth surfaces, sharp corners, and the smell always of cleanliness, intense, pungent, shaded over with the scent of fresh-cut flowers or a simmering stovetop.

Despite all her prewedding glamour, Alice quickly became the most quiet, the most demure of a quiet and demure set of junior investigators' wives. She was the first to bring the tuna noodle casserole to the new family that moved in, or to the household with the sick mother. She attended church with Bill and often me, turning the pages of the hymnal with her immaculate white gloves, apologizing that her half-Catholic, half-Pentecostal upbringing hadn't prepared her for the Lutheran service we attended.

Almost instantaneously it seemed, Alice, with her fresh and lovely looks and her handsome, upstanding husband, had made friends in the neighborhood. It was not long before she and the other women in the cul-de-sac began buying each other things, visiting gifts, housewarmings. They bought each other mint julep sets made of aluminum and cork, copper fruit bowls, tidbit stands, pink Polynesian chop plates adorned with a black palm frond pattern, spun aluminum nesting bowls with neat reed handles, Pyrex hostess sets for picnics on the back lawns, Klise Frosted Oak relish boats and cheese boards with Lucite inserts, Manta Ray centerpiece bowls with a chic black glaze or elegant figured white, canapé rosettes with three banked levels which as the pretty box said, "make this tray an ideal serving accessory for 'after bridge' and for afternoon teas."

For months, it seemed all she did was bake. She was learning by doing, with Betty Crocker perched on the counter, with *Joy of Cooking*, with our mother's dog-eared collection of country cookbooks. She made a raspberry-coconut jelly roll for a brunch with the Leders and Conlans. A rum-and-cherry-cola marble cake for a cocktail party. Caramel-apple chiffon cupcakes soaked through with Dry Sack cream sherry for the Halloween party. On Bill's birthday, she spent hours making cream-puff swans shaped from what she carefully pronounced as a "pâté à chou." For a block party, almond icebox cake and cornflake macaroons. Chow mein–noodle haystacks and fried spaghetti cookies for a neighborhood association bake sale. For a dinner party, white chocolate grasshopper pie still foaming with melted marshmallows and doused with Hiram Walker. More dinner parties and still racier items, ambrosia brimming with Grand Marnier, a fruit-cocktail gelatin ring nearly a foot high and glistening. As the parties grew more elaborate, more frenetic, bourbon balls studded with pecans and Nesselrode pie with sweet Marsala and chestnuts. Strawberries Biltmore covered with vanilla custard sauce. Baked Alaska drizzled through with white rum. Peach Melba suffused with framboise.

Soon, she had no rival. In the neighborhood and among the investigators' wives, she set all the trends, and everyone else followed.

It was as though she had waited her whole life for this.

As the months passed, however, I began to see glimpses, odd, awry glimpses of a different Alice, an Alice somewhere between the girl in the picture of Breuer's Chocolates and this matchless homemaker. At parties or bridge gatherings, in the ladies' room after three stingers, she'd lean over to me, hot alcohol and perfume, and whisper something like a clue, "When I was a department store model, a customer once paid me seventy-five dollars to come home with her and put on her dead husband's clothes, piece by piece. She played 'I'm Forever Blowing Bubbles' on her turntable over and over all night. She never laid a hand on me, but she might have. Love is funny, isn't it?"

Or "This old roommate of mine, Lois, she bathed every night in rubbing alcohol. She'd bathe in it for hours, and then come out and coat, *coat* her body in jasmine lotion—together, the smell was like a punch in the face.

"Then—listen, Lora—then, one night, my other roommate, Paulette, had a date over and he—his name was Dickie—was on the fire escape smoking. Next thing we hear this scream, horrible, like an animal under a car. Apparently, Dickie had thrown his lit cigarette down the alley and the wind carried it up and through the bathroom window. Lois was just getting out of the bath covered with the alcohol. We ran in, and we got the bath mat around her, rolled her on the floor, like they tell you to do in school.

"Her skin felt like crinkled paper. I could barely look at her. I kept thinking her flesh was going to fall off in my hands. Then it turned soft and shiny, like wax. The bath mat was cheap, and bits of it stuck to her. When Paulette looked down and saw what was happening, she started screaming. I had to slap her three times.

"Lois was okay, some second-degree burns on her stomach and her thighs. What was funny was that Dickie felt so bad, he kept visiting her at the hospital, and the next thing you know, they were a couple. Things happen like that sometimes. It didn't last, those things seldom do, but when I would see them, out in Santa Monica or Hollywood or something, they'd be sitting together, smoking like chimneys, and I would laugh, and Lois, one tough nut, she'd laugh back and wink and say, 'Where there's smoke there's fire, honey.'"

It is after one of Alice's triumphal dinner parties. Alice and I are washing dishes while Bill drives a few intoxicated guests home. As she leans her face over the steam rising from the scalding dishwater she favors ("Splendid for the complexion"), we laugh about how enamored of Bill his senior coworkers seem.

"I guess they're especially glad they have someone young enough not only to run after witnesses but also to play first-string quarterback for them against Glendale PD."

"He's the youngest by six years." I smile, trying to be careful drying Alice's new china. "The second youngest junior investigator ever to work in the D.A.'s office."

"I didn't know that. How did he get such a position so young?" Alice turns and looks at me, face piping red and dappled, eyes lit.

"You mean he never told you?" I say. Then, shaking my head, "That's so like him."

"Never told me what?"

It is then that I tell her how Bill was promoted after an incident that received a great deal of local attention.

It was his fourth year on the force, and Bill's partner had just retired. A rookie officer named Lester was assigned to him. Only a few months out of the academy, Lester was thrilled to have such a hot beat.

The first night they rode together, they received a call from a fiercely angry woman who claimed her teenage son was spending time with a street gang and probably had been involved in recent vandalism and maybe even the latest stickup in the neighborhood. He had been a good, churchgoing boy, and now he was on his way to being a hoodlum, plain and simple. It was all on account of this *pachuca* girl he had fallen for who had been to reform school and only dated boys who proved their street mettle.

Bill and Lester went over to her apartment, which was heavy with die-cut crosses on the walls and a plaster saint in one corner. Bill was dubious. The woman, tightly wound and incessantly gesturing with the large tinted photograph of her son at age four in her hand, seemed unreliable and maybe even a little crazy. Bill started to wonder whether or not her son was still even in the picture. Maybe he had run away; he'd seen lots of things like that, lonely-sad or lonely-mad people worried about or seeking revenge against spouses, friends, lovers who were actually long gone.

The woman decided, tossing the photograph on the worn couch, that Bill and Lester should help her search her son's things for evidence of criminal activity. Aching for action, Lester started up to his feet, assuring her that they would find something, if there were something to find.

Bill couldn't get over his doubts, and watching the woman tugging at the hem of her cotton shift dress over and over and bemoaning her fate to have such a rotten son with her own blood, *her own blood* running through his veins, he paused a long second before following Lester toward the bedroom.

The small room was immaculate. Not a boy's room at all, Bill thought, still working on his theory that this boy had beat town months, years before, or had been killed in Korea or maybe died before he'd reached adolescence. He'd seen stranger, after all.

The twin bed was tidily made. A chair against one wall had a football resting on it. A snapshot of a pretty girl with a scarf sat on the dresser top, along with a small trophy. As Lester bent down to look under the bed, Bill moved to the trophy out of curiosity. He was thinking, This doesn't look like a sports trophy, more like a—

It was at this moment that the closet door slammed open with a deadly clap and a boy of about fifteen stormed out with a thick Louisville Slugger in both hands. Before Bill could get his gun, the boy was on him, pounding. They both fell to the floor with a thud, and the mother was screaming in horror as Bill shouted to Lester, "Shoot him, shoot him," with the blows coming straight to his head. He could feel his skull cracking, denting like a melon before everything went blurry, then black.

In what was actually only a few seconds later, Bill's eyes shot open just as the bat was about to come straight down on his head. He found himself shooting, and the boy fell backward, like a duck in a shooting gallery. The mother, apparently just as surprised as Bill that her son was in the apartment, fainted in grand style. Fighting to keep conscious, Bill managed to radio for backup right before he passed out again.

It turned out that Lester had panicked. When the boy began pummeling Bill, he ran out of the apartment, and they found him several blocks away, hiding in an alley.

Bill was in the hospital for two weeks with a fractured skull, dislocated shoulder, and lacerations on his face and chest.

The boy was seriously wounded but not killed. Bill, even in

his half-conscious state, had managed to hit him in the shoulder to disable him.

After he was discharged from the hospital, Bill was honored by the chief of police. His attacker turned out to have been involved in the murder of another officer earlier that day, and Bill became a minor hero, which enabled his dreamed-for reassignment to the prosecutor's office, unheard of for a twenty-seven-year-old.

I tell Alice all of this, and she is silent, washing slowly, eyes focused, mascara dewy, flecked. She listens as I try to tell her in a way to make her understand, understand everything. I know the way I tell it is everything: There is so much to know about my brother. Some things she might already understand, some things she should, she must recognize. When I finish, she looks at me with an expression heavy with meaning, about what she now knows about her husband and somehow, somehow what she now seems to think she knows about me.

Suddenly, we are jolted out of the moment by a knock on the kitchen door. I walk over to the window, expecting to see a partygoer returning for a forgotten coat. Instead, it is a tiny, dark-haired girl who looks about sixteen.

"Neighbor?" I ask, beckoning Alice.

Alice looks past my shoulder. When she does, I see something pass over her face quickly but unmistakably.

Recovering quickly, she assembles a smile of happy surprise at the intrusion and, nearly tumbling into the dish rack, moves past me to open the door.

"Lois." She waves the girl in, wiping her hands on her

apron. "Come in. Um, Lora, there's someone I'd like you to meet."

With a sharp red grin, the girl enters. Closer now, I can see she is older than she first appeared, perhaps in her mid-twenties. And, as if in some slapstick silent movie about a misbehaving wife, she wears an unmistakable black eye.

"Hi, honey," she hums with a vaguely southern intonation. "Got a steak?"

"Lois, Lora. Lora, Lois," Alice says tightly as she opens the refrigerator. Alice, being Alice, does have a steak on hand. She hands it to Lois, who slaps it across her cheek and slumps down at the kitchen table.

Not sure what to make of the scene, I mentally reject a series of things to say. Each one sounds ridiculous, given the circumstances. It is at this point that I remember Alice's story about her friend Lois: *Where there's smoke there's fire.*

As I try to find my voice, I notice a starburst of broken blood vessels between Lois's lid and temple.

"I got socked," she burbles, smiling lazily under the steak.

"I didn't mean to—"

"It's okay. I'd stare, too. It's a peach." She doesn't move as she speaks, as if determined not to let the steak budge an inch. As if doing so might allow her face to fall off.

"Lois is a friend from the studios. She's an actress."

"I'm an actress, all right," Lois slurs, staring straight at me with a sad smile.

"In pictures?"

"That's right."

"Have you been in any I might know?"

"You can see me jerk a soda next to Dana Andrews in one. In another, I wave a big peacock feather over Maria Montez. And if I knew how to swim, I'd be wearing a tiara in a tank right now over at MGM in the new Esther Williams picture."

"That's great," I say. "I mean, so many actresses can't get any work."

"They don't know the right people," she replies, still smiling. Alice looks at her, turning the water off at the sink.

"I guess it's connections along with the talent," I say, removing my apron. "And luck."

"Lois makes her own luck," Alice says.

I turn to Lois, who looks back at me with a wink.

One Sunday, I receive a message from my building manager that Alice called while I was out and is desperate for me to come over.

When I arrive, feeling a twinge of trepidation, what I find is both less and more worrying.

There are huge platters of food everywhere—on the large Formica table, leaves out, on the kitchen counters, on the seats of the chairs, even on the top of the refrigerator and the windowsills. Round plates of deviled eggs, quivering tomato aspic, large glass bowls of seven-layer salad, smudgy glass tureens of trifle, copper molds filled with fruit-studded Jell-O—where is the suckling pig, I wonder. And then Alice amid all this, hair pulled tightly back, flushed almost obscenely, glassy sheen of sweat on her face, neck, collarbones. The radio, teetering precariously on the windowsill next to a dish of creamed spinach with bacon, blares jazzy Cuban love songs. Her eyes, my God, her eyes are very nearly radiating, blinking spasmodically, pupils pulsing.

"It's a surprise party, Lora! A party for our darling, our Bill."

I gather my breath. "What's the occasion?"

"I had this revelation, Lora." She tears out at me, smile like a pulled rubber band. "You don't even know. I woke up with it. He works so hard. And that story you told me. Oh my God."

She clutches her hand to her chest before continuing. "He carries this crazy city on his shoulders, and what does he get? We take him for granted. Well, *I* do. Look at what he does, each and every day.

"This is for him, Lora. I just leaped out of bed and headed for the grocery store. I still had my slippers on, Lora. The store manager followed me around the whole time. He was afraid I might fall. He carried my groceries to the car. I've been cooking, baking all day. All day. I hope Bill doesn't get home before it's all finished.

"I need you, Lora. I need you to hang those decorations in the bags over there. And make the phone calls.

"We need to hang the lights, arrange the tiki torches, pass out the ashtrays, the bamboo coasters I bought. These wonderful coconut tumblers that I'll fill with daiquiri. Can you make daiquiris, Lora? I don't know how, but I bought ten pounds of ice."

She can't stop moving, stop talking. She is like a windup toy, or dominoes falling, unstoppable.

At no point do I stop and ask Alice anything. I just put on

my apron. There doesn't seem to be anything I can say to stop her. I don't know what I *would* say. So, within a few minutes of first seeing the spectacle, I am hanging palm fronds from streamers to the sound of ukulele music, listening to Alice make phone call after phone call, her voice pressed and hot.

Somehow, somehow—for Alice alone could make something like this work—it all comes together, and by the time my brother comes home, wide-eyed and weary, Alice's whirring energy melds seamlessly with the larger excitement of a group of neighbors and a handful of fellow teachers and my godparents, all swept up in Alice's frenzy and heads bobbing under pulsing tiki lights and the purple and red luminescence of dozens of bright lanterns.

And all of them, everyone she invites, show up. And they all eat and they dance and they toast Bill as if they had actually started that day thinking of what they might say about his hard work and strong character. And Bill keeps looking around dazedly, not knowing what to say, biting his lower lip and spinning slightly, plate sagging in his hand, dripping pineapple glaze on the patio, too stunned to lift his wrist and steady himself.

As Alice drags out a tub of firecrackers to the delight of the crowd, I sidle up beside him. He looks down at me, putting a drowsy arm around my shoulder, his finger tickling my ear. We stand there, without saying anything, watching Alice dart around like a firefly. It seems like we are both thinking the same thing. Or at least, what I am thinking in full, he is wondering in part. *How long can this go on? This fever pitch, this spinning, quaking thing before us. Forever or a little less?*

. . .

And then, so soon after it might have been the following week . . .

"But, Bill, you're telling me Alice is qualified to teach high school?"

"She is. I mean, she's qualified to teach home economics. She studied it. At Van Nuys Community College." He's followed me into my car after lunch, sits down next to me on the bench seat.

"Well, she'd have to get her teaching certificate." I shrug. "It takes months of coursework and student teaching." I wonder if Bill's sudden urgency has anything to do with the surprise party.

"No, no. She has her teaching certificate. She got it to teach in Lomita about four years ago. But then she finally got in the seamstresses' union and started working for the studios instead."

"Really? Well, that's great, Bill," I say, meaning it, really meaning it. Alice content means Bill content, after all.

And anyone could see Alice was desperate to channel her energy into a new project. "Long afternoons," she'd say to me, eyes a little too bright, neck a little too straight, teeth a little on edge, "the afternoons, Lora, are *endless*."

"So do you think you could talk to Don Evans? Maybe offer to bring her in so he could meet her? I'm sure if they met her, they'd see she'd be a great addition. I'm sure she'd charm the pants off them. And the kids would love her."

"But I'm not sure what I say means much. For hiring, especially. I'm not senior faculty."

"But you'll try?" He looks down at me, squeezing my fingers gently.

"She's my sister now, isn't she?" I smile.

As it happens, it is all too easy. Principal Evans is eager to make a quick hire, with Miss Lincoln ready to leave and begin planning her wedding. It seems like the whole process unfolds effortlessly, with Alice coming for an interview and receiving a modest offer two days later, contingent on her submitting appropriate credentials. Within three weeks, she will be in the classroom.

"Tell me everything about these girls, Lora," she says, the table in front of her papered with open books (*Mrs. Lovell's First Book of Sewing, Teaching Domestic Arts to the Young, The National Association of Home Economics Teachers Presents a Guide for Lesson Plans*), pads of paper, notes, an oversize calendar filled with notations like "Begin pillowcase" and "Basting work." Two pencils poked out of her upswept hair.

"What do you want to know?"

"Anything. I don't even know what to ask. What do I say? Will they do what I ask them to?"

"You taught before, to get your certificate. Just do what you did then."

"But these girls . . . are they very . . . what are they like?"

"They're just girls. They do what they're told. Just don't let them get the better of you. You know, passing notes, talking behind their hands to each other during class."

"I'm going to start with a simple project: napkins. Then a

pillowcase. We'll work up to grander things: an evening jacket with shirring."

I bite my lip. "That's fine, Alice. But I don't think you can have fourteen- or fifteen-year-olds make evening jackets. They're not spending their time at nightclubs."

Alice looks up at me, eyes wide. "No, no, of course not. But they might wear it to a dance. They go to dances, after all, don't they?"

"Yes, but these girls aren't as . . . sophisticated as the ones in Los Angeles. They're small town girls, really. What if you made a nice flounced skirt instead?"

"Is that what Miss Lincoln had them make?"

"No. No, I think they made middy blouses or jumpers."

Alice looks down at her calendar, hands shaking slightly. "You think I'm a fool." She smiles weakly.

"Of course not, Alice." I lean forward, toward her. "You're going to be fine."

"They'll love me," Alice says, looking up at me for a moment, then back down at her lesson plan decisively. "You'll see. They'll absolutely love me."

It is all as Alice predicts. She begins teaching and everything proceeds fluently. It strikes me that a focus for Alice's queer restlessness was all she had needed: just apply the same fervor to teaching that she had to the house, to being a new wife.

The girls are intimidated by her, not surprisingly. The intimidation that comes with intense infatuation. Even Nonny Carlyle, the most popular girl in school, settles in her seat, focused on the sewing machine, listening closely as Alice explains the different stitches, how to thread the new machines.

Alice wears her hair in straight-cut bangs, and within a week Aileen Dobrowski, Linda Fekete, Mary Carver, even Nonny Carlyle herself all come to school with freshly shorn bangs. They stay after class, circling Alice's desk, showing her pictures in magazines, in *Vogue* and *Cineplay* and *Screenstar*, pictures of dresses they want Alice to look at, ideas they want her opinion about. Alice, eyes jumping, is only too glad to indulge them, although her interest runs on an egg timer and it is never too long before she smiles and tells them they can discuss it more tomorrow; she has a husband to get to, a pot roast to make, a house to clean.

Each day, we drive home together, chatting about each classroom interaction, each charming or charmless student comment. Still, it is only a few weeks when the rush of the performance, the velocity of daily events, seem already to have worn off. I guess I am surprised at how quickly things turn. While she doesn't say so, it's clear that the pleasures have waned. She still talks ceaselessly, but no longer about school, about anything but school. When she settles in the car at the end of the day, her whole body seems deflated, like she has peeled herself out of some awful costume and tossed it aside.

At Bill's encouragement, Alice and I begin going out for "girls' nights" once a month. Nights that are at least as much about getting ready—radio moaning, hair spray buffering the air, Alice with needle and thread fitting me into new dresses she's made from studio-scrapped gossamer—as they are about the destination.

Having Alice in our life makes me think of what it might have been like to have sisters or close girlfriends. Here we are in our slips and stockings, laughing and running around, cigarettes dangling (only with Alice do I smoke) as we try to get ready. Alice plucks my eyebrows for me, cursing me for what she calls my "crushingly natural arch."

One night, Alice is putting delicate finger curls in my hair when she starts to talk about how her mother had the most beautiful mane, like sealskin. Mae Steele née Gamble was dismissed from her place of employment when it was discovered she was eight months pregnant with Alice—a fact she had concealed through increasingly painful physical measures for nearly six months. She'd been a chambermaid for a rich Los Angeles family—"not the Chandlers, but close."

Mae confided in her daughter Alice the toil of the job, and the many indignities. Especially, the monthly job of dyeing the woman of the house's pubic hair. "Once, she asked me if I'd ever done it to myself," Alice's mother told her daughter. "I said no, but that I once shaved mine in the shape of a heart for a man. Her jaw dropped to her knees. For about three seconds. And then she decided she liked the idea and she asked me to help her do it. It wasn't for her husband, of course. The Jap gardener. Who was a big favorite in the neighborhood, let me tell you.

"Of course, the man who asked me to shave mine was her

husband. When he finally saw what she had done, weeks later, he was furious. Because he knew. He knew that I had something over him, that she and I were that close."

These sidelong revelations, conveyed so casually, and then an hour later we are seated in sparkling, red-hued nightclubs in Hollywood, nights with cigarette after cigarette, cracked crab on silver plates, and maybe one too many Seven & Sevens.

Three hours later still, my head slung down, chest ringing, I can't stop the quaking fun house feel, bright pops and tingling sparkles, hand clutching, fist twisting in my belly.

Suddenly, Alice's enormous black eyes are looming beside me.

"Hold on there, darling," warm and then pealing into a laugh. "Haven't you ever been tight before?"

Not like this, I try to say, but the thought of speaking seems unimaginable, Alice's hand on my neck, in my hair, trying to hold me up like a ventriloquist's dummy.

"—get you home safe and sound before one of these pretty boys can get his hands on you when my back is turned. Bill will wonder where we—"

And driving home and lights passing over me and I sit in the passenger seat trying to listen, trying to listen to Alice's rustling voice. She is telling me how she saw her mother on television the night before, her long dead mother, and had nightmares all night. It was an old musical and she couldn't remember the name, never remembered the names. As Alice watched the movie, her mother's face suddenly popped out of a row of dancing girls in satin bathing suits. "Like some horrible jack-in-the-box." She laughs, her voice rising, quavering uncomfortably.

"This was in the early thirties, before she hung it all up. She couldn't keep up with her union dues, and there were other problems, too." Alice's voice jingles in my ears, and I try to concentrate, try to hold on to her words, the secrets she may be revealing.

"She moved us out to Hermosa Beach and laid low for several months before getting her maid job. Hard times, and no one suffered more than that woman. At everyone's hands, but especially her own."

She pauses, looks out the window into the hills, eyes heavy with dread. Then adds, "If she'd had more of a taste for pleasure, like her husband, she'd have been better off."

Then adds, "Did you know. She committed suicide by eating ant paste."

Then, "Don't take this the wrong way," she confides with a ghost of a smile, leaning over as we pull into the driveway, mouth nearly to my ear, "but it wasn't soon enough."

For two months, we all fall into an easy schedule. Alice and I carpooling to school. Thursday night dinners. Sundays spent at my brother's, ending with a big Sunday dinner. Sometimes, bowling on Fridays. A double date. The main difference is I spend more time with Alice and almost never see Bill alone for more than a few minutes. It is jarring at first, but I know that it is only natural. They are newlyweds. And Alice is working so hard to make a home.

During the school day, if I have a free period, I sometimes walk by Alice's classroom, just to see. Occasionally, I notice a faraway look in her eyes as she teaches. She is very present, talking seamlessly, directing everything. But her eyes are slick, silver things not connecting to anything, just hanging there, unfixed. And sometimes her body starts to look that way, too. Not tight and taut and jumping like usual, but loose, with slow and elongated movements, punctuated by hands touching everything lightly, running along the sewing machines, sliding along the windowsill, passing over the girls' shoulders, touching everything, but only faintly, fleetingly, like a ghost.

It reminds me of my days volunteering at the county hospital, and the way some patients would always touch you, and the touch was warm and slippery and the morphine tanks dripped endlessly, endlessly.

"Don't you ever get tired of it?" Alice is smoking and driving with equal intensity. It is a bright Monday morning.

"Of what?"

"Of having to be at school. Of having to be in front of them, of having them come up to your desk, in the hallways, in the cafeteria. Always wanting to talk to you. And then, the other teachers, always talking about their classes, about lesson plans, about the students, about the principal, about faculty meetings and curriculum. All the time. All day long."

I wave her smoke out of my face and say, "Well, it's the nature of the job. Everyone takes these jobs, chooses teaching because they *do* care, right?"

She looks at me, blowing smoke from her lower lip and smiling faintly. "I notice you didn't say 'we.'"

"What do you mean?"

"You didn't say, 'We take these jobs because *we* care.'"

"I was speaking generally," I say.

She doesn't say anything, her eyes darting at the traffic. I can't tell if she is thinking of a response, or if she's already moved on.

"I've always known I was going to be a teacher," I add.

She nods vaguely, hitting her horn lightly as a car threatens to force its way into her lane.

"You'll get used to it," I say.

"You'll come to enjoy it," I continue. "Truly. You'll come around."

I can't stop talking. Somehow, it's me now who can't stop.

The sense always that there is a ticking time bomb . . . and then, quite suddenly, it seems to be ticking faster.

It is a month or so before final exams, and I'm in the main office, where the attendance secretary is helping me track down an errant student.

"Don't take it personally, Miss King." She clucks her tongue. "Peggy's been missing all of her classes. We're going to have to call her mother."

"All right," I say. As I turn, I collide with Principal Evans, his vested chest nearly knocking me down.

"I thought I heard you, Miss King," he says. "Come into my office for a moment, will you?"

He opens the door for me with his usual formality.

"Have a seat. I have a small favor to ask."

"Yes, sir."

"When we hired your sister—"

"Sister-in-law."

"Sister-in-law. When we hired her last fall it was under the precondition—the state-dictated precondition—that we would receive a copy of her certification from . . . what was it . . ." He began thumbing through the file in front of him.

"Van Nuys Community College," he reads aloud, then looks up at me, over his reading glasses.

"Right."

"Well, somehow we never received the paperwork from Van Nuys. Or from Lomita, where she taught for . . . a semester."

"Really." I want to be more surprised than I am.

"I'm sure it's merely an oversight." He smiles serenely.

"I'm sure. Why—may I ask, why are you asking me and not Mrs. King herself?"

"Well, you see, I didn't want her to feel we doubt her," he says. "She's very sensitive, you know. A fairly green teacher."

"I see. I'll be sure to bring it up with her."

"And I'd hoped to take care of it today, because I have a lunch meeting Wednesday with the superintendent about next year's renewals. Do you know, will she be back tomorrow?"

"Pardon me?"

"Well, I might have broached the subject with Mrs. King herself, delicately, but her illness—"

"Illness?" Alice had seemed fine when we drove to school that morning.

"Oh, I assumed you generally drove in together. She's out sick today. Apparently some sort of flu."

"Right," I say, rising. "I'll speak with her tonight."

"Righto."

As I walk out, head suddenly throbbing, I try to guess at what point Alice might have slipped out of school. At what point she gave up her pretense of coming to work and drove away. Perhaps she felt ill once she arrived.

"Miss Harris, have you seen Mrs. King today?"

"No, no," she says, thumbing through her card file. "She called in sick." She waves a card in front of me. "She phoned when I first arrived, seven A.M."

"Thank you," I say.

That night, I call my brother to tell him about the missing paperwork. I speak to him in simple, even tones, trying to keep my voice free from any concern or doubt or judgment.

Like the detective he is, he asks a series of questions I am in no position to answer, questions about how the school or the college must have bungled the process, why he and Alice hadn't been told sooner. Then, he assures me that he will take care of it.

"There must have been some mistake, some kind of filing error or something," he says, and even over the phone I can somehow see his brow wrinkled in a gesture so old it seems timeless.

"Don't worry," he says, for the third time.

"I'm not worried, Bill."

"I'll drive to Van Nuys myself if necessary," he adds.

"Fine. How was work—"

"—Gee, I wish they'd called me sooner. Evans, I mean. I hate for him to think . . . I want everything to go smoothly."

"Is Alice there now?" I ask, as casually as I can manage.

"No, she's out. She's got some meeting. A neighborhood thing, I guess. Couldn't be school-related, or you'd be there, too, right?" he says, and I'm not sure if it is a question or not.

"Right," I say, deciding, in an instant, not to bring up that Alice had left school before it began. I don't know why I don't tell him. Something in his voice. Instead, the revelation hovers in my throat, too momentous to spill forward. I say nothing.

Then, not a week later, the next head-jerking puzzle.

I am walking into the home ec lab to meet up with Alice for our carpool home. The cavernous room, with its half dozen kitchen units for students to practice making beef bourguignon, is dark, lit only by faint late-afternoon sun. Past the kitchenettes and through the set of sewing machines, I can see Alice standing in front of her desk, my view partially obstructed by sewing dummies.

I pause for a second, because I think I hear her speaking to someone and I wonder if it is a student she might be reprimanding, or counseling, and I don't want to interrupt.

Quickly, however, I can see she is distraught in a way she

wouldn't be with a student. The low murmuring becomes more fervent. I step slightly to my side and see the profile of a man leaning against the edge of her desk, facing her. The dark furrow of his brows juts out, and as I inch closer, I can see the edges of a steel blue sharkskin suit.

"Well, how would I know she wasn't going to go through with it? I only know what she told me."

Then, the deep, indecipherable tones of the man. Then, her again:

"Did she give you the rest? I told her not to do it. I knew it would turn out this way."

She raises the back of her hand to her forehead. I twist around one of the kitchen counters and see him. He doesn't move at all as they speak, but she moves constantly, winds her arms around herself, scuffing her heels on the floor anxiously.

"She's digging her own grave as far as I'm concerned. That's his story, anyway. I can't promise anything, but she knows better. Christ."

Her head bobs wildly. I still can't hear him, even as I pass the kitchen units and near the sewing machines, about twenty feet from them. He never moves at all, so still, issuing the low tones of confidence and placidity.

"Christ, why do you think she . . . damn it, anyway. Well, she's made her bed and now . . ."

Alice's foot taps staccato, and suddenly she looks up from her own frantic tapping to the man. He meets her gaze, and then, as if feeling my struck gaze upon him, looks over to me.

"Hello there," he says calmly, pausing a cool, languorous moment before moving out of his leaning slouch and standing upright. The eyes are the thing— like a Chinaman's. The heaviest lids you ever saw, barely any pupil can squeak through. Cushiony lids and puffy lower rims unbalanced by angular black brows.

Alice's head turns suddenly, jarringly to me, her eyes wide and glassy. Then she quickly smiles and runs over.

"Oh, honey, Lora," she coos sweetly, and with surprising sincerity. "Let me introduce you." She hurries over to me, grabs my hands in her frosty ones, and tugs me back with her.

The man, hat in one hand, holds out his other toward me. "Good to meet you, Miss King. I've heard . . ." He trails off, touching his mouth to my hand, fingertips touching the back of my wrist so fleetingly I wonder if I imagine it.

"This is an old friend," Alice says, tugging at the sleeves of her dress and standing very straight.

"Oh?" I say politely, taking my hand back and burying it safely in my dress pocket.

"I know Alice from when she was a little girl with curlicues and pantaloons." He winks at me, eyes, face impenetrable, voice soft and low. Utterly unreadable. Is he teasing? Is he lying? Is he sharing a sweet truth?

"Family friends?" I find myself asking, when no one says anything.

"You could say. Seems we've always known each other." A soft pause and a long arm out to Alice's shoulder as Alice smiles indecipherably. "But I've been living in Mexico for a while."

"But you're back now." Alice looks up at him. "Isn't it wonderful that you're back? Make new friends but keep the old, as they say."

Alice wrings her hands and rubs at her watch, pretending not to look at the time, and then abruptly, broadly, she does look, as if in a stage gesture.

"Oh, Lora, it's late, isn't it?"

"Yes," I say. "Should we go?"

Alice nods anxiously and grabs her purse and gloves from the desk, navigating her way behind him.

"I never did get your name," I find myself asking.

"Joe Avalon," he says serenely, putting on his French gray felt hat. "Miss King, the pleasure has been mine."

In the car afterward, Alice chatters away about her troublesome fifth-period class, about Nancy Turner, who is going to perform a monologue at the state drama competition, about the Handler girl with the dirty neck whose mother seems to have left town with a marine. She unleashes a stream of talk the likes of which I haven't heard since the night I first met her. A long rant filled with comments, thoughts, and questions for which she leaves no room for answers. Finally, "Isn't he the nicest fellow? He's an old family friend and he's always helped me out of jams. He just always seems to turn up when I'm in trouble, and for that, I'll always be grateful to him."

"So you're in trouble now?" I ask, turning the steering wheel as we enter their drive.

"No, no, of course not. I didn't mean *now*. Just in the past, things I owe him for. Not that he expects more than a thanks. But I say it all just to suggest what a fine fellow he is. My friend Maureen, who dated him for a while, used to say, 'a stand-up guy.' That's what he is. Though I'm sure you couldn't tell that from the quick exchange, but even though he looks a little . . . *you know*, he's really the *kindest* man you'll ever meet. I should have him over for dinner some night now that he's back in town. I'd really like Bill to meet him. They'd get along like a house on fire, I *know*. Don't you think? Well, maybe not. Oh, here we are."

And I remember this: a slow, slow turn of her head from me to the house. I remember it occurring in actual slow motion, dragged out, and her head turned and her lit, blazing eyes transforming instantly into coal weights, her face a slow, pale blur studded with heavy, inkblot eyes turning to the house, turning and turning off like a windup toy shutting down and shut . . . ting . . . off.

That night in my apartment, and other nights, too, burrowed under the covers, I watch the shadows on the wall and think of meeting men, meeting men like in movies, and meeting men like Alice and her mysterious friends seem to—seem to at least in Alice's stories—men met on buses between stops, in the frozen foods aisle, at Woolworth's when buying a spool of thread, at the newsstand, perusing *Look*, in hotel lobbies, at supper clubs, while hailing cabs or looking in shop windows. Men with smooth felt hats and pencil mustaches, men with Arrow shirts and shiny hair, men eager to rush ahead for the doors and to steady your arm as you step over a wet patch on the road, men with umbrellas just when you need them, men who hold you up with a firm grip as the bus lurches before you can reach a seat, men with flickering eyes who seem to know just which coat you are trying to reach off the rack in the coffee shop, men with smooth cheeks smelling of tangy lime after-shave who would order you a gin and soda before you even knew you wanted one.

These men weren't like the men with whom I went to the pictures: Archie Temple, the chemistry teacher, who never got further than rubbing his rough lips halfheartedly against mine, or Fred Cantor, the insurance salesman who sold Bill his policy and took me to Little Bavaria once a month or so for long, cocktail-drenched dinners. While I seldom got past the first, small glass of sweet wine, Fred could go for hours, jollily imbibing and telling stories of his combat duty in the Pacific. Not always but often there would be an awkward, searching embrace in the front seat of Fred's burgundy Buick. A few beery kisses and Fred would get ideas, and before I knew it, he was pressing my hair against the side door window as I tried to peel away from him.

Where were the golden boys of my high school days, the boys with sweet breath and shy smiles, with proud gaits and long lashes, the boys who sat with you for hours in the booth at the local five-and-dime just hoping for a promise, a promise to go to a dance or listen to records with you at Dutton's Hi Fi or to share a paper plate at the church social?

Though I knew these boys, held their sweet, damp hands in mine only a handful of years ago, they were now like sketches in a yellowed paperback, a photo album from many generations past. When we moved to Los Angeles to live near our godparents, we were only sixteen and nineteen. What we left behind remained a half-imagined reverie of half-opened adolescence, caught now forever between curiosity and harsh awakening.

The thing about Lois . . .

Alice's friend Lois Slattery has a kind of crooked face, one perpetually bloodshot eye just higher than the other, and that Pan-Cake makeup you often see on what Alice calls "girls on the make." She begins periodically appearing at Bill and Alice's, each time without warning. Somehow, I end up, over and over again, having conversations with her. Each time thinking, Poor Lois, in a few years, she'll have a slattern look to match her name.

Her clothes are sometimes very expensive but never look like her own, are either too big or too small, or are well-cut and well-made but someone has stepped on the hem, or the collar has a cigarette burn on it. These flaws aren't, as I first thought, because Lois can only afford secondhand clothing. In fact, the garments are often new, bought that day and already with splatters on the lace edging, or the heel loose. It is as simple as this: she has a complicated life and her clothes can't help but show it. It is all part of her unique disheveled glamour.

As it turns out, Lois is less an actress than a professional extra and a sometime dancer. She takes acting classes in West Hollywood. But most of all she seems to go out dancing and drinking with girlfriends or enlisted men or publicity men.

She is the kind of woman whose face you try to commit to memory because you feel something might happen to her at any minute and you'll have to remember that left dimple, the burn mark from a curling iron on her temple, the beauty mark next to her eye, the small tear in her earlobe, from an earring tugged too far.

"I hooked up with this fella lived in Hancock Park," Lois says out of the corner of her mouth, cigarette dancing lazily. "Had a gold telephone, that was how high-hat he was."

I've never heard a real person talk like this.

"How long did you date?"

"We never dated," she says matter-of-factly, unstrapping her high heels as ashes fly from her hanging cigarette. "But he was a swell guy. He used to take me dancing and to fine parties up in the Hills, and then, very late, we'd drive over to Musso's for an omelet and one last martini. He once introduced me to Harry Cohn, the big studio guy. Oh my, was he a real blowhard. But it ended badly. With this fella, I mean."

"What happened?"

"Let's just say"—she flings her shoes onto the floor and props her feet up on the coffee table—"he had some bad habits."

"Other women?"

"Even more pressing interests, honey. I'm an open-minded gal, God knows, but even I got my limits."

"Do you ever run into him?"

"Nah. He moved to Mexico last I heard. I was looking for him to get back some of my clothes and a brand-new straw hat when I ran into Joe Avalon. He was staking out his place looking to collect on some debts owed. It got pretty complicated."

"I didn't know you knew him, too." Hearing her say his name gives me a start.

Lois punches out her cigarette and begins to apply a bright lipstick without a mirror. "Everybody knows Joe, honeybunch. *Ev*-erybody."

"Did Alice introduce you?"

"Oh, gosh, peach, it don't work like that."

"What do you mean?"

She places her palms together and twists her wrists in opposite directions in a gesture that seems as though it is supposed to mean something to me.

"Time, Lora, works different in your world." She twists her wrists back again.

"To me, I've always known Joe Avalon. He was the number-one cherry picker on my block. He changed all our diapers, tweaked our mamas' teats. He was the glimmer in my papa's eye. He lived on the rooftop of every house on our block, and could slither down the chimney at night. He was, is, and always will be your four-leaf clover and dangerous as hell. He's always been here. This town will always have guys like him, as long as it keeps going."

This is the longest speech Lois has ever given me. I won't forget it.

As we hurtle toward the end of the school year, I see less of Alice on the weekends. Her teaching and her swelling social schedule fill every minute. Still, she seems unable to stop. It is around this time that she begins suffering from what she calls her "old affliction," migraine headaches, hissing pain so severe she feels her own skull will crush her. These headaches send her into dark rooms with cool, oscillating fans for hours, even days on end. "It's related to my cycles," she confides nonchalantly. "So there's nothing I can do about it."

The headaches are almost daily occurrences by the time Bill's baseball league starts up its season. She makes most of the games, putting on a brave face, but I fill in when the pain becomes too much. It helps make Bill less worried. He never wants to leave Alice alone, but she insists, setting a cramped hand on his chest and swatting him away.

Long hours in the bleachers, hands wrapped in knitting or spread out over *McCall's*, the investigators' wives sit, and often I sit with them. Tonight, it is with the blond and blunt-nosed Edie Beauvais.

"Lora, I'm *desperate*. I've got to get pregnant. We've been waiting for so long now."

She runs her tiny hand up and down her arm, which is flecked with goose bumps from the chilling night air. "We had this fantasy of getting pregnant on our wedding night. That's what I expected. But now . . . I just want it so bad, Lora."

Edie is the young wife of Charlie Beauvais, one of Bill's coworkers at the investigators' office. Although he was always willing to take a coworker who'd had a hard day out for a beer, and he'd always stop in at the local tavern when an after-work gathering was under way, Bill never had many friends. Besides, most of the men in his department are either heavy drinkers or gamblers or both, or are wrapped up in the politics of the office.

But Charlie has been a kind of mentor to Bill, showing him the ropes when the other men resented Bill's quick rise, which they attributed to luck or imagined connections.

"But you're so young, Edie," I say, watching the action absentmindedly, watching Charlie waving his hat, waving a player in, laughing mightily, big white teeth against his stubble-creased face. "You've got plenty of time."

"I know," she says. "I've got nothing but time." She stifles a long sigh by dipping her chin and tucking her mouth into her collarbone.

Edie is twenty-three, Charlie's second wife. Born in Bakersfield, she was straight out of modeling school when they met four years before. She had talked her way out of a speeding ticket, claiming a "feminine emergency."

"Are you going to help out at the fund-raiser again?" I ask.

"Sure, sure," she says, eyelashes fluttering, trying gamely to focus on the action. "Where's Alice?"

"She wasn't feeling well," I say.

Edie nods vaguely, watching Charlie bounding in from the infield, removing his hat and rubbing his crew cut vigorously.

"Looking good, honeybunch," she coos, waving and twisting in her seat. Charlie's face bursts out into a grin. It seems to explode over his whole rubbery face as he turns to join his teammates on the bench.

"When are you going to get yourself one of those? A husband, I mean," Edie asks as we watch Bill take a few practice swings.

"So you think I'm in danger of old maid status too?"

She turns to me with a smile. "Don't you want to have a house and kids and nice things?"

I look at her with her blond lashes, eyebrows penciled with delicacy, face so fresh and flat and empty, as only California faces can be. "It's hard to find a man like Charlie, though, isn't it?"

"Hmmm," Edie says, eyes roaming dreamily back to the game, to the shoving match that seems about to unfold between Bix Carr and Tom Moran, who always fought, over sports, old debts, patrol assignments, cars.

I am supposed to say these things, the things I should want. It is what you say. I look at Edie, looking at the other tired, careless faces on the bleachers, hair tucked in curlers under scarves, bodies straining or flaccid, pregnant or waiting to be.

We watch as Bill and Charlie separate the men, and Bill talks them down, his hand on Bix's shoulder, Bix nodding, cooling. Tom abashed, kicking the dirt.

"I'm going home, sugar." Edie sighs, stumbling forlornly down the bleachers.

I wave good-bye.

An hour later, the game finally over, Bill wanders over. "Where's Edie? Charlie's looking for her."

"She left," I say.

"Oh. Really? That's funny. Charlie—"

Tom Moran comes running up behind Bill, slapping him mightily on the back. "Billy, where's that gorgeous wife tonight?"

Bill extends a hand to help me descend the bleachers. "Under the weather."

"Too bad. Don't mind gazing up at her."

Bill looks over at him for a second, as if caught between annoyance and good humor.

"You know." Tom shrugs, grinning at me anxiously. "She's different than the others. Than the other wives. Ain't she?"

I smile faintly, and Bill tilts his head, unsure how to respond.

I know this isn't the first time he's heard these comments. I've seen the way they look at her. They watch her when she comes to City Hall, they watch her at the social events, they watch the way she walks, hips rolling with no suggestion of provocation but with every sense that she knows more than any of the rest. A woman like that, they seem to be thinking, a woman like that has lived.

Their wives come from Orange County, they come from Minnesota or Dallas or St. Louis. They come from places with families, with sagging mothers and fathers with dead eyes and heavy-hanging brows. They carry their own promise of future slackness and clipped lips and demands. They have sisters, sisters with more babies, babies with sweet saliva hanging and more appliances and with husbands with better salaries and two cars and club membership. They iron in housedresses in front of the television set or by the radio, steam rising, matting their faces, as the children with the damp necks cling to them, sticky-handed. They are this. And Alice . . . and Alice . . .

Charlie Beauvais, he once said it. Said it to Bill in my earshot. He said, Don't worry, pal, don't worry. It's not that they want her. It's just they have this feeling—and they're off, Billy, they're way off—but they have this sense that, somehow behind that knockout face of hers, she's more like the women they see on the job, on patrol, on a case, in the precinct house. Women with stories as long as their rap sheets, as their dangling legs . . .

Struggling to sleep in the guest bedroom after helping clean up the damage from a late party, I can hear Bill and Alice talking on the back porch, talking soft and close.

"How is it that Lora hasn't been snatched up, anyhow?"

"What?"

"You know. I'm just surprised she isn't married. I mean, you could say the same about me, until I met you. It's just that she seems the type to be married."

"She *is* the type to be married. She'll get married."

"I'm sure. I just wondered why she hasn't yet, darling. Just curious. She's so sweet and such a warm girl, and—"

"She was almost married once. About three years ago."

I am listening as if it isn't me somehow they are speaking about, as if it were someone else entirely. I hold my breath and pretend to sink into the very walls.

"Oh? Did you scare him off, big brother?"

"It wasn't like that. He was a good friend of mine. A guy who used to be on the force when I first started."

"Did you play matchmaker?"

"Sort of. It just kind of happened naturally. We'd all spend time together, go to movies. He was a good guy, and it made sense."

His tone is shifting, from cautious to grave, and she begins to respond accordingly.

"So what happened?"

"They began getting serious just as he had to leave the force. TB. It was rough, but she stood by him. You know, that's how she is."

"Oh, dear. Did he—"

"No, no. He eventually had to go to a sanatorium, way up by Sacramento or something. He didn't want her to wait for him. He was a shell of the guy he'd once been. Down to a hundred and twenty pounds. He couldn't bring himself to continue with her. He did the right thing. He said, 'Bill, I can't let her tie herself to me like a sash weight,' he said. So he broke it off."

"He isn't still up there—"

"No. They wrote to each other for a while, but it wasn't the same. Last I heard, he married one of the nurses there and they settled. He works for an insurance company or something."

It really wasn't like this, was it? Was that how simple it was, so explicable in a few sentences, a few turns of phrase? Wasn't it months of high drama, so wrenching, so unbearably romantic that I'd conveniently forgotten that I never really cared that deeply for the amiable, square-jawed Hugh Fowler to begin with?

It had absorbed all the emotional energies of Bill and myself for a fall and winter and an early spring, and then, suddenly, it was as though he'd never been a part of our lives at all. His second month at River Run Rest Lodge and we couldn't remember when we'd next be able to make the long drive up the coast.

And then other things emerged, other things that left no room, no time, no space for that sweet-faced young man who, so ill, would shudder against me despite his height, his gun holster, his still-broad (but not for long) shoulders. Was that it?

"How very tragic," says Alice. "Like out of a movie. It could be a movie. Poor Lora."

"She'll find someone and it'll be right," Bill says firmly. I feel my eye twitch against the pillow. I press my hand to it, hard.

"Well, I'm going to help."

"Oh, Alice, I wouldn't—"

"I know lots of wonderful men. Men from the studios."

"I don't think Lora would want to date anyone in the movie business. That's not Lora."

"Oh, brothers don't know," Alice says. "And I can't bear to see her with these sad sacks from school. These men with the saggy collars and shoes like potatoes. I'm going to get her with a real sharpshooter. If you had your way . . ."

"Alice, you don't know Lora. She won't—"

"Just watch me."

I can hear her smile even if I don't see it. It doesn't seem real, that this is me they are talking about. I look out the window, at the heavy jacaranda branches trembling gently against the pane. I think, for a moment, about the men Alice seems to know and it's hard to believe they really exist. That they could enter my life, my small world. What would it mean if they came crashing in the same way Alice has?

As my cheek leans against the glass, I realize suddenly how hot my face is. I press my hand to it, surprised.

It is a long time before I fall asleep.

. . .

With this forewarning, I am prepared when, after one of what Alice refers to as my "sad sack" dates, she phones me and announces she is ready to play matchmaker.

"His name is Mike Standish. Can you believe it? I call him Stand Mannish."

"What does he do? He's not an actor."

"No, no, of course not. He's with the publicity department. He's delicious, Lora. He's a huge, strapping man. He's like a tree, a redwood. He's a lumberjack."

I am always surprised by what Alice thinks might make a man sound attractive to me.

"I don't know."

"Lora, he's very smart and accomplished. For God's sake, he went to Col-*um*-bia University."

"He doesn't want to date a schoolteacher in Pasadena."

"He wants to date *you*. I set it all up. He's taking you to Perino's and then to the Cocoanut Grove. The only question is what you should wear."

"When is all this supposed to happen?"

Why not, for God's sake. Why not.

"One thing, Lora, one thing," she says, and it's almost a whisper, a voice burrowing straight into my head. "This is what he does: first thing, he warns you that he's going to charm you, and that warning becomes part of his charm."

✠

"Hey, Shanghai Lil, come over here," my brother says, waving his arm toward Alice.

"I think that you no love me still." She pouts, imitation geisha, as she pads over in her brand-new Anna May Wong–style silk pajamas.

"See how nice it can be staying home on a Saturday night." He smiles peacefully, tucking her into his arms.

"Until you get the call." She sighs.

"Not tonight. Promise."

"Your sister will have fun enough for us all." She turns from inside the serge curl of my brother's arm and looks to me.

"Oh? Where are you going?" He straightens up suddenly and peeks out over Alice's blue silk to see me.

I pause.

"Just to dinner, I think. And then dancing maybe." I stare at my lipstick, then dab a bit more on for good measure.

"Mike Standish shows a lady a good time." Alice slides out from Bill's arms and slinks over to me.

"We can go out, too, Alice. I just thought—"

"That's not what I meant," Alice says, curling up in front of me as I sit in the wing chair.

"Maybe we can join them. I—"

"No, no, no, darling." She reaches out for my lipstick to add still more. Her face looms over me, and her eyes hang big as saucers. "Besides, they don't want old marrieds along, believe me."

"I'm sure we'd be glad for the company," I say, blotting with the handkerchief she holds out to me. "The more the merrier."

"I'd like to meet this Standish guy," my brother says suddenly. "Have him in for a drink."

Alice shakes her head and slides back into his lap. "Easy, Judge Hardy. You're not her father, after all. You'll meet him soon enough. Besides, doesn't Lora want *some* privacy? Some life separate from family."

She looks at me as she says it, and there is a wistfulness there, a kind wistfulness that, despite everything, I find myself warming to, and secretly thanking her for.

Two hours later, this:

"I could tell you stories, honey." Mike Standish smiles. "Stories to make Fatty Arbuckle blush. The four-o'clock-in-the-morning calls I've gotten, the places I've had to peel them off of the floor, the circus freaks I've had to pay off to keep these little indiscretions, these quaint peccadilloes out of the papers."

"You sound proud of yourself."

"As they say, life is too short to bother with Puritan hypocrisies. Besides, it's not me racking up time in the booth with Father McConnell. I just clean up," he says, still smiling, rubbing his hands together as if to wash them.

"My grandmother would have called those devil's dues," I say noncommittally, removing the maraschino from the bottom of my drink.

"Your grandmother didn't know what she was missing." He winks, cuff links flashing in the soft light, summoning the waiter over for another round.

. . .

A few days later, as I arrive to help Alice make cookies for the senior banquet, I see that Lois Slattery is back again. I take a chair as Alice fusses over the moon and star shapes. The cookie cutter, in her frustration, keeps slipping from her hand.

"Lois, if you get one cigarette ash near these cookies, I'm going to tear your hair out."

"Better men than you have tried," Lois slurs, unaccountably nodding to me before leaning back in her chair.

"I just don't have the patience today." Alice sighs, wiping her face with the back of her hand.

"Can't the blue bird scouts or whoever manage with store-bought?"

"No, no." Alice's crimson-tipped fingers steady themselves and she manages to get the first perfectly cut star safely onto the sheet.

Lois turns and looks at me. "She gave up Tinseltown for this."

"What a sacrifice," Alice says with a faint smile. "I saw enough of the business from my mother to know where it gets you. I didn't even want to end up working for the studios, but who would turn down union wages?"

I nod, as she seems to want affirmation.

"Still," she adds, "it was a rotten job, running measuring tape over starlets all day."

"That was how we met," Lois says, eyeing me.

Alice, intently at work, raises her hand to Lois to ensure silence as she lifts a pair of moonbeam cookies onto the sheet.

Lois bends forward again with a deep red smile. "You know what that looks like?"

Alice looks at Lois expressionlessly but with a firm lock of the eyes.

Lois breaks the gaze and turns to me. "Do you recognize it, Loreli?"

"I guess that'd be a moonbeam, no?"

"Does it remind you of anything?"

"No," I say, feeling like the girl at school who was never let in on the game.

"Relating to a certain brother darling?" Lois waves her cigarette over the cookie and then toward the kitchen door. Alice stares motionless.

"Pardon?"

"You *know*. I can't say I've seen it myself, but . . . the scar, doll."

"Oh, the scar from his accident," I say, trying not to picture the horrible night of the assault. The scar came from the sharp edge of the radiator when he fell after the baseball bat blows from the young suspect. It is right above his hip.

"I haven't seen it since the hospital," I add. "I suppose I've never seen it as a scar. Only as a wound." I feel my throat go a little dry. It seems strange to have us all sitting here, dwelling on this.

"Lois," Alice says with an edge, hands still, hovering over the cookies. Lois returns the tough gaze, bites her lip a bit, shrugs with effort, and looks down at her pointy, scuffed shoes.

Later that night, at the fabulous Alice-inspired cocktail party at the Beauvais house, Alice and I drink gimlets together, and the heat wilting us, the crowd pounding in, we draw closer and I've forgotten everything but how much, everything else aside, she only wants it all to be good, to be good and fine.

"Lois, I told Lora to—I mean"—Alice giggles, correcting herself tipsily—"*Lora*, I told *Lois* to stop coming by."

"Oh," I say, helping her steady her tilting drink.

"Bill doesn't really like her around. He thinks she's bad news. Which, of course, she is."

"She is?"

"Nothing serious, of course," Alice assures. "I'm just trying to wean her off me, but it's hard because we've known each other so long."

Then Alice tugs me closer to her, nearly pressing her mouth to my ear as we nestle on the Beauvaises' sofa. It is then that she tells me how they met, years before, at the studio.

Alice was fitting Lois, a young extra, into an Indian Girl costume, feathered headband, short tunic straight from a gladiator picture, pure Hollywood. When she was adjusting the hem, she saw the abrasions on the insides of Lois's thighs, shallow like slightly large pockmarks.

"So glamorous," Lois had said, not even looking down at Alice, kneeling beside her, needles in her mouth. "I didn't know the skirt would be so short."

"It won't pick up on camera," Alice had said.

"I thought that once, and the next thing I knew, the camera was moving under my spread legs."

Alice hadn't said anything but smiled just enough to keep the needle in her mouth as she pinned the hem.

"You can never tell when a camera's going to be between your spread legs," Lois had continued, seeing Alice's smile.

"You sure can't," Alice said, dropping the pin too fast. "Oops! Did you get poked?"

At that, Lois had let out a long, quiet, drawllike laugh, and Alice had laughed too.

"You have a lot of history," I say.

Alice sighs and raises her eyebrows. "That we do." Then, suddenly, "I'm sorry about earlier, though. About what Lois said about the scar."

"What do you mean?"

"I don't want you to think I tell her all kinds of private things about Bill."

"I don't," I say, even as, for the first time, I wonder if she does exactly this.

"Truth is, Lora . . .

Truth is, Lora . . .

Don't think I'm trashy . . .

Truth is, I think his scars are beautiful, Alice whispers, face
red.

I think they're beautiful, she repeats. Don't you?

Then comes the first step from which there is no turning back.

As the final bell rings for the day, Alice grabs my arm in the corridor.

"I know we have a staff meeting, but can we miss just this one?"

"You go on. I'll make excuses and get a ride home with

Janet," I say, wondering what arch looks will fly at Alice missing yet another faculty meeting.

"Actually, Lora, I was wondering if you could come with me."

"Come with you?"

"I have to go see Lois. She's sick and I want to check in on her."

"That's fine, but why do you need me?"

"Please, Lora? I'm worried. It would be such a relief to have you there."

I look over at her, fingers clasped tightly over the clipboard in her hand. There is such forceful concern that I can't help but agree. I feel glad that Alice would go to such lengths for her friend, that the intensity with which she approaches being my brother's wife is not the only force surging through her.

It is a long drive that involves threading through a series of shaggy and ominous neighborhoods. Alice talks the entire time, almost as though trying to distract me from the gray-boxed bars and barred-window pawnshops that stud the roadways as we finally land on Rosecourt Boulevard. She sings along to the radio when she isn't talking, mostly about the shopping she needs to do and how late she is going to be for dinner guests but that fortunately she has prepared everything in advance, from the cold potato soup to the slow-cooking roast.

"What a horrible name for a place to live," I murmur as I notice a thickly painted apartment complex to our right. Its large, red-lettered sign darts out from behind a heavy blur of swaying pepper trees, "Locust Arms Apartments."

Alice laughs loudly and suddenly, like a bark. Covering her mouth, she says, "That's where Lois lives."

I feel my face redden but say nothing as Alice pulls the car into the small lot. We step out and begin walking toward the courtyard.

Watching Alice three steps ahead of me, gliding serenely past each blistered door while I find myself sneaking only furtive glances, I wonder about the places she's lived. Places even worse than the Bunker Hill rooming house.

The place is run-down, but it isn't that. It's something else. Something I can't quite name. The paper-thin doors, heavily curtained windows, the faint sound of someone chipping ice, relentlessly, the winding drone of a radio playing music without rises or falls, just a sporadic beat, the vague murmur of a neglected cat. Behind all these doors there is something finishing. Dead ends.

Alice knocks pertly on the door marked 7.

"Lucky seven," she says to me unreadably.

There is the sound of feet running anxiously, and the door flings open so quickly that Alice and I both jump back with a start.

Lois's white face pokes out of the dark interior with an energy I've never seen in her.

"Get in, get in." She half-stumbles backward, waving at us furiously.

It is hardly larger than a hotel room: a small seating area with a chair and settee, both covered in thick, lime-colored bark cloth, a tiny kitchenette with a counter and two stools, a sagging bed. My eyes keep shifting from one detail to the next:

the chipped, brown-ringed porcelain sink, the upturned liquor bottles in the corner, the two chalky glasses that seem, as far as I can tell, to be stuck to the shelf paper adhered to the counter.

Alice, as if to shake me out of it, grabs my arms and sits me down beside her on the unforgiving couch.

"How are you feeling?" she asks as Lois, wearing an expensive-looking appliquéd kimono, paces before us anxiously.

"How do I look?" She turns to us, sweat streaked on her face and neck, raccoon eyes. I can hear the ice chipping again. And a long, low drip tapping from Lois's bathroom.

She turns to Alice. "Why did you bring her here?"

I look at Alice embarrassedly.

"You called and said you were running a hundred-and-four-degree fever. I thought she could help." Alice seems eerily calm, even opening her purse and tapping out a cigarette.

Lois's eyes narrow. "I know why you brought her."

Alice lights her cigarette and shakes the match out, tossing it on the coffee table.

Standing on the balls of her bright white feet, Lois waits for a response.

Alice merely smiles and exhales a long curl of smoke.

The silence becomes unbearable, and I venture, "Alice was worried about you."

Lois looks at me for a second, then fixes her gaze back on Alice, cool, implacable Alice.

"That's not why she brought you, Sis," Lois says, as if turning something over in her mind. "She's just calling a bluff." She rubs the side of her face with the back of her hand, then adds, "You think you can leave us alone for a minute?"

Although she doesn't look away from Alice as she speaks, she seems still to be talking to me.

Alice's and Lois's eyes are locked, Lois's are working, Alice's possessed of an unreachable calm.

"Okay," I say, dreading the thought of waiting in that courtyard. I rise and walk to the flimsy front door, shutting it behind me.

I take a few cautious steps to the old concrete fountain in the courtyard's center, bone dry. I have the vague sense that I'll never approach an understanding of what I've just witnessed. Something between women who've known each other for centuries.

Waiting, I watch a tiny, birdlike woman with one shoe in her hand and none on her feet make her quiet way from the parking lot, through the courtyard and to Number 4. Walking with purpose, her eyes focused on the ground, with the funny gait of the barefooted. She pushes on the door with the hand that holds the shoe, and it pops open like the top of a hatbox.

I rise again and walk in slow circles back toward Number 7.

I lean against the outer wall of the apartment, not intending to—but quickly realizing I can—hear Alice and Lois.

It is only patches, fragments.

". . . not afraid to bring her . . ."

". . . bring him next time . . ."

". . . is the end of everything . . ."

". . . watching over me to keep me doing what you . . ."

". . . everything she says. You know what he'd do . . ."

". . . Don't you see? . . . the end of ev-erything . . ."

". . . that what you want?"

The words, their whispery, insinuating tones, their voices blending together—I can't tell them apart, they seem the same, one long, slithery tail whipping back and forth. My head shakes with the sounds, the hard urgency, and my growing anxiety at being somehow involved in this, even if by accident, by gesture.

The voice—as it seems only one now—becomes abruptly lower, inaudible, sliding from reach. The more I strain, the more I lose to the ambient sounds of the courtyard, the radio, a creaking chair, the cat, the vague clatter of someone knocking shoes together, a bottle rolling.

Suddenly, the door bursts open and Alice is right in front of me.

"All right, she's fine. Let's go." Alice grasps my arm lightly and begins marching us both across the courtyard.

Surprised and confused, I turn around to see Lois leaning against the doorframe.

"Bye, Sis," she murmurs, looking calmer and quite still, voice returning to its usual vague drawl.

Alice moves me forward fast, and I keep looking back at Lois until Alice turns us around the corner and Lois disappears behind the faded yellow hacienda wall.

In the car on the long ride home, Alice assures me everything is fine.

"She needs my attention sometimes and will do a lot to get it. It's hard for her to have me married and with my own commitments and not always able to be there. Once I saw she wasn't sick—not really sick—I knew she only wanted to see me *concerned* about her. It's hard for her since I married. But, truth told"—Alice puffs away on a new cigarette—"she's just going to have to get used to it.

"Right?" She looks at me, waiting for a response.

"Right." I nod, without knowing to what I am agreeing. The more she speaks, the more I feel convinced that there is an entirely separate narrative at work here, one to which I might never have access. Nor should I want to.

At the polished bar at the Roosevelt Hotel. Corner booth. Gimlets.

Mike Standish leans back and puts forth a long, rich smile.

"Everyone knew Alice. Everyone in Publicity especially. Most of the women in Costume were old ladies, pinch-faced old maids or pinch-faced young virgins. But Alice . . . Hell, maybe they all seemed more pinch-faced because Alice was so . . . unpinched."

He pulls a cigarette from his gleaming case, fat onyx in its center. As he taps it leisurely, his smile grows wider. "She would be there at all hours, walking toward you, slow and twisty, a ball gown hanging off one arm, sometimes a cigarette tucked in those red lips. Jesus."

He lights his cigarette and blows a sleek stream upward.

"Of course, she wasn't really my type," he concedes with a half shrug. "Too much going on all the time. Made you really nervous. Once you started talking to her, she made you feel like the threads in your suit were slowly unraveling.

"Still, she was awfully fun. We'd take her out, the fellows and I. She'd bring along a few friends. We'd go out drinking, to the Hills or on the water, Laguna Beach. To Ensenada once. Once even to Tijuana. No, twice. That's right. Twice."

"Did you meet Lois Slattery?"

"Who's that?"

"A friend of Alice's."

"What's she look like?"

"Dark hair, short."

"That doesn't really narrow it down. Alice seemed to know a lot of girls."

"Very young-looking. And with slanty eyes, kind of crooked."

Mike grins suddenly, his hand curling around his face in sudden recollection.

"Oh, yeah. One eye higher than the other. That B-girl." He squints one eye and looks up. "Lois? Are you sure? I thought her name was Lisa—or Linda. She came out with us one night. Slumming in . . . Jesus, some bar in Rosecourt. Oh, yes. Lois, huh?"

He looks at me suddenly. "You've met her?"

"Yes."

"I can't picture that, angel." He hands me his cigarette. "Well, what do you know?"

I take a quick drag and hand it back. "What do you mean, 'B-girl'?"

"Oh, what the hell do I know?" he says, shrugging handsomely. "I even had her name wrong."

"Didn't you think it was strange that Alice would know a . . . someone you'd call a B-girl?"

He looks at me, eyes dancing, revealing nothing. Then, he opens his mouth, pauses, and says, plain as that, "No."

Suddenly, it is commencement, and then begins a long, rich summer with no classes to teach and lately so much to occupy evenings. I see Mike Standish once or twice a week, but there are also the parties those in Bill and Alice's neighborhood circle hold, and especially Alice herself. These parties always include me, the married couples eager to invite a young single to play with, to engineer setups for, to pepper with questions, reminisce about being young and unattached, an entire life path still unwritten.

As for me, suddenly the world is so much larger than it had been before.

There are gin-drizzled evenings with a few neighbor couples, some of the other teachers and their spouses, a few of Bill's friends from work, along with their wives, everyone laughing and touching arms and elbows, and the bar cart creaking around the room and no kids yet, or the few there are, safely tucked away in gum-snapping babysitters' arms.

Almost every week there is one, usually on Saturday evening. They are cocktail parties, rarely dinner parties, yet they can stretch long into the dinner hour, sometimes beyond. Once in a while, arguments flare up, typically between couples, at times between Bill's friends from the D.A.'s office.

Sometimes there is intrigue spiraling out, whispered conversations by guests slipping into dens or rec rooms, the far corners of the darkened lawns, out by the hibiscus bushes beside the carport, on beds soft with piles of coats.

At first, I go to these parties with Archie Temple, the geol-

ogy teacher, or Fred Cantor, the salesman, or some setup, usually an awkward one, given the high energy and heavy drinking
of these parties.

But when I start seeing Mike Standish more frequently, he
comes along, and then we go out afterward, to Romanoff's or
even Ciro's.

At all of these parties, Mike thinks everyone there is a hope-
less square, except for Alice. But he likes to watch, seated
amused on the sofa, sipping his Scotch and making sly comments to me.

Sometimes, a woman flirts with him and he strings her
along, winking to me, flashing his gold cuff links, his sleek
watch, his slick and slippery eyes. Later, he makes fun of her
Mamie Eisenhower bangs or her twitchy eye or her flat accent
or her off-the-rack décolletage. And I laugh and laugh no matter who it is or what kindnesses she's shown me. It doesn't matter. I laugh and laugh anyway and don't care.

Alice sometimes dances with the dashing school drama
teacher. They do Latin numbers, Cuban routines. She pulls
the edge of her satin skirt to her side, tosses her head back, grins
darkly, hotly, and everyone watches in admiration as he twirls
her, as they twist and lean and then swing back upright and
taut.

Bill claps most loudly of all. He watches her, transfixed, and
shakes his head with a smile, and when she finishes he walks
over to her, puts an arm around her tiny shoulders, looks down
at her and marvels, just marvels. How did it happen, he seems
to be wondering, that I married this person?

By the evening's third trip to the bathroom, a face caught in the mirror, a smear of what you were a few hours ago. You totter, you catch a smudgy glimpse, you see an eyelash hanging a bit, lipstick bleeding over the lip line. Heel catches on back hem, hand slips on towel rack, grabbing tightly for shell pink guest towel.

There are more than a few times Mike walks me out of the house and we end up back at his place before we head out for a nightclub or show.

The thing about Mike is he is always ready to go back out again. He knows just how to rub a cold towel on his face and yours, how to fix you both hot coffee and dry toast, how to make a few calls, shift a few reservations, and you both, not a full hour after arriving at the Hillock Tower Apartments, find yourselves sitting straight-backed and freshly groomed in Mike's buttercup yellow roadster.

During the summer, during every past summer so why not this one, I go to the courthouse and have lunch with Bill a few days a week. If he is very busy, it is a quick lunch cart break, the two of us settling at his desk or in the Plaza Las Fuentes over liverwurst or a hot dog. He leans across his desk, shirtsleeves up and suspenders, and tells me as much as he can about a case he is working on. Three times out of four it seems like he is looking for someone who is likely, he says, long gone.

When he first started, I remember always asking him if it was like in the movies, with finger men and stool pigeons and rats. He'd always laugh and say it both was and wasn't like that, but he could never really explain. When he spoke about his job, it was usually as if he were just a man shuffling papers and making phone calls and conducting interviews across desks and through doorways. This was the way he chose to talk about it.

These lunches seem more important now that Bill is married. They are nearly the only times I see him alone.

Soon, however, Alice begins to have lunch with Bill too and there aren't enough lunches to go around, given Bill's schedule, which often means eating lunch on the job, driving around and doing his work, whatever it is that day. So, at first, Alice and I drive out together. This doesn't last too long, however, because it feels like a big production. Alice is always perfectly outfitted, with a new hat, silk flowers on her lapel, her hair done at the salon that morning. By the time we make it to the courthouse, it is late and we draw so much attention that Bill begins to feel as though it looks too "fancy."

So we start visiting on alternate weeks. Sometimes, at the last minute, Bill realizes he is going to be free for a quick tuna sandwich if I can come down, and sometimes we meet at Gus's, a diner halfway between work and home. This way, we can have our talks without trouble. We don't need to tell Alice.

These times remind me of how things were before, after Bill returned from the war and we moved to Pasadena together. Everything had settled beautifully. He was so busy with his police training, and I was so busy with my classes and certification training and teaching. But it worked well because we helped each other, and we knew how to unwind at the end of the long days, listening to *Molle Mystery Theatre, This Is Your*

FBI, and *Inner Sanctum* on the radio, playing Scrabble, Monopoly, Chinese checkers.

He told me some stories of overseas. He brought back a small stack of photos, and he would explain everything to me, saying, "This was Tom, he was from Virginia and he had a wife and new baby at home, he wrote letters every day," and "This one is of me and Popeye, that's what we called him because of the way his jaw stuck out to the side, he was from the Ozarks and he got shot in the neck by a sniper in Berlin, the first one I knew to get it."

He also had some souvenirs, which he kept in the top drawer of his sideboy. His army-issue pocketknife, a pewter stein, some medals and stripes, even a small, toylike pistol—a Walther PPK, he informed me, not letting me touch it—that he had been allowed to keep when he disarmed a German officer in a skirmish.

The war had been nearly over by the time Bill made it to Europe. He was one of the last drafted, and most of his time overseas was spent in occupied Germany, supervising the rebuilding. He was shot at more than once, mostly in encounters with hostile civilians or stragglers. But he considered himself very lucky, and the experience was, he always said, fundamental to his decision to enter law enforcement. "Seeing what I saw, people driven to bad things. It made me want to . . . I don't know how to put it, exactly. It's just, you realize, most people wouldn't go bad either if . . . if the *really* bad people, the real animals could be stopped. You stop them and you can save all the rest, Lora. You really can."

So rare to hear him speak like this, to speak about himself and what he believed. He curled his fist and lightly punched his thigh with it as he sat beside me and spoke. Where did this come from, my brother feeling things so strongly, knowing things so fervently?

When we were children, a man ran over the bicycle of the little deaf girl next door to us. The man plowed over it, and crushed it to the quick. Nancy, that was her name, was only seven and didn't understand it at all, thought nothing could be so wretched as this. She kept crying, and Bill, who'd seen the whole thing, seen the man take the corner of the road too quickly and swerve onto the shoulder and knock it down with a crunch, became so angry that he didn't know what to do. He kept pacing, kicking the dirt as Nancy cried and my grandmother comforted her. The next day he traded in his bicycle, only two months old, for a small girl's bicycle to replace Nancy's. When my grandparents and Nancy's, and Nancy herself, crying her big blue eyes out, tried to thank him, he wouldn't even look at them. It embarrassed him. That's how he was.

"I think you like Mike Standish a lot." Alice smiles, shaking crushed coconut into the bowl.

"Sure." I smile back, handing her a wooden spoon.

"I think"—she plucks two oranges from the glazed fruit bowl—"that you're falling for him."

A hot jolt sails through me.

"Don't be silly, Alice." I help her remove the pith, slicing the membrane from its glaring rind with a knife. "We're just friends. We enjoy each other's company."

She begins peeling the pineapple, her fingers heedlessly diving into the spikes. "It's something else. There's something there," she says, her hands now sticky with the juice, and my own stinging with the orange flesh. "Something you like."

Something about how you are with him.

She splashes some liqueur into the bowl. It drizzles over the sugar crystals, swirled in with the vanilla extract. Our hands are matted with pulp, with juice, with the soft skin of coconut beneath our fingernails. I turn my hand around and lick the heel, feeling the sweet sting. *Why not?*

Mike working a room, patting men on the back, running his softly used hands on the backs of women's necks. It is clear he will go further, rise higher than some of the other men in the publicity department because he never seems too eager. And because he never has the look of a man with something to sell. He is always on the make, but only in the most general, most genial way, a way that suggests he is enjoying the ride while it lasts and shouldn't we all, too?

He can play tennis with the actors, go hunting with the directors, golf with the producers, make the nightclub scene with the new talent. He is always willing to put an ingenue on his arm for the premiere, or walk in with the mistress while the big shot walks with his wife.

He can tell bawdy jokes and read racing forms. He knows

the right restaurants to be at and the right times to be at them, he knows the drinks to order, the maître d's to grease. He can tell the studio folk the best place to vacation; he has the steamer trunk company number on hand, the dealer to go to for the latest cars, the company from which to rent the yacht, the tailor to get just the right cut. He knows which lawyers to call and when, which reporters to leak to and which to throw off the scent. These are valuable things for a thirty-two-year-old climber to know. And it always helps that he is from Connecticut and went to Columbia (and nearly graduated) and has the sheen of class and breeding everyone he works for lacks.

There is something very easy about Mike, about being with Mike, about Mike's whole existence. He never has a wrinkle on his suit. His hair is cut once a week, though one never need know how it happens, or where or when, because it occurs in the margins between when I see him and when I see him next. I never see a restaurant check, or worry about hailing a cab, or imagine how it happens that Mike pays his bills or his rent, or his cleaning lady. All the practicalities of his life seem to go on invisibly, effortlessly.

How does he come to own the clothes he wears so immaculately—when does he shop? When does it happen that orange juice and Coca-Cola end up in his refrigerator or the plate of perfectly arranged Kentucky pralines on his kitchen table or the Seagram's and soda water on his bar cart? Even if his cleaning lady purchases these things, or the stores deliver them on a regular order, when does Mike place the order or sit and think about what he wants? When does he deal with the mail on the table? I've seen him run through it, eyes darting at the return address names, and then toss it back down. When does it all happen? Where is all the offscreen time?

It is barely possible to imagine Mike taking a shower. Isn't he always perfectly groomed, crisply cologne-scented, freshly shaved and ready to go? What a disappointment it would be to become truly intimate with him, to stay over past the deliciously mechanical grope on the bed after the long string of martinis and have to see the behind-the-scenes efforts that produce such a clean and cool container of a man.

Exactly when—in what order—these things happened, the *structure*, is hazy, muddled. The moments pop forward, spring out suddenly, and there I am, sometime early that summer, coming by to visit with Bill, maybe go for a drive together. Instead, I find Lois, whom I haven't seen since that day five weeks before at the Locust Arms. She is making herself at home in the bedroom, wearing a lavender feather boa, parts of which are stuck to her face. It looks as though she's been wearing it for days, some of it still fluffy and sleek, like an excited bird, other parts knotted and fraying.

"Lois, each time I see you . . ."

Lois, each time I see you, I think I've discovered the body.

"Fuck a duck, Lora King, I got it bad," she slurs, then as if just noticing it, she lifts the edge of the boa and examines it. "This belonged to Loretta Young until Wednesday."

As her arm stretches out, I see a footpath of bruises and welts.

"Lois."

"These men I know . . . they wanted to have a party. I thought it'd just be booze. Sometimes you can't tell. One of them had eyebrows that ran together," she says, dragging a ragged fingernail across her forehead. "He looked like out of *Dick Tracy*, you know?"

"Does Alice know you're here?" I ask, remembering what Alice said about telling Lois to stop coming around.

"She told me to come. We ran into each other last night at this place over on Central Avenue, before my date with Big Harry."

"Who?"

She taps the flaccid skin of her blue-white arm as if in response.

I want to confront her with what is an obvious lie. I want to say, There is no way in the world you saw Alice on Central Avenue. No white woman from Pasadena would— Instead, I say, "Let me put you in a bath and get some food in you."

"Bath sounds good. You got any chop suey joints around this neck? I go crazy for chop suey. I think the last thing I ate was a fried bologna sandwich around two o'clock yesterday."

Her eyes shining like clanging marbles, she laughs as I start to peel the boa from her face.

"Honey, you must really wonder how the hell you got messed up with me."

✺

Looking in Mike Standish's mirror at 2:00 A.M., my face, neck, shoulders still sharp pink, my legs still shaking, I see something used and dissolute and unflinching. How did this all happen so quickly?

And it has nothing to do with him at all. It is as if this girl in the mirror has slipped down into some dark, wet place all alone and is coming up each time battle-worn but otherwise untouched.

A late dinner at Lido's by the Sea, all cracking seafood, clamoring jazz, squirts of lemon in the air, the clatter of dozens of docked party ships on the water, long strings of lights stretched out into nothing.

Now, back at Mike's apartment, he uncharacteristically down for the count, dreaming heavily, stunned into sleep after a day-into-night of cocktails and courses, a director's wedding, a premiere, a party, and finally dinner with me.

I decide to phone for a taxi.

Tiptoeing into the impeccably tailored dark green and tan tones of the living room, I sit down at the desk, on which rests only a phone, a pad of paper, and a set of fountain pens. I slide open the desk's sole drawer to find a phone book.

As I pull it out, I see that I have inadvertently picked up, along with the phone book, a tidy pack of playing cards. The pack falls soundlessly into the deep carpet. Reaching down, I accidentally knock the cards, and they slide out of the pocket into a near perfect cardsharp's fan.

I kneel on the floor. As I collect the cards wearily, a few flutter again to the carpet, flipping over from the standard navy blue pattern to their reverse sides.

There, instead of the mere jack or diamond, I see slightly grainy, hand-tinted black-and-white photographs.

I bite my lip and faintly recall Bill's army buddies joking about the decks they picked up in France, where, they'd laugh, "women understand men."

The cards are filled with naughty open-legged shots of women, and I avert my eyes, shoving them back into the box. As I do so, however, one catches my eye.

It is two women, wearing only garters, kneeling, hands cupping each other's breasts. Unlike what I had seen in the flash of the other cards, these women are facing not a man just out of frame or their own plump forms. Instead, they look openly into the lens, heavily made-up eyes gazing out.

I stare for a hard thirty seconds before realizing I am looking at Lois Slattery and my sister-in-law.

Lois's unmistakable crooked face.

Alice's brooding eyes—eyes so intense that not even the thick layer of kohl could conceal them, a virtual fingerprint.

They are kneeling on what looks like a cheap Mexican serape.

Their fingernails are painted dark.

They look younger, with a little of the roundness that especially Alice now lacks.

Their mouths are open, Lois's lewdly, like a wound.

Though their bodies and faces are tinted a rosy shade, the photographer hasn't bothered to tint the insides of their mouths, so instead of red or pink, the mouths give way to a gray-blackness like something has crawled inside them and died there. Like their insides have rotted and the outside has yet to catch up.

Suddenly, I hear stirring in the bedroom. Before I know it, I've palmed the card, shoving the rest of the pack back in the drawer.

Mike Standish is standing in front of me, trousers pulled up, suspenders hanging rakishly.

I am still kneeling on the floor, fortunately holding the phone book by way of explanation.

"I'll take you home," he says with a casual yawn. "Sorry I fell asleep, King. Bad form."

"All right," I say, looking up, knees brushing painfully into the carpet.

He holds his hand out, and I grab it, and as he lifts me to my feet, I feel like the sin could never be greater. Who is this man? And—his hand now casually curved around my lower hip, my buttocks—what have I fallen into, eyes half open or more?

That night I think about the picture of Alice and Lois for a long time. I think about telling Bill. I think about asking Alice. Or Mike. But I know I will do none of these things. I know I will hold on to it, hold on to it tightly. The strangest thing of all is how unsurprising it is. It has a haunting logic. I suppose Alice had been desperate for money. Hadn't she always been desperate for money? How can I know what it was like? I don't know how bad things may have gotten before she had Bill to turn to. I don't even know if the photos were doctored. I don't know anything. But I know I will hold on to the card, tuck it in my drawer under three layers of handkerchiefs, just in case.

Within two weeks, I've banished the thought. After a few awkward encounters, I can finally see Alice again without the image shuddering before me, raw-boned, grimy black and a stark, sweaty white. But I don't forget it.

One weekend, Bill and Alice canceled plans with me at the last minute to go to Ensenada. They came back glowing, brown as café con leche and with a duffel bag filled to bursting with mangoes, melons, passion fruit, ripe and fleshy. Bill pretended to be mad that Alice had snuck the fruit through customs while he, a member of law enforcement, no less, sat beside her. He spoke to her sternly and refused to melt at her lippy pout. But when she made her signature ambrosia dripping with honey and coconut, spelling his name with cherries on top, he ate heartily, pulling her onto his lap and kissing her with a sticky mouth.

A few weeks later, Alice suggests a weekend getaway to Baja, Bill and Alice and Mike Standish and myself.

"You know Bill hasn't quite warmed up to Mike, and I think this would be a good opportunity for everybody," Alice says to me in a confiding tone.

"Bill doesn't like Mike?" I say plainly, wondering what she knows.

"I wouldn't say that. I'm sure it's hard for a brother. No man is good enough for his sister, right?"

"It's not as though we're serious," I say carefully. "He's just someone I can go out with."

"All the better." Alice smiles. "No pressure, then. Wouldn't it be divine? Swimming, dinner at the waterfront restaurants, dancing."

"It sounds expensive."

"Mike can afford it. He's got pockets full of dough."

"What about Bill?" I say, purposely light.

"Oh, he needs to splurge more. He's too careful. His work is so stressful. It's important that he have fun."

"I don't know if Mike . . . we see each other during the week. I think he has more glamorous commitments during the weekend. I wouldn't feel comfortable asking him."

"I've already asked him. He wants to go. And don't worry" — she grins at me sidelong — "I've booked separate rooms for you two, to keep up appearances."

"Alice," I say, with a feeling of dread. "I don't think it's such a good idea."

"Why not?"

"Many, many reasons. And you *know*." Because, in truth, I know Bill doesn't like Mike Standish. I can tell by the careful way he speaks about him and to him, or the freighted tones with which he asks, "How was your evening with the publicity man, Lora? Did he see you home after the party, Lora?" Once I heard him say to Charlie Beauvais, "What kind of man wears a pink shirt, anyway?" And Charlie laughed, and Bill, rubbing his bristle cut, did not.

"What do I know, Lora?" Alice says blankly but with a faint glimmer in her eyes.

"You know. Let's not go through it all."

"I don't know what the problem is. I'm suggesting a lovely weekend trip. You should be thanking me," she says with no apparent guile, only a pretty Alice-smile.

"Bill will not want to do it, Alice."

"True, at *first*. He didn't want to, at first." Alice smiles. "But then he settled down about it."

And then we are on the highway, in Mike's convertible. Alice is playing Louis Prima loud on the radio and holding her wide-brimmed straw hat to her head, ribbons blowing behind in the breeze. There I am, watching Mike and wondering why we are all here. A cigarette hanging from his mouth, sunglasses shielding his eyes, he smiles lazily at me, as if getting a kick out of the entire improbable thing—what a gas. Here he is with a cop and his schoolmarm sister, two squares who should be sitting on some porch swing in Pasadena, twiddling their thumbs.

It starts with mai tais. We girls are drinking mai tais on the long deck that wraps around the hotel. The sun is setting, burnishing everything, and the rimy drink sets our teeth on edge, and we are leaning back and the drink is churning slowly and warmly inside.

The men have ordered Scotch, which they are nursing quietly. They are trying to find things to talk about. UCLA football. The best way to get to San Diego. Mike's new coupe.

But Alice is skilled at making it work. She beams at Bill and brings up "topics" and laughs at all Mike's jokes. She tells a long, funny story about a dress she worked on for Greer Garson. She'd had to take it out, and out, and out. They kept sending the dress back, saying the actress was "er, retaining" and needed more "room to move."

Mike has a second Scotch and begins to swap studio gossip, and he places his hand on my leg under the table and it is fine and relaxed.

There is a lengthy discussion about where we should eat and where the best seafood is supposed to be and when is the best time to go.

A sloe-eyed torch singer takes the stage in the bar and begins crooning. Suddenly, there are more mai tais and I notice myself giggling and can't remember why I've begun.

There are two men in panama hats at the table across the aisle who are playing cards.

A trio of couples behind us are arguing raucously about moral rearmament.

A man in the far corner is moving closer and closer to his date, a young Mexican girl who looks uneasy, her thin-slitted eyes darting around.

"Is anybody hungry?" Bill is saying. But the rest of us don't seem to answer, and then there are more drinks and Mike's arm is around my waist, fingers grazing my midriff.

"Don't forget that actor who was sweet on you." Mike is laughing.

Everyone looks at Alice, who stares blankly.

"Don't you remember? That English fellow who kept saying, 'Measure the inseam, darling. The inseam.' "

Alice smiles noncommittally, not meeting Bill's gaze.

"Remember how he made you run the tape measure?" Mike chortles, and Alice suddenly laughs, too, despite her efforts. I think maybe I laugh, too.

"I'm glad you don't have to do that anymore," Bill says, determinedly lightly.

"They called her the Girl with the Tape." Mike sighs. "And they meant it fondly."

"Oh, Mike," Alice says dismissively. "Where should we eat?"

"Let's dance," I find myself saying, the music from inside swelling sweetly.

"Wonderful!" Alice clasps her hands together. "Why eat when you can dance?"

"Shouldn't we eat first?" Bill says. "These drinks must be falling hard on you."

He is looking at Alice, but it is Mike who laughs. Laughs as if Bill has made a hilarious joke, and turns to me and holds out his hand and I take it. I take it.

And the next thing I know I am pressed against him on the small dance floor, the orange-gold lights of the bar cloaking us, tucking us closely together. The music is so beautiful I think I'll never hear such beautiful music again.

Later, I won't remember what was playing. But I remember one lyric buzzing hot in my ear over and over, "It was a night filled with . . . desperate."

Later, the lyric won't make sense.

Later, I'll try to remember how it went. But I can't match it. Can't make it work. Can't make the words hang together right.

I'll just remember that we danced and then he seemed to know everything about me and seemed to see everything and he was so limited, such a horribly limited person, but that night he seemed like he knew everything and I would take it. Who was I not to take it?

At just past midnight, Mike deposits me at my door and says good night to us all. My brother and Alice, arms around each other, walk into their room, and I walk into my adjoining one. A few minutes later, I stumble into the shared bathroom. Holding on to the sink, dizzy with drinks and dancing, I laugh at my own reflection, its frenzied gaiety. How has all this happened?

Alice comes in a few minutes later, dress half off, hanging in front of her like a silky bib. I resist the sudden flash before my eyes of her, laid bare, on the dirty playing card. Dizzy with drink, I literally shake my head to knock the image out.

Giggling and hiccuping, she walks toward me, arms out. "Help me, Lora. Bill's all thumbs."

Five minutes of giggly fumbling, of her buttons going in and out of distended focus, and I undo her.

She tugs the top half of the dress down to her waist and shakes her arms free, facing the mirror. After a long look at herself, she reaches past me to my cold cream on the counter.

"I always wash the makeup off," she stresses, waving past my face. "No matter how smashed I am. If I can barely stand—if I have to hang on to the sink with one hand to see the mirror—I still do it."

I nod gravely and watch her scoop the cream with two fingers.

Suddenly, we both hear a knock from my adjoining room.

"Someone's at my door," I say. Alice's eyes widen. Then narrow.

"Honey, you'd better get it," she says in a whisper, turning back to her reflection with a faint grin.

"Is it Mike?" I ask as she covers her face in white.

"Go get it, darling," she says, her red lips still visible. "I won't tell."

Vaguely, I want to tell her she has the wrong idea, that I haven't invited Mike Standish back, that I don't know why he might be there, and that there is no secret to keep. Tell whom? But I can't form the sentences. It seems too exhausting. I manage only "Maybe it's the bellboy . . . room service by mistake . . ."

She keeps looking straight into the mirror, her face a big blank now. I walk back into my room, closing the bathroom door behind me. My left shoe dragging in the carpet, I make it to my room's front door and say, touching the blond wood lightly, "Who is it?"

"Little Jack Horner," Mike says.

I open the door partway.

"Is that the one with the thumb and the pie," I ask.

"Sure, baby." He reaches a hand from behind him and shows me a bottle of champagne. "Nightcap, room 411, five minutes or, if you'd like a personal escort, presently."

When he speaks, his eyebrows rise and his round shoulders tilt forward and I stare at him for a moment, leaning hard against the rough edge of the door, and then I extend my hand without thinking. And I take his arm. And my hand doesn't even seem to make it halfway around its thickness. And his smile is so loose and so easy and only a half smile really, and I don't even stumble because, you see, he wouldn't stumble. He never stumbles at all. And as we walk along the red and tan diamonds on the carpet, the sconces releasing only a soft golden shadow for us, I think this might be all right.

Two hours later, staring up at the shadows of the banana leaves on the ceiling . . . *This is the end of everything.* The phrase rings out and shoots through the air and quavers tightly, suspended, and does everything but dive into my chest. Could six words ever sound so ominous?

The following night, after a long day at the beach and the markets, we enjoy what becomes a nearly endless dinner on a commercial yacht anchored a few miles from shore. The service is so slow that it is two hours before the food arrives and, along with those at nearly every other occupied table, we become unintentionally fuzzy with drink.

I have never seen my brother drunk before, and he is very charming.

We eat lobster tails and drink champagne, and Mike pays for it all by charging it to the studio. Bill is too softly intoxicated to notice.

Later that night, we end up at an old cantina with Wild West doors. Their feet gliding along the sawdust-covered floors, Mike and Alice dance to a thrumming mariachi band, and Bill and I lean back in rickety chairs and recover from the flush of the dinner.

Somehow, although the music is roaring, we can hear each other perfectly and we recall—together and in impossibly great detail—a favorite Fourth of July from our youth, from the hornet bite on my throbbing leg to the splattery fireworks to the splinters Bill got from skimming along the boat dock as he ran, feet first, into the lake.

—I'm a little drunk, so don't listen to me.

   —You're a little drunk, I smile and listen anyway.

   —I'm a little drunk, Sis, and feeling like I want to tell you something.

   —Anything, I say, chest suddenly, strangely pulsing, rippling.

   —You know, right, even if I don't say it, that I'd do anything for you. Anything.

   —I do know, I say slowly, solemnly, so he'll know I mean it.

   —We're each other's family and I feel

   (His eyes luminous, severe, relentless: saying, Listen to me now because I may never be able to say this again, may never be able to tell you like this what I feel—what I feel and live every day and you do too.)

   —I—I'm yours, Sis. You know that, right? I'm all yours and I'm responsible for you and that's what I want.

   —I'm glad, Bill

   is all I can say, all I know how to say.

   He tilts his head against mine, like when children swinging hammock, and gripping hands hard.

And it is there, and happening, and then it is over, gone.
But it breaks my heart it is so beautiful.

I will never forget it.

It is in the middle of that same long, messy summer, before we even know she is pregnant. Amid all the fun, even with its dark edges, Charlie and Edie Beauvais slip unnoticeably off the dance card. We are all too busy to see, to stop for a second. And now, this:

What could be sadder than seeing Edie Beauvais there, white fluffy cloud of hair against the pillow, eyes like two fresh wounds?

I take a long time arranging the lilacs in the vase, unsure what to say.

Her arms lay flat out in front of her, palms facing up, a tissue crumpled in one hand.

"I'm awfully sorry, Edie. I know how much you and Charlie . . ."

"Hmm," she says noncommittally, staring out the window.

"If there's anything I can do . . ."

"Thanks."

"Would you like me to get you a movie magazine? The new *Photoplay*?" I offer weakly.

She looks over at me without moving or even turning her head.

"Will they let you leave soon?"

"Day or two. I lost a lot of blood. You should have seen it. It was everywhere."

"I'm sure you'll be back to your old self in no time." I don't bring up what Charlie has told me, about her not being able to get pregnant again.

Such a little blond thing wasn't meant for this, like wet snow on the pillow, sinking fast and nearly disappearing.

But as I look at her, she all of twenty-three, I wonder what she will do for the next forty years of her life. I know she too is seeing her future spread out before her, years and years of Charlie working long hours and growing older and saggier, and she decorating and redecorating and gardening and going on long drives through the hills and fine lines etching in the corners of her bright eyes and watching other women with their baby carriages and their toddlers and long-lashed schoolchildren and awkward, shiny-faced teenagers and eventually downy, glassy-eyed children of their own. She will have none of this. It will not be hers. And her life feels over at twenty-three. How could one possibly fill those years, days, hours? One sharp slash and her future shriveled up into itself. How could one fill one's life?

This from a man so impeccable. But there it is, in the tipped-over bag Mike has left for the laundry, an effluvium of white sheets with a long, hot streak of fuchsia lipstick. I can picture a swirl of candy-colored hair pushed face-first into the bed linen. My stomach turns.

Mike is fast behind me, scooping up the sheets and shoving them into the bag and yanking it closed with one swift gesture. Like a magician.

I had been about to light a cigarette, even though I don't really smoke. He had already pulled his lighter out of his pocket. And there it is, or was.

I feel something slip inside me, fast and hard, and then suddenly regain its footing before hitting bottom. The shaking hand, cigarette loose between fingers, that had seemed about to move to my face returns instead to my side. Then, a second later, am I really leaning casually against the wall, managing even to finish lighting the cigarette, lifting my head to the still outstretched lighter?

He snaps the lighter shut, looking down at me with watchful eyes. Then, he slides the lighter into his pocket and leans against the wall too.

"Lora King, you continue to surprise me. You really do."

I look up at him, blowing smoke from behind my lower lip. He turns his head, appraising.

"I really had you pegged for one of those who would be wrecked."

I let the smoke fill my lungs, giving shape and texture and spine to the moment. My jaw sets itself, and the warm flush I'd first felt around my eyes, tears waiting to happen, vanishes. I am sucked dry in a heartbeat and feel funny, like I am on strings.

"I thought you'd be a finger pointer, or an hysteric, at least a crier," he says, not smugly but thoughtfully, like he has just read something unanticipated in the morning paper, something that happened between sundown and sunup.

"Is that the usual routine?" I say, walking toward the center of the room, then turning and facing him again.

"Not always, but with you . . ." He smiles suddenly and, head still tilted against the wall, he twists around to catch my gaze. "Aren't I a bastard? Or maybe I'm a powder puff. You see, Lora King, turns out I'm surprising myself this time. Turns out I'm disappointed how little you care."

I find myself offering a sharp giggle of shock.

"Hard-boiled." He winces.

Covering my mouth, I concede, "You're rotten," before letting the smile spread, blowing smoke. I run the tip of my thumb along my lower lip, brushing away a stray wisp of tobacco.

"Well, then." He folds his arms and matches my stare, grinning like a snake. "Put out that cigarette, beautiful, and take off the fucking dress."

It is the middle of August when it happens, when I can't ignore it any longer. It is a postcard of the famous pier, a shadowy couple on the edge, waving in the moonlight. It is lying on the floor of my vestibule. The words "Welcome to Santa Monica Pier" are punches of light in the sky. The handwriting awkward, as though written from a strange angle or position, or maybe while riding in a car, fast.

Your brothers wife is a tramp, she's no good and she'll rune him. if you dont beleve me, ask at the Red room lounge in Holywd.

I read it over three or four times, squinting at the scratches. There is no postmark. Somebody has just slid it under the door. I sit down and read it one more time.

I turn it over, look at the picture again, and then read it even more slowly, studying the address, the turned corner. What could it possibly . . .

I take a long pause, then pick up the phone. Then put the phone down. Then grab the phone book for Hollywood. Dragging my finger up the page.

Redux Stereophonics

Red Tag Appliances

Red Sam's Pawn

Red Rose Florals

Red Rooster Coffee Shop

Red Room Lounge

Red Room Lounge. 12614 Hollywood Boulevard.

"Hello. I'm trying to find someone. I think she may be a customer."

"Honey, we're a bar and grill, not an information service."

"You just might know her name."

"I don't know names. I don't know nothing. You want a drink, come on by."

My chest is vibrating. It is six o'clock, or nearly so. If I change and leave immediately, I can be there by seven, but for what? An employee eager to tell me something? A customer? If so, why doesn't the card specify a day and time?

I put the card down and start peeling potatoes for dinner.

Soon, however, I begin to feel a tug in the back of my head. Something on the postcard keeps ringing in my ears, but I can't place it. I find myself thinking about Joe Avalon and about the playing card. About many small, taunting whispers in my ear, whispers I'd heard and keep on hearing.

Within fifteen minutes, I find myself in the car, driving toward Hollywood.

Tucked between an Italian restaurant and a peeling office building, the Red Room Lounge is a basic shoe box building distinguished only by a heavily painted crimson door and a chain of paint-spattered lights across the dusty window.

The curtains are pulled across, but as I draw nearer I can see through the gaping edge. There is a mirrored bar, Naugahyde booths, and a few bustling waitresses with red scarves and blank expressions. My hand on the varnished wood handle, I take a breath and walk in.

Youngish to middle-aged men in cheap shirts and flashy grins turn to the door when it shuts behind me, and a few of the dull-faced girls with tightly curled haircuts and painfully arched brows glance over casually.

I guess I must have expected an immediate response, a stranger approaching me, an unmistakable clue. When nothing happens, I find a small table and sit down. A grim-faced waitress with a painfully shorn poodle cut takes my order and brings me a Seven & Seven.

I sit, brushing off the occasional offer of a drink from pointy-jawed scenesters. I sit for nearly two hours, feeling the smoke and grease and desperation fill my pores, wondering what in the world I am doing there, how I happened to fall for this.

"Fuck a duck, it's Big Bill's baby sis."

It is a long, blue drawl followed by the sharp clack of brightly polished nails on the table in front of me.

I look up: Lois. In all her crooked-faced, ruby-lipped glory.

She sits down, rakishly tugging her tiny evening hat over her eye. Plastic cherries dangle from it, over her shiny white forehead.

"What you doin' here?" she says, dragging the words slowly, looking me up and down amusedly.

"Oh, I don't— I just wanted a drink. I stopped by on my way to meet a friend."

"Is that a fact? Funny. Don't seem like your type of haunt."

"It's not really. I just— I didn't know. I . . ."

Her twisty grin suddenly turns broad and her eyes light up.

"Oh! Oh, I get it. Don't worry, honey. I won't tell."

"Won't tell what?" I say, my mind racing over what it might mean that Lois is here. Could she have sent the postcard? But if she wanted to tell me something about Alice, why not come right out with it?

"You got a secret admirer," she murmurs. Then, "Scotty, another," pointing to her lipstick-rimmed glass.

"No."

"A randy-voo. Don't worry, sugar cake. I won't tell."

"I don't. I just wanted a drink and—"

"And you just thought with your stiff hat and your starched gloves you'd dip into this dive. Don't worry, honey. I'm not bracin' you."

"Are you here alone?"

"I'm never alone." She brings the fresh drink to her lips.

"I'm with that party over there." She points to a corner table filled with raw-boned servicemen and one baby-faced woman whose brightly gartered leg is tucked beneath her, flashing a half mile of creamy, gleaming thigh.

"Friends of yours?" I say.

"Sure."

Looking over at us furtively, the girl at the table mouths Lois's name. Or at least I assume it's Lois's name. For a split second, I think she's mouthing "Lora."

Lois merely waves and turns back to me.

"Who's that girl?" I ask.

"Some gal I met at a casting call. Why? You looking to join the party?"

One of the servicemen slams his glass down, sending ice everywhere. The others laugh even as the girl jumps in her seat, smile stuck on her face. Another grabs her leg and rubs it under the table. Her expression betrays nothing, and he keeps rubbing roughly, eyes fixed on her. A trace of fear skims across her face, but she quickly suppresses it, shifting her leg and slightly shaking herself away, bouncily downing her drink.

She looks back over at Lois fleetingly, eyes jumping anxiously. Lois merely winks back at her.

"No. I . . . I wondered if, well, if Alice might have been with you tonight. Do you— Did you ever come here with her?"

"Alice?" Her painted-on brows shoot up and she laughs. "I don't think so." So, I realize with something like relief, it isn't Lois who sent the postcard.

She looks over at the increasingly loud, throbbing table of

soldiers, then rises, sliding her drink into her other hand, along with her cigarettes and lighter. "Looks like I should rejoin my party, angel face. Don't miss me much."

"Okay. Good-bye, Lois." I hunch my shoulders together, suddenly wishing she wouldn't go. Suddenly afraid for her to go, to join those boys with their hard, tight, coiled hands, shoulders, faces. They look ready to pounce.

She pauses a long, silver moment, looking at me, the comb in her hair glittering in the low lighting. Her smile slides away and she just looks at me, thick, fringy lashes casting shadows across her face. I feel something. I feel something fall away.

And then the smile returns, at its usual half-mast. "Hey, be careful, peaches. You know?"

"Right," I say, watching her and watching the servicemen behind her, now all pounding their glasses hard on the table, red-faced and primed. "You, too."

She turns, the back of her shiny purple dress sliding after her, swaying like a fish tail, swaying after her as I watch and feel a keen shudder.

I grab my purse, take a sip of my now-watery drink, and stand up. I am out the door before Lois slinks back into that murky red corner.

Later that night, I think about the postcard. Probably just a bitter old boyfriend of Alice's or a romantic rival trying for some measure of revenge. The image of sharkskinned Joe Avalon passes through my head. Were he and Alice once lovers? One thing feels sure: The writer of the postcard didn't expect that I'd actually go to the Red Room Lounge, figured

that the postcard would be enough to stir suspicion. I decide
that I'd better forget it.

Three hours of cocktails and crowded dancing in Bill and
Alice's living room, their Labor Day party just kicking up at
nearly eleven o'clock, a cutthroat game of canasta in the
kitchen, an impromptu dance contest on the living room's
wall-to-wall, a gang watching a boxing match on the Philco, a
bawdy conversation spilling from the powder room into the
hallway. And there's my brother standing to the side, looking
like a wrung rag, shirtfront wet from crushed rumbas with tire-
less Alice. He is nearly a foot taller than Alice when she is in
her stocking feet, but she exerts so much presence that you
never think of the height difference. Bill is always receding into
the background, leaning back on the couch, hanging back
from the circle gathered in the middle of the party, while Alice
looms forward, saucer eyes and manic energy, her red-ringed
mouth huge, like a beautiful fish against the glass.

Finally, Mike, an hour late, arrives with an orchid as delicate as a doll wrist.

"My apologies, King. Budding starlet, too much dope, car
tipped over half into the canyon. You didn't hear it from me."

"Can I take your hat?" I hold my hand out.

He smiles, handing me both his hat and his attaché. "Girl's
had a few?"

"It's just the atmosphere. It's like a sponge."

I walk down the hall to the bedroom and deposit his things

on the bed, where a small mound of ridiculously out-of-season fur chubbies and cowls sit. I set his hat on the bedside table and turn around to see Mike standing in the doorway.

"These bulls sure can swing," he says, as he says many things, as though almost wanting to yawn.

"That they can." I move toward the door. With a clean gesture, he steps in and shuts the door behind him.

"You are fooling yourself, sir," I say, "if you think I would kiss you in my brother's bedroom."

"Any brother who throws parties like this could hardly care." He nudges me backward with a thick forefinger. The backs of my legs brush up against the silk coverlet.

"It's Alice's party," I say, knowing he is playing me.

"Is that how you frame it?" He places the heel of his hand on my collarbone and actually shoves me this time. I fall back onto the bed, the span of furs curling under me, bristling against my neck and arms.

"Tough guy now," I say, waiting for him to break into his characteristic ironic grin.

"That's right." He looks down at me, no grin.

I feel suddenly hot with shame. All the things that happen in Mike's cool, self-contained apartment start to flash before me.

"Don't—"

His mouth untwists and releases itself into a self-aware smile. "I'm just kidding, King. You know I have your number. I wouldn't hold it against you."

I manage a return smile, and take his hand. As I rise, my shoe hits something soft, and my ankle wrenches. We both look down to the floor and see a small steel-blue book slide out from under my foot.

I pick it up and set it back down on the bed.

"I don't think that was on the bed," Mike says. "More like under it."

"No?" I pick it up again, running my finger along the gold edges of the pages.

"See if there's a name in it."

I open it up and see pages and pages of what appear to be some kind of strange shorthand, all initials and numbers.

"Not another Red," Mike says.

"It's an address book," I say, gesturing to the small lettered tabs on the page edges. "In code."

"Lots of people don't want their numbers getting around. Especially in this town," Mike says offhandedly as he opens the door.

"Should I just leave it here?"

Mike shrugs, already halfway out the door, eyes thirsty for a drink.

Suddenly, Alice appears in the doorframe, almost as though she's been hovering just outside of view.

Without knowing why, my heart jumps and I find myself gripping Mike's arm. On instinct, I tuck the address book between the folds of my skirt.

"Look who I find in my bedroom. My, my," Alice says, shaking her head.

"I was dropping off Mike's hat," I say.

Alice nods with a teasing smirk. But something in her eyes—

"Where's these drinks I keep hearing about?" Mike says, dropping an arm around each of our shoulders.

"Oh, I see . . ." Alice laughs with low, raw tones.

Mike laughs too, and we walk together down the hall. We walk with the address book sliding, as if not by my own hand, into my pocket.

Later that night, back at my apartment, I try to steady my party-clogged, smoke-drenched head by lying down. The address book slips out of my pocket onto the bedspread. I pick it up. On the inside cover are the words "Deau Stationers." And the tiny address: "312 Hill Street, Los Angeles." I think about the postcard, trying to see any possible connection.

It isn't the next day, but the day after that I find myself at a small shop with old-fashioned green shutters just around the corner from the funicular railway that creeps up and down a yellow clay bank from Hill Street. The store looks the part of a once-grand remnant of the sagging, shaggy Bunker Hill neighborhood.

As I walk toward it, I wonder what exactly I am doing. Isn't this likely just some party guest's item, fallen from a coat? But the code is so strange, and the book so fancy, fancier than a schoolteacher or a policeman or any other likely party guest would have. Too ornate for any of those men and too masculine for the women.

I open the door and see a horseshoe glass counter filled

with buttery leather-bound books, pale-hued stationery blocks, and sterling silver fountain pens.

A young woman with cat's-eye glasses looks up from her sales sheet.

"Yes?"

I move closer to her, suddenly very self-conscious. What is my plan here?

"I'm wondering if you could help me," I all but whisper.

"A diary?"

"Pardon?"

She pulls a small, cream-colored leather book from the glass case to her left.

"It has a gold lock and key, gold edging, the most charming gold studs in the tufted padding." She runs her hand across the top of the book, then looks up at me.

"I . . . I don't understand."

"Oh," she says, setting the book down. "Usually I have a good sense about these things. You look like the diary type."

I feel my face warming. "Sorry, no. I really just have a question."

I take the address book from my purse and set it on the counter in front of her. "Is this from your shop?"

She tilts her head at me and then looks down at the book. She flips the cover open to the stamp on the inner leaf.

"I guess you already knew that," she says.

My face grows warmer still. "I do. I guess . . . I suppose what I'm asking is if you might, somehow, know anything about this purchase. If you might remember making this sale."

"Do you know how many of these we might sell in a given week?" she asks with a clipped voice, looking back down at the Deau stamp.

"I'm sorry. Of course. Really, I have no idea. Pardon me," I say, reaching out to retrieve the book.

"We sell less than one in a given week, on average," she says, holding on to the book with pressed-together forefingers. "Actually, we sell maybe one or two a year."

I look up at her.

"It's not a comment on business, which is fair, all things considered," she continues. "It's just that this is a custom-made book, sewn with special French thread, hand-pressed leather. We had to order it specially."

I nod, not seeing.

"This book," she says, holding it up between two fingers. "This tiny book costs two hundred and fifty dollars."

"Two hundred and fifty dollars," I repeat.

"Yes. This tiny book cost *us* two hundred and fifty dollars when the check bounced."

"*Oh.*" I see at last.

"Oh indeed. Would you mind telling me how you came upon this book? We'd obviously be very interested in finding its owner." She holds the book still, despite my unthinking effort to take it back again.

"Don't you know, from the check?"

Pursing her lips, she pulls out a small clipboard from under the counter. To it are attached a few checks and a list of names.

She slides the clipboard toward me, her finger pointing at one of the checks.

"*This* person does not exist. We don't know who passed it."

It reads, John Davalos.

I feel a wave of disappointment. The name means nothing.

"Ring a bell?"

I say, "No."

I say no. But, on a hunch, I take the book from her tight little fingers.

And wish her a fine day. I leave too quickly for her to try to take the book back.

I have the thought it might come in handy.

I do try, at first, to forget about the address book, too. What, after all, do I really know? But it keeps bumping up against me, shoving itself in front of my face like a carnival huckster trailing after you as you hurry past, avoid eye contact, resist the spiel, the hot, fast patter of infinite and gaudy persuasion. Somehow, it lingers with me even more than the dirty playing card. That photo seemed part of Alice's ancient past, but this is Alice's—and Bill's—present.

It is with a vague twitch of guilt that I begin watching her. Before I know it, I find myself watching her everywhere. At Sunday dinner, at social events, at the new school year's first department meetings, I keep waiting to see a connection, a clue. A clue to what, though, really, after all.

There is a string I am pulling together, a string of question marks so long they are beginning to clatter against each other, and loudly.

I count them on my fingers, beginning to feel the fool: the missing credentials, the unexplained absences, the playing card, the postcard, and now the address book. And perhaps most of all, Alice herself. Something in her. The hold so tight over my brother, and suddenly it appears more and more as though she is this brooding darkness lurking around him, creeping toward him, swarming over him. Her glamour like some awful curse.

"Mr. Standish is on set right now. If you'll wait." The receptionist with the silver fingernails gestures toward a long row of chrome-trimmed leather chairs.

Guests of publicists and press agents don't rate too highly with the front office staff, or so I've come to learn in recent months. I sit down, back straight, as awkward as I always feel anywhere near the studio.

I watch the top of her foamy blond head tilt this way and that as she answers calls on her headset, fingers tapping the earpieces with each turn and swivel of her chair.

I look over at a rough-hewn boy seated four chairs down. He has a scar like a lightning bolt over his left eye and wears a sweater and gymnasium shoes.

When he spots me looking at him, he nods, straightening in his seat. Reaching into his pocket, he pulls out a packet of cigarettes, gesturing toward me.

"No. Thank you."

He nods again and slides one into his mouth. "Do you mind?"

I shake my head and smile slightly.

Blowing a shallow stream from his mouth, he looks back toward me. "You in that college movie? The one with all the football scenes?"

"Pardon?"

"Sorry. I just know they're shooting this afternoon and I thought I seen you over there before."

"No." I shake my head. "I'm just visiting someone."

"I did a few stunts over there," he says, leaning forward. "Those pretty boys in the letter sweaters can't take a tackle to save your life."

I smile. Sensing he expects a reply, I say, "Did you get that scar from doing stunts?"

He touches his forehead self-consciously, and I feel bad. I assumed he'd be proud of it, like a battle wound.

"No, I got this a long time ago. Old bar fight. But I've been working here for a while now."

He looks at me expectantly, and I can tell he is waiting for a response.

"How did you get into stunt work?" I offer, hoping Mike will show up.

"Oh, I was knocking around, trying to find a way to make some money for taking punches, rather than taking them for free," he says. It sounds like he's said it many times before, to great effect.

I try to stop the conversation politely with a closing smile.

"I been doing it for four years now."

He takes another drag. "I did a stunt for Alan Ladd once. Frank Sinatra even."

"Well, well."

Suddenly, the foamy blond head of the receptionist pops up, and her nasal voice rings out, "Teddy, Mr. Schor is through with him. Mr. Davalos is on his way out. He wants you to bring the car around."

The boy jumps up, suddenly flustered.

"On it," he shouts, dancing on the balls of his feet for a second before nodding his head toward me and heading to the door.

Mr. Davalos. Suddenly, I see the arched brow of the woman at Deau Stationers as if she were right before my eyes. Mr. Davalos. Could this be the owner of the address book in my sister-in-law's bed? No. I must have misheard. The name has occupied my thoughts so much in the last few days that I must have imagined hearing it aloud.

I take the opportunity to pick up a *Modern Screen*, in case the boy returns and wants to continue the conversation. Burying my head behind it, I wonder how long Mike will be and if I should really keep waiting.

A few minutes pass before I hear a quiet, faintly familiar voice. "Is Teddy out there?"

"Yes, Mr. Davalos. He should be waiting for you."

"Thank you."

As the voice trails away, I glance up from the magazine just in time to see Joe Avalon, resplendent in sharkskin, passing the reception desk and through the office doors.

He doesn't see me.

I rise as he steps out. Walking to the window, my heart jumping a bit, I look out. Tugging his hat down, he opens the door of a sleek black roadster. I see a flash of deep maroon interior as he pulls the door shut behind him and the car leaps to life and drives off.

Joe Avalon is John Davalos.

Shaken out of my shock by the nervous buzzing at the reception desk, I turn around on my heel, almost losing my balance.

Foamy-head is watching me. "Mr. Standish says he's coming."

"Fine," I say. Ticking my finger lightly on the window, I ask, "Who was that man? I think I know him."

She pauses and looks at me for a moment. "That's Mr. Davalos."

"Does he work for the studio?"

She pauses again. "He's not a casting agent, if that's what you mean."

"No, no." I smile. "I'm not an actress. I just think I've met him before."

I then add, "Maybe through Mr. Standish."

"He doesn't work here. He's a business associate of Mr. Schor's."

"I see," I say, just as Mike pushes open the glass doors.

"Let's go, doll," he says, tipping the hat in his hand to Foamy-head. "Before the gray fellows call me back. I gotta talk to a few columnists at Sugie's."

＊

Joe Avalon. What more do you need, I ask myself. What more do you need to know you must do something? The next morning, as Alice gathers her sewing samples for our first day back to school, I grab her phone book and pass through it as quickly as I can. I'm not sure which number is his. There is nothing under A or D that fits. I end up looking under J, and there is a number without a name attached. In my haste, I end up scribbling it on the inside of my wrist.

That afternoon, during my prep period, I call the operator, who tells me that the name listed with the number is J. Devlin. Given the multiplying names, I feel sure that it's Joe Avalon. And then, she actually gives me the address. As I write it down, I wonder what exactly I think I'm going to do. But something keeps telling me I've waited long enough, let enough strange glimmers accumulate in the corners of my eyes. It's time to stop blinking.

After dropping off Alice after school, I drive into Los Angeles and find the house on Flower Street. I sit in my car for three hours, and he never appears.

I go back the following evening. I sit and watch. I think about Bill. I think about Joe Avalon in my brother's bedroom. I think about Alice and what she has brought with her, what she's carried into my brother's world. Our world.

At a little past ten, a car pulls up his driveway. I duck down in my seat and then wait, watch.

Joe Avalon, in a shiny raincoat, emerges and heads for his

front door. I ask myself, Could this man really be Alice's lover? And if not that, what?

He is alone. Here is the opportunity. There is no reason to wait. I banish the strumming refrain in my head. The one that keeps asking what I think I'm doing here, after all.

As he unlocks his door and walks inside, I slide out of my car and walk to his house. There is no use thinking about it, I just have to do it, without thinking, just go . . .

I am suddenly there, knuckles rapping the pine door.

And it's a long minute before he opens it, coat off, collar open, blast of cologne in my face. He doesn't know what to make of it.

"Miss King, right?"

He opens the door wider. "Come in," he says. He says, "Come in."

I step past him and into the darkly paneled hallway of the pristine, cocoa-colored bungalow.

"I can't guess why I'm so lucky," he says softly. He always speaks softly, and low, so you have to lean in to hear. A trick like a southern belle's.

The hallway spills into a living room, Oriental rug, teak-colored blinds, amber lamps, and a large, plush sofa in deep rose.

"Have a seat." He buttons his collar, twisting his neck. "Can I get you a drink?"

I shake my head, but he begins pouring two glasses from the mahogany bar cart. Whiskey and two quick sprays of soda from a smooth green bottle.

He hands the drink to me and gestures for me to sit on

one of the damask chairs. Opposite me, he settles on the sofa.

My hand curls around the glass, and I'm suddenly glad I have it to hold on to. I finally look at him straight on. I can't avoid it. His eyes, glossy dark like brine, fixed and waiting.

"I couldn't be more surprised, Miss King. I'm sitting here thinking that I don't even know how you know where I live. Is this about our mutual friend Alice?" He says this all nearly tonelessly, only the vague lilt of someone very conscious of how he speaks, the words he wants to use.

"*I have something of yours.*" This is what I say. I just say it, and that's it.

"Is that right?" he shoots back more quickly than I anticipated.

"I have something of yours." I look him straight in the eye this time, and his right lid twitches for just a second.

"And what is that, Miss King?"

"You can't guess?" I watch his face. I want him to admit something, confess to something, betray something.

"Miss King, I really can't imagine." He smiles vaguely, unreadably. "But I'd really like to know."

"I bet you would." How I manage to say this, I don't know. *It's like a movie scene. This is what they say in the movies.*

"This could go on forever, Miss King." He slouches back in his seat. "Do you have a direction in mind for this exchange?"

I open my purse and pull out the address book, keeping it close to my chest.

He looks at the book and doesn't flinch.

"Do you want it back?"

"That's supposed to be mine?" He gestures toward it.

"I know it's yours."

"Let me see it. I'll tell you if it's mine." He looks down at me, not making a move.

"It's yours, but that's not the interesting part." I feel a strange bravado lurching up in my chest. I can't guess where it's coming from.

"I'm waiting, Miss King. Don't think I'm not curious."

"I found it in my sister-in-law's bed," I say squarely.

He pauses and manages a slight grin. "*That's* the interesting part?"

"How did it get there?"

He leans back, setting his glass on his knee and spreading his arms along the back of the sofa.

"This is about your brother's wife. This is about you wanting to pin something on your brother's wife." He can't hide a smile.

"No. No," I say, reacting instantly to the strange allegation. What does he mean? What could he possibly mean? "I'm just trying to find out what . . ."

My mouth inexplicably goes dry. Pin something on my brother's wife? *Why would I . . .*

I hear some sound come from within me. My jaw begins shaking suddenly. It seems to be rattling.

He takes a sip from his drink, smile still suspended there. The glass has left a faint ring on the knee of his cream-colored pants. I stare at it, trying to regain my focus.

"I just want to know . . ." It's hard to talk with my jaw doing this. I can't make the words sound smooth.

He raises his eyebrows expectantly, waiting for me to finish my sentence.

". . . what it was doing there. I just want to know . . ."

I wonder, can he hear that? Can he hear how loud my jaw is? It seems so loud I can barely hear myself. A horrible rattling like a dying snake.

"Why didn't you ask your sister-in-law?" He smacks his lips ever so slightly, holding the glass with its still popping soda water. "Why don't you?"

"Maybe I did," I blurt, fixing my hand on my jaw to keep it in place.

"I don't think so." He smiles.

"No. I . . . I just want for you to tell me. I didn't want . . ." It's hard to answer because I don't know what the answer could be. To tell the truth, I'd never even thought to ask Alice. To tell the truth, it is as if, lately, as everything keeps surging forward, it is as if I am seeing her through glass, through dark water three feet deep.

"You wanted something over her?" he says, tilting his head.

He watches me squirm and shake my head fervently, but then his smile slips away for a moment, as if he has just realized something.

"How did you know it was mine, anyway?" My jaw finally settles a bit. If I clench it, I can speak.

"That doesn't matter," I say.

"I might decide that." His voice turns cooler. "You'd better just spill it all, Miss King."

Then he says, "You, honest, don't know what you're getting yourself into."

Then he says, "And I think you better give me the fucking book."

Then, finally, "It's mine, after all."

I stand up, my drink nearly slipping from between my fingers as I press the book to my chest. I feel foolish. If he really wants it, my little grasp isn't going to stop him.

I set the glass down.

Things suddenly feel far more complicated.

And all the reasons for not bringing the book with me, much less coming at all, swirl through my head. I wonder exactly what I am doing here.

I turn on my heel, intending, I suppose, to get as far as I can. Thinking, I guess, that it would be too embarrassing for him to overpower a woman.

But then thinking he might overpower a woman every day.

I can feel him watching me for a moment, then I see him, from the corner of my eye as I begin to walk to the door, calculatedly break into a shrug.

"You want it, you got it, Miss King," he says, standing, his thin-lipped smile hanging from one side of his face.

Then he adds, "I don't need it."

And finally, "It's been more than an even trade."

I open the door, and my hand is shaking like a string pulled taut and plucked hard.

On the drive home, my jaw buzzes, hums, nearly sings. I jam the heel of my hand underneath it, steer with one hand, and turn the radio as loud as it will go. The zing of the brutish jazz finally vibrates hard enough to drown it out.

My head clogged with incomplete revelation after revelation, I avoid Bill entirely. Any other time, he would be the one I would go to, would have long gone to, for help. But this time I can't.

Instead, the next night, unable to sleep, I end up at Mike Standish's apartment.

"You're awful dirty, Lora King. I wonder if anybody has any idea what a dirty girl you are."

I don't answer, don't like him saying it, even if I am curled against the edge of his bed, my knees on the floor, persuaded not to put my stockings on, persuaded to stay right where I am and look up at him, straight into his laughing eyes.

I sit there and I try to frame a question. But I can't.

"I'm going home."

"Why go home? No one's keeping tabs on you. Come on."

"You don't need me to stay." I reach for my stockings, pull them slowly from the tangle of sheets.

"I do." He sighs, stretching his arms above his head. "I really do."

"You like to sleep alone."

He seems—it is dark and hard to tell—to smirk a little before he says, "I think you should stay. You are the one I like to stay."

I almost ask why and then I don't ask why and my stocking, via my own slightly trembling hands, is streaming up my leg.

"Come on. I like you here and I like the way you smell. I like making you stay." He yawns.

Here he is, the man who knows things and who should

want to help me. But it is so hard to bring up things with any weight at all to a man like this. A man like this doesn't have real conversations.

He is lying there whistling contentedly, and I just close my eyes. For weeks, I've been deciding whether to ask him, ask him anything about what I've learned, or almost learned. Now, with what I have seen, with Joe Avalon and more and more questions, it seems I don't have anything to lose.

"I saw some pictures, Mike," I say, biting my lip a little, snapping my belt, adjusting my collar, feeling the need to straighten myself.

"It's all about pictures, King. Don't you forget it. It's my bread and butter." He reaches over and touches my belt lightly with a finger, leaning in and sending a shot of peppery cologne to my face.

"I mean specific pictures. Bad ones. Here in your apartment." I look at my gray shoes, pointy-toed and confident. Teacher shoes.

"I got pictures like that, sure," he says, and I realize, with regret, that he is scrambling, dancing.

"Pictures on playing cards. One of them, it was of my sister-in-law. Of my brother's wife. And Lois Slattery."

He smiles. He nearly grins, but it's an effort. "Oh, right. Yeah, I really didn't want you to see that. Not—not because . . . Frankly, King, I thought it would hurt you." The voice almost soft. "Because of your brother."

I can barely stand it. I honestly feel my knees buckle. There he is, this cold, rather limited man with—is it?—a distinct look of kindness in his eyes.

"How did you get those pictures?" I manage, recovering.

"Lora . . ." He sighs and sinks back into the bed.

"Tell me where you got those pictures."

"Listen . . . listen, we live differently, in different worlds. Truly, Lora, your world, your world is kind of beautiful. Why bring my world into it? Why—"

"Tell me, Mike. You'd better tell me." I look down at him.

"She gave them to me," he says, firmly, deliberately, but unable to look me in the eye for long. "To show me. She wanted me to see, Lora. She wanted me to see."

Later that night I lie in bed and think about what he said and how far I was able to push him and the point at which I couldn't ask any more questions. *Wanted you to see what?* I wanted to ask, but didn't. *And did you? Did you see what she wanted to show you?* Somehow I knew he had and now I had, too.

As the days pass, there is nothing else I can think about. I'm not sure when my suspicions about Alice slipped from the ambiguous to this, to an instinctive desire to know, to know what had found its way into our family, our life. But it happened, and not a few days later, I am back at Joe Avalon's neighborhood and then at his house.

I sit in the car, with *Photoplay, Look*, anything they had at the drugstore, knowing it could be hours before I see anything, if I see anything at all. I feel like Girl Detective from the serials, my Scotch plaid thermos filled with black coffee, a scarf over my head. Am I close enough? Am I far enough away? What if I do see something? Would I know what to do? Could I follow another car, if I needed to? What if I were spotted, what then?

It doesn't take hours, only forty-five minutes. The door to Avalon's bungalow opens, and I am watching as it happens. I see the pine green door open and see the woman come out with Joe Avalon's hand delicately on her back. With a quick verbal exchange, he disappears back into the house. The woman walks down the small path to the street, down the sidewalk, and on. Her gait is slow, strange, dreamy.

Although she is on the other side of the street, she is moving hazily in my direction, and I duck quickly as she walks past. Then, I turn around and get a better look as she continues her slow way down the street. She wears a navy and white suit, and a white hat with a large brim. Her handbag swings neatly, a fine circle of white patent leather hanging from her arm. A purchase from Bullock's that ran her nearly forty dollars.

I know because she told me soon after she bought it. I know because it is Edie Beauvais sashaying out of Joe Avalon's house and down Flower Street.

At a safe distance, I start the car and turn it around, moving slowly. Inching along, I watch her reach her own car, parked three blocks away.

I wonder how in the world Edie Beauvais could come to know Joe Avalon. Edie Beauvais, whom everyone knew was still suffering from "the blues" after her summer miscarriage, Edie

Beauvais, cop's wife. I don't wonder for long: the only possible link between this Pasadena housewife and this Los Angeles shark is Alice.

As she drives away, I follow her as discreetly as I know how for several miles, until it becomes clear to me that she has no destination. She takes me high into the hills and then down again, and finally straight to the ocean. As I drive, I consider whether Joe Avalon is Alice's lover or Edie's. Or how it came to be that Alice introduced the two.

I keep telling myself that she must notice me. There are too few cars on the road, it has gone on too long. But I can't stop myself. I follow until she finally pulls into the lot of a stucco establishment with a sign twice as big as the place itself: "Recovery Room Inn." Apparently so named because a run-down charity hospital is across the street.

I know I can't follow her inside. The place is too small. So I wait. This time for two hours.

It is nearly eight o'clock when she emerges, hat in hand, hair blowing in the breeze, pink smile wide as she chats with a tall man in a gray suit and a dark woman with the kind of high-topped veiled hat popular ten years ago. Well past tipsy, Edie and the man laugh heartily, hands to bellies. The veiled woman lights a cigarette and throws the empty pack into the street, tapping her shoe as if ready to go.

They wind their way to Edie's car, and the man gets in the backseat, and the woman sits beside Edie, who keeps laughing, hands on the steering wheel. At last, as the woman smokes long, slow, flat clouds, Edie starts the car.

It is getting dark, and I'm not sure how long I'll be able to follow, but I figure I'll try. It requires all my attention as Edie's car weaves and meanders and keeps accelerating and then slowing unexpectedly.

Finally, Edie stops at a bungalow court on Pico Boulevard. The lot is too small for me to enter unnoticed, but by parking on the street out front I can see into the courtyard through its overhanging arch. All three suddenly appear underneath it and then seem to turn into one of the apartments.

I wait a moment and get out of my car. Walking over to the floored patio, I step under the arch and see a dozen apartments laid out in a rectangle. Along one side there are a series of mailboxes. I look over in the direction the trio walked and guess they entered either Apartment 3 or Apartment 5.

Then I move over to the mailboxes for a closer look. Apartment 3 has the name Chambers listed and Apartment 5 has the name Porter written in unconfident pencil.

Suddenly, the door marked 5 begins to open. Frantic for some excuse for my loitering, I remember in a flash that I have Alice's cigarettes still with me from a few weeks before, when her clutch was too small to hold them. Plucking the pack out, I fumble one to my mouth. Swiveling a little, I make large gestures of trying to look further into my purse.

The man from the car emerges from the apartment. He wears a tan suit, and his skin is very pale and looks clammy. He stands a moment and wipes his cheeks with a handkerchief.

Still stalling, I nearly shake the contents of my purse to the ground, pretending to be looking for a lighter or matches. This is a mistake.

"You need a light?"

I turn to him. He looks about thirty years old, with hair prematurely steel-edged. I try to fix his face in my mind, but there is little to hold on to: pencil-thin mustache, weak chin, twitching, blinking eyes.

"Yes, thank you."

We move toward each other, he with an extended hand. He holds a gold-colored lighter under my nose and flicks it. I puff anxiously, having smoked perhaps a dozen cigarettes in my life.

"You live here?" he asks.

I begin walking away. "I was just visiting a friend."

The thought that Edie might, at any minute, step outside, keeps flashing through my head.

He nods. "Me, too. I just needed some air. These apartments are sweatboxes."

"Thanks for the light," I say, backing away a bit.

"We're having a party in that apartment," he says, waving his handkerchief at the door. "You know?"

He looks at me levelly. "Maybe you'd like to join us."

"No, no." I back myself nearly to the mailboxes, my elbow hitting one metal box hard.

"Sorry," he says evenly, with a shrug. "I thought you were . . . someone else."

"Someone else?"

"Never mind." He shakes his head. "I got it wrong."

He offers a tilted head and a grin, and then I watch as he opens the door, disappearing inside.

It is at this moment that I realize I am smoking so deeply my throat feels raw, thick with tar. By the time I get to my car, I have finished the cigarette and feel my stomach turn. There is this sense that the closer I come the more things slip away.

I sit in front of the wheel for maybe fifteen minutes, trying to explain things to myself. Edie. Joe Avalon. Alice. What kind of sticky web connects these three? I drive around the block a half dozen times. Then I park back in the lot and get out of the car again, not sure what I am going to do.

I find myself approaching Apartment 5 again with a sick feeling in my stomach.

I decide to walk behind the building into the wide alley. Overcome by the mingling smells of ripe garbage and heavy jasmine, I put my hand over my nose. There is a white apartment number painted on each overflowing trash can, and I quickly locate Number 5. There is one small window facing the alley. I walk over to it, conscious of every small tap and scuffle my shoes make.

I peer in between the shutter slats, seemingly drunk on my own sense of invisibility.

I can't see much, but I can see this.

I can see Edie, her whipped cream hair piled high on top of her head, sitting on the edge of a bathtub wearing a half-slip and stockings. Her hands cover her face, but I know it is her.

At first I think she has a scarf tied jauntily around her upper arm.

And then, feeling foolish, I realize.

This, of course, is what could bring together a vulnerable Pasadena housewife and a Los Angeles shark. If nothing else, this.

If there's a way to describe it, it's like the world, once sealed so tight and exact, has fallen open—no, been cracked open, and inside, inside . . .

I am ready to tell him, to tell Bill. To tell him at least what I have seen, if not the lengths I've gone to see it.

Even if I don't know what the clues point to, the clues themselves are troubling enough. Joe Avalon in his home, his bedroom. Edie Beauvais. God, does Charlie know? Shouldn't Charlie know? I tell myself it is Bill's job to string clues like this together. I can, as tenderly as possible, give him the clues, and he can see what they add up to. As hard as it will be for him to hear, I have to tell.

That night, Alice suggests an evening out at a dark-walled Latin dance club.

At first, I decline her invitation. But, knowing how hard it is to get Bill alone anymore and knowing Alice will be the one dancing while Bill will mostly sit and watch, nursing one watery drink for the entire evening, I decide to go.

As I sit there with him in the curved booth, however, I am frozen. How do I say these things to him? I try to imagine how he would tell me.

"Sis," he says, head turned, hand lightly on my forearm. I can't look into those eyes. I look down instead at the slightly dented knuckles on his cop hands. When he was on the beat, they'd often be grated raw across the joints from rough arrests, from holding men down while his partner cuffed them, from climbing fire escapes and breaking up bar fights and dragging drunks through cracked doorways.

His hands are smoother now but still studded with small, healed-over tears, flecks of white from old scars, old stories mapped onto him, some stories he won't tell even me.

His hand rests on my arm. "Sis."

"Yes." I manage a sidelong glance at his sharp, focused eyes.

"How are things?"

"Fine, Bill."

"You like this Standish guy, huh?" The familiar strain to sound casual. Even after all these months, Bill still turns away, teeth clenched, when he sees Mike with his hand on me.

"He's fine. That's all. You know." *This is what we do.*

He shrugs a little, softening. "Well, Alice says he's okay, so."

"She should know," I say. *I have to do it now. Now.*

As if on cue, Alice flits by on the dance floor, bottle green dress throbbing, a man with a pencil-thin mustache leading, but just barely.

"Doesn't that bother you?" I say. "Her dancing with other men?"

"No, I like it," he blurts out, eyes fixed on her until she slips out of sight. "I mean, she enjoys it," he quickly adds with a shy smile. "I'm no match. I can't keep up with her."

His eyes tracing her, sparking with energy. *No I like it. This is my wife. Look at her. Christ would you look.*

Is there no end to the devotion? What dark corners would it furrow around and where would it end? What are its limits?

"You know what Charlie said to me," Bill says. "He said, Billy, you couldn't have dreamed up a wife like that."

"Yes, Bill." I steal another look, and I see he's glowing. He's nearly red-faced with—what is it? Pride.

"She's very special, Bill," I add. A sharp pain, my own nails into the heel of my own hand. What am I waiting for?

"I remember, on our honeymoon . . ."

He can't possibly—

"Sis, she was so beautiful it hurt to look. On the beach, hand over her eyes, looking out on the water and talking gentle and low, dizzy from the sun, talking about how I'd changed everything for her."

"You did." I nod.

"I must be going soft from that last drink," he apologizes with a grin, tapping his fingers lightly on my arm.

"No, I know." I'm ready. I am.

Lost in his own thoughts, he turns his face away from me suddenly. Then, "Lora, I do know she's not like the other girls. Like Margie, Kathleen . . . I know she's not like them. But . . ."

He knows. He knows she's something foreign. Something not us. He tilts his head thoughtfully. "She's been knocked around a little. And I've seen, from the job, what that can do. I know what that can do to a girl. Even the best girls."

He looks at me, his face lit by the candle on the table. His eyes darken a little. I see it.

Then, decisively, he thrums two fingers on the table. "But it hasn't done it to her. She fought it off. And, really, isn't that something?"

He smiles, waiting for me. For my reassurance.

"Bill." I can't bear it. I put my other hand on his. "I want—"

Then, just as he is about to lean toward me, to hear what I am saying, he spots Alice again on the dance floor.

I can see his eyes catch, lock. I can see a change sweep hard over his face.

She is looking at him. She's dancing with some man, any man, and looking at my brother. Her eyes like black flowers. She places one white hand across her collarbone, her mouth blood red. It's so open, so bare, I can't look.

How could she know? But she does. She knows and she's watching, waiting, marking time, seeing what I will do. And then Bill . . .

He is rapt. He is mesmerized.

It's like this: she's on the dance floor, eyes tunneling into him, and then she's in front of him, right next to me, crushed satin skirt skimming my own legs as she presses toward him, leans down with that great gash of a mouth, and with one long finger under his upright, always upright chin, she kisses him with her whole charged little body. So close I can feel my brother shudder.

And then, before he—or I—can take a breath, she has disappeared back onto the swarming dance floor.

One hand on my stomach, I feel strangely sick.

This is when I realize there are some things you can't tell.

This is when I realize:

He wouldn't tell me at all. He'd just make it go away.

I know what I have to do.

That night, desperate to forget for a while, I call Mike. I don't tell him about anything that has happened, especially not about seeing Edie Beauvais. But something in my voice, he hears something in my voice that makes him know he should say: "Tonight I'm taking you out of this burg."

When I get in his car, he smiles. "Hey, kid. We're going to the Magic Lamp."

And before I know it we are on Route 66, and we keep going and we pass the Derby and the Magic Lamp and suddenly we are deep in the desert.

Light breaking up in the clouds as dusk gives over, and we're driving and we're driving and it seems we'll never get anywhere, but with my hands resting in the creamy folds of my dress and with the sound of Mike faintly tapping fingers on the leather steering wheel as the music burns off us both, as the radio sounds not tinny but like a movie score streaming over us, like in a movie, like a movie where they're driving and the red dusk envelops them in gorgeously fake rear screen projection, the car jumping not like real cars but like movie cars, carrying you away with the lush romanticism of the night, the sharp jawline of the leading man, the soft curls of the ingenue who has all the promise of turning siren or vamp by the night's end.

It is that evening that he tells me, after rounds and rounds of drinks in a far-off roadhouse, leaning over and whispering into my ear, the thing he couldn't bring himself to tell me before. I know, even as my own head is swirling, that he will regret telling me this. Even Mike Standish sometimes slips. But he does tell me. And the whole ride home, I feel sick with it.

He tells me this:

Time was, a few months back, he couldn't believe what he'd gotten himself into. Yes, he'd had a few jaunty turns on his mattress with costume girl Alice Steele, he'd admit it. But who'd have guessed a year or so later she'd ask him to take out the schoolteacher sister of her new cop husband?

Truth was, he'd done it as a favor, but he'd never liked Alice all that much. She spooked him with her heavy eyes and the strange stories he'd heard.

He remembers seeing her once in a colored nightclub on Central Avenue. He knew why *he* was there. A fast detour, giving a dark-meat-loving matinee idol a guided tour of the city's murkier regions. But Alice, she was in the middle of everything, her stark white face looming out from a crowd of colored jazz musicians and one slick-faced white man puffing hard on reefer. She wore a low-cut velvet dress hanging by two long strings off her shoulders, and her mouth was like one gorgeous scar across her face. He remembers thinking she looked as though she might slide out of that dress and slither across the floor, and caught by the image, he found himself inexplicably terrified. Then, feeling embarrassed and foolish, he recovered. He waved over at her, he sent her a drink.

She stared at him with eyes like bullet holes, stared at him like she'd never seen him before, and he felt his blood pulsing, the vein in his neck singing. She wasn't just a B-girl, she was carrying the whole ugly world in her eyes.

Two hours later he had talked her into the alley and he'd

had her for the fourth and last time since he'd met her, and hands so hard on her white thighs that he thought his fingers might meet right through her, he knew he could never see her again.

He did, but never like that.

The next time he saw her she was married to a cop and wore a scratchy wool suit and sensible pumps.

And her new sister was set out for him like fresh meat.

I avoid Bill all week, unable to face him. It is not until the following Sunday that I drive over to his house for a twice-postponed dinner. My chest surges as I walk in and see him sitting on the sofa with his head in his hands.

"What is it? Is Alice—"

At that moment, Alice walks into the room with a brandy. She hands it to Bill, placing her hand gently on my back.

"Did he tell you?" Alice gives me a heavy stare.

"Tell me what?" I sit down beside him and touch his arm.

"Edie Beauvais. She's dead."

"What?" I feel my voice shake. I saw her just over a week ago. Even if she didn't see me.

Bill raises his head, face flushed, and looks at me. "She killed herself with pills. Can you believe it?"

"No," I say. "I can't."

"The miscarriage and everything." Alice sighs. "I think she felt everything had turned bad for her."

"It can't be," Bill says. "Poor Charlie."

I try to figure it, try to figure this into what I saw. I want to watch Alice closely, to see what she might know. Does she know all that I do, or much more? Does she know how far Edie Beauvais had gone? Had she watched her go?

But all I can focus on is Bill's wrecked face.

"We'll go see him, Bill. We'll bring him dinner. Be with him," I say, thinking of how much Bill relies on Charlie, his only real friend. And, ever since Bill married Alice, there has been that special closeness between them, both always watching their lovely, baffling wives from the sidelines, perpetually bemused and lovestruck. Always, I realize now with a wince, always so many steps behind.

"He's gone," Alice says. "He left the hospital and got in his car, and Bill hasn't been able to reach him."

"I was at the morgue with him," Bill mumbles, clenching the table edge with his hands, almost wringing it. "He didn't really seem to react at all. And then suddenly he bolted out of there. I tried to follow him, but he just took off. I don't know where he could be."

Sitting beside him, I place my hand on his back. He grabs my fingers, tugging at them. We sit that way for several minutes. I wonder if Bill is thinking what I am: that there might be some lesson one should draw from this, from what happened to his friend. About the price one might pay for a love so crushing and for a woman so filled with secrets.

It reminds me of a conversation I witnessed between Bill and Alice right after Edie's miscarriage. Bill had talked about how these women, they were so delicate, like those flowers that look too heavy for their stems to support, that seem to defy their very structures.

"I'd say you men are the fragile ones," Alice had replied. "Too soft for this world."

When she said it, I thought she was teasing, but I could tell Bill was affected, that he found the remark surprising, penetrating. Even if he couldn't quite put his finger on why.

The look in Bill's eyes had been: *She knows things. Things I can't begin to know.*

As I remember it now, with my hand on Bill's shoulder, I lift my eyes to see Alice standing there, her face a hieroglyphic.

✳

"Is Alice there, honey?"

I know it is Lois on the phone, but it is Lois even more slowed down than usual, her voice dragging by its hind legs, barely making it from her lips to my ears.

"She'll be back around eight. She's gone downtown to buy some fabric—in Chinatown, I think." I had stopped by hoping to see Bill, to console him. But he was gone, too, working late again.

"Oh, God . . . for real? Is she going to be home soon?"

"Not until about eight," I repeat. "Is everything all right, Lois?"

"Don't even ask . . . that creep. That son of a bitch. I can't even believe . . . Can you . . . So she's downtown, huh? She's . . . I'm in Culver City, I think. I don't even know."

The eerie, wavering pitch of her voice unnerves me. Shivery like a zither in a monster movie. She sounds as if she can scarcely hold on to the phone, barely make the words come out of her mouth.

"Is there anything I can do, Lois?" I find myself asking.

"Sleep tight, baby. Sleep tight, let's call it a day," she murmurs, half-singing.

"What were you calling Alice for?" I say. "Did you need some help? Is everything okay?"

There is a pause, a faint sound of contorted humming, then a clicking sound, like a drawer sliding on its runners, open and shut.

"Lois?"

I clutch the receiver as my stomach rises anxiously into my chest. I get a sudden feeling of monumentality. I whisper one more time, hardly a whisper even, "Lois, are you there?"

"Yeah?" she says at last. I take a breath.

"Lois, why don't you tell me where you are and I can come get you and bring you over here?" I can't believe I'm saying it. But if not me, who would go? Who would go?

"Me? I'm on a fast track to nowhere, baby," she says, then laughs lightly. Then, suddenly, "Would you come by? Would you?"

Then, "God's honest, I'm afraid he's gonna come back, and he said if he did he'd bring the pliers this time."

The car keys I've unconsciously palmed drop to the floor

with a clatter and I nearly lose the phone. Breathing deeply, I force out, "Tell me where you are, please. Please tell me"—and I am suddenly half out of breath—"where you are."

The Rest E-Z Motel in Culver City. I drive by it three times, hands tight on the steering wheel, trying to steel myself. On the phone, Lois said she didn't know what room she was in. She said she couldn't get up to look at the door. I will have to try to find her by talking to the clerk.

The place looks about as I had guessed when she told me its name. The shaggy carport leading to the lobby hanging so low it seems nearly to hit the tops of the stray cars that move underneath. Gray shingles cracked in the sun, and bloodred trim caked around each window and awning of the dozen or so rooms.

My legs shake as I walk across the parking lot. It doesn't strike me until that moment that there is every reason to believe this sort of thing happens to Lois five times a week and she emerges each time with only her usual number of scratches.

The clerk, a Mexican with a cigarillo and a bowling shirt, looks me over dubiously from behind a grimy counter. He scratches the back of his neck.

"Hello. I'm looking for a friend. She called me from here, but she was ill and wasn't sure which room she was in."

He blinks slowly and raps his fingers on the counter.

"She's small, maybe five feet two or so, with dark hair." I gesture with my hand.

His lips twist around the cigarillo. His fingers rap more slowly, and he shakes his head.

I open my purse, hands shaking slightly. "I'd be so grateful for any help you can give."

He shakes his head again, raising his hand to me.

"Really." I slide ten dollars across the counter, Mike Standish style, not knowing if it is what Lois might call a bum amount or the real deal.

He sighs, rubbing his hand along the bristle on his chin, then takes the bill, slipping it into the waistband of his pants as he steps from behind the counter. I jump back with a start, but he is only gesturing for me to follow him. We walk out the glass door and across the flyspecked parking lot, over to Room 12.

He knocks once on the mud-colored paint of the door. No sound.

He looks to me expectantly.

I knock this time. "Lois? Are you there, Lois?"

No response.

"Look"—I turn to the man—"she's really sick, can you—"

He pulls a passkey out of his pocket and unlocks the particleboard door.

My eyes adjust to the dark room, with its nubby curtains pulled tight across the bulging screen of the window to block out the late-afternoon light.

Mounds of sheets piled on the bed, a faint red-brown spatter curled into one of the rivulets.

"Lois," I blurt, unable to make it past the threshold. The clerk begins muttering loudly in Spanish.

Abruptly, amid the piles of sheets, a torn-stockinged leg surfaces. "Whossit?"

I push past the clerk and move quickly to the bed. Lois is huddled in one corner, locks of hair matted to her face and clotted in a thin sheen of dried blood.

"Are you all right? God, Lois."

Her dark-ridged eyelids slide open, and a sheet-creased breast slides out from under the covers.

"Alice?" She squints.

"It's Lora. Lora King," I say. I turn to the clerk. "Thank you."

He pauses a long second, deciding something, probably about whether or not to call the police. Then he points a finger at me, turns, and leaves, closing the door behind him.

The room is in near darkness again, a dusty, heavy kind of late-afternoon dark. Street noises radiate in and out, carried by the hot winds.

I sit down on the edge of the bed, next to her.

"Lois, let's go. Let's get you your clothes on and I'll take you over to Alice and Bill's. Or to my place. Your pick."

She puts a hand over her eyes and says nothing.

"We can call a doctor from there," I add, trying desperately to see the source of the blood in the darkness.

"No doctors, sugar pie." She rolls over and tries to prop herself up a bit.

I reach across to the bedside lamp and switch it on.

Lois rubs her eyes and manages one of her crooked smiles. A cigarette burn snarls from her collarbone.

"Oh, Lois!"

Her eyes widen a bit, then she looks down at the burn. She smiles.

"Oh, no, that's old, honey. It got infected, never healed right."

She struggles a blue-veined, dimpled leg out from under the sheet. A garter hangs loosely atop her thigh.

"Now *that's* new." She smirks, pointing to a long, crimson strand down the inside of her upper thigh.

"Lois," I murmur, feeling dizzy and sick, suddenly aware of the smells of the room, the bed, a fulsome mix of bodies, drink, the slime of a lost evening and half day.

"Ah, it ain't so bad. You should have seen the other guy." She chuckles wryly, tiredly, and gestures to the spray of dried blood. "Busted his nose."

"What happened?" I cover my mouth and nose with the back of my hand, unable to hold back my nausea. "Lois, what happened?"

Her eyes light up and she is onstage, the cameras are rolling, *something*.

"The kind of dance you're lucky to make it out of, toots." She reaches over to the bedside table and, with a growing jauntiness, pops a cigarette in her swollen lips. "It just happens. And then happens again. But it's a walk into the lion's den. We've all got our soft spots."

Taking a puff, she squints at me and says, "Did you ever feel something in the dark and it gives you tingles, pinpricks under the skin, like ice on your teeth followed by a warm . . . a warm, velvety fist?"

I don't say anything. I feel my stomach and face go suddenly hot. I run the back of my wrist along my forehead.

Lois reaches under the sheets to pull out a silky violet dress. Throwing it over both her head and her sagging cigarette, she wriggles into its wasp waist, then turns to me.

"Honey, don't worry. I've had my insides scooped out clean after four bad turns and the clap. I've seen things and done things, had things done to me, things that . . ." She slides out of bed, looks down at her legs, scaled a bit on the shins with dermatitis. "There's a lot I can get through. You, you'd best deal with your demons just the way you do now."

I turn sharply, all the way around to face her.

"You know," she says, through the smoke. And that is all she says. I don't know what she means, but I feel, with a shudder, that whatever she thinks she knows is probably true.

"Where are we going?"

Slouched down in the seat, Lois shifts a bit, eyes closed to the glare of passing headlights.

"La Cienega. And Manchester. With the donut on the corner."

"Why don't you let me take you to Alice's? I think you really need to see a doctor."

She fumbles in her ruched pocket, eyes still shut.

"Lois?"

I try again. "Lois? Can't you let me take you to Alice's at least?"

She plucks a fresh cigarette, partly crumpled, from her pocket and punches in the car's lighter.

"I'll get taken care of where we're headed, honey. Don't worry."

We drive in silence, listening only to the dull thud of the car over the ridges in the road. Eventually, Lois, now sucking her cigarette with vigor, turns on the radio. As the brassy music leaps out, she begins to gain energy, sitting up straight and humming along.

Finally, we approach Manchester and the ten-foot-high pink-frosted donut, sprinkles the size of baby legs.

"Turn left. It's the bungalow on the right there. The one with the chair."

There is an orange velvet armchair on the front lawn, a magazine on its cushion, pages rippling in the evening breeze. A large radio is perched on the bungalow's porch and is billowing out what sounds like old Tin Pan Alley.

Lois is halfway out the door as I turn off the ignition. I begin to step out of the car when she swivels around and looks at me.

"Thanks, kid. Don't think I don't appreciate it."

"Let me make sure someone's here to take care of you," I say. As I head toward the porch, I think suddenly, as I see her there bone white and battered, that she is slipping away right in front of my eyes and that nobody will take care of her at all.

It seems to me, for no reason I can name, that if she walks up those porch steps and sets her shivery foot across the threshold, she'll sink into something even more terrifying than what I found at the motel. The jabbing strains of the radio—was it "Tiny Bubbles"?—seem to be pulling her in through sheer hypnotic force.

"I'm okay, honey." She turns and nearly falls up the steps onto the porch. With this, the screen door gapes open with a groan, and a tall woman with a tepee of dark red curls appears. She offers a long glance at Lois.

"Oh, it's you." Her eyebrows rise. I move a few steps closer to the porch. Lois smiles crookedly at the woman but says nothing.

"And who's that?" She gestures at me imperiously. Closer, I realize she is an older woman, maybe fifty.

"I'm a friend. I think Lois needs a doctor."

Lois, making her way past the woman and through the doorway, looks back at me without expression.

"I'm fine," she slurs with a brittle edge, turning back away from me and disappearing into the deep red shadows of the house.

The woman looks down at me with her hard, made-up features.

I return her gaze, unsure what to say.

She appraises me a few seconds longer, then turns, the bustle folds of her dress swinging behind her as she, too, disappears into the house. The screen door sighs back into place.

I stand there for another minute, even lean against my car and pretend to fidget for my keys. I don't know what I think might happen, but nothing does. Nothing I can see.

I settle into my car and, before leaving, jot the address down on a scrap of paper, not knowing why.

As I make the long drive home, all the women's faces along the boulevard seem to have the same look as Lois. Every one.

How can it be that, two days later, I'm in my brother's car, feeling ugly with fear, and Bill . . . Bill, still numb from Edie's death and Charlie's abrupt exit, wants to talk, inexplicably, about sister-wife relations.

"Sis, I know you love Alice to death." He turns the wheel delicately, with two fingers. "But can you try to show it a little more?"

We are driving to our godparents' for dinner. Alice is in bed, the middle of a new round of daily migraines. It makes it easier. It lets me puzzle things out without the distractions of her sidelong gaze.

"What do you mean," I say.

"Lately, she feels like you don't want to spend time with her. That you're distant," he says, eyes on the road, voice soft and coaxing.

The day before, when I ran into her in the teachers' lounge, she stopped me, one spiky hand on my shoulder. "I hear you helped Lois out."

"Yes."

"Thanks. Thanks for that."

Her face was as static and flat as a photograph. I felt a quiver dancing at the base of my spine.

"For what? I'm sure you would have done the same," I replied, and as I said it I realized it was filled with meaning for her.

"Oh, yes. But she's my burden, not yours. And thanks for not telling Bill."

In a flash, anger came over me. I wanted to say, *How dare you?*

"That's not why I didn't tell him," I said, voice brittle. "Not for you."

Struck, she flashed a brilliant smile. "I know, Lora, honey. But thanks. You're such a good sister to me."

As I sit with Bill now, however, all I say is: "I don't know where she gets the idea that I'm distant."

Bill smiles faintly. "I told her that she shouldn't have set you up so well if she didn't want to lose you to a boyfriend."

He turns to me briefly, stopping the car at the traffic light. When he looks at me, the smile, barely perceptible, fades.

I am not smiling.

"He's not my boyfriend," I say, gesturing to the changed light.

"Well, if he's not your boyfriend, what is he."

He hits the gas pedal.

"Really, Lora. If he's not your boyfriend, what is he."

It isn't a question; there is no rise at the end of the sentence.

"I see her all day at work and then on the weekends and sometimes on Wednesday nights for bridge," I point out. "How can you see that as neglect."

"It's just she feels you don't confide in her like you did. Girl talk, I guess."

"We never did that," I say, resting my head on the heel of my hand and looking out the window. "She's my sister-in-law."

"Your sister, really. The most family we have."

"I know. Okay." It is like saying, Point taken. But it is no commitment. No commitment.

"She doesn't have many friends, and you were her friend."

"Let's get some flowers on the way." I point to a store.

I can't tell him—not with what I've seen, not even with this feeling of sickly dread vibrating in me.

There are things Bill can't hear. Things about her. He just can't. All I can do is find out everything I can, know everything there is to know, all she's laid her fine white hands on. It is the only way.

Looking back, I see that it was all such happenstance.

Maybe if I hadn't seen it, I would eventually have let go of the things I had seen and learned in those past few months. If I hadn't been waiting so long for Alice to show up for our ride home, I might never have picked up the newspaper's metropolitan section, sitting harmlessly on the coffee table in the teachers' lounge. And I might so easily have missed the first article, which struck me only as very sad and somehow closer than it might have a year or two ago.

Kansas Honeymooners Find Body in Canyon
LAPD Work to I.D. Jane Doe, Dead Three Days

(HOLLYWOOD)—A pair of newlyweds on vacation from Wichita, Kansas, were in for a grim welcome from the City of Angels Saturday when they discovered the body of a dead woman in Bronson Canyon.

Fred and Lorraine Twitchett, married less than a week ago, were on a morning stroll by the Hollywood Reservoir when they noticed what Mr. Twitchett described as "something satiny" in the brush. Closer inspection revealed it to be a torn green dress. A few yards from the dress, they came upon the corpse of a young woman wrapped in what they described as a silver shawl and naked from the waist down, except for shoes and stockings.

The woman, estimated to be between the ages of 25 and 35, was shot in the face and apparently dealt a blow to the back of the head. About five feet one and 100 pounds, the woman had dark, shoulder-length hair. Detectives will search dental records and fingerprints to determine her identity.

The corpse also had several scars of different sizes on her arms and legs that are believed to have been premortem, some weeks or more old. Several appeared to be cigarette burns, others looked to be caused by use of intravenous needles.

Police urge the public to contact them with any knowledge of a missing woman matching this general description, possibly mistreated by a husband or boyfriend, and with a possible history of narcotics use.

The next day, however, I find myself looking through the newspaper to see if there is any further information. If I hadn't seen the second article, I don't even know if I would have thought any more about it—after all, there were thousands of Hollywood girls fitting that forlorn description.

But there it is on page two.

(HOLLYWOOD)—Police have identified the Jane Doe found in Bronson Canyon just above Hollywood two days ago. A fingerprint check identified the body as that of Linda Tattersal, 27 years old, most recently of Rosecourt.

Detectives matched the victim's fingerprints through police records showing three past arrests for shoplifting, public drunkenness, and solicitation, and one conviction, last February, for resisting arrest at a roadhouse in El Segundo.

Ms. Tattersal was a member of the Screen Actors Guild from June 1953 until four months ago, when her membership was revoked for nonpayment of dues. Her last known address was at Locust Arms Apartments on Rosecourt Boulevard in Rosecourt.

"She was a nice girl," said a neighbor in the building, who did not wish to be identified. "But she kept bad company."

There it is, building through paragraph one, through paragraph two, and then, my heart in my throat by the time I reach the name Locust Arms. In a flash, I see the dark tangle of pepper trees swaying out front like a warning.

I spent only ten minutes there, months ago, and yet I suddenly can see myself walking with Alice along its cracked pavement. The door of Lois's room hanging partly open and her quavery singing voice calling us closer, beckoning us in.

Alice didn't even blink. Alice had been there many times. Alice, it struck me, had lived in dozens of places like this all her life, and for her, it was like going home.

I spread my hand over the article in the paper. I push my

fingertips into the smudgy print. I wonder what I would do. I don't know anything for certain, after all.

Could Linda be Lois? Surely, Lois wasn't the only wayward girl lost in the Locust Arms, the only girl who seemed doomed to end up in Bronson Canyon or some other desolate place.

I try calling the Locust Arms, but no one will speak to me.

—Our tenants like to keep to themselves.

Or

—I don't know who you're talking about, honey.

Or

—Try Missing Persons, lady.

The next morning, I drive by the courtyard. I can't get out of the car. I stare at the row of wan doors. I wait for signs of life.

I realize I should be talking to Alice. If the girl in the paper isn't Lois, Alice could assure me that she'd just seen her friend, just got off the phone with her not the night before. Talked together confidentially just that day about the sad fate of the girl who lived across the courtyard in, say, Number 8.

That afternoon, having promised Bill, I find myself helping Alice bake cakes for the Rotary Club bake sale. As she frantically prepares three cakes for the sale and one for dessert that night, I take a seat at the kitchen table and begin peeling apples.

"Oh, Lora, I feel like we haven't talked in weeks. And first with the Beauvaises and . . . Well, we both get so caught up with the rest of our lives," she says. Then, smiling, "You with your big romance—"

She must see me bristle at the characterization because she quickly adds, "—your busy life, and we haven't made time enough lately. I want to hear everything that's been going on."

"How's Lois?" I ask it. I ask it abruptly, like a shot to the heart.

Alice stops for just a split second, almost unnoticeably, but I see it. She stops for a hairsbreadth of a second in folding the cake batter.

"Oh, you know Lois."

"I do," I say, watching. Then I wait, still watching, until she has to say more. She sees I will keep waiting.

"Funny you should ask." Alice shakes her head like a vaguely disapproving older sister. "I guess she's gone off on another one of her tears. From what I hear, she's headed off to San Francisco without so much as a forwarding address." Her voice, the words she chooses, seem unreal, like dialogue from a movie.

"She told you she was going to San Francisco?"

"No, not even that. A friend of hers told me. I wonder if I should put a little nutmeg in this. Do you think Bill would like that, or would it be too strong."

"Gee, Alice, I don't know. So who told you?"

"This girl who used to work at the studio." She puts the nutmeg back in the spice cabinet unopened. Then turns to me and smiles.

"Oh, how did you happen upon her?"

"We ran into each other at the Apple Pan."

I look at her. Look at her and can't figure out a thing.

"With Bill," she adds. "We went to get a quick sandwich, and she was leaving as we were arriving."

Just daring me to ask still more.

"What's her name?"

"I can see you're a cop's sister." She laughs, the sound like an unbearable silver bell. "Ina. Her name's Ina. Now do your sister-in-law a favor and hold that pan for me while I pour."

I hold the cake pan steadily, watching her coolly, watching her watch me, wondering what I know or what I think I know. She empties the batter with great precision, twisting the bowl, shaking it just right to dispense everything evenly. Not a drop is left when she finishes. It is all very simple for her, and for every shake of my hands, hers become steadier still. I have nothing on her.

The next day, I stop by Bill's office with a surprise box of gingerbread and the excuse of needing to renew my driver's license nearby.

"So I heard you ran into an old friend of Alice's."

He turns and looks at me.

"She told me you ran into a friend of hers."

"She's got old friends everywhere," Bill says, wiping his fork off with a napkin. I can see him thinking, but I'm not sure about what.

"Hmm. But this one you ran into together."

"Yeah?"

"Ina. Her name's Ina."

"Ina?"

"At the Apple Pan."

"Right. That's right. Ina," he says. I can't read him—can't read Bill, whom I always, forever could read. But I think I detect a whiff of confusion.

"So I guess she told you that Lois Slattery took off for San Francisco."

"I don't know." Bill swipes a large forkful into his mouth. "They were talking while I was paying the bill. They went to the ladies' room together."

"Did you know Lois had left town?"

"I don't really keep tabs on Lois Slattery," he says, shaking his head. "I leave that to her probation officer."

He hooks an arm around me. "Just between you and me, I'm kind of glad she's not around, needing Alice to take care of her all the time."

"Was Alice giving her money?" I blurt out.

"Money? No, I don't think so. No." He wipes his hands with his napkin.

His brow furrows ever so slightly, and my heart rises in my chest.

I struggle with the urge to put my arms around him and comfort him as I see cracks appearing all around him, spreading. He does see them spreading, doesn't he? How can he not?

Two days after seeing the second newspaper article, I determine to carry out an idea that I've formulated all night long, lying in bed, unable to sleep, hoping against all reason that Lois will call, her voice sizzling in my ear.

Was it all about Joe Avalon? Was he the center of this ugly story? He was in my brother's home, maybe in his bed. Edie

Beauvais gone. And now, maybe Lois, too. Of course, Alice was the one everyone had in common. Everyone.

Remembering now, at parties, Alice and Edie huddled in a corner, smoking conspiratorially, giggling and flashing glances, legs swinging, rocking as they shared an ottoman, so close they were like one grinning, dangerous thing. Alice in common.

And there was mostly this: a D.A.'s investigator with a wife caught in the middle of something so lurid? However peripheral her role, it wouldn't matter. In the papers, in City Hall, it wouldn't matter. Years of hard work shot through.

As I leave my apartment that evening, I put on an old hat with a veil that hangs over my face, cobweb thick. When I arrive at the police station, I remind myself that this is not Bill's precinct, is a world away. No one will recognize me, I tell myself. Nevertheless, the dove gray veil hangs low and I try not to make eye contact with anyone as I walk into the dingy, sticky-walled station house.

I ask to speak with the detective assigned to the Linda Tattersal case, and the squinty-eyed deputy at the desk gives me a long look.

"That'd be Detective Cudahy, Miss. Can I tell him what it's about?" His finger is poised on a button on the control board.

"It's private," I say quietly, through the veil. "Is he in?"

The deputy looks at me again, then pushes the button, speaking into the microphone: "Cudahy . . . someone to see you."

I sit on the adjacent bench to wait. It is several minutes before a shiny-faced man with a gritty scrub of red-blond hair walks toward me, sleeves rolled up over his red forearms. He pauses at the station desk for a moment, conferring with the deputy.

"Miss? Come with me," he says at last, waving his arm.

He lets me pass in front of him, then guides me into a small office that smells of burnt coffee and Lysol.

He leans against the front of the desk as I sit down across from him.

"So . . . ?" he says.

"I'm not sure . . . I hope I'm not wasting your time."

"Not yet," he says with a faint smile.

"This Linda Tattersal. From the papers. I may . . . may know her."

"But you're not sure," he says, pushing the door shut with his outstretched leg.

"I know a woman named Lois who lived in Rosecourt."

"That so?"

"At the Locust Arms."

"I see," he says, arms folded across his chest. "You always wear a veil like that in this heat?"

I feel my face turn warm. I try to lift the veil, catching it on my eyelashes.

"Let me help," he says, reaching out and pushing the veil up. My hand wavers.

"So you know a Lois in Rosecourt, huh?"

"I do. I mean, she did live there, at those apartments. And she fits the physical description."

"She's a friend of yours."

I pause, looking at him. "Listen. All I'm suggesting is that I think it may be her. They may be the same person."

"How do you know this Lois?"

"I'm sorry, I . . ." I tug at my skirt. "I guess I don't see how that matters. Don't you want to find out if it's the same girl?"

"Why? Did someone want to hurt your friend?" He cocks his head.

"I just . . . if it's Lois, *my* Lois, she . . . she had scars."

"Lots of people have scars, Miss . . . I'm sorry, what's your name?"

"Okay, she'd have *specific* scars. She'd have lots of them. On her arms. Needle marks."

"That was in the papers, yeah."

I twist in my seat. "She'd also have them other places."

"Yeah?"

"She'd have them all kinds of places. Behind her knees. Between her toes. On her neck." I find myself pointing two fingers to my own neck.

"She'd have them everywhere," I finish.

His arms drop a little.

"And she'd have a cigarette burn, right here." I touch my collarbone lightly.

"And dermatitis on her legs. Maybe old burns on her thighs from a fire."

His arms fall, and he reaches out for a pad of paper and pen.

"And she'd have scar tissue from . . . from several abortions." This is little more than a guess but a confident one (*"I've had my insides scooped out clean after four bad turns . . ."*).

He meets my eyes.

"Okay, Miss, we'd better start here," he says as he grabs the phone, barking into the receiver, "Get me the morgue."

And it's this. It's this:

Could that thing there, that block of graying flesh, be Lois? Could it be a woman at all? The morgue attendant picks pieces of dust and gravel from the place her face had been. He's trying to get a footprint.

"I think after he does her, he kicks her over on her face with his foot," the attendant says.

He says this to Detective Cudahy.

I'm standing in the corner.

"I didn't know you were working on her right now," says Cudahy. He looks at me.

From the side, from where I've backed up, nearly to the far wall, it looks like she has a big flower in her hair, like Dorothy Lamour. A big blossom, dark and blooming.

If I don't focus, don't squint, I can pretend it's a flower and not a hole, a gaping cavity.

"It's going to be hard to tell," he says. "But try your best."

He reaches his hand out, summoning me over with low-ered eyes.

"She was a mess even before," the attendant notes, tilting his head. "Her skin . . ."

I touch my fingertips to my mouth as I walk over. I wonder if there's any way at all that I will be able to look long enough to tell.

"There's no . . ." What I want to say is that there's no face there. There's nothing there at all. But I can't quite get the words out. Instead, I just stare down into the shiny, blackened pit before me.

"You want to focus on the rest of her," Cudahy says quietly. "Body size, shape. The places you remember scars."

I look at the stippled body, I look at its pocks and wounds. I look—knowing this will be it for me—at the hands. Lois's stubby little hands, her doll fingers with her strangely square fingertips. They're there, right in front of me. They're little doll hands, and they're covered with ink, torn at the tips in places, ragged and stringy at the edges but definitely hers. They're Lois's hands.

I teeter back slightly on my heels. Cudahy's hand is pressed on my back, holding me up. My head swims and then I see the welts on her breasts and below her belly. I see them and I remember the Rest E-Z Motel. I remember everything.

"So it's her, huh?" A voice sounds out.

"It's her," another voice answers.

It's my own.

"We'll need to start at the top," Detective Cudahy says, uncapping his pen and smoothing a rough hand over a pad of lined paper.

"Right."

"What's your full name?"

This is when I realize the extent of what I have done. And this is when I find myself not knowing why I feel the need to lie. But I do feel I need to lie.

"Susan. Willa. Morgan," I say slowly, pulling each part

from my class roster. Susan Wiggins, Willa Johnston, and Eleanor Morgan will never know the dark tunnels into which their names have been thrown.

"Age?"

"Twenty-eight."

"Married?"

"No."

"How did you know the victim?"

"She used to come into a nightclub I go to sometimes." I am on eerie autopilot, unsure from where I am getting the words coming out of my mouth. My voice even sounds different: vaguely brittle and with a slight lilt.

"What nightclub?"

"The Red Room Lounge."

"In Rosecourt?"

"No, Hollywood. It's on Hollywood Boulevard."

"She told you her name was Lois?"

"Yes."

"Last name?"

"She never said." I don't know why I lie about this. I'm going solely by instinct. Somehow I want him to think I didn't know her well, not well at all. *If I knew her well enough to know her last name, wouldn't I have known enough to stop—*

"What was she doing there?"

"Passing the time," I say with a shrug.

"Is that what you were doing there?" he asks, scribbling, not meeting my gaze.

I straighten in my seat. "I would go with my girlfriends. Sometimes on a date."

"What kinds of dates?" He looks up at me with a slight pause.

"Kinds of dates? What do you mean?"

He looks at me for a moment. "Skip it," he says, returning to his writing pad. "How regular would you see her there?"

"Once or twice a month."

"How'd you happen to talk with her?"

"I don't know. I think maybe someone I was with knew her or vice versa. I really can't remember."

"What kinds of things did you talk about?" He continues writing.

"Girl stuff. Hair, men." I try a smile. "She was doing some acting and modeling."

"Modeling?"

"That's what she said."

"What do you do?"

"Pardon? What?"

"Do you have a job?"

"Yes, I . . . I give sewing lessons." I don't know where this comes from.

He writes something down. Then, "Did she ever tell you about any men she dated? Men she knew?"

"Yes." Here is my chance. "She told me once about a man who would . . . do things to her."

"Things?"

"She would have burn marks. He would burn her."

"With cigarettes?"

"Yes."

"Did they use narcotics together?"

"I don't know."

"But you knew she used them."

"I saw the marks."

"And you knew what they meant?"

"I don't use narcotics, Detective, if that's what you mean."

"Was she very scared of this guy?"

"I guess. She must have been. But she'd been, you know, around the block a few times. Nothing much surprised her."

"Did she tell you anything about this man? What he did? Where he lived?"

"He worked in the movies," I say, tightening my fingers over my purse. "He worked for a studio."

"Which studio?"

"I don't know. She worked for RKO and Republic. I do know that."

"So you think he did, too? Did you get the idea he might have got her jobs?"

"I don't know."

"Did she tell you anything else about him?"

"No."

"When was the last time you saw her?"

"A few weeks ago." Here, because it seems easier, safer, I just lie. Somehow telling him about the recent episode at the Rest E-Z Motel seems too risky, too involved.

"At the Red Room Lounge?"

"Yes. Right. The Red Room."

He pushes a piece of paper over at me.

"I want all your information and any names you can remember of anyone you ever saw her with. Don't forget your phone number and address."

I stare at the paper for a second. Then, I take the pen and begin writing.

"So." He leans back, stretching his arms a bit as I write. "How do you think she ended up in water?"

I look up with a start.

"Water?"

"So you don't know everything, Miss Morgan?"

I feel my hand shake around the pen.

"I don't know anything. What water?"

"You tell me. Your friend drowned."

My head is throbbing when Detective Cudahy hands me the glass of warmish water. I can't keep my lies straight. I slide my hat off my head and into the palm of my hand. It is moist where my forehead has strained against it.

"You're telling me she didn't die from being . . . from being shot." Unconsciously, I touch my hand to my own face.

"The shot was postmortem."

"So it was all an accident? She just drowned?"

"I don't think so. Accidental drowning victims don't usually end up with their faces blown off."

"Why was she shot then?"

He tilts his head. "Could be to try and prevent identification of the body. Or he's just in a violent rage. It's hard to tell just yet. She wasn't in the water that long. Just long enough to fill her lungs and sink her like a stone."

I twitch, involuntarily. "But the papers . . ."

"She was found in the Hills, but we kept the water stuff out of the press. It may help down the line."

"So she drowned and then someone shot her and then just . . . just dumped her there?"

"Far as we can tell."

"Drowned in the ocean?"

"Salt water."

"What would Lois have been doing in the ocean?"

"Thought maybe you could tell me. Her boyfriend have a boat?"

"I don't . . . know," I say, trying to process it all. Trying not to think of Lois, face in dark water, floating.

"Maybe you'll ask around for us." He looks at me hard in the eyes. "In your circles, you might be able to find out things we can't."

At this, I almost want to laugh.

"I'll try. I will," I reply, not knowing what I mean by it.

You have to ask it: Who would cry for Lois Slattery, with all her slurry glamour, her torn and fast-fading beauty—beauty mostly because you could see it vanishing before your eyes? Her loss meant nothing and she would not be missed, not even by me. I wouldn't miss her—not in a way as true as she deserved.

But there was something that lingered, her whole life a dark stain, spreading. A pulsing energy racked tight and always threatening to burst through its borders, its hems, its ragged, straining edges. She would have been happy to know how ripely powerful she would become in death. She had been waiting for it.

The next day . . . the next day, very early, I am walking from the office to my classroom. I'm thinking of how many days it's been since I've seen Mike Standish, how many calls of his I've left unreturned. He is filled with the promise of distraction. But now is not a time for distraction.

I'm walking through the still-empty hallways when I feel her. I feel her even before I see her, hear her. She's leaning against the door of my classroom, humming and patting her nose with a powder puff from the ivory compact in her hand.

"So our carpool days are over," she says evenly, looking only in the mirror.

"I have a lot of new responsibilities," I say, walking closer.

"I understand," she says, snapping the compact shut and looking at me.

I try so hard to read her, to read the look in her eyes. I try so hard I feel I'll bore through.

But she just smiles impersonally, superbly, like a showroom model, a beauty queen.

"Well, let's not forget, Lora."

"Forget what?"

"About us. Sisters," she says. "About how we're sisters."

Alice pulls open my classroom door for me. A draft whistles through from within.

"Who could forget?" I say, hard. "Who could forget that?"

She only smiles in return, and in her smile I can see nothing, not a stray flicker of fear or anger or anything at all. But what I now know is this: There's a reason she's wearing this blankness, this mechanical look stripped of her heat, energy, her intermittent chaos. There's a reason she's wearing this face. And I'm the reason.

Ellie Marbury, fifteen years old with gum in the corner of her mouth, wearing a sloppy joe sweater the vague color of store-bought pound cake, is whispering feverishly to Celeste Dutton as I try to keep the attention of twenty girls on a warm Friday afternoon.

When I confront both girls after class, Ellie, with all the petulance of a teenager unaware she is already at the height of her rather wan beauty and it will all be downhill from here, asserts, "Mrs. King sure was acting funny today."

"Oh?" I say, emptily.

Ellie's eyes grow wide. "Y-e-a-h," she says, stretching the word out and spitting her gum into the trash can I hold before her.

"She kept running over to the window and running all around the room."

"It was like she had ants in her pants or something." Celeste, always acting younger than her age, giggles.

"And then she told everyone that one day we'd understand how hard it is to be a woman," Ellie adds, half snickering and half eyes popping. Both girls seem torn between laughter and discomfort.

"She said wait until they come sniffing around you," Celeste burbles. "And Ellie said who, and Mrs. King said be glad you still have to ask."

"And she meant *men*," Ellie nods. "I *knew*. We *all* did. I just wanted to see if she would say it."

And then I realize, abruptly, that Ellie, for all her bravado, all her eye-rolling teenage sarcasm, is about to cry. Despite the bubble gum pink smirk on her face, I can see tears are itching to pop from the corners of her powder blue eyes.

I know I should put my hand under her chin and reassure her somehow. But I don't.

"And then . . . and then . . ." Ellie's face is just seconds, mere seconds from bursting. "She said that once they find the dark holes be-be-be-between our legs, no matter how good it is, everything turns to s-s-s-s-shit. Excuse me, Miss King, but that is what she said."

Celeste's eyes grow wide with pleasure at her friend's daring, but I know better. I put my hand sharply on Ellie's shoulder and direct her out of the room.

She's just made it into the hallway, the classroom door has just slammed shut behind us, when glassy tears tear open her once-smug face. Somehow Ellie has understood something about what she has seen, about what Alice has shown her. Why she understands, I don't want to know.

"It's okay, Ellie," I say, leaning against the lockers. "You're not in trouble."

"Thanks, Miss King," she says, tears jetting unabated. "I know I'm not."

She rubs the long sleeve of her sweater over her face. "Don't tell, okay?"

Then she pulls her old face together, tight and contemptuous. "Don't tell."

And I won't. It would be one too many private dramas, after all.

It is late, after nine, after a long student assembly, and my head is still ringing from the sounds of throngs of teenage girls straining gracelessly to mimic Kay Starr.

I make my way quickly through the noiseless lot, where only a handful of cars remain.

As I near my car, a dark sedan lights up suddenly and veers over toward me. I scramble for my keys, guessing it is only a colleague wanting to share a commiserating good night but not wanting to take any chances.

As I slide into my front seat, the car pulls up beside me.

"So . . . this is where you work. I wouldn't have guessed girls who moved in your circles taught school."

I turn my head, recognizing the familiar voice.

"Hello, Detective," I murmur.

Cudahy faces me with a grim-eyed stare. "Get in," he orders, reaching across and opening his passenger side door.

I do as he says, trying not to meet his eyes.

"Isn't this out of your jurisdiction?" I bluff.

"Yes," he says.

"Oh."

"I had you pegged for a liar, but not that kind of liar," Cudahy says.

I feel my face burn and wonder what he knows, other than that I am obviously not the kind of girl who is a regular at places like the Red Room Lounge.

"You don't understand."

"Sure I do, Miss Morgan. You figure, What's the harm? What's a dumb cop going to know? I'll have a little fun with him. Get my kicks."

"No. No. I wanted to help, but I had these . . . responsibilities."

"Who to?"

"No, you've got me really wrong here. Horribly wrong."

"You just protecting yourself or someone else too?"

"I've got nothing to do with it," I say, still not looking at him directly. "I know Lois through someone else. Lois is a friend of someone . . . close to me. Lois *was* a friend of someone close to me."

"Don't you think it's about time you started spilling it? Honest, I'm three seconds away from booking you. You've hampered a police investigation, lied to authorities—"

"Please. I do know Lois. I told you: I know she used narcotics. I know she was selling herself." I pause, deciding whether I should hazard a guess about Joe Avalon's role. "And I know that she had a . . . someone who arranged things."

"And who'd that be?"

I can't think fast enough. All I can think of is my face, blazing with shame. "Don't you already know? I can't be the only person you've found who knew that."

He looks at me long and hard, rubbing his chin and glaring. "I don't know what you're doing to me here. I don't know— Look, I'm a real sap not to just bring you in. I'm doing you a big favor, but only if you can give me something."

"He lives in Bunker Hill. You must know who he is. He takes care of everything for RKO, maybe others."

I feel the weight of the gaze from the corners of my eyes.

"I don't know . . ." A horrible pressure on my chest.

He reaches into his glove compartment and pulls out a folder, tossing it over to me. I open it with shaking fingers.

It is a photo of a man I've never seen before, with a lanky mustache and yellow eyes.

"I don't know who this is," I say, relieved. I start to hand it back to him when the photo slips and another appears behind it.

There he is.

Droopy eyes, bushy black brows and lashes. I turn the photo over and see, in small type, "Joseph Nathanson alias Johnny Davalos alias Joe Avalon 06/25/12."

"Okay," Cudahy say. "Okay, then. Lucky guess."

I look up at him. "I don't know anything specific. I just figured . . ."

"So who's this person who introduced you to Lois Slattery? Davalos?"

"No, no."

I feel my throat go dry. A voice, some voice, rises up from inside. "You won't involve me at all?"

He sighs and looks down at the photo hard. "I can't promise I won't need to contact you. But I won't push you."

I breathe in fast.

"Edith Ann Beauvais." It is a chance. I take a chance.

He writes the name down. "Who's she?"

"She was someone who . . . I saw her with them a few times."

"Davalos and the victim?"

"Yes." I am losing track of my own distortions.

"Where does she live?"

"She's dead."

"Convenient."

"She killed herself."

"We'll see how what you say checks out. Does she have any surviving relatives?"

"I guess. I mean, her husband."

"Name?"

"Charlie Beauvais."

"Where might I find him?"

"He's gone."

"He's gone. Of course. Where'd he go? Hop a ship to the Orient?"

"No one's sure. Maybe Mexico."

"What are you doing to me?"

"Telling you the truth."

He sighs again, looks out the window for a minute, then turns back to me.

"Don't you want to ask me something?"

I look at him.

"Don't you want to know how I found you?"

I swallow hard, although I'm not sure why. "How did you find me?"

"Police business."

"Oh."

"But you might think about this: I found *you* by accident. Because I was following someone else. Imagine my surprise. You get it?"

"I'm not sure."

He gestures with his eyes to the Avalon photo. "Watch your back, Miss."

Like out of a movie. Like out of a movie, and I clutch my chest. I clutch my chest and shake my head. I didn't see it coming, but I should have.

The next day at school, I keep worrying about when I will see Alice for the first time, for the first time since this most recent conversation with Detective Cudahy. These days she seems to be lurking around every corner.

As I make my way down the stairs after fifth period, I am surprised instead to see my brother standing in the front vestibule, kicking his foot in short strokes against the blasted brick of the wall. *My brother*, I almost say it aloud.

He must have heard my approach, or somehow sensed me descending, because he immediately turns to see me.

His face has a pinched, anxious look I know very well. It is the face he wears when he feels helpless. Seeing it, I stop short. I can't bear to move closer.

"What's wrong, Bill?"

"Nothing's wrong, nothing. Why do you ask?"

I am still a few steps from the bottom, but somehow I can't get any closer. Why is he here? Has something happened? Has he found something out?

I can't say anything. It is long past saying anything.

He runs the back of his hand over his face. "It's nothing. It's nothing. It's just— When you drove Alice to school today, did she seem all right to you?"

I make the words come out. "I didn't drive her today. I had an early meeting. I've had a lot of early meetings lately."

He turns toward the wall, touching it with his fingertips. Suddenly, he is nine years old again and facing the profuse tears of his sister, who doesn't want to leave for girls' camp the next day.

"What is it, Bill?"

"And she's not here. She hasn't been here all day. They said she called in sick. They called me at work to see if I could pick up her students' assignments and take them home. They . . ." He trails off.

"She's probably at home in bed. A misunderstanding—"

"Yes." He lifts his head. "I'm sure. Obvious. Thanks, Sis. You know me, overreacting as usual."

I try for a smile and walk the final steps, moving toward him.

"She's just been a little sick, so I've tried to keep a close eye on her."

"Yes, of course. I'm sure she appreciates it." Then I add, touching his arm lightly, "It's what you do."

He turns his head and looks at me, his eyes fastening on mine, *my eyes*. "That's right, Sis. You always know. You always knew."

After he leaves, I shut the door to my classroom and lock it. I sit at my desk for ten minutes, ignoring the students gathering in the hallway. I don't even hear their rising clatter. I sit at my desk, hands folded, looking out the window, thinking, knowing things. Things I will have to do.

He wouldn't tell me. He'd just make it go away.

I haven't seen him in ten long days, since before seeing Lois's body. Have been avoiding him, not wanting to feel tempted to tell him about Lois, afraid, in part maybe, that he might already know. I haven't returned the calls he's left with the front desk of my apartment building. I don't let myself think about it. If I start to think about it, I remind myself who introduced us.

At night, when I'm trying to sleep, pictures of them together gather in my head. Mike and Alice in the far corner of the room, her head thrown back in laughter as he talks in her ear. Mike and Alice smoking on the back porch at one of her parties, each making droll faces, telling old jokes. Who knows how many conversations? Who could guess all that had passed from his wry mouth to her tilted ear? Then from her mouth to . . . anywhere. There is something so horrible in the thought of that, so horrible that I shut it all down. I shut it all down until I feel nothing.

And then there he is.

Standing in the hallway in front of the door to my apartment. His hat is pushed back, and he is fishing through his coat pocket.

He looks up and sees me, eyes dancing. "So what, you're finished with me, is that it?" But smiling, always smiling.

I don't say anything. I reach into my purse to retrieve my key.

"Kind of a shabby way to let me know. Hearing from the building manager that I'm no longer allowed in when you're not here."

Leaning his shoulder against the wall, he pulls out a cigarette and lights it.

It is true. Two days before, I told the manager not to let him or anyone else in. After what Detective Cudahy said, I couldn't take any chances.

I unlock the door and walk in, leaving it open for him to follow.

I turn on a lamp, and he sets his hat down on a table.

"Why would you want to be here when I'm not here?" I say as I walk around the back of the sofa and flip on two more lights.

He sits down and returns to his cigarette. "To wait for you. Like you do at my place. Or like you used to do."

I sit down on the arm of the chair across from him, folding my hands in my lap.

"And now you don't even offer me a drink." He throws his

hands in the air and shakes his head. "That's how it is, is it? I gotta tell you, King, this is not something that happens to me all the time."

"Not with someone like me, you mean."

He meets my gaze and talks through the cigarette. "That's right. That's exactly right."

"If you wanted to get in my apartment so badly, what stopped you? Don't all you press agents have ways to get in places you're not supposed to be?"

"I didn't know it was a place I wasn't supposed to be," he says, blowing a gust of smoke at me. "I guess if I had, I would have brought my set of pick locks and just— You think I'm a real snake, don't you? Jesus, Lora, how could you have sullied yourself so long with me?"

He is good. His face displays genuine injury. Of course, I remind myself, putting on a first-class front is his bread and butter.

"Why would you want to be here when I'm not?" I say again, my mind continually rotating back to his connection with Alice, his history with Alice.

He twists his head from side to side with irritation. "I told you, King. I came to see you. You weren't here. I was going to wait. Scandalous."

"Why would you think I would be here? Did you call first?"

"I guess I didn't give it all that much thought," he says, with more than a little annoyed sarcasm. "Call me irresponsible."

"What did you think you might find?"

"Find?" His eyebrows lift.

"I'm not as naïve as you think."

"Jesus." He punches out his cigarette. "Okay. If that's how you want to play it. If I wanted to come when you weren't here, why would I be waiting for you?"

"How do I know you were waiting for me?"

"This could go on forever. I don't know what dark secrets you think your apartment holds for me, but to tell you the truth, I'm not that interested. Maybe it's me who should be asking you questions. Why don't you just tell me who the guy is?"

"What guy?" I say.

"The one you're tossing me for. I hear he's a badge."

"A badge."

"A cop, or a police detective. Which makes for a kind of poetic justice." He pushes out a faint wrinkle in his gabardines and leans back, folding his arms behind his head.

"Poetic? . . . I don't . . ." Has he seen me with Detective Cudahy?

"What, did you think Alice wouldn't tell me?"

I feel a cold blast across my chest. She is always so many steps ahead.

"Alice . . ." My mind reels. I slide down off the arm onto the chair cushion. How much could she know about Detective Cudahy? I realize suddenly that whatever she has figured out, or guessed at, she is determined to make sure that I know about it. Know she is watching.

"So when did you decide you preferred hot dog stands and chop suey joints to Ciro's and Mocambo?" Mike continues.

Alice. I try to pull myself together. I close my eyes, place a hand on either side of my head, and try to focus. *Don't think about it now, don't think about it now, just find out how, why, anything you can.*

"What are you so upset about, King?" I hear him get up and move over to the bar cart. "I'm the one who got played."

He pours me a short drink and walks it over to me before getting one for himself.

I gulp it and look up at him.

"Who's being played?" My voice sounds funny. "For God's sake. Are you just some kind of spy? A snitch? Did she tell you to take me out, *seduce me* just so she can keep tabs on me?" It doesn't sound like me. It sounds fast, hard and crackling, my teeth chattering with nerves.

"Seduce you?" He chortles. "King, is that really how you remember it?"

"What, do you tell her everything about me, about us?"

He stops laughing and throws me a severe look I've never seen on him. "That's right. I tell her ev-erything. Let's see." He looks up, as though trying to recollect and begins counting off on his fingers. "I told her how I had you in my bed within three hours of meeting you. I told her how you'd come by my place for a late-night fuck after you'd been on dates with other men. I told her how you liked to be flipped in bed and how you like it when I push your face into the pillow. I told her how—"

"You're a real bastard."

"King." He shakes his head. "I didn't tell her a thing. I don't know where you got the idea that I'm such a cad. The worst you could say about me is I don't mind keeping secrets. Including yours."

"I'm sorry," I say, because suddenly, forcefully I believe him. Something raw in his eyes amid all the polish and flash. Something I've never seen before.

"Now," he says, reaching for the bottle he'd set on the coffee table and pouring us both another drink. "Isn't it time you told me what's going on?"

I pause for a moment, but there he is, there he is. And I do it. I tell him what I know about Alice and Lois, and then I tell him about going to get Lois at the Rest E-Z Motel. And then I tell him about Edie Beauvais and Joe Avalon, and about seeing the articles in the paper and, last, about seeing Lois's body in the morgue. I tell him many things, but not everything. Without thinking, I instinctively leave out anything about what I have done and said to keep Bill's name as far out of it as possible.

Mike listens to it all, smoking a new cigarette and not speaking. When I finish, he leans forward, squinting through the billow in front of him.

"Is that everything?"

"Isn't that enough?"

"There are some things I can help you with. Some things I can tell you."

"I thought maybe."

"So why didn't you talk to me before?"

"I didn't trust you." There is no kind way to say it. And I am through with being kind.

He looks at me. "But you do now?"

"I'm not sure how much of it is trust and how much is desperation," I say, truthfully.

"Nobody ever is," he says, stubbing out his cigarette. "Joe Avalon, that fellow, he hustles women for people in the business. I guess you figured that out. I've seen him before. In my line, he's one of the numbers you call. Some of these guys can be counted on more than others. Some end up in the blackmail business."

"Is he one of them?"

"Maybe. I don't know. Sure, I wouldn't put it past him. But I can't be positive."

"Did you know he knew Lois?"

"No."

"What else do you know about him?"

"He worked for Walter Schor a lot."

"I know." I tell him about seeing Joe Avalon coming from meeting a Mr. Schor at the studio. "Who is Schor exactly?"

"A big gun. Very high up at the studio. Avalon must be doing well for himself. He gets to skip the go-betweens. Like me," he adds. "But you can't be surprised by any of this."

"No. Is that all you can tell me? Do you think Lois worked for Joe Avalon?"

Mike rubs his eyes and pauses. Then, "Of course."

"Do you think Alice worked for Joe Avalon?"

He pauses again, eyeing me. "Of course."

I feel my torso lift suddenly, as if in shock, but I am too numb to feel shock. "Why . . ."

"How else would she know a guy like that? Even if she also bought drugs from him, I'd be surprised if she hadn't worked for him at one time."

"Bought drugs?"

"He sells dope, too. They all do. Or at least he's a middle-man. Don't you think he's the one who was so good at keeping Lois half bent?"

"I see," I say. "And Alice?"

"Alice used to take bennies—Benzedrine—when she worked at the studio. All kinds of pep pills. A lot of them do. I don't know if she still does."

I think about Alice, about her manic hostessing, her frenzied housework, her rabid energy, and her occasionally surging speech. And I think about her days in bed with "migraines," her disappearances from school, the thin enamel of sweat that often gleamed off her body.

"And what did Alice do for him?"

"What do you think?" He rakes a hand through his immaculate hair. "She found girls. She found all the girls, Lora. I saw her do it. She knew them all, the Girl with the Tape. She met them that way. Word was she'd pick out the ones she thought would sell. Is that what you want?"

An image flashes before my eyes: Alice on her knees, pins in her mouth, measuring Lois for her Indian Girl costume. I swallow hard and push forward. "What else?"

"Let's stop here for now." He straightens his tie and jacket. "I'll tell you a few more things on the way."

"On the way?"

"We're going to the studio."

"Why?"

"It may not be as exciting as tailing people, but old-fashioned bureaucratic files can do a lot of talking."

• • •

As we drive, my mind swirling, Mike talks.

"She'd call me and want to meet for lunch, and then she'd ask me if we'd slept together and what it was like, what I did and what you did. Did you know that?"

"What did you say?"

"I generally don't kiss and tell, but that rule doesn't usually apply to telling women, or women like Alice. But somehow I couldn't tell her. Somehow . . . I just didn't," he says, then laughs. "Maybe some kind of press agent instinct."

"What did she want to know?"

"Everything. And she'd want to know if you would feel bad about what you'd done. And she'd want to know if you ever liked it to hurt, liked it rough, you know?"

"What did you tell her?"

He looks over at me with his lazy smile. "I lied. But I don't think she believed me."

"No," I say, feeling my face turn hot. "I guess I wouldn't either."

He grabs my hand lightly, fingertips touching my palm. It is so genuine a gesture that it startles me. I resist both the urge to pull my hand away and the urge to seize his tightly.

"D-d-does"—my mouth inexplicably tripping me up—"does my brother know about you and Alice? Your history?"

"Oh, God, no. I'm sure he doesn't. She is nothing if not careful about what your brother knows."

"I suppose that's right."

The warren of offices has an eerie silver chill at night. The sound of our shoes seems unbearably loud. Even though I know Mike is allowed to be here—this is his work, after all—I can't get past the feeling we are trespassing. I speak barely above a hush.

"You don't need to whisper yet." Mike smirks. "We're still in legit territory."

We pass through several winding corridors without seeing a soul.

"Some people are around, but not in this building. They'd be over on the soundstages—or else the writers in their building across the street. I doubt we'll see anyone."

I follow Mike into a suite of offices. SECURITY is etched in glass on the first door. We move through an outer office and up to a door marked WARREN DIXON, CHIEF OF SECURITY.

Mike reaches into his pocket and pulls out a sterling key ring.

"You have a key to his office?"

He smiles again. "It's my job, King. When that barrel-chested all-American box office champ gets caught pants around his ankles in the back room of Café Zombie, sharing a needle with a twelve-year-old hustler, I need to be able to fix it fast."

He unlocks the office door and pushes it open before me. "And this is the place to start."

I walk in, my feet sinking into carpet as thick as a sponge. "Here?"

He breezes past me and moves to the other side of the dim office, illuminated by large set lights across the street. As I follow, he raps his fingers on a paneled door. "Files. Secrets enough to bury an industry."

"You don't have to impress me," I say. "And if you're allowed in here, why can't we turn on the lights?"

"No need to draw extra attention." He grins, opening the door.

I was expecting a closet, but it is a large windowless room, twice as big as the office that led into it, filled with filing cabinets with mahogany fronts.

Before my eyes can adjust to the bright lights, Mike is opening a long drawer marked "Personnel—Costume—1950–52."

"I think she moved here from Universal in 'fifty-one," he says, his fingers dancing along the colored tabs.

"And there she is." He whistles, pulling out what strikes me as a disproportionately large folder marked "Steele, Alice."

As if reading my mind, Mike says, "She worked here for, what, just two years and her file is bigger than Joan Crawford's."

"May I see?" I say, tiptoeing over his arm.

"Yeah, yeah," he mutters, paging through furiously. "Just let me pull out the relevant stuff. There's a lot of administrative material we don't want to waste our time with."

"Maybe I should decide that," I say.

He stops for a second and looks at me, raising an eyebrow. "Still don't trust me, eh?"

"I trust you enough," I say. "Enough for some things."

"Well, fasten your eyes on this." He hands me a document bearing the black stamp PERSONAL AND CONFIDENTIAL. "If I got caught showing you this, I'd be on a plane back to Connecticut. That's trust, King."

It holds a copy of a police report. Alice P. Steele, 9/14/52. Suspect was arrested outside the Black Flamingo nightclub.

Pandering. Solicitation. Public drunkenness. Suspected narcotics use. Assaulting an officer.

"But she was never formally charged? She'd have been fired."

"She must have had friends in high places. Friends within these walls. We may take care of the talent, but costume girls don't normally rate such treatment."

"Joe Avalon and his . . . clients?"

"You got it." He pulls out another document. "Didn't you say Alice graduated from someplace in Van Nuys?"

I remember my conversation with Principal Evans. "Well, that's what she said."

"According to her personnel papers, she never graduated high school."

"I guess I knew that was a lie," I say.

"A reprimand."

"Pardon?"

"This memo shows that her bosses in Costume reprimanded her for what they call 'improper conduct and questionable behavior.' I'd have to talk to Costume to find out what that was about. Could be anything from tardiness to giving head to the grips—" He stops himself and smiles at me. "Pardon me."

I pull out a cache of paper from behind the memo. Paging through, I can't find anything relating to Joe Avalon/John Davalos, Walter Schor, or Lois Slattery.

"Would Lois have a file?"

Mike returns Alice's to the drawer and walks over to a set of cabinets entitled "Extras."

"No . . . ," he says, shuffling through the folders.

"Try Linda Tattersal."

"Bingo."

The folder is slim. It has only a carbon copy of basic personnel information.

"The police probably took the rest," I realize.

Mike looks at me briefly, then looks back down at the form. "Not much here."

I look at the form.

"Five five one seven oh six Manchester."

"What?"

The address strikes me suddenly. Lois lived so transiently that I didn't expect it to have any significance, but it does.

"Where is that?"

"Hell if I know." Mike shrugs. "Not my part of town."

"Could that be Manchester and La Cienega?"

"I don't know, why?" His eyes look strangely bright, his hand on the folder I'm still holding.

"Just wondering," I say. I look at the name listed next to the address, the spot usually reserved for landlords or landladies. It reads, "Olive MacMurray."

"What are you looking at?" Mike asks, placing his other hand on my shoulder.

"Nothing," I say. I wonder if she is the woman I saw when I dropped Lois off at the house on Manchester after picking her up at the Rest E-Z Motel.

But somehow I don't want to tell Mike that. The more he asks, the less inclined I feel to tell. He seems too eager to leave, to wrap things up.

He takes the folder from my hands.

"Sorry this wasn't more help," he says, opening the drawer and slipping the folder back in its place.

"That's okay."

"Let's go grab a nightcap, King. Sit on this a little."

"I'm tired. Maybe we'd just better call it a night."

The next day, I leave work early and drive the same route I had with Lois, along La Cienega, all the way to the large display donut, its slightly rusting candy sprinkles nearly shaking from it.

At the door, I take a deep breath and ring the shrill, over-sprung bell.

It is the same tall woman with the crimson cone of curls on top of her head, her brows pinch-knitted red on her forehead. She appraises me with cool suspicion through the screen door.

"Miss MacMurray?"

Squinting, a cigarette wedged in her scarlet-edged lips, she mutters, "It's Mrs. What do you want?"

"I wondered if I might have a moment of your time."

She surveys me, from the pale, custard-colored hat on my head to my pigskin pumps.

"No God stuff here," she finally says, starting to shut the door.

There doesn't seem to be any way to get into that house much less get the information I want. In the basted pocket of my dress, I grasp my only bargaining chip.

"Oh," I say, waving my hand. "I'm not one of those. I just have some questions for you."

"That's how it always starts."

"It's about Lois Slattery," I blurt out, just as the closing door nearly blocks my view of her.

She pulls the door back with a jerk, raising an eyebrow in a way that looks painful, like risking the opening of a wound.

"Don't know who you're talking about."

"But you do." I try to fix a stare.

She pauses, then says, with a faint snarl, "Who are you to me, anyway? I don't talk at all and I don't talk to just anybody."

"I'm an acquaintance of Joe Avalon."

She smirks so bodily that the powder on her chalky bosom rises, hangs in the air for a minute, and then falls again.

"I don't think so, honey, but that's just funny enough to get you inside."

She props open the door with one acid green slipper. I hurry past it and into the darkened living room.

"Twenty and I'll listen," she says, sitting down on a worn velvet armchair much like the one on the front lawn.

I can barely see in the dim space, but what I can discern seems strangely unlived in. A sofa that matches the armchair, a large radio of the kind common before the war, a fringed lamp wrapped in dust. Otherwise, the room is bare.

Through an open door I can see a bedroom empty save a bed with a bare mattress on top and a pile of towels at the foot.

Nobody lives here. They pass through.

"Twenty," she repeats.

"Pardon?" I sit down on the low edge of the sagging sofa, my knees nearly reaching my chin. "Oh, of course."

I reach into my purse and hand Mrs. MacMurray a bill, hoping that money won't be her sole bartering interest. If so, the meeting will be over soon after it starts.

"You don't know Joe Avalon," she says, sliding the bill into the pocket of her robe and folding her maroon-tipped talons in her lap.

"I do."

"How?"

"That's not important."

"I'll be the judge of that," she says, hard as the edges of the bulbous jade on her right hand. The ring looks real.

"You don't live here," I say. Her eyebrows pitch up suddenly.

"No." She shrugs, as if deciding that this particular fact bears no weight. "Of course not."

Leaning forward, the dust in the air mingling with the powder on her chest, she fixes me with a steely stare. "I'm losing interest. Tell me who you are and what you want or I'll make things ugly. You don't throw that name around lightly."

As she speaks, she moves her face so close I can see the bleeding edge of her painted mouth. Inexplicably, it makes me shudder.

"Lois Slattery," I say quickly. "She worked for you?"

She doesn't respond but looks ready to say or do something that I am pretty sure I won't like. I know I have to move quickly.

"She's dead," I say. "Murdered. Don't you care?"

She leans back, pursing her lips and nearly curling herself into a purring smile.

"That no-count bitch. How do you know I didn't kill her myself? She caused me enough trouble."

"You didn't," I say, suddenly realizing I have no idea if she did. "But you know things."

Her back stiffens. "You better have a bankroll the size of my fist if you want that kind of information."

"No bankroll. But something that might be worth more." I reach into my pocket and pull out Joe Avalon's address book. The book that has been sitting in my dresser for months.

I can tell from the hitch in her eyes that she recognizes it on sight. In a flash, however, she puts on a poker face.

"Is this where the music rises and I clasp my chest like Kay Francis?" She is tough, but she shows more than she means to. She wants the book.

"You need to tell me everything you know about Lois and what happened to her," I say coolly. "And then you get this. And you don't need to waste my time. I know you know what it is."

"Is that so—"

"Now *I'm* losing interest." I feign brusqueness, gathering my gloves and bag. "I know other people who will give me information *and* a fat bankroll to boot for this."

She sighs, eyes continually darting toward the address book.

"What good does that book do me? I don't need addresses, phone numbers."

This is what I am afraid of. Is that all the book contains? Even with its funny code? The shorthand that I can't crack?

"I think you know it's more than that," I bluff.

"Let me see it."

"I'm listening," I say, leaning back for effect, even as I feel the sofa's dust seal itself to my back.

She pauses, running her pointy fingers from her throat to her ample cleavage.

"Fine. Fine. Slattery. A no-good whore. What else do you need to know?"

"You're going to have to do better than that."

"She was a party girl. I take care of party girls. They stay here when they need to. They get taken care of"—she gestures ominously to the bedroom—"when they need to. Lois was one of dozens. She was especially popular because she was especially . . . agreeable. Some girls have rules. Lois had no rules."

Suddenly, her cool breaks, for a split second. Her face visibly darkens. "No rules," she murmurs grimly, looking down at her hands.

Shaking herself out of it, she continues, "Girls like that don't end well. She must have made the wrong date."

"She had a date the night she was killed?"

"That book in your hand better be damn good," she says coldly. "Come here."

She rises and wearily walks me over to the door adjacent to the bedroom. Stepping in, I see a small room dominated by a large, sagging bookshelf.

"Girls leave things here. When they're flopping. They leave valuables, personal items. I let them," she says, reaching down to the bottom shelf. She grabs a large shoe box that has "Lois" scrawled across it in loopy script. I guess I've never seen Lois's childlike scribble.

I take the box from her outstretched hands.

"Didn't the police seize this?" I ask, before thinking.

"They're looking for Linda Tattersal, wherever Lois got that name. They haven't been here. They don't know anything." She eyes me frostily. "Do they?"

"Not as far as I know. Which is good luck for us both," I say. I carry the box back into the living room and open it.

Somehow I thought it would contain revelations, by magic some proof—like a photograph of her own murder.

The first thing I see is a gold shell compact I recognize as my own. I had presumed it lost months ago. There are a handful of swizzle sticks from places like Dynamite Jackson's and Café Society. In one corner a sticky-looking syringe has wedged itself.

"That can't be any surprise," Mrs. MacMurray growls. "She didn't just use. She booted it."

"She what?"

"She booted it—hit the needle real slow, pulling back and pumping the blood again and again to get a bigger fix. Tough stuff, that one. And I only know tough."

A few lipsticks roll from one end of the box to the other. I notice a small, pocket-size pad of mauve paper beneath the syringe and slide it out.

"That's the idea," Mrs. MacMurray says blankly, one eye searching for the address book, which I have temporarily returned to my pocket.

It is a list of hotels and motels and nightclubs, as far as I can tell. Next to each is a set of initials. The printing is in neat black grease pencil.

"Favorite haunts of her regulars. Hard to keep them straight. I told her to log them to help her remember which name to call out."

"These are just initials."

"And those are just numbers and addresses, right?" she says, pointing to the address book.

I scan the list quickly, looking for the Rest E-Z Motel. If any of Lois's dates were dangerous, that was one of them.

On the third page, there it is: "Rest E-Z: WS."

"Walter Schor," I say out loud, remembering Mike's comment about Joe Avalon's main studio client.

"Why not? Walter Schor, William Shakespeare. Why not look for Louis B. Mayer in there while you're at it? Darryl Zanuck."

"You want this?" I finger the address book.

"You want this?" She reaches into her robe pocket and pulls out a small, shiny revolver. The gesture is so cinematic that I feel no fear. Just a cold rush of adrenaline.

"You don't want to use that. You would have used it already if that's what you wanted."

She smiles lightly. "Sure, I don't want to use it. That's not a mess I want to clean up. Look, I'm a lying, cheating grifter. But I play fair, within reason. I promised you information for the book. I've given you all you need. Now give me the book and you can take that box and get it far, far away from me. I've washed my hands of her. She stains badly, little girl. I don't need it."

I hand her the book, as happy to be rid of it as she is to be rid of Lois's things. She opens it immediately. As far as she is concerned, I'm already gone.

"Thank you, Mrs. MacMurray," I say, rising, tucking the shoe box under my arm. "I'll show myself out."

Her eyes tear across the pages as I head toward the door. As I open it, I decide to take one last shot. From over my shoulder, I call out, "Oh, and where's Alice Steele's box?"

Without looking up, ravenously consuming each mystifying page, she mutters, "She picked that up long ago."

It is hours later, with the box set on my tufted bedspread, that I understand why I was so struck by Lois's name on the top. It had been tingling in the back of my head ever since.

The writing in the pad did not match. It had been written by someone else—maybe Joe Avalon, or likely Mrs. MacMurray herself. As for the scrawled name on the box, I suddenly recognize the hand. The same looping, wavering, slanted scribble.

Your brothers wife is a tramp, she's no good and she'll rune him. if you dont beleve me, ask at the Red room lounge in Holywd.

The postcard of the Santa Monica Pier that had led me to the Red Room Lounge.

Lois had been trying to tell me something. Maybe she lost her nerve once I arrived. Or maybe she was just seeing if I'd bite. Maybe she was showing Alice how close she could get to me. Or maybe, maybe she was looking for help.

If WS was Walter Schor and he was the man who had beaten up Lois, it wasn't hard to believe he was the type of man who could also have killed her. I wonder if Alice knew and if she did, why she didn't do anything about it. And if she didn't, then why she was content to let Lois just disappear.

I think of Lois's torn body at the Rest E-Z Motel. I think of the look in her eyes, of despair and wry defeat, or provocation and surrender. She wanted me to *see*, to know the kind of world she—and by extension, Alice—lived in. Was she blackmailing Alice or just refusing Alice her own escape?

Pushing aside my doubts from the night before, I call Mike.

"Can you tell me something about Walter Schor?"

"Sure. What are you looking for, sweetheart?"

"Would he be the type who would hurt women?"

He doesn't even pause. "No, no. He's not the one you're looking for, Lora. You're on the wrong track. Besides, I heard that Lois was running up and down Central Avenue every night. Far more likely this has to do with drugs and a bad scene."

The feeling I had in the file room as he snapped up Lois's file folder returns, but with more intensity—a bristling up my spine, rough as a razor. "When did you hear this?"

"Asking around. She was moving in a very rough crowd. These things happen."

"What's wrong?" I nearly gulp, straining for air. When Mike saw Olive MacMurray's name in Lois's file, he somehow figured it all out. Figured out that this wasn't just about Alice and a two-bit thug like Joe Avalon, an easily replaceable pimp. This went higher, sunk deeper. He is lost to me.

"Wrong?"

"You sound different from last night, at my apartment."

"Different? No, baby, not different. Listen, I had an idea. How about you and me and a drive up the coast this weekend? Or Catalina and all that? Get our minds off all this. Forget about it."

I try to get some control of my voice. I want to sound casual. I want to sound like nothing is wrong.

"That sounds wonderful, Mike. But I've got a lot of work to do this weekend, stacks of student papers and lesson plans. Listen, I'll call you later."

"Okay. What are you doing tomorrow?"

"Just cleaning house," I say as I hang up. I am going to have to do it alone.

Lois lying, facedown, in dark water. Born only to die and to die like this, lost, forgotten, brutalized, released, left faceless, nameless, alone. Somebody had to speak for her. That night, I dream of her. Of her speaking to me. Hair twisted with seaweed, face swimming out of dark water, eyes imploring, mouth coiled darkly, queerly into a smile. *Lora,* she would say, *Lora, you know more than you think. You know everything.*

These are the things I barely remember: Calling in sick. Driving to my bank. Waiting twenty minutes for it to open. Withdrawing my savings—only four hundred dollars, but a world of effort for me. Driving back to the ghostly house on Manchester, the long, long drive past countless streets baroque and scarred, nondescript and ominous.

The next thing I know I am looking at Olive MacMurray's startled expression as she peers at me from around the corner of the sofa, ten feet and a screen door separating us.

There must be something in my eyes, something hanging there, dangling dangerously, because she stands, not moving closer, only hissing faintly, "What are you doing here?"

"I need to see you."

"We finished our business," she says in clipped, hushed tones, stripped of the prior day's wile.

"I have money. I need to know some things about Alice Steele."

She rushes to the door, her face stretched tight, and hastily ushers me in with trembling hands. "Listen, you, you don't know what you've gotten yourself into. I don't want any part of this."

"What do you mean? What happened?"

"How much do you have?" She twists her fingers anxiously.

"Four hundred dollars. But only if you can answer all my questions."

She waves me over to the sofa. Someone has gotten to her. Joe Avalon has gotten to her. I feel my teeth set on edge.

"I'll take that money. I need that money now." The powdered flesh of her bosom mottled today, her hands clenching.

"Who wrote Lois's schedule of dates? Was that you?"

"No. It was your sister-in-law," she snaps.

"Why?" I snap back, only then realizing what she has said: *Your sister-in-law.* She knows who I am, maybe has known all along. But there is no time for this revelation. I repeat, "Why?"

She takes a deep breath, then, "She was one of the girls, fancy ambitions but dangerous habits. She had an arrangement with Avalon. She helped control Lois. Helped keep her jumping—Lois and her big mouth. Joe wanted to dump her or worse, and Alice kept her alive. She was her lucky piece, as they say."

"I guess she couldn't keep her alive forever," I murmur, my head throbbing.

"Once Alice hooked up with her lawman, she had more of an interest in keeping herself in the pink. Lois was a drag on her. It turned out pretty lucky for Alice in the end. But her loose ends may trip us all up yet," she says, wringing her hands over and over.

I pull the Santa Monica Pier postcard from my pocket.

"Did Lois write this?"

"How should I know?"

"The handwriting?"

"Could be. Lots of the girls write like that." She reads the card more closely. "Ah, I get it. She was looking to have something over Alice's head. A bargaining chip."

"You think Walter Schor killed Lois."

"I cleaned her up enough times after dates with him," she says, voice lowering. "And this sure is worth that four hundred: He sent another one of my girls to the hospital after a night of monkeyshines."

"Because . . . because . . ." I wonder if I can ask it. "Because Alice would never . . . never hurt Lois." I couldn't look the woman in the eye.

"I gave up long ago guessing what people were capable of," she says. "But my money's on Schor. Question is, How many times did Alice need to put Lois in harm's way before the party girl turned up cold? And I do know this. And then I'm done. Joe Avalon isn't about to be a patsy. And *he's* capable of just about anything when his back is against the wall."

Her eyes meet mine, and I feel something very weighty has been communicated to me—but its full meaning is as yet unclear.

"It was Joe Avalon?"

She shakes her head. "You're missing it. Listen close, and then I'm closing the shutters on the information booth. Joe Avalon isn't about to be a patsy. And, *right now*, he's capable of just about anything.

"By the way," she adds, rising. "It was Alice Steele, couple years back, who got put in the hospital at Walter Schor's hands. You don't forget that kind of dinner date.

"Before we took her in to County, she spent two days in there"—she gestures to the bedroom—"filling it with blood."

I park my car three doors down from Olive MacMurray's house, trying to unravel all she said for my four hundred dollars. I don't trust myself to drive yet.

I sit for about twenty minutes thinking about Lois and why she let herself fall into Walter Schor's poisonous arms over and over again—one long death scene. *"The kind of dance you're lucky to make it out of,"* she'd said, not so lucky herself.

And I think of Alice, Alice serving herself up to countless men and now sunk deep, heels dug in, in my brother's home. And Alice once lying on that bed in that fetid house, lying there, body twitching, more blood with each spasm, more pain with every move. Lying there in a doomed attempt to hide, to hide this, to hide all this. And it was to hide, to conceal, to bury, that she sent Lois up to the pyre and watched as the flames ate her alive.

My God, Bill, what you've let crawl into your bed . . . you poor, hapless thing . . . must you pay so much for your fine innocence?

I sit for about twenty minutes

I sit for about twenty minutes and then

It is then and there it is. There is no one there, and suddenly, blinking back at the house, I see him flicker up Olive MacMurray's porch steps out of the corner of my eye.

I have his picture in my head and then he is there. And me

Like a sleepwalker

As someone hypnotized

And there I am, now out of my car, fast and without thinking, slinking past the three houses

Back to 551706 Manchester

Walking in a silence so deep it is as if all sound has been sucked out of the world

I walk along the side of the house

lean up against the wall, against the pitted shingles

along the window, open, paint-flecked

through all this I pretend I didn't see *who I saw*, pretend it was just a trick of the light, the eye

like the old adage, Speak of the devil, and he shall appear

I press my hand, my palm against the heat-curled shingles

I might have even whispered it aloud

not Bill it couldn't be Bill not my brother not

then I hear the voice through the screen window

"We're talking a lot of money here," he says. "And all the protection you could want."

Could that hard, anxious sound possibly be my brother's voice?

"How much money? My life wouldn't be worth a plug nickel, Detective."

"He wouldn't be able to touch you, Mrs. MacMurray. I can promise that. We're talking serious money."

"I'd need five grand."

"Fine. I'll arrange to have it wired to your bank account this afternoon."

"Do I look like a landlady? I don't have a bank account."

"I'll get it to you." A quaver tilts into his voice, and *it is Bill and my God—*

"He's going to find out I gave him up to you."

"He won't. And if he does, it won't matter. He'll be in county jail and then prison for life. Murder first-degree conviction for Avalon. I promise."

"And I get all his girls. And I get all his studio johns."

"Right. Who else but you?"

"I suppose even Walter Schor, if I want him."

"Because you've got what I need to pin this on Avalon?" Hot desperation in his voice.

"We can make it work. He's dirty enough for any frame to work."

"He's an animal." Quaver gone and now a hard bark. "I got into the law to beat guys like this." *Oh, it is horrible.*

"Whatever you say, copper," a low, amused drawl.
A loud noise, a sound like a blood howl
and it is me

As I watch him walk rapidly out of the house, my body begins moving too. He passes his car and keeps going until he reaches the donut shop. I follow at a distance. *Don't think about it now, don't think about it now, just find out how, why, anything you can.*

Looking furtively to his right and left—*my brother, like a criminal*—he ducks into the phone booth out front. I move quickly around the back of the shop and then sidle along the far wall, inching as close as I can to the front of the building while still remaining hidden by both the corner and the meager hedgerow that wraps around it. He has shut the phone booth door, but I can still hear.

His voice is loud, raked raw. "I did it. Don't worry. I took care of it. I told you I would."

His effort to control his voice, sound strong is painful.

"No," he says. "It's just like I promised. She'll pin him for it. She'll claim he came to her that night talking about how he'd dumped her in the canyon. She'll say he did it to keep her in line. She'll say Lois was terrified of him. Once she has the money, she'll tell more."

He pauses for a moment, listening. Listening and, I can hear it, jabbing his fist rhythmically against the door of the booth.

"Yes, yes. I did it all. You know, Alice, you know, he's done enough bad things he never got caught for. So he can pay by paying for this. He can pay for this. He should pay. This is about the kind of man he is and those things he made you do. He can't hurt you anymore."

He can't stop. He isn't talking to her. He doesn't know it, but he's talking to me.

"He's going to pay for the things he made you do."

I want to protect you from all that, my brother Bill once said to me. I had returned home crying. Some boy who had cornered me in his car, pressed himself so close, so roughly his watch had caught on my sweater and snagged it from collarbone to waist. The sweater was a favorite, was the perfect aquamarine. It was the softest thing I'd ever owned. It felt like pussy willows against my skin. It was the ruined sweater that brought me home with tears stinging. But my brother assumed it was the boy.

—Did he hurt you? Did he force himself on you?

—He tried to. He kept . . . trying.

It was true, after all.

It took nearly an hour to persuade him not to go to this boy's house. I knew he wouldn't hurt the boy, just frighten him, scold him. But I was too embarrassed. And part of me would rather listen to him. Listen to him say things like

—I want to protect you from all that. I don't want you to have to know these things. About men. I want you to be safe forever. I will make you safe forever.

I want to protect you.

From somewhere in the dark murk of my head, the phone jumps at me.

"Lora? It's Bill. I'm glad you're there. We've been kind of worried about you. Alice says you missed school today."

Images of my brother at Olive MacMurray's that very afternoon crackle through my head. I can't remember anything else I have done in the last six hours. Did I really drive home, park my car, walk up the stairs to my apartment, pour the glass of water in front of me, light the cigarette—whose cigarette?—I seem to be smoking now?

Gathering myself, stopping my pounding heart with my hand, putting on a face, a voice, I say: "I wasn't feeling well."

"Well, we thought maybe you forgot about the party. It starts soon."

"Party?"

"The charity event Alice is hosting, remember? For the Police Benevolent League?"

"Right." I vaguely remember agreeing to bring a tray of rumaki.

"People are supposed to get here in half an hour."

"I'll be there," I say.

I say it as though nothing has happened. And then it becomes as though nothing has happened. My brother is the same. I am the same. Somehow we've all agreed. It is the only way to go forward, to speak, to move. I can do it. There is some strange steel to me . . .

I open the refrigerator door. I don't have any chicken livers for the rumaki, so water chestnuts will have to do. As I stand wrapping the bacon around each piece, sliding in a pineapple chunk, my mind keeps shuttling back to seeing Bill again, how I'll see his face and know. Know what? There is nothing to know.

I set my jaw, focus my eyes.

The busier I make myself with the food, the slippery pineapple and the frilly toothpicks and the sticky honey glaze on my fingers, the more I am able to send myself back to my Bill, the Bill who never surprises me except with the extent of his flinty decency, his goodness, his deathless integrity.

The more I think of this, the more I think of what he might do for me if I were so ensnared. The more I think of this, wrapping the rumaki in wax paper, the more the fog in my head clears, my thinking becomes razor-sharp. I can go to the party and I can see what she has brought upon him, what she has brought him to. I can look the damage in the face and then I will know what to do.

The staggering thing is this: amid everything, amid all Alice's efforts to conceal a murder, to entrap her husband in the treachery, to bribe one partner in crime and frame the other, she still manages to orchestrate another one of her extravagant spectacles.

Japanese lanterns have been artfully positioned to spread a pink haze everywhere, over the platters of egg rolls and plum sauce, fried wontons, fortune cookies, glistening pork on bamboo skewers, and the tureen of chow mein, over the tall vases filled with moon lilies and bamboo stalks, the hanging temple bells tingling serene music from the patio, over the sandalwood fan party favors in the basket by the door, the paper dragon stretched across the fireplace. It is pitch perfect. It is almost obscene.

And there is Alice, her dark hair pulled back tight and her eye makeup straight out of a Charlie Chan movie, emerging from under one of the cherry blossom parasols on the patio in a searing turquoise cheongsam dress, all the rage since Jennifer Jones wore one in *Love Is a Many-Splendored Thing*.

As she moves across the room to greet me, I feel a hard chill drag down my spine. Can I really do this, be here, see them? It is as though time has slowed to a hypnotic crawl as she makes her way toward me, the silk of her cheongsam shushing, her feet, in wooden sandals, making no sound on the thick carpet, her head lowered like a good geisha. Then, as she approaches me, her darkly lined lids rise and she looks at me and in that look . . .

In that look, perhaps for the first time since I've known her, she conceals nothing. Her gaze—filled with rage, terror, shame, ugliness, and still, her keen beauty—scissors through me, and I feel I have been gored.

"Lora! And you remembered the rumaki," she coos with a kind of honeyed slither. "I can always count on you."

I can't speak, can't bear to, then—

"Sis."

I feel the familiar warm, heavy arm on my shoulder, and something in me, something held tight, collapses.

"Hi, Bill." I can't look up at him. I merely feel him, smell his old-fashioned aftershave, the scent of which is pressed, warm and peppery, into everything he owns.

And then they are both gone, people coming in behind me and Alice whisking my platter off to the kitchen.

It is only then that I notice the dozen guests already in the room, drinking Singapore slings and mai tais, the women waving their fans languorously and the men lighting cigarettes and the Four Aces crooning, "Your fingers touched my silent heart and taught it how to sing," on the stereo and everything going on as if nothing . . .

I float around the space like a ghost, avoiding conversations, speaking to no one, trying to disappear into the crimson haze of the decor.

Looking at Alice from across the room, I see that, although her face is powdered an impeccable white, a faint sheen of perspiration is beginning to pearl on her skin. She is laughing and talking and mixing drinks and adjusting the lanterns as men's heads hit them, but she isn't pulling off the performance with her usual élan. And it both thrills and frightens me.

As for Bill . . . Bill is no good at all, half-hiding in a corner chair, continually, compulsively running his hand through his hair, rubbing his jaw until it turns red, tugging at his pants legs, reaching for his drink and then changing his mind and returning his hand to his knee, to his ear, which he tugs, to his tie, which he loosens, then straightens, then loosens and straightens again. Oh God, Bill.

The things I heard him say, only hours before, to that woman, that horrible woman:

"We're talking a lot of money here. And all the protection you could want."

". . . you've got what I need to pin this on Avalon?"

But then I look back at him, at the tightness around his eyes like when, like when there's things going wrong, things he can't control. *Like when a masher grabbed me in the movie theater or when a teacher scolded me in front of the class or when my grandparents pillaged my forbidden box of Dubarry face powder and the only bottle of perfume I'd ever had—Soul of Violet—or when . . . or when . . . a very bad and dangerous criminal slipped just out of reach.*

I reach over to the bar cart and pour myself a small glass from the first bottle I touch. The feel of it fresh in my throat, I walk across the room to him.

He just wants to save us all, I think. It sends him down some very dark alleys. He can't help it. He never could.

"Hi."

He looks up at me and when he does

And when he does and I can't forget this

it is with unbearably guilty eyes.

I think I might burst into tears.

"Sis," he says scratchily, one hand to my arm, soft. "I'm glad you're here."

This is what he is really saying: *"I had to do it, Lora. Otherwise, it all would have meant nothing."*

And suddenly I understand.

Then, he averts his eyes from mine, rises, and walks away.

I think I might die.

• • •

Moving past guests, pretending not to hear anyone who might call my name, I step out onto the empty patio and around the corner to a darker patch of the small yard. A shot of brisk air tingles on my face, and I take another long drink.

"I didn't think you'd show."

Jumping, I turn and, through the growing dark, make out Mike Standish leaning against the jacaranda tree, hands in his deep linen pockets.

"Likewise," I say, catching my breath.

"Well, as you know, I've always been a great supporter of law enforcement."

Peering through the tree's feathery leaves, I think I can see him smiling. He makes no move to indicate he plans on coming out from the shadows.

"Why are you here?"

"I've been asking myself that a lot lately. Almost every time you ask it of me, King."

"I can't talk to you," I say, my chin faintly trembling. I remind myself that everything he says is at least half a lie.

"Why not," he replies, cool as ever.

"I can't talk to you at all." I feel my hands jerking, and surprising myself, I see that this moment may in fact be about Mike and Mike and me and I can't do it, not now, and I feel the supple, insinuating warmth of his voice as he says my name and I want him to come out from the shadow of the tree, but I'm afraid if he does, I will be lost.

(*One thing, Lora, one thing, Alice had said, he warns you that he's going to charm you, and that warning becomes part of his charm.*)

"Just stay away," my voice, somehow, rings out.

"You think you know things, but you don't." At last, he steps out of the heavy darkness of the low black branches.

For the first time since I met him I can almost see a path of stubble, a slight wrinkle of the collar, a hair out of place. It's heartbreaking.

"King—*Lora*, you don't know anything. At least not where I'm concerned," he says.

This is too much. Something slips in me and there's no going back. "Don't come any closer!" I say, my voice at a higher timbre than I'd meant.

Mike's eyes widen and he stops short.

Out of nowhere, a hand on my shoulder.

"Is he bothering you?" And it is Bill's taut, broken voice.

Before I even turn around, I feel it in the blood. I feel him straining against his own skin, so desperate for something to fix, to make right. *If I'm not this, then what am I?*

I turn and look up at him. Both these men and their creased white collars and scruffy faces and this is not how it is supposed to be . . .

"Perfect." Mike shakes his head.

"No, no," I say quickly to my brother. I can't manage him, too.

"Do you want me to get him out of here? I will, Lora. What do you want, Lora?" Bill stutters, unsure, never looking at me, looking only at Mike, jaw newly set. "What has he done?"

What has he done? What have they all done to us both, Bill?

"Skip it," Mike mutters, seamlessly lighting up a cigarette.

"I was heading out anyway. The police don't need my support these days."

I put my hand to my mouth at the insinuation and turn my eyes away. Does he know, too? Does he know about my brother, too?

"You know, they take care of themselves now," Mike adds— needlessly—tossing his match behind him.

As I watch, arms to my sides and mouth slightly open, he walks away, around the side of the house, disappearing into the trapped darkness there.

I turn back around even as I know Bill too is gone, swallowed up by the party, by Alice, or just not wanting to look me in the face.

Inside, everyone is dancing, waiting for Alice to take her usual position at the center, leading the group. But instead she keeps vanishing into the kitchen or the back bedroom or the powder room, a cigarette always in hand, the sweat now coating her skin, seeping into the white geisha girl powder, scattering her black eye makeup.

"Alice! C'mon! Alice, are we going to mambo?"

"Let's go, Alice! We don't know any Oriental dances, unless you count the cha-cha-chopsticks!"

She begs off, mouths an excuse, heads back into the kitchen.

"Bill's in there, too," I hear Tom Moran bark to two other cops. "Washing dishes! In the middle of a party!"

Doris Day's voice belts out, "Oh, why did I tell you it was bye-bye for Shanghai? I'm even allergic to rice . . ."

"For God's sake, Alice," someone shouts out. "We need you."

I turn around to see that Tom Moran and Chet Connor each have one of Alice's arms and are walking her to the center of the makeshift dance floor.

The look in her eyes is that of a cornered animal, but she quickly reassembles, and inhaling hard, she hoists a dazzling red Alice-smile on her face.

"All right, boys, all right. You can't take no for an answer."

"Or so Tom's girlfriends say," Chet guffaws, grabbing Alice around the waist and into position.

All cherries and foamy milk, Doris Day prattles on, "Why don't you stop me when I talk about Shanghai? It's just a lover's device . . ."

Alice leans back and grabs a fan from the basket as Chet twirls her. Her distracted look evaporates, and as she twists her wrist and spreads the green fan out in sync with the music, I can see her pleasure, blunt and maddening.

"Who's gonna kiss me? Who's gonna thrill me? Who's gonna hold me tight? . . ."

Chet laughs delightedly, and everyone steps back to let them have the floor. Eyes glittering, Alice begins singing along, the sultry counterpoint to Doris, "I'm right around the corner in a phone booth and I want to be with you *tonight!*" Every line Doris belts with cheery vim, Alice matches with tantalizing venom. Everyone is clapping and cheering, packed tight together, maybe twenty-five of them, to see the show.

I feel caught between admiration, awe, and fury. Whipping around the room, fan snapping and hips swiveling in the tight dress, she's utterly alive, and even when her eyes pass over me, they practically spark with unabated energy, and then, as the last stanza begins . . .

She almost trips. She's looking, eyelashes shuttered open wide, past me and to the left, at the door.

Her face is sliding off.

That's what it looks like, because it *is*.

I jerk my head around to see what she's looking at, what has so dissembled her. Peering through the throng and smoke, I think I see— And then I see it is.

There is a man standing in the vestibule.

I fix on the lightning bolt scar over his left eye. It's the boy from the studio. The one who drove Joe Avalon. The tough kid seated four chairs down from me as I waited. Teddy. That is his name.

Alice's eyes fix on him for a split second. Only I—and probably Teddy—see. And she finishes the final twirl and then, trying glamorously to catch her breath, clutching her hand to her chest with all the drama of Bette Davis, she fashions a breathtaking smile.

I look back at Teddy, and by the time I turn around again, Alice is gone.

Pushing past the energized dancers, I try to get to Teddy, not knowing what I can possibly say to him. But he has already thrust through the other way, to the patio doors, presumably after Alice.

I squeeze through the oblivious revelers and out the doors,

but by the time I'm outside I can't see Alice or Teddy or anyone.

I begin thinking. Avalon sent Teddy here to scare Alice, or abduct her, or worse. He knows she's setting him up. He will do anything he can to stop her. Alice has to have known that this would happen, that Joe would find out about the frame. What's her plan now?

In my head, flashbulbs smash in front of me, and Bill is squinting, covering his face, running down the City Hall steps. *Cop Fired in Disgrace, D.A. to Prosecute His Own.*

On a guess, the only guess left, I walk quickly and purposefully back through the house and into Alice and Bill's bedroom.

I have no idea what I might find. None at all.

Some part of me is sure she is too smart for this, too smart for me. There can be nothing to find. She has spent a life covering her tracks. Passing time in one darkened hotel room after the next, peeling masks off only to expose other, still brighter masks beneath. She knows how to leave no trace.

But time is running out, and I have to take the chance that she is scared and desperate. As it turns out, I am lucky.

It is almost too easy. There in the drawer of the bedside table is an oblong envelope with a drawing of chocolate-colored natives on it, flowers in their hair.

I sit down on the bed and open it. It is the itinerary for a boat trip—the SS *Tarantha*—headed to Brazil. Mr. and Mrs. King. Mr. and Mrs.

The boat leaves tomorrow at six o'clock.

I feel my stomach rise. *How could he go with her?*

I stare at the envelope for several minutes. Then I walk over to the closet and open the top drawer of the tall highboy inside. In it is the dainty Walther PPK pistol Bill brought back from Europe. I put it in my purse.

I'd like to say I have everything planned, but I am just running by pure instinct, some throbbing voice inside me saying, *Don't take any chances.*

I exit the bedroom unseen and leave quickly through the patio door and the black, echoey yard. As I do, I think I might see Teddy lurking in a far corner. I half-expect to see his fleshy scar, feel his hard arms.

For two hours, I drive mindlessly, unable to think. I drive out of Pasadena and its endless, pungent groves all the way to the Sepulveda Dam, all quivering cottonwoods and glittering sycamores, and the new golf course carved in the middle, and then back through Burbank, by the blazing Hollywood Bowl. I drive and as I drive, slowly, with the radio mourning haunted hearts, I find I'm making plans.

Finally, I find myself on my block and then at my building. As I walk from my car, I hear someone walking briskly to catch up with me. I turn with a start, waiting for the lightning bolt, or Joe Avalon's coal-eyed stare. Lately, it seems like I am always turning with a start.

"Detective Cudahy," I blurt, not entirely relieved.

"You're not playing straight, even after our little talk," he says with a creeping coldness in his voice.

"I don't know what you mean."

"Where's your sister-in-law?"

I guess there are few secrets left. I lock eyes with him. He looks tired, frustrated, impatient. "Where is she, Miss King?"

In my head, I start to say, *Sister-in-law? I don't know what you mean.* But I can't bear to keep playing. I can't stomach putting on the front.

So instead I say, "I don't know. I came here looking for her."

He looks slightly relieved at my bluntness. "She knew we were closing in. We were tailing her."

"And you lost her?"

"She lost us. I was staking out the party and she just disappeared. One minute she was there, the next she was gone. Must have left on foot. We're guessing she's on her way into hiding, or skipped town. This may come as a big surprise to you, Miss King, but she knows even more than you."

"I thought maybe," I say, inwardly relieved. He has figured out a lot, but not everything.

And then he pauses as if deciding something.

"We'll keep your brother out of it," he finally says, nodding toward me.

I feel my eye twitch. I don't know why I wasn't expecting him to mention Bill. I don't know why I thought Bill was still safe.

I consider, fleetingly, telling him about the tickets to Brazil. But I have no real reason to believe Cudahy would, or could, keep my brother out of it. And, more pressingly, I have no reason to believe Bill would, or could, stay out of it.

"We know he doesn't know what he married into," Cudahy continues. "The circles your sister-in-law moved in."

"Right."

"You should have told me about him. About who you were."

"I know."

As I walk up the stairs, my head is blank. It crosses my mind that I can't be sure I'm not being followed now. Still, what choice do I have? I have to take my chances.

When I enter the apartment, the phone is ringing. Somehow I know it has been ringing for hours.

"It's Alice. Don't you think it's time we spoke?" I hear the roar of the ocean in the background.

I say, "Where?" and she tells me.

On the long drive to meet Alice, I am careful to watch my rearview mirror. I take some winding detours and don't notice anyone.

I am thinking that there are so many things about Alice that I will never know. An airless gap between the stories of her low-rent childhood and her years working for studio costume departments. And do I even know if these exotically sketched narratives are true?

She made herself into someone you didn't ask questions of because somehow you didn't know the right questions to ask.

Or the questions you wanted to ask seemed impossibly naïve in the face of the dark maw that lay behind her finely etched wife face.

Once I thought she was trying to escape a darkness, and she found rescue in Bill. Now I know that she wanted both. She liked the double life. It kept her alive.

I arrive at Miramar Point as the moon shows its full size; giving off a faint glitter on the water, whose waves cream forward into sleek spit curls before straightening out to stretched silk again. A lone boat knocks around the Santa Monica breakwater. Past it, the colossal gap of the ocean hangs a steely purple.

I park on a small ridge off the highway and make my way to the top of an endless flight of wooden steps. My hand moist on the nickel rail as I ascend higher and higher, I make the final turn to reach the restaurant. Its round booths, hung over with fairy lights, are uninhabited except for a young man with a shock of white-blond hair nodding off over his drink. A cat twined at his feet suddenly arches his back at me as I walk over and slide into a booth, ordering a short glass of red wine.

It is twenty minutes before I hear someone call. Looking out, I see her making her way up the long set of steps.

Through the brown-violet dusk, I can see her waving, waving as if somehow—against all reason—glad to see me.

As she walks up the last stretch, I think of nothing but the faint sound of passing cars on the highway below. It is the only way.

Moments later, we are leaning, small glasses of anisette in

hand, over the terrace rail behind the bar. Her hair, long and undone, swirls around her as she turns to face me. Every moment feels unutterably significant.

"Remember that night when I told you I felt like someone was following me?" she says evenly.

Before I can say I don't remember it at all, she adds, "Isn't it funny that it was you?"

Taken aback, I say, "I'm not following you."

"No?" she says, and suddenly I'm not so sure.

She taps out the final cigarette from her creased pack, her fingers sallow at the tips.

"It's you who's followed me," I insist severely. "Telling Mike Standish things that you couldn't know."

She only smiles.

"You wanted to scare me off this. But you can't." I feel my nerve rise the more I speak. If she wants it straight, I'll give it to her. "Why did you keep letting Lois go to Walter Schor when you knew the kind of man—"

I wasn't expecting the response.

"Why not?" Her eyes ringed red. "If it wasn't him, it would have been someone else. Girls like us—" she begins, then lifts her shoulders almost in a shrug. The *us* is painfully, devastatingly vague.

"But you were out of it all. You could have been out."

"There is no out." Her eyes like fresh teeth, hooking into me. "Don't you know?"

I ignore her question, try once again to shift the conversation to the immediate, the practical.

"So Mike told you," I say. "What I'd found out." I'm not

sure if it is a question or not. The conversation feels unreal, unmoored. I feel drunk, nerves hot and tingling.

"Everything. He told me everything," she says, and runs a finger along her lips, blue under the lights. "He couldn't help it. He had to give me all of it. He was in love and he couldn't distinguish."

"In love."

"With you, my girl. I figured on a lot, but not on that." She draws in the smoke.

"I should have," she adds, almost kindly. The tone sets something off in me.

"Why don't you just tell me. Why don't you just tell me. Was it you? Did you kill her." My voice is like a knot unloosing too fast, uncontrollable. Even as I say it, I don't really believe it. But I want to see. I want to see how bad it is.

"I didn't kill her." Alice shakes her head. "But I might have, it's true. If I had to. She knew I couldn't leave everything behind. Not everything. Or couldn't yet. I still liked the perfume of it, even if I sometimes hated myself for it.

"Walter Schor, you know all about him, I guess? She showed up at his house. She knew you were never supposed to do that. She wasn't following any of the rules anymore. Schor called us both. Said get her out of here or there's going to be trouble. He was through with her anyway.

"When Joe and I got there, his flunkies, they said they didn't know where she was. But you could feel something in the air, something awful.

"We kept looking through the entire house, walking down corridor after corridor, in and out of over a half dozen bedrooms and sitting rooms and a projection room and pantries and a room, Lora, a room just for arranging flowers.

"The longer it took to find her, the more we both saw our futures shuddering before us. He could see trouble with cops and all the bad business that comes with it. I could see worse. The end of everything.

"It was a half hour before we found her. We'd already looked at his famous saltwater pool and hadn't seen her. But when I was upstairs in one of the bedrooms, I stepped out on a balcony and looked down at the big kidney shape, and there was something in it, floating.

"It looked like a big black rose, like those aerial shots in old musicals, round black-stockinged chorus girl legs fanning out into big flowers."

She spreads her blue-lit hand out over the water beneath us.

"It was her dress blooming.

"Joe and I ran down, and he kneeled over and he saw too.

"Neither of us jumped in. Isn't that strange?" She turns to me, as if wanting an answer.

I don't say anything. How can I say anything? I look down past the railing, into the surf. I look down and listen to her buzzing, relentless voice.

"And, Lora, it was so funny. Lois was leaning over herself, facedown, curled over like the top of a cane. Joe reached out and tugged her toward the pool's edge. I can still see him lifting her head up. Her eyes were wide open. I wasn't expecting that. They were beautiful.

"Before I passed him off to Lois, I was Schor's girl for a long time, with the scars to show for it. He wasn't even as rough as they come. I've had rougher. But I knew it could have been me. In many ways, it was me: Alice Steele, folded up upon herself, and Alice King waiting there, ready to cut her losses, reborn free of old ties, old stories, old desires . . .

"Joe called two of his boys and told them to dump her but first make her hard to identify. They didn't do much of a job. They didn't think they needed to. Who would stand up for Lois? Who would even look for her?"

She reaches out and grabs my face in her hand. "You really want to know?" Her grip is cold marble on my skin. "Listen"—she holds my chin more tightly, forcing my eyes to hers—"listen, Lora. Isn't this the kind of thing you've always wanted to know? Isn't this the kind of thing you've been touching with your fingertips since we met? Touching in the dark?"

No.

"They busted a cap together, he beat her raw, and when he was done, he pushed her in, and let her sink like a stone. Maybe he held her under, forcing all that hot dirty life out of her.

"Listen, Lora, listen."

The way she looks at me—I remember what Mike once said: *She wasn't just a B-girl, she was carrying the whole ugly world in her eyes.*

Then she finishes me off. "When we got there, Schor was reading the racing form. Drinking cognac and circling sure things with a little blue pencil."

My hand darts out, knocks her arm away from me forcefully. Then slaps her face with a sharp crack. Her face shoots backward, but she doesn't even blink. I think she might smile.

"Just tell me. My brother—" I start, then feel all the sound rush out of me—*when did he fall when did he fall so far*—blood beating in my brain. It is too much.

"Of course." She nods, and now she is smiling but softly, a streak of red seared to her cheek. "Of course. That's what you really want to know. That's all you really want."

She shakes her head. "Lora, that doesn't matter."

"I don't. I don't," I say, shaking my head, shaking it loose.

"I came to him when I had no choice left. Bill, he . . ." She starts, then stumbles.

"He was in love and he couldn't distinguish," I say, turning away from her, eyes brimming. I say it not for her but for him. Only for him.

We each take a long drink from our glasses. The liqueur snakes down my throat, steeling me.

"I'm not stopping," I say in a scratchy voice I don't recognize. "I have to help him. He can't see . . ."

Her expression turns from loose to tight, a flat mask. "You'll bring him down. Is that what you want? That bum cop you're spilling to. Joe told me all about him. You do know he'll have your brother's badge. Lock him up and throw away the key. It'll be your fault. Is that what you want?"

I've never heard her talk quite this way, quite this hard.

"Is that what you want?" she prods.

"You—you crashed into him," I suddenly, incongruously say, then furl my brow. *What am I saying?* The words make no sense.

"I can save him." I recover. *He's saved me.*

"Listen," she says, brittle and dangerous. "The only way you can save him is by letting this go. Just let it get handled and shake the cop off us."

I feel my hand gripping the rail. I swivel toward her.

You think you can . . . infect him. You think you have the right. You have no right. I can protect him from you, from it, from whatever this is that you've tried to . . . pollute him with.

I think all this, my head throbbing, vein pulsing in my brain. But my only chance is in her not knowing that I found out about the plan to frame Joe Avalon and, most of all, the plan to leave the next day. I can't let her know that I learned he is risking everything and doing things he'd never, never do.

So all I say is, "Okay. Okay, Alice Steele."

He wouldn't tell me at all. He'd just make it go away.

The puckering anisette still in my veins, her voice still hot in my head, I drive straight to the only place where I have a chance, even though it is a slim one.

Parking my car half a block down on Flower Street, I walk quickly to Joe Avalon's house, rehearsing in my head what I will say.

He doesn't seem surprised to see me, even though it is nearly three in the morning.

Not saying a word, he jerks his unshaven jaw to gesture me in, a highball glass in his hand.

Somehow—I would never understand this later—I am not afraid. Not of him, at least.

All the blinds are closed, and I sit on the edge of one of the thick leather chairs.

"Olive told me you might be by," he says gruffly. "I can't figure out what you're up to, Miss King. Not for the life of me. I oughta call your fucking brother and threaten you dead if he doesn't stop."

I think of clever Olive MacMurray playing both sides, working Joe Avalon while agreeing to help frame him.

"You could call him," I say evenly. "But I don't think you will."

"Why not?"

I pull my brother's pistol out of my purse and direct it toward his stomach.

His smudge-circled eyes barely widen. "You gotta be kidding me," he mutters. "I've lost all instinct about you girls."

"I want to know what happened. To Lois."

"You aren't going to use that." He gestures toward the pistol. "I could get it from you in under a second."

"Maybe." I nod. "But like you said, you've lost all instinct. I think you'd rather be careful. I think you're nothing if not cautious. I'm asking very little."

He sighs, sitting on the arm of the sofa, resting the glass on his knee. He is a very tired man. All these men are so, so tired.

"I knew Schor might end up doing something like it, but Alice kept saying, Lois can take care of herself. Don't want to lose the butter and egg man."

"Alice?"

He smiles. "For toughness, I got nothing on her, honey. You

don't even know. I'm a fucking ingenue. Never saw one like it, and that includes three dances in San Quentin. You have no idea."

"But—"

"Schor did her, but Alice and I, we took care of it. Alice didn't want to stop the gravy train. She was ready to keep Schor happy."

"Why did she do it?" I demand. "She had everything. Why didn't she just cut ties?"

He shrugs, his eyes suddenly dreamy. "Never could explain her. Not that one. She couldn't step out of it. And it served her. But Lois was getting too close. Talking too much. To everyone. To you."

His eyes turn harder, quite suddenly. "Those girls, they'd have been nothing without me and they both fucked me. Even if I slip out of this frame, I still gotta leave town."

"And Edie Beauvais?"

"You know about that one?" He seems almost impressed. "Alice introduced us. She had a liking for some bad stuff, had been sampling it with Alice, two housewives sitting on the patio in the middle of the day doped up to their pearl necklaces. It ended up getting the best of her. There's no darker story than that, as far as she goes. It was one long suicide."

"I see."

I'd never imagined Edie as anything more than the slope of her stomach, waiting to be a mother. To me, she was still Sunday dinners at Charlie's table, flitting around, arms bending under serving dishes. Somehow, that wasn't her, not really, cracked and tilted, on the bathroom floor of the bungalow apartment on Pico Boulevard. One long suicide. All these lost girls . . .

"Well, Alice and I were cleaning everything up. But then you, little girl." He points a long finger at me. "You sicced the law on us. It fucked everything up. The cop you've been dancing with started following me. He was following Alice. I had to start playing for myself, and apparently so did she. But she had the D.A.'s office on her side. At least one member of it. Tough competition. She told her daddy—your brother. Fessed up to a version of the truth, far as I can tell. And what do you know, he's come out guns blazing to save her skin."

"You don't—"

"Hey." He leans back, touching his chest lightly with his fingertips. "Is it my fault your brother developed such a taste for trash? Too many years tunneling through it on the job and it's in him."

I feel my knuckles shake against the pistol. It is all I can do not to squeeze the trigger. The feeling is so strong that I terrify myself.

"Should I let you out of here?" he continues, not noticing my hand, my quavering fingers. "How do I know you're not out to fuck me, too? You don't even know how to use that thing."

"I don't care," I say, my voice tremulous, eerily wailing like something inhuman, trapped. "I'll keep pulling the trigger until I get it right."

He watches me closely. "I think I know what you could do and what you couldn't."

"How could you?" I say with a keening hum. "How could you when *I* don't know?"

I feel an awareness nearly come crashing in.

"Look at what I'm doing. Look at me," I find myself saying, my face hot.

His eyes fix on mine. In the dark room, I can see them glistening, reading, piercing. I let him see it all. I let him see everything.

He holds my gaze for a long twenty seconds, then, with a twitch, he shakes it off. Narrowing his eyes suddenly, he barks, "But I think you got something for me. I think this goes two ways."

"It will all happen tomorrow."

My brother's voice, tingling through my head, touching lightly every nerve—no, like ink spreading:

"I had to do it. Otherwise, it meant nothing."

. . . like a door shutting somewhere . . .

I pick up the phone and hold it in my lap for a moment. Then I take a deep breath.

"Gardenia two–five four three five." I read the number off the small card Joe Avalon has given me.

"One moment."

I let it ring twelve times. No answer.

I walk around my apartment three times. I wash my face and hands. I stare in the mirror, smoothing my eyebrows, my hair.

I call again.

No answer.

I walk into my kitchen and pull out a mop. I clean the floors with extra bleach. Open a window. Notice the sheen of dust on the sill. Pull out a dust rag and dust every window in the apartment.

I call again.

No answer.

I run the carpet cleaner over the figured rugs. I straighten the shoes in my closet, adjusting the shoe trees. I run down to the lobby to get my mail. It hasn't arrived.

I call again.

"Yeah?" Joe Avalon's voice, but even harder, icier than the night before.

"Are you ready?" It isn't me talking, but someone is talking. Some cool, measured voice with firm enunciation. Fine as piano wire.

"Go."

"She's going to be at the San Pedro Port, boarding the SS *Tarantha* at 6 P.M."

And I set the receiver back down on the base curled in my lap.

Later, I remember looking in the mirror for a long time, struck.

I imagine it in advance. My brother's pleading voice.

—I have to go, Lora.

—You said you'd protect me.

—You don't need me now. Alice does. I can save her.

I imagine it and know it won't work, not like that. To make him believe he needs to stay, I have to make it so that he can't leave.

. . .

Timing is the linchpin, and luckily I know the schedule. I make several calls to the D.A.'s office to track Bill's movements. I figure he plans to meet Alice by 5:30, but by then, if everything falls as it should, he will be speeding his way, siren on, to my apartment in far-flung Pasadena.

I go to the Western Union office first and write the telegram to be delivered the following day.

I return to my apartment, mind racing, imagining scenarios, plotting as though I've been living this way my whole life. I look at my watch and wait for the minute hand to strike five minutes to five—the time his shift is supposed to end.

I pick up the phone and dial him.

"Bill."

"Lora. You just caught me on my way out." How can he try to sound as if everything is normal, thinking, as he does, that he will be abandoning everything within a few hours?

"Bill, it's over." I feed a light sob into my voice.

"What? Lora, what's wrong?"

"Don't blame . . . don't blame . . ."

"*Lora*. Is this about Standish? I knew last night . . . Did he hurt you?"

Out of my mouth, the half-remembered lyric.

"*This, my darling, this is the end of everything.*"

And as I hang up, I can hear him say, "I'll be right there. Don't do anything, Sis. I'll be right there."

The irony is blissful. He thinks it is he who is saving me.

. . .

I walk out my apartment door and head toward the stairwell, my feet clattering on the tiled floors.

Something inside me jerks, and it feels like a surge of cold air slicing through me.

I stand at the top of the first flight, twelve steep faience-covered steps. I look down at the shining lobby floor.

I can't say there is even a thought.

I can't say I pause at all, somehow knowing I can't.

The second my heel hits the top of the stair, I swivel it around and twist my body as hard as I can, my hip hitting the railing and my body rising and then crashing and then

How like the astonishing leaps my brother and I used to take off the warped and quivering dock at our grandparents' house. Leap after leap into the sludge-thick water. It was easy, as true and as ancient as anything I'd ever known.

By the time I limp back up the stairs to my apartment, a throbbing wound is hanging heavily over my right eye. My ankle is swelling neatly. The sharper pain in my chest makes me think I probably cracked a rib or two.

I make it to my living room. My head growing foggier, my stomach pitching with nausea, in a flash I am no longer upright.

By the time he arrives, like some Wild West sheriff storming through my door, my head feels strangely suspended, refusing my body entirely.

I can barely feel his hands on me when he lifts my head off the floor and slides a pillow underneath. He is careful not to move me. Even in his rage, his gorgeous, frustrated rage that nearly terrifies, he knows what to do and not do. Or he's remembering.

The sounds from his mouth fade in and out. ". . . did this to you . . . I knew . . . I knew . . . what happened . . . can't you tell me . . . doctor . . . hospital . . ."

And then, as he winds down, as the ambulance comes and as he curls up beside me before they place me on the gurney, grave whispers, breath on my ear, heart pressed against my chest, sighing promises, and I know I have him.

I am in the hospital for three days with bruised ribs and a concussion and a sprained ankle. How could I know my brother would go to Mike Standish and break his jaw, two teeth, and his own hand in doing so?

Mike took the beating and kept his mouth shut. That is what Mike does.

When urged to press charges, I merely turn my head to the side and look away. In this way, I never have to tell another story.

Within a week, we are home. Bill moves my things into his house and closes out my lease. He tells me he has filed a missing person's report for Alice King née Steele, who apparently has left town.

I listen to his lies, all of them, with sympathetic eyes. Bill tells me he has found out that Alice bought a ticket to South America. That she planned to leave him. But that she never showed up on the ship's passenger list, so she could be anywhere.

"Are you going to try to find her? Take a leave of absence?"

His expression stiffens, in his eyes something distant and unbearably close at once. "No. No, she'll come home when she's ready."

"Of course she will," I say, pouring him his morning cup of coffee.

His eyes float over to the window above the sink, as if she might suddenly appear there.

What is he thinking happened? That she, feeling abandoned by him when he didn't show up at the dock, has disappeared as a way of punishing him?

He never says a word about the telegram I sent in her name (Darling—I couldn't bring this upon you too. Stop. It's better this way. Stop. I can start over and you can go on. Stop. I love you. Stop. Alice. Stop.).

I like to think that somehow he knew everything I had done, knew and understood. That this is ultimately, secretly what he wanted, too. He is free now, free of everything she brought and everything she drew out in him.

I hate to think that we can never speak of it, that both of us hold and will continue to hold and hold secrets so dark that to ask questions of the other might risk contaminating everything.

But standing there beside him as he waits for me to finish filling his coffee cup, standing there in the sun-drenched kitchen so white it glows, I feel that in an instant everything can be erased, that we are, in a quick breath, born anew and time has disintegrated and then rebuilt itself and a new world has formed that is the same as the old, the world before the accident, that awful collision and everything it brought.

I have one last, strained phone conversation with Mike Standish. He is gentlemanly about the jaw and the split teeth. And he says he won't ask me any questions about it.

"I guess I don't want to know, King. I imagine you're probably glad that Alice split."

"It's been very hard for my brother."

"I'm sure it has. But, you know, I bet you're taking awfully good care of him."

"I'm trying to," I say, ignoring something strange in his tone.

"So is this it? You're through with me?"

"Aren't you through with me?" I say.

He pauses briefly, as if deciding.

Then, "I don't know, King. Last night I read a book. What do you make of that?"

I feel something knock loose inside me, I feel his face in front of me, eyes on me and silky hands warmer than they should be, than they have any right to be.

"Your world . . . it's so dirty," I whisper, as if to him in the dark, as if to myself. "How do you live in it?"

I hear him laugh softly to himself, and in that laugh are things that are tender and things that are harder, meaner, truer. It is both at once. Always both at once.

"Lora," he says. "One last thing."

"What?"

"Didn't you ever think that maybe I was just trying to protect you?"

"From what?" I shot back.

"Never mind. Never mind." His voice trails off, and then I hear the receiver click. I hear it click over and over again. I think I held the phone in my hand, pressed to my ear, forever.

The letter is forwarded to me from my old address. It is postmarked the very day the ship was to leave dock. She must have mailed it on her way to meet my brother. I read it three times very fast and then I tear it up and then

Listen, Lora, when I told you what happened with Lois, it wasn't to boast and it wasn't to come clean, to confess. I told you because I wanted you to see. It was time for you to see.

You never trusted me, not once. How could you, given what your brother is? Who could be good enough, special enough, worthy enough, righteous enough for a man like your brother? God, he could make me shudder long after no man could make me shudder.

I guess I can tell you now: I started working you right away. I knew what I was up against. I was careful how dark my lipstick was, how low I'd wear my neckline, how I hung the drapes, made his dinner, danced with him at parties, and looked at him across rooms, across oceans, across crowded cocktail parties. I was beyond reproach.

But then I saw that you liked my dark edges. Here was the surprise long after anyone could surprise me. You liked it.

You liked the voile nightgown you saw in my closet, touched it with your milky fingers and asked me where I'd gotten it. When I bought you one of your own, your face steamed baby pink, but you wore it. I knew you'd wear it.

From there it was simple. I can't deny the kick I got out of putting you and Mike Standish together. The giddiness at the thought of you being wedged between the same corded elbows I was. *She'll never know he's such a bad lay,* Lois growled at me. *After me, he was better,* I said, not wanting to feel it, not wanting to enjoy it so. What would Bill . . . I turned hot with shame. I was obscene.

Of course, I had to be careful, had to watch. Was I letting you see too much? How far was too far? How much too much? Would I know?

Please understand. Trying to sleep all these nights, I'd lie in bed and think: There are things you can never tell these people. Things they can't hear. Things like what you will do if you have to, if your back is against the wall. Men you'll open your legs to. The open cashbox. Please. And if everything around you is runny and loose and awful, why shouldn't you take that hard shot of tight pleasure, that dusty tablet, that loaded bottle? A little inoculation, ward off the stained mattress, the time clock, the mother feeding you rancid mush?

How could I tell you and your brother any of that? Always huddled together, all flax and Main Street parades, pressed against each other on the patio steps, always so absorbed, so caught up in your own blood-closeness that you can't believe anything—anyone—else exists. Oh, there's a lot to be told about that. And then there was me, this damaged thing.

The things you can't tell—well, most of all, it's this: *The hardest thing in this world is finding out what you're capable of.*

My hands in your yellow hair, helping you get ready for a party, every party, I felt this was a sister, my sister, and I loved you, even your terrible judgment (on me, no less!) and, still more, your own terrible weakness. When I touched you, dug my fingers into your hair, it was as though you were a part of him, even smelled like him, all great plains, fresh grass and prairie. Because he was mine, so were you.

And so we shared everything, didn't we?

The main thing, darling: When you get this, your brother and I will be gone. It's best this way even if you can't see it. Try to understand. You must know you can't possibly give him what I can. And you know damn well why.

I won't say what I want to because you won't believe me. You can't see it and wouldn't see it. Not even when I showed it to you.

I guess I understand because maybe I wish I didn't

see everything, all the time. Even now, writing this, I can see your flat gray eyes. They're his.

Alice

Several weeks later, I drive to the Los Angeles Public Library and spend the day scouring newspapers from the previous month, crime beat stories in newspapers throughout the area.

Stories of mutilated starlets, scorched bodies, pregnant suicides, lost girls leaping, falling, and being pushed, strangled, shot, stabbed, and set in flames. All of them somehow in flames.

When I have nearly given up, my eyes catch a small headline in the Santa Ana *Register.* It reads, UNIDENTIFIED WOMAN FOUND DEAD IN RAVINE.

The article notes that the woman's body was virtually unrecognizable from having lain in several inches of standing water for so long. The only clue to her identity was a small card, an identification card of some sort, with the text nearly completely effaced by the water. All that remained were the letters L o.

L o

The irony is so rich as to be painful. Whose identity—Lois, Lora, Lora, Lois—had Alice planned to wear, and did it matter?

her face faded away, erased by water, cold and dark and

I can see them both down there, one face wiped clean, made new, and one split apart, turned inside out. If I could, I'd give them back their faces, like in the solemn, lurid photograph lying

on the carpet, the photograph that gives them tawdry life still,
their twin faces turning out to face, always turning out to face me
and say

＊

Months before, before everything, this . . .

It was at Calisto's, after two hours of sidecars at a tiny table
in the corner, Mike Standish with one arm around each of us,
king of the castle, smoking and laughing.

Alice and I standing side by side in front of the mirror in the
powder room, packed with primping women, music scattering
through the door with each entrance and exit.

Suddenly, as she stained her lips hot red, Alice seemed
struck by our matching images. She stopped and watched, as if
transfixed. Then:

"Do you ever feel like you're being followed?" It was a bullet shot in my ear.

"What? What?" I said, tucking a stray strand of hair behind
my ear and then tucking it again as it slid out, and then again
once more.

She stopped and smiled dreamily, ashamedly. "I'm sorry.
I'm drunk, Lora. So drunk."

"What? But what did you say?" I said, standing straight.

She looked around at all the preening women. "Come on,"
she said, scooping my arm in hers and pulling me out into the
hallway, and down past a clanging kitchen toward the open
door to a back alley.

"Alice, I . . ."

"It's okay. You don't have to pretend with me."

"Pretend what?"

"That you don't like it. All of it and more still. Darker still."

"I never think about it," I said, even as I didn't know what she meant, or what I meant. "I don't like it. I never thought about it once."

She put her face close up to mine, peering hard at me. Heavy and confused with liquor, I thought she might somehow be able to know, to read my thoughts by staring hard enough, to know things about me I didn't even know.

"You don't have to talk about it, but it's something we both have, Lora. It's something we've both got in us." She rapped her chest, her décolletage, glaring at me.

"I don't have it in me," I found myself saying with sudden fierceness as the music swung mightily around us, pouring out loudly from the club, kicking up suddenly with the tempo, and the crowd swarming.

"I don't have it in me," I said louder, trying to rise above the cacophony.

She said nothing but kept staring, her hand resting on her chest, her gaze unwavering.

"*I don't have it in me.*"

I don't have it in me.

I could feel my face contort, my voice rise and crack, fighting the band for all it was worth, fighting the street sounds streaming through from the alley, the clattering dishes from the kitchen, those hard eyes boring through me.

I don't have it in me.

Not at all.

POCKET
BOOKS

Mark Gatiss

The Vesuvius Club

Presenting a thrilling plunge into Edwardian low life and high society.
England's most dashing secret agent investigates the greatest mysteries
of the age: who is killing Britain's most prominent vulcanologists –
and which tie goes best with a white carnation?

Lucifer Box is the darling of the Edwardian belle monde: portrait painter,
wit, dandy and rake – the guest all hostesses must have. And most do.

But few of his connections or conquests know that Lucifer Box is also
His Majesty's most daring secret agent, at home in both London's
Imperial grandeur and the underworld of crazed anarchists and
despicable vice that seethes beneath.

And so, of course, when Britain's most prominent scientists begin
turning up dead, there is only one man his country can turn to.

Lucifer Box ruthlessly deduces and seduces his way from his elegant
townhouse at Number 9 Downing Street (somebody has to live there) to
the seediest stews of Naples, in search of the mighty secret society that
may hold the fate of the world in its claw-like hands – the Vesuvius Club.

ISBN: 978-0-7434-8379-7
PRICE £7.99

POCKET
BOOKS

Mark Gatiss

The Devil in Amber

Lucifer Box – the gorgeous butterfly of King Bertie's reign, portraitist, dandy and terribly good secret agent – is feeling his age. Assigned to observe the activities of fascist leader Olympus Mons and his fanatical Amber Shirts in a snow-bound New York, Box finds himself framed for a vicious murder.

Using all his native cunning, Box escapes aboard a vessel bound for England armed only with a Broadway midget's suitcase and a string of unanswered questions. What lies hidden in the bleak Norfolk convent of St Bede? What is 'the lamb' that Olympus Mons searches for in his bid for world domination? And what has all this to do with a medieval prayer intended to summon the Devil himself?

From the glittering sophistication of Art Deco Manhattan to the eerie Norfolk coast and the snow-capped peaks of Switzerland, *The Devil in Amber* takes us on a thrilling ride that pits Lucifer Box against the most lethal adversary of his career: the Prince of Darkness himself.

'Lucifer Box is the most likeable scoundrel since Flashman'
Jasper Fforde

ISBN: 978-0-7434-8380-3
PRICE £7.99

POCKET
BOOKS

Mark Gatiss

Black Butterfly

With the young Queen Elizabeth newly established on her throne,
Lucifer Box Esq is now by Appointment to Her Majesty. But the
secretive Royal Academy seems a very different place and, approaching
retirement, Box decides to investigate one last case . . .

A series of bizarre accidents has claimed the lives of some of the world's
most important people. Lucifer Box discovers that they were all
members of the mysterious Widows' Circle, headed by the delectable
Melissa Ffawthawe. He soon finds himself in the Transylvanian forests
on the trail of boy assassin Kingdom Come and his deadly masters in the
Anarcho-Criminal Retinue of Nihilists, Incendiarists and Murderers –
A.C.R.O.N.I.M!

What is the mysterious Black Butterfly?
Who is Gottfried Clawhammer?
Why is the world's biggest scout jamboree taking place on
a fortified island in the Caribbean?

All will be revealed as Lucifer Box takes his artistic licence to kill into
the sleek, bleak era of the Cold War . . .

'Delicious, depraved, inventive, macabre and hilarious . . . More,
I want more!' STEPHEN FRY

ISBN: 978-0-7432-5711-4
PRICE £12.99

POCKET
BOOKS

This book and other **Mark Gatiss** titles are available from your bookshop or can be ordered direct from the publisher.

978-0-7434-8379-7	**The Vesuvius Club**	£7.99
978-0-7434-8380-3	**The Devil in Amber**	£7.99
978-0-7432-5711-4	**Black Butterfly**	£12.99

Please send cheque or postal order for the value of the book,
free postage and packing within the UK, to
SIMON & SCHUSTER CASH SALES
PO Box 29, Douglas Isle of Man, IM99 1BQ
Tel: 01624 677237, Fax: 01624 670923
Email: bookshop@enterprise.net
www.bookpost.co.uk

Please allow 14 days for delivery. Prices and availability
subject to change without notice

OFFENDER PROFILING SERIES: Vol IV
PROFILING PROPERTY CRIMES

Edited by

DAVID CANTER and LAURENCE ALISON
Centre for Investigative Psychology
University of Liverpool

Ashgate

DARTMOUTH

Aldershot • Burlington USA • Singapore • Sydney

© David Canter, Laurence J. Alison 2000

Published by
Dartmouth Publishing Company Limited
Ashgate Publishing Limited
Gower House
Croft Road
Aldershot
Hants GU11 3HR
England

Ashgate Publishing Company
131 Main Street
Burlington, VT 05401-5600 USA

Ashgate website: http://www.ashgate.com

British Library Cataloguing in Publication Data
Profiling property crimes. - (Offender profiling series)
   1.Offenses against property 2.Criminal behavior, Prediction of
   I.Canter, David, 1944- II.Alison, Laurence J.
   364.1'6

Library of Congress Control Number: 00-130068

ISBN 1 84014 785 7 (Hbk)
ISBN 1 84014 787 3 (Pbk)

Printed and bound in Great Britain by MPG Books Ltd, Bodmin, Cornwall

Contents

Series Preface

'Offender Profiling' has become part of public consciousness even though many people are not really sure what it is and the great majority of people have no idea at all of how it is done. This ignorance is just as prevalent in professional circles as amongst the lay public. Psychologists, psychiatrists, probation officers and social workers all have an interest in how their disciplines can contribute to police investigations, but few practitioners are aware of exactly what the possibilities for such contributions are. Others, such as police officers and lawyers, who seek advice from 'profilers' often also have only the vaguest ideas as to what 'profiling' consists of or what scientific principles it may be based on. The army of students who aspire to emulate the fictional activities of psychologists who solve crimes is yet another group who desperately need a systematic account of what 'offender profiling' is and what the real prospects for its development are.

The public fascination with the little understood activity of 'profiling' has meant that no fictional account of crime, whether it be heavy drama or black comedy, seems to be complete without at least one of the protagonists offering as a 'profile' their opinion on the characteristics of the perpetrator of the crime(s) around which the narrative is built. This popular interest combined with widespread ignorance has generated its own corpus of urban myths: such mythical 'profilers' produce uncannily accurate descriptions of unknown killers, solve cases that had baffled the police and seem to know before the criminal where he would strike next.

Sadly, like all myths not only do they only have a very loose connection with reality but they also distract attention away from a range of other significant and more intellectually challenging questions. These are the important questions that are inherent in the processes of criminal behaviour and its investigation. Such considerations include assessments of the quality and validity of the information on which police base their decisions and subsequent actions. This also involves assessing the possibilities for detecting deception. There also exist questions about the consistencies of a criminal's behaviour and what the crucial differences are between one offender and another.

Group processes of criminals raise other questions, which surprisingly are seldom touched upon by 'profilers' in fact or fiction. These ask about the form such groups take and the influence they have on the actions of the criminals, the role of leaders in crimes or the socio-cultural processes of which they are a part. There are also important issues about the implications and use of any answers that may emerge from scientific studies of crimes and their investigation.

These and many other questions are raised by the mere possibility of psychology being of value to police investigations. To answer them it is essential to go beyond urban myth, fiction and the self-aggrandising autobiographies of self-professed 'experts'. A truly scientific stance is necessary that draws on a wide range of social and psychological disciplines.

Many of these questions relate to others that are central to any psychological considerations of human actions, such as the nature of human memory, the processes of personality construction, group dynamics and interpersonal transactions. Therefore the systematic, scientific study of the issues relevant to 'offender profiling' are recognisably part of a burgeoning field of psychology and related disciplines. In an attempt to make this point and distinguish the steady accretion of knowledge in this area from the mythology, hyperbole and fiction of 'offender profiling' I labelled this field *Investigative Psychology*. This term seems to have taken root and is now evolving rapidly throughout the world.

Yet in the way that labels and terminology have a life of their own 'offender profiling' and its variants will just not lie down and die peacefully from a robust youth and dissolute old age. So we are stuck with it as a somewhat unhelpful shorthand and therefore the term has been kept for the title of this series in the hope that we may gradually re-define profiling as a systematic and scientific endeavour.

The books in this series provide a thorough introduction to and overview of the emerging field of Investigative Psychology. As such they provide a compendium of research and discussion that will place this important field firmly in the social sciences. Each volume takes a different focus on the field so that together they cover the full range of current activity that characterises this energetic area of research and practice.

David Canter
Series Editor

Acknowledgements

We are grateful to Cathy Sanders and Anthony Lundrigan for the level of organisation that they have brought to pulling these volumes together, and to Julie Blackwell, Steve Deprez and Julia Fossi for their help in compiling the volumes.

1 Profiling Property Crimes

DAVID CANTER AND LAURENCE ALISON

The psychological issues that form the foundations for answering a number of important questions in criminal investigations are considered in this volume. These are shown to have their roots in the psychological study of individual differences. In the criminal context these differences relate to important variations between types of crimes and also within any type of crime. The notion of a hierarchy of criminal differentiation is introduced to highlight the need to search for consistencies and variations at many levels of that hierarchy. Consideration of this hierarchy also lends support to a circular ordering of criminal actions as a parallel with the colour circle. In developing the constituents of this 'radex' structure, it is proposed that the chapters in this volume support distinctions between criminals in terms of the intensity and seriousness of their crimes, the nature of their transactions with their explicit or implicit victims, the amount and type of expertise they bring to their crimes and the organisational and social contexts within which their crimes occur. The studies in this volume, then, show a slowly evolving behavioural science of crime that approaches the study of criminal actions from an objective, often statistical viewpoint rather than one based on personal intuition and clinical experience

David Canter is Director of the Centre for Investigative Psychology at the University of Liverpool. He has published widely in Environmental and Investigative Psychology as well as many areas of Applied Social Psychology. His most recent books since his award winning *'Criminal Shadows'* have been *'Psychology in Action'* and with Laurence Alison *'Criminal Detection and the Psychology of Crime'*.

*Offender Profiling Series: IV - **Profiling Property Crimes***
Edited by D. Canter and L. Alison. © 2000 Ashgate Publishing, Aldershot. pp 1-30

Laurence Alison is currently employed as a lecturer at the Centre for Investigative Psychology at the University of Liverpool. Dr Alison is developing models to explain the processes of manipulation, influence and deception that are features of criminal investigations. His research interests focus upon developing rhetorical perspectives in relation to the investigative process and he has presented many lectures both nationally and internationally to a range of academics and police officers on the problems associated with offender profiling. He is affiliated with The Psychologists at Law Group - a forensic service specialising in providing advice to the courts, legal professions, police service, charities and public bodies.

1 Profiling Property Crimes

DAVID CANTER AND LAURENCE ALISON

Fundamental Questions

Three psychological issues form the foundations for answering a number of important questions in criminal investigations:

1. *The selection of behaviours (information collection).* What are the important behavioural features of the crime that may help identify and successfully prosecute the perpetrator?

2. *Inferring characteristics (deriving conclusions from data).* What inferences can be made about the characteristics of the offender that may help identify him/her?

3. *Linking offences (identifying consistencies).* Are there any other crimes that are likely to have been committed by the same offender?

All three are derivations of questions crucial to other areas of psychology. They involve concepts associated with the significant differences between one person and another and the features of one individual's behaviour that remain constant over different situations. It is therefore not surprising then that many of the concepts developed by psychologists over the last century, particularly in the field of personality and individual differences have relevance for the study of crime. Importantly, these issues are relevant to the investigations of all crimes, not just those that catch the newspaper headlines, like serial murder.

There may not appear to be any important psychological issues to explore when a robbery is committed for financial gain or a building set on fire to claim the insurance or exact revenge. The actions will appear to be explained as merely criminal mentality in the pursuit of gain. But any such explanations only touch the surface of the investigative questions

3

noted above; questions about the salient qualities of the crime and the relationship of those qualities to other crimes and other characteristics of the offender. These questions and the psychological issues from which they grow are as relevant to the investigation of property crime as they are to crimes against the person.

Profiling and its Roots in the Psychology of Individual Differences

The study of the differences between individuals has been a concern of psychologists since the earliest emergence of modern empirically based psychology. It can be traced back at the very least to Sir Francis Galton in the late nineteenth century who measured variations in the aspects of people's size and weight as well as their intellectual functioning. Out of this work grew the development of intelligence tests and other assessments of people's abilities and aptitudes. Further explorations of differences in the way people relate to others and see themselves emerged later, under the general heading of the assessment of personality. More focused studies of the variations between people in the opinions they held about particular entities, referred to as 'attitudes', also became an aspect of the study of the important ways in which one person differed from another.

What is particularly noteworthy about these studies of individual differences is that they examine the actions and verbal reports of people directly. They do not attempt to infer some hidden engine driving people, a 'motive', that is the explanation of their deeds. Instead these studies recognised that for a variety of reasons, that have their roots in individuals genetics, upbringing and life experiences there will be observable and measurable differences between one person and another. There are many forms of explanation that are offered as to why these differences occur. The explanations go beyond the reason that individuals themselves may offer for their actions. As such they recognise that the motivation that a person may put forward for their actions is only one of a number of possible explanations and not necessarily the explanation most useful for understanding that person's actions.

In relation to criminals this psychological perspective gives much more emphasis to a careful consideration of what offenders do, their actions, and the salient characteristics that distinguish one criminal's actions from another's, rather than an attempt to build explanations on inferences about putative motives.

An especially clear illustration of this in the present volume is Lobato's study of the relationships between measures of personality and the types of weapons used by offenders [5][1]. She uses standard measures of personality used in many areas of psychology and shows how the correlations they have with type of weapon use help us to understand the processes that give rise to the use of weapon. In essence, not too surprisingly, extroverts are more likely to use powerful, rather dramatic firearms, where introverts have a tendency to use knives. In what sense is degree of introversion a 'motive'? Yet knowledge of the personality characteristics an offender is likely to have can be combined with other inferences to help winnow down the most likely suspect from a number of possibilities.

Psychologists as the Original 'Profilers'

Sadly, the mass media fascination with violent, sexually related crimes and criminals has encouraged the belief that the study of the differences between criminals, and the making of inferences about their characteristics, is some unique area of expertise quite divorced from the main currents of contemporary psychology. The myth that is promulgated, attempts to characterise this process as originating solely from the speculations of US special agents of the Federal Bureau of Investigation. These speculations have been termed 'profiling', or more fully 'offender profiling', 'psychological profiling' or 'criminal personality profiling'. Yet a moment's reflection makes it clear that the description of the general characteristics of a person on the basis of a limited amount of information about them, has scientific roots in the concepts of psychometric testing. These concepts existed long before the FBI was created.

As Delprino and Bahn's (1988) survey of psychological services in US police departments shows, psychologists were giving opinions to their local police forces about the characteristics of criminals before the FBI 'Behavioral Science Unit' was established. This was a natural outgrowth

---

[1] Numbers in [ ] refer to a chapter in the present volume.

of their major involvement in the development of predictive profiles of people applying for jobs in the police force. This procedure, otherwise known as 'assessment of applicants', as well as their advice on clinical matters relating to suspects, such as fitness to plead and other aspects of their mental health status, has been an enduring contribution for some time.

Artificially Imposed Limitations on the Nature of Profiling

Along with the myth that the process of inferring offender characteristics from criminal actions had its genesis in the FBI's work is the suggestion that psychological insight into a criminal is most valuable when the offence does not appear to be 'normal'. The usual characterisation of an abnormal offence is one in which there is no obvious motive, such as crimes that do not have a clear instrumental, probably financial, purpose. This tends to put the emphasis on rape, and the murder of strangers and other violent crimes. Indeed, in their introduction to *The Crime Classification Manual* Ressler et al., (1992) quote with obvious approval Bromberg's (1962) finding that 'Those behaviour patterns involved in criminal acts are not far removed from those of normal behaviour'. It is therefore perhaps not surprising that their 'Manual' is little more than the codified opinions of a wide range of police officers. It therefore offers somewhat less than the legal definition of crimes. However, the classifications are confused by the apparent focus on 'the primary intent of the criminal'. For, as has already been indicated, scientific psychology moved away from attempts to infer intent over 100 years ago precisely because of the ambiguities that caused. Furthermore, the emphasis on 'intent' unnecessarily restricts the consideration of the psychological issues involved to the most lurid and bizarre[2]. The studies reported in the present volume demonstrate that the three questions outlined at the beginning of this chapter are relevant to the investigations of all crimes.

A further restriction that is commonly thought to apply to the crimes that can be 'profiled' is that they must be part of a series. This is somewhat akin to a psychologist saying that guidance can only be

---

[2] The specific research base for contributing to investigation of those types of crime is covered in a further volume in this series (Canter and Alison 2000b).

provided in the selection of a job applicant if that applicant applies for a number of jobs. Of course, the more relevant information available about a person the more effectively can inferences be drawn from that information. This is not a function of the number of crimes but of the amount of information available in total.

As can be appreciated, then, these restrictions on the possibilities for 'psychological profiling' are derived from the misconception that there are some special sets of skills and knowledge available only to those who have worked with criminals, or who have considerable experience of police investigations.

The following chapters provide many illustrations of how offender profiling can be seen as a natural part of the broader discipline of *Investigative Psychology*. As Canter and Alison have illustrated elsewhere (Canter and Alison, 1997), investigative psychology is simply a development of an existing range of psychological concepts and methodologies that may be applied to increase our understanding of offence behaviour and of the psychological processes that occur across criminal investigations.

A Hierarchy of Criminal Actions

In considering the actions of criminals the major premise for developing scientifically based profiling systems is that there are some psychologically important variations *between* types of crimes and also *within* any type of crime. This principle may be illustrated with the example of arson. In looking at the differences between crimes, are arsonists any different from any other offenders who commit crimes against property? Secondly, in considering the differences within crimes, are there differences between arsonists?

Expressed in this way it may be assumed that there are only the general questions about the differences between the types of crime and the particular questions about the differences between arsonists. But it is more productive to acknowledge that there is actually a hierarchy of possible distinctions. At the most general level there are the questions about the differences between those who commit crimes and those who do not. In contrast, at the most specific level there are questions about very particular sub-sets of activities that occur in a crime, say whether a particular type of weapon was used. Between the most general questions and the most particular are a continuum of variations that can be examined. This would include questions about different sub-sets of crimes, such as the comparison of arsonists and burglars, as well as questions about particular patterns of criminal behaviour, such as the comparison of offenders who prepare carefully in advance of a crime with those whose actions are impulsive and opportunistic.

Figure 1.1 provides notional levels in this hierarchy. However, the linear ordering of this table is an over-simplification. The description of crimes is clearly multi-dimensional. Consider as an illustration a crime in which a house was burgled and at the same time a fire was set with material taken from the house, giving rise to the death of an occupant. Would this crime be best thought of as burglary, arson or murder? The charge made against the accused is usually for the most serious crime, but psychologically that may not be the most significant aspect of the offender's actions. The difference between an offender who came prepared to set fire and one who just grabbed what was available may be crucial. The murder may have been an accident or unfortunate coincidence. One central research question, then, is to identify the behaviourally important facets of offences. Those facets that are of most use in revealing the salient psychological processes inherent in the offence are often also of value to help answer questions posed by the investigators.

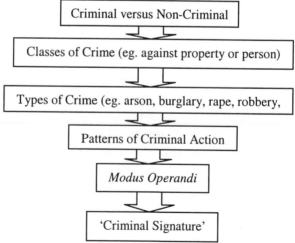

Figure 1.1: A Hierarchy for the Differentiation of Offenders

The Radex Model – Beyond 'Types'

There is one particularly important implication of the hierarchy of criminal actions. This is the challenge it presents to the notion of a criminal 'type'. There are some aspects of a criminal's activities that are similar across many other offenders. These lie at the most general end of the 'hierarchy'. They involve the actions that define the individual as criminal. But there will be other actions that s/he engages in that are located further towards the specific end, the activities that identify a particular crime. Furthermore, some of the actions will overlap with those of other offenders, for example whether s/he carries out his/her crimes on impulse or plans them carefully. Indeed there will be relatively few aspects of his/her offending, if any, that are unique to him/her (these are known as 'signature'). Even those may not be apparent in all the crimes that s/he commits.

The actions of any individual criminal may therefore be thought of as a sub-set of all the possible activities of all criminals. Some of this sub-set overlaps with the sub-sets of many other criminals, and some with relatively few. It therefore follows that assigning criminals to one of a limited number of 'types' of criminal will always be a gross oversimplification. It will also be highly problematic to determine what 'type' they belong to. If the general characteristics of criminals are used for assigning them to 'types' then most criminals will be very similar and there will be few types. But if more specific features are selected then the same criminals, regarded as similar by general criteria, will be regarded as different when considered in relation to more specific criteria.

This is the same problem that personality psychologists have struggled with throughout this century. Their research lead to the identification of underlying *dimensions* of personality. This 'dimensions' approach assumed that there were distinct, relatively independent, aspects of personality that could be identified. The best known of these are the dimensions of extroversion and of neuroticism. However, in recent years rather more complex models have emerged that do not require the simplifying assumption of independent dimensions.

An analogy that helps in understanding this debate is the problem of classifying colours. Clearly colours come in a virtually infinite variety, but in order to describe them some points of reference are necessary. These points of reference must cover the full spectrum of colours and they must be distinct enough for people to understand the reference. So, for instance, it would be unhelpful to try and discriminate colours merely on the basis of how much grey they contained and how much turquoise. Many differences between colours could not be accommodated in this scheme and many people may be unclear as to what colour turquoise actually is.

Another approach may be classifying colours along dimensions of blueness, redness and greenness. Indeed, many computer colour manipulation systems use just such a dimensional approach. These three hues do account for all colours and they do have very clear meanings to people who are not colour blind. The psychological parallel of personality dimensions of extroversion and neuroticism, or in intelligence of spatial, numerical and verbal ability, also seeks to describe people in their combined position along all the identified dimensions. As with colour naming, a great deal of research has gone into determining what the major dimensions of personality or intelligence are and of specifying how they may be measured as clearly as possible.

But even though the dimensional classification scheme can be very productive it does have a number of limitations. This can be illustrated by considering yellow in our colour example. Most people regard this as a distinctly different colour from red, blue or green. Yet the computer, say, only gives us one of these three dimensions to use. How can yellow be produced? It takes special knowledge of the system and how colour combinations work to realise that red and green will generate yellow. The reason why this difficulty arises is that colours are not perceived along distinct dimensions, but rather as blending into each other. Various oranges sit between red and yellow, browns between yellow and green, turquoises between green and blue, purples between blue and red, and so on. Indeed for some purposes, such as printing, it is more useful to think of the 'between' colours, or 'secondary colours' as they are known as the defining dimensions, i.e. cyan, magenta, and yellow. This switch from one set of axes to another is only feasible because they all merge into each other in a continuous colour circle (as first pointed out by the artist Albert Munsell, 1960).

The existence of a circle of colours does not deny the value of defining the major points of this circle. But rather than treat them as independent dimensions they are dealt with as emphases from which other combinations can be readily derived. The parallels with criminal actions are very strong. In order to describe those actions we need to identify the dominant themes, but it would be unproductive to regard these themes as independent dimensions. It would be even more misleading to regard them as pure types, just as it would be misleading to think that colours can only be red, green or blue.

The hierarchy of criminal actions also lends support to a circular ordering of criminal actions as a parallel with the colour circle. At the centre of the colour circle are those aspects of colour that all colours share. This is the degree of greyness. It depends on whether lights or pigments are being considered, but for simplicity it is just necessary to remember that Isaac Newton showed that white light contained all the colours. So if all lights of all colours are combined they produce white. This is the centre of the colour circle. As the colours move out from this central position they become more specific and more distinctly one colour or another. The same mathematical process can be thought of in criminal behaviour. At the centre, are actions typical of all the criminals being considered. These are the general aspects of the sorts of crimes that are the particular focus. As the actions become more specific to particular styles of offending so they would be expected to be conceptually further from the 'centre' of general criminality.

It can thus be appreciated that this consideration of the variations between criminals has two facets to it. One is the facet of specificity, moving from the general shared by all offences and therefore conceptually in the middle to the specific at the periphery. The other is the thematic facet that distinguishes between the different qualities of the offences, conceptually radiating around the 'core'. This model was recognised by Guttman (1958) as a powerful summary of many forms of differentiation between people and named a *radex*. It turns out to be more than a conceptual abstraction but is actually a testable hypothesis.

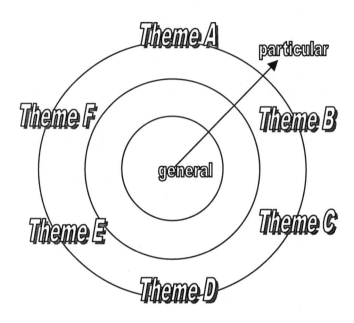

Figure 1.2: A General Model for a Radex as Applied to the Actions of Criminals

The crucial discovery in testing such a hypothesis is the identification of the dominant themes that can be used to classify any set of crimes. In the process it is often possible to give more substance to the meaning of specificity in that criminal context. In other words, the research may allow a determination of what the aspects of crime are that reveals the differences in the thematic emphases. For example, is it the degree of planning, or the forms of contact with the victim, or the intensity and legal seriousness of the actions, or some other underlying aspect of the crime, that produces the salient variations between crimes?

In the following chapters a number of different researchers explore these possibilities in a variety of ways. Not all of them follow through the details of the radex hypothesis, either because of the weaknesses of the data they have available or the current impoverished levels of conceptualisations of criminal actions. But most of the researchers who have contributed chapters to this volume do find value in attempting to determine the dominant themes that can be used to distinguish between sub-groups of offenders.

MDS Analysis as a Test of Aspects of the Radex Hypothesis

The quest to find the underlying themes that will be most productive in answering the investigative questions and help determine the characteristics of offenders can be conducted in many different ways. As will be apparent from a number of chapters in the present volume many researchers do find it fruitful to use an approach that relies heavily on what is known as non-metric multi-dimensional scaling (MDS). It is worth emphasising that this is not the only procedure available and that every procedure has its own strengths and weaknesses. Doubtless as research develops in this area other procedures and approaches will be explored and a productive debate as to which is most worthwhile will ensue. However MDS, and especially its non-metric forms, clearly has much to offer this field.

MDS procedures in general and the particular ones utilised in the present volume do have a long and very wide history of use in psychology, the related social sciences and other areas of the biological sciences. They have been used for everything from; the classification of *cetacea* (whales) to the examination of neonatal heart defects; from the study of the genetic basis of behavioural differences in mice to reasons for taking up dieting; the effects of drug addiction in parents on their children to architects' development of the concepts of style, and so on. The ideas and algorithms for using this approach were first published in the 1950's and have been steadily developing ever since.

In essence the procedures consist of calculating the correlations between a set of variables then representing these correlations as distances in a notional 'space'. This has the great advantage of being able to examine each of the variables in relation to every other as part of one general visual pattern. The discerning reader will also have recognised that the consideration of the facets that differentiate the actions of offenders, that was discussed above by analogy with the colour circle, required the examination of the way every action related to every other in some notional space. MDS procedures therefore allow direct test of the radex hypothesis and simplifications of that hypothesis.

To carry out these tests the correlations between the actions need to be established. Often the best that can be hoped for, given the crudeness of the data, is that the co-occurrence of actions across a range of crimes can be examined. These co-occurrences are taken as the basis for measure of association between the variables.

Another aspect of the approach that has been emphasised is that it is the dominant themes amongst these variables that are important. In other words, it is the relative distinctions between one set of actions and another rather than where they may sit on some absolute values of an underlying continuum. It is the relative associations between actions that needs to be represented. To illustrate from our colour analogy, it may be the case that all the colours in our sample have a bluish tinge to them because of faults in the process used to reproduce them. We would still want a technique that would produce the colour circle, not one that was greatly biased to show us the results as merely aspects of blue.

The preferred MDS procedures are thus ones that represent the rank order of the associations as rank orders of the distances in the notional space. It is this representation of the relative degrees of associations, through ranks, rather than the absolute or 'metric' values that gives the procedures the label of 'non-metric' MDS. This is an important technicality. It greatly facilitates the interpretation of what is often less than clear data but as Lobato shows in chapter [5] care must be exercised when interpreting these results for practical applications.

Differentiation Within and Between Property Offences: Narrowing Down the Parameters

A number of the studies reported in the following chapters deal with aspects of the radex model in relation to different areas of property crime. They each focus on different ways in which the crimes considered can be fruitfully distinguished on the basis of what actually happens in the crimes. Overall seven psychological issues emerge from the studies in the present volume and from the other related studies that have been published.

1.   Criminals differ in the intensity and seriousness of their crimes.

2.   Criminals differ in the style of transactions with their explicit or implicit victims.

3.   Criminals differ in the amount and type of expertise they bring to their crimes.

4.   Differences in the organisational and social contexts within which crimes occur provide a framework for understanding the actions of particular criminals.

5.   All of these differences allow inferences to be made about;
        a) the offender's criminal history,
        b) the offender's distinguishing personal characteristics, crucially including the location in which he may be living, and
        c) other known crimes that may have been perpetrated by the offender.

6.   There is a prospect of extrapolating the inferences that can be made about an offender to predict how they may deal with the interview process.

7.   There is also the prospect of extrapolating the inferences that can be made about an offender to predict where and what type of crimes they may commit in the future.

Cognitive and Affective Aspects of Offending

Intensity and Seriousness

The radex structure of criminal actions is clear in Merry and Harsent's study of burglary [2]. They show that the general aspects of burglary in their sample are forced entry into a house near a main thoroughfare in which many rooms are searched and readily saleable items are stolen. This is the white light of burglary. The distinctions emerge in terms of the transactions that take place during the burglary; the different forms of the more focused and intense aspects of the offence. Some burglars, for example, show their violation of the house by malicious damage, where others may do it by preparing their escape. Yet others will reveal the care with which they have searched the house by stealing valuable antiques. All these actions can be seen as more intense forms of transactions with the house beyond forced entry. It is the variations in these more intense aspects that provide the major thematic differences between burglars, which show what their true colours are.

Merry and Harsent's results show how the variations in intensity of burglaries are variations in the degree of 'defilement' of the home. This is likely to be mirrored in differences in the experience of the intrusion. As many commentators have pointed out, for some people the home is an extension of the self. For such people a burglary can be experienced as a defilement of and domination over the private aspects of identity. At the extreme victims report that the invasion of the property was like being raped (Bennet and Wright, 1984). The extremity of the reaction of the victim appears to increase with the amount of damage caused, and mess left (Brown et al., 1989). This shows how the actions in a crime can be differentiated in terms of their emotional intensity and consequences.

Other studies, including those reported in this volume also draw attention to the crucial significance of the intensity and seriousness of the actions in providing the basis for discriminating between offenders. For example in Canter and Fritzon's (1998) study of arson the intensity of the actions is revealed in the target of the arson. Whilst the general setting of fires without any attempt to alert people, during a weekday, can be seen as the general nature of arson its passion comes from what is set on fire, a car, a public building, a school, or an inhabited dwelling. These targets give the meaning to the actions. In chapter [6] Fritzon develops these ideas to show their investigative implication.

One very interesting and practically very significant example of crime being distinguished in terms of the focus of their intensity is the study of where criminals commit their crimes. Barker reports in chapter [3] one of the first studies to examine the individual choices that small town burglars make of where to commit their crimes. Since her initial study, over ten years ago, a number of her leads have been followed up with quite remarkable consistency (Canter and Larkin, 1993; Canter and Gregory; 1993; Canter et al., 2000). These all support Barker's initial demonstration that, for many criminals, the day to day focus of their home acts as a core to their mental geography. They move out from that to commit the more intense actions of their crimes on the periphery of their home range.

Interpersonal Emphasis

The consideration of the intensity of the criminal actions draws attention to the ways in which even property crimes are, in effect, interpersonal transactions. As Merry and Harsent suggest, following Canter's seminal (1995) argument, the variations in the activities of burglars may tell us something about the personal narrative of the offender and his/her/their perception of the offence. But this is a perception of the others who are being dealt with during the course of the criminal activities.

As mentioned, in arson these others are often symbolised by the building or object that is set alight. So the patterns of activities of arsonists can be shown to take on distinct forms in relation to their targets. Fritzon [6] discusses the practical significance of these differences in the explicit and implicit interpersonal transactions that characterise arsonists' activities, showing that guidance to investigations are far more likely to emerge from a careful consideration of the offender's actions than from disquisition on his or her motivations.

However, Fritzon's chapter also draws attention to the value, for some classes of crime in considering distinctions at the more general end of the hierarchy of offence behaviour. There do seem to be consistent differences, in general, between arsonists and other forms of offenders. Fritzon highlights the indications that there is something unique to arson subgroups of offender populations. For example the majority of young fire setters are part of severely disruptive family environments with many disruptive changes (early parental separation, illegitimacy, death of close relative or brought up in children's home). In Hurley and Monahan's (1969) study a comparison of arsonists with other inmates revealed that the arsonists had 8 times as many property convictions than comparison group, spent less overall time in institutions but significantly longer in institutions prior to age 14. Similarly, Rice and Harris (1991) note that the arsonists that they studied within institutions were more socially isolated (i.e. hobbies, marital status, living arrangements), less likely to be physically aggressive, less intelligent, younger, less physically attractive, and had a more extensive psychiatric history than individuals convicted for other offences.

These studies suggest that there is some underlying psychological pattern that is peculiar to arson. However, instead of the popular psychoanalytic examination of 'motivation' that relies on the assumption that arsonists experience sexual arousal to setting fires, a relative lack of social skills appears to be a more appropriate analysis. For example, Lange and Kirsche (1989) noted that of a sample of 243 fire setters only 2.5% were sexually aroused by fire stimuli, whilst Quinsey (1989) found no differences between normal subjects and firesetters' sexual arousal to fire related stimuli. Instead, Rice and Harris (1991) established in their sample that social skills in general and assertiveness in particular, are important correlates of firesetting. Jackson (1987) formulated a displaced aggression hypothesis, where feelings of hostility were redirected from people to objects. Further, this group appeared to have less stable or well-defined constructs of the seriousness of property vs. person offences since there was no significant bias in rating crimes against the person as more serious.

These findings serve to illustrate that just as differences between patterns in behaviour can be fruitfully differentiated on the basis of the different interpersonal styles they reveal so the differences between broad classes of crimes may also be a reflection of different interpersonal styles.

Skill and Professionalism

The distinctions in interpersonal style that emerge in studies of burglars and arsonists combine with more overtly cognitive processes in the more demanding crime of robbery. Alison and his colleagues show this clearly in the thematic emphases they reveal in their intriguing study of 144 British robberies. Once again a radex structure is clearly present in their results, but because of its obvious practical significance they chose to emphasise the distinguishable themes. These themes reflect the mix of interpersonal styles and skill that the offenders exhibit during their crimes.

Alison et al. draw on criminal patois to label the regions they find, but their underlying discovery goes beyond the insults of criminals. They show that the distinction between the planned, strategically sophisticated robber and the impulsive, violent 'cowboy' is clearly reflected in their actions during the crimes. A third theme characterising people who are more haphazard and violent than the first group but with more strategy than the second, bandits, can also be recognised in the results.

The differences in what might be regarded as levels of 'professionalism' in robbers can also be seen in the workplace crime that Robertson describes [7]. His studies similarly revealed three thematic interpretations of behaviours that occurred in a courier and distribution company. His data allowed him to take the analysis a stage further than Alison et al. were able to. Robertson showed the three themes were each broadly associated with various identifiable features of the individual's personal circumstances. A 'criminality group' was defined by a deviant career and was associated with stealing courier traffic despatched by banks and smuggling intact items from the factory floor. The 'opportunity group' was identified by behaviours such as stealing small amounts of cash or low value goods, and finally the 'responsibility' group with behaviour such as abandoning consignments or taking packages home and hiding them.

Robertson established the age ranges for the groups as early 20's - early 30's, mid 20's - mid 50's and under 25's respectively. Further, none of the opportunity group had pre-convictions, whilst the responsibility group were linked more to lack of capability, all of them having had less than 4 years' experience. Future careful comparison of workplace theft and robbery may reveal some important parallels in the variations found.

Dodd [8] draws attention to the overlap between crimes that are legally very distinct and the consequent possibility that similar psychological processes underlie the differences between offenders. He argues that what many criminals share is a predilection for fraud. Whilst fraud is a relatively neglected area of research it underpins many other areas of criminality and is often a more general feature of a criminal's life. Thus, much of our understanding of this offence may help inform us as to the broad features of individual variation in more frequently studied offences. Again, we are drawn back to the issue of intentional, sophisticated and organised forms of behaviour vs. opportunistic, seemingly random and ill-organised actions. Dodd highlights this as possible differences between opportunistic and sophisticated offence styles.

Opportunistic offence styles do not involve the initial intention to defraud and may begin by initially exaggerating a claim. If successful, the individual is likely to defraud again. This pattern of behaviour is exemplified by those cases where the offender tries to secure small amounts and where the individual is frequently in financial difficulty.

The sophisticated pattern involves the individual knowing their way around the system and creating their own opportunities rather than abusing those already in existence. Successful fraudsters, as Dodd states, have a good knowledge of the system that they are defrauding. Therefore, the configuration of other influences on the individual's life, the contextual features of the offence landscape and the personal predisposition and knowledge the offender has all combine to colour the particular features of the way in which the offending behaviour is carried out.

The Relevance of Context

As we have argued in another volume (Canter and Alison, 2000a) crime is a social process that can only be fully understood in its interpersonal and institutional context. The relationships between criminals and their victims as well as the significance of the particular skills and knowledge they bring to bear therefore only make sense within particular contexts. Robertson [7] shows the importance of understanding the influence of context in theft from work. This view is rather more controversial than might be realised. There is one school of thought that emphasises individualist explanations in preference to socio-cultural ones. The former relies on the assumption of continuity in the individual's life history and predisposition towards crime, whilst the latter proposes that the management and climate of the workplace create a criminal culture. In support of the former come Hogan and Hogan's (1989) studies of 'organisational delinquency', which incorporate a host of correlated behaviours including theft, drug and alcohol abuse and assault. Moreover, Jones and Terris (1983) note that dishonesty scales correlate positively with lateness, higher absence rate and mishandling of company cash. These studies suggest an extended pattern of behaviours that spill over into the offender's everyday transactions and are a consistent, stable trait that impacts on and is reflected in all aspects of the individual's lifestyle. This brings us back to the similarities between crimes. The importance of context is not peculiar to workplace crime. As we have mentioned Barker [3], for example, notes that burglars leave a trail of geographic, physical and temporal information about themselves at the crime scene and that these issues emanate from their normal, non-offending patterns of behaviour. The proximity of the home base to the offence location is a positive indicator of the comfort of offenders in staying close to home (White, 1932; Pyle, 1974).

The Development of Empirical Models

The studies in this volume, then, show a slowly evolving behavioural science of crime that approach the study of criminal actions from an objective, often statistical viewpoint rather than one based on personal intuition and clinical experience.   The debate at the heart of this distinction is not a new one for psychology. Many years ago Meehl (1954) reviewed the evidence for clinical versus statistical prediction of judgements about patients seen in clinical psychology therapy. Somewhat controversially, for his time, he argued that the evidence was heavily in favour of the statistical approach.   In a more recent review he has demonstrated, on the basis of 136 research studies that the clinical approach is invariably the weaker than one drawing on objective assessment and quantitative calculations (Grove and Meehl, 1996).

There are other arguments beyond the parallels to psychological therapy for challenging the clinical approach to profiling (see also Alison and Canter, 1999b). The first is that if it relies on experience then this, by definition takes years to gain. In an experience-led system police officers should simply ask for the opinions of the most experienced clinician. The knowledge would therefore be peculiar to an elite group of practitioners who cannot easily impart their knowledge to others unless those others have had the same history of experience.   This relates to the second problem of the 'experiential school'. The inability to clearly articulate *why* they have made certain assertions about a case. This presents at least two major problems. Firstly, as we have suggested, increased efficiency cannot be handed on or quantified. Secondly, the profiler may feel great personal responsibility if a gut feeling was in fact wrong. This is not to say that any individual should not accept personal responsibility for opinions given but the argument in the empiricist case would be that any other practitioner using the same process would have given the same answer. In other words the expert's 'ego' does not interfere in the actual content of the account. Furthermore, because the reasons for coming to a particular conclusion are known others can learn from their failures as much as their successes.

Quality of Information

One of the prime features that any statistically driven approach to profiling relies upon is the quality of information. As Farrington and Lambert point out [9] the reliability of police information varies considerably. Comparing C10 forms, they note that the most reliable forms of information are ethnicity, age and eye colour. Other forms of information in the archival records obtained from witnesses or victims are considerably less reliable. We have discussed how opportunities for distortion across enquiries may profoundly influence the types of information that end up in these statements and they are potentially riddled with inconsistent, and selectively eroded or acquired information (Canter and Alison, 1999b). This will be a recurrent problem until police forces recognise the power of effective information. In the final chapter [11] police superintendent Merry takes off the casual research clothes he wore in chapter [2] to put on his official uniform and show how research ideas can be turned in to practice. He demonstrates that the first, and probably most powerful step to take, is to collect information about crimes in a more systematic and objective way.

Although generally police information is not collected for the purpose of scientific examination, in tightly controlled laboratory conditions, it can still be the basis of valuable research as this volume illustrates. Webb, Campbell, Schwrest and Sechrest (1966) refer to this type of information as 'unobtrusive or non-reactive measurement' because it does not have the researcher's input at the early design stages. Psychological considerations may be able to make many contributions to aid the police in the way in which information is collected and processed. One might refer to this as a process of 'guiding' effective unobtrusive measurement protocols. Part of this may lie in advising the officer on what they do *not* need to collect - thereby helping reduce the 'dross' rate.

The three broad categories of unobtrusive measurement are physical trace measurement, the use of archives and simple observation.

Physical trace methods are perhaps the most obvious form of police information. Examples include DNA, ballistic assessment, orthodontic records and fingerprint assessment. However, as well as providing sources of evidential utility they may reflect certain behavioural qualities peculiar to the way in which an offence is carried out. For example, the geographic areas in which an offender has chosen to attack a victim may reflect a topographic bias in movement that directly relates to generalisable features of the offender's lifestyle. These measures help to ascertain certain behavioural traces laid down 'naturally' without interference from the social scientist. Barker [3] gives a clear example of this in outlining the spatial patterns of burglars. Research within the Centre for Investigative Psychology is currently using such material to great effect in developing computer models of offenders' geographic patterns of offending (Canter et al., 2000).

Archival data involves an examination of the documentation of information over specific periods of time. The amount of and variation in the quality of archival data held by the police is vast and includes many potentially rich reports. These include many reports of the same incident: victim and witness reports, interview tapes, informer's reports, expert reports, court transcripts, social enquiry reports etc. It may involve extortion letters, tapes of undercover liaisons or documentation relating to police officers' employee records. Both Robertson and Dodd have relied heavily on such types of information in constructing their research on workplace crime.

In simple observations the observer plays an unobserved, passive and non-intrusive role in the research situation, and has no control over the behaviour in question. A major advantage of unobserved methods of data collection is that the investigator has had no part in structuring the situation, and therefore, protects the research from reactive validity threats. This reduces what Campbell (1957) refers to as the 'reactive effect of measurement'. This is the problem that no one ever acts in quite the same way when they know they are being studied as when they think they are observed. Another advantage is the fact that the data is collected first-hand, which reduces the probability of contamination of the data.

Similar types of 'measurement' are the concern of police investigators involved in undercover surveillance and 'stakeouts' where a high priority is placed upon fitting in with the individuals being observed. Though studies such as Whyte's (1943) participant observation study of an Italian street gang in Chicago are rare in engaging with criminal activities and the concerns of the investigator there is much to learn from observing the advantages afforded by such approaches.

However, useful though these methods may be there are certain disadvantages. These include (i) variations between collection protocols, (ii) the promotion of guided statements for increasing the probability of prosecution in court, (iii) potential distortions within accounts and (iv) disregard for the meaning of behaviour within different contexts.

Variation in Collection Protocol

In burglaries, SOCOs (scene of crime officers) are generally asked to write a narrative account of what has been stolen, what damage has occurred and what the movements were of the victim in relation to the relevant period when the offence was thought to have occurred. There is no strict protocol that must be conformed to so there is, in all likelihood, considerable variation across the accounts. This may vary as a function of individual differences in thoroughness or, more likely, contextual features such as time pressures. However, this is gradually changing as constabularies adopt empirically validated coding checklists for examining potentially relevant information. This is evident in Merry's work in chapter [11].

The drive towards developing the collection process in line with social science requirements is already taking place in certain constabularies nationally and internationally. As a result a far more effective relationship between social scientists and the police force is very gradually emerging. A major step in this direction is to familiarise researchers and investigators with the limits and benefits of using such information as well as to outline and define the framework within which such research is set. Whilst these are encouraging developments, proformas are not consistent across all UK constabularies and will require thorough reassessment after each tranche of analyses. This presents the research with the thorny problem of internal validity. It is quite possible, for example, that there are profound differences within, let alone across, constabularies.

Guiding the Account for the Courts

A second issue involves the fact that certain features of the account may be guided into a format that enhances their value as part of the prosecution case. Where the burden of proof relies on the intention and coercion of the victim it is very important that there are no shades of grey. Therefore, there may be a pressure on an interviewing officer, in taking a statement, to ignore any indications that the victim is admitting some culpability for the offence occurring in the first place. Thus, accounts may have been shaped by selective attrition (or accretion) of certain potentially important behavioural features. Additionally, psychologists and police officers often only have partial information. Without the *full* details of any event, there is potential for distortion in the analysis of the offence. Further, many distortions occur as a product of the different agendas of the individuals involved in giving the accounts.

The Effect of Context

Psychological meaning is frequently imposed on behaviour without considering the conditions under which it evolved. However, single actions are rarely indicative of specific causal associations. For example, is the use of a hammer to bludgeon a victim indicative of forensic awareness (in that blunt objects are relatively more difficult to trace to specific woundings than, for example, knives), or the convenient and opportunistic use of an object close at hand (i.e. the offender retrieved it from his garage)? This relates to our original comment regarding the nature of investigative psychology research where we often do not have the luxury of being able to control the parameters under which behaviour evolves. Thus, whilst there has been some success at examining a unitary mapping of offence behaviour to offender characteristics, the research is likely to be somewhat limited and quite theoretically arid without a consideration of the situational parameters that surround the event.

Given the difficulties and challenges of using information collected by the police as data for research it is remarkable that so many consistencies and other scientific results are emerging in investigative psychology. Nor are such fruitful findings limited to the sort of research strategies illustrated in the present volume. For example, using much more basic research procedures Davies (1997) has made some progress in determining specific behavioural variables that relate to particular preconvictions and other background characteristics.

One of the keys to these successes is to work with those aspects of the police records that are reliable enough. Farrington and Lambert [9] point the direction in establishing which features of an offence most reliably relate to predictable features of offenders' characteristics. They established in an assessment of crimes in Nottingham that the key dimensions underlying property offence behaviour were location and site. In other words, offenders consistently attacked the same approximate locations (i.e. suburban or central areas), consistent sites (for example residences) but were not consistent in the times or days that they chose to attack. Similarly, there was weak agreement on place of entry, method (smash window, force entrance) instruments used and going pre-equipped, yet near perfect agreement on method of escape. Violent offenders were more consistent on locations, sites, time of day and day of week, weapons used, being pre-equipped and disguise.

Similarly, the Centre for Investigative Psychology has examined a variety of offence behaviours through multivariate approaches with some success (Canter, Hughes and Kirby, 1998; Canter and Heritage, 1990; Canter and Fritzon, 1998). The facet framework employed in such research is an important tool in helping the psychologist select consistently reliable variables. Because there is a close correspondence between hypothesis formulation and testing, the facet framework forces the researcher to develop a conceptual understanding of the variables within the context of other behaviours.

The Scientific Solution

Many researchers start off by collecting too much information. Being unsure what they are going to do with it they collect material 'on the off chance' that it may be useful. But blind collection of any and all information wastes time and may confuse the picture, making an investigative focus even more difficult. Yet often quite simple readily available information can be very powerful. For example, there are high probabilities of any new offence occurring as relating to an offender that is already within the police data bases. In Farrington and Lambert's [9] study, 89% of burglars and 79% of violence offenders had preconvictions.

Similarly, in trying to trace co-offenders, investigators may wish to consider the finding that co-offenders are similar to one another in terms of their home base, sex, occupation, ethnicity, age, and tattoos but not similar in height, build, or marital status. However, as Farrington and

Lambert point out many of these characteristics are often hard to retrieve because of missing data and considerable variation in the collection protocol. However, he does at least demonstrate those features that might, most reliably, indicate some utility for a profiling system. This would also serve to guide researchers to develop manageable coding systems where it is not necessary to code every type of available information. The pragmatics of policing do not allow officers to spend hours filling in coding sheets. Psychologists may be able to contribute to developing the most efficient and quick proformas to find out the most relevant information for establishing and developing hypotheses as well as detecting criminals.

As Dodd [10] points out, this principle is also applicable to the investigation of crime in organisations where similar problems exist in extracting the most useful material. Part of the problem, as Skyrme and Amidon (1997) state is that the organisations collecting the data (a) do not know why they are collecting it and (b) have no *systematic* method of collection. Skyrme and Amidon point out, the first principle of organising such systems is to 'know what you know'. After assessing the integrity and reliability of the information, such material may be of direct utility in predicting subsequent patterns of loss and in identifying the behavioural features of offending that correlate with their particular background characteristics. Some guidance may also be given to redesigning those features of the organisation that may, unbeknownst prior to an evaluation of the information, have contributed to encouraging criminal behaviour in the first place.

Conclusions

This volume provides some initial steps towards the profiling of property crimes on the basis of an objectively tested investigative psychology. The opportunistic streak that drives much of this work demands a use of existing material and records held by various law enforcement agencies. It this regard it has more in common with anthropology or archaeology than conventional laboratory based psychology. But the well-springs of the research are fundamentally psychological in their explorations of how people differ from one another, how consistent they are in those differences, and why.

Emerging from these early studies are some encouraging results, notably differences in the implicit and explicit relationships offenders set up with the people who suffer from their crimes and in the levels of cognitive processing they apply to their criminal activities. All of these variations have to be viewed against a back-drop of the offender's commitment to their criminal actions, their involvement in them. These emerging results raise interesting questions about variations between people as well as having practical implications for the investigating of crime.

But it is clear that such findings will only increase in clarity and precision if the information on which they are based also improves in quality. The problem is that the effort required for such improvements relies on support and the goodwill of law enforcement agencies. Such support will only be forthcoming when the benefits of the extra effort are apparent. This is an interactive cycle, the quality of the data relying on the value of the results and vice versa. If the cycle is pursued without commitment it becomes self-destructive. Unreliable results produce a loss of faith in the process, leading to less effort being put into the collection of the raw data with consequent increased unreliability of the results.

However, if the findings explored in the present volume can be seen as the first, even faltering steps, towards police investigations of the future they will set in motion a self-fulfilling prophecy of the best kind. The efforts that all the contributors to this volume, and all the people who have supported them, will thus have been worthwhile.

References

Alison, L.J. and Canter, D.V. (2000a), 'The Social Psychology of Crime', in D.V. Canter and L.J. Alison (eds), *The Social Psychology of Crime: Teams, Groups, Networks, Offender Profiling Series Vol III*, Aldershot: Dartmouth.

Alison, L.J. and Canter, D.V. (1999a), 'Profiling in Policy and Practice', in D.V. Canter and L.J. Alison (eds), *Profiling in Policy and Practice, Offender Profiling Series Vol II*, Aldershot: Dartmouth.

Bennet, T. and Wright, R. (1984), *Burglars on Burglary* Aldershot: Gower.

Brown, B.B. and Harris, P.B. (1989), 'Residential Burglary Victimisation: Reactions to the Invasion of a Primary Territory', *Journal of Environmental Psychology*, **9**, 119-132.

Campbell, D.T. (1957), unpublished report cited in E.J. Webb, D.T. Campbell, R.D. Schwartz and L. Sechrest, *Unobtrusive Measures*, Chicago: Rand McNally.

Canter, D.V. and Alison, L.J. (1999b), 'Interviewing and Deception', in D.V. Canter and L.J. Alison (eds), *Interviewing and Deception, Offender Profiling Series Vol I*, Aldershot: Dartmouth.

Canter, D.V. and Alison, L.J. (2000b), 'Profiling Rape and Murder', in D.V. Canter and L.J. Alison (eds), *Profiling Rape and Murder, Offender Profiling Series, Vol V*, Aldershot: Dartmouth.

Canter, D.V., Hughes D. and Kirby S. (1998), 'Paedophilia: Pathology, Criminality, or Both? The Development of a Multivariate Model of Offence Behaviour in Child Sexual Abuse', *Journal of Forensic Psychiatry*, **9(3)**, 532-555.

Canter, D.V. and Heritage, R. (1990), 'A Multivariate Model of Sexual Offence Behaviour: Developments in "Offender Profiling"', in *The Journal of Forensic Psychiatry*, **1(2)**, 185-212.

Canter, D.V. and Fritzon, K. (1998), 'Differentiating Arsonists: A model of Firesetting Actions and Characteristics', *Legal and Criminological Psychology*, **3**, 73-96.

Cohen, L.E. and Felson, M. (1979), 'Social Change and Crime Rate Trends: a Routine Activity Approach', *American Journal of Sociology*, **73**, 73-83.

Davies, A. (1997), 'Specific Profile Analysis: a Data-based Approach to Offender Profiling', in J.L. Jackson and D.A. Bekerian (eds), *Offender Profiling: Theory, Research and Practice*, Chichester: John Wiley and Sons.

van Duyne, P. (1999), 'Mobsters are Human Too', in D.V. Canter and L.J. Alison (eds), *Profiling in Policy and Practice, Offender Profiling Series, Vol II*, Aldershot: Dartmouth.

Festinger, L., Riecken, H.W. and Schachter, S. (1956), *When Prophecy Fails*, Minneapolis: Univeristy of Minnesota Press.

Hogan, J. and Hogan, R. (1989), 'How to Measure Employee Reliability', *Journal of Applied Psychology*, **74(2)**, 273-279.

Hurley, W. and Monahan, T.M. (1969), 'Arson: The Criminal and the Crime', *The British Journal of Criminology*, **9**, 4-21.

Jackson, H.F., Glass, C. and Hope, S. (1987), 'A Functional Analysis of Recidivistic Arson', *British Journal of Clinical Psychology*, **26**, 175-185.

Jackson, J.L. and Bekerian, D.A. (eds) (1997), *Offender Profiling: Theory, Research and Practice*, Chichester: John Wiley and Sons.

Jones, J.W. and Terris, W. (1983), 'Predicting Employees' Theft in Home Improvement Centres', *Psychological Reports*, **52**, 187-201.

Lange, E. and Kirsch, M. (1989), 'Sexually Motivated Fire-Raisers', *Psychiatrie Neurologie und Medizinische Psychologie*, **41**, 361-366.

Munsell Colour Company Inc. (1960), *Munsell Book of Colour*, Baltimore: Munsell Colour Company Inc.

Pyle, G.F. et al. (1974), 'The Spatial Dynamics of Crime', *Department of Geography Research Monograph*, **159**, Chicago: University of Chicago.

Quinsey, V.L., Chaplin, T.C. and Upfold, D. (1989), 'Arsonists and Sexual Arousal to Firesetting: Correlation Unsupported', *Journal of Behaviour Therapy and Experimental Psychiatry*, **20(3)**, 203-209.

Rice, M.E. and Harris, G.T. (1991), 'Firesetters Admitted to a Maximum Security Psychiatric Institution. Offenders and Offences', *Journal of Interpersonal Violence*, **6(4)**, 461-475.

Skyrme, D. and Amidon, D.M. (1997), *Creating the Knowledge Based Business*, London: Business Intelligence Ltd.

Webb, E.J., Campbell D.T., Schwartz, R.L. and Sechrest, L. (1966), *Unobtrusive Measures: Nonreactive Research in the Social Sciences*, Chicago: Rand McNally.

White, R.C. (1932), 'The Relation of Felonies to Environmental Factors in Indianapolis', *Social Forces*, **10**, 439-467.

Whyte, W.F. (1943), *Street Corner Society: The Social Structure of an Italian Slum*, Chicago: The University of Chicago Press.

2 Intruders, Pilferers, Raiders and Invaders: The Interpersonal Dimension of Burglary

SIMON MERRY AND LOUISE HARSENT

The authors discuss whether house burglary, commonly considered a property crime, may be better regarded as an interpersonal interaction. The basis for this argument is the evidence that shows the psychological effect burglary has on the victim. They discuss the home as an 'extension of the self' and the psychological effect intrusion upon the home has on the victim. The authors move on to discuss their own research investigating two proposed facets of craft and personal narrative. Thirty-four crime scene behaviours were analysed using a SSA on 60 crimes. The authors identify four themes: Intruders, Pilferers, Raiders and Invaders each displaying its own level of craft and narrative. They conclude that there is evidence for discussing burglary in terms of an interpersonal interaction, that the four themes found each display had different qualities of interaction and hence hold a different significance for the victim.

Simon Merry completed a BA degree in Social Science with the Open University before obtaining his MSc in Investigative Psychology at the University of Liverpool. He is a Superintendent with Dorset Police and is a part-time PhD student conducting further research into the crime of house burglary. Both authors have been responsible for transferring academic research into the operational policing sphere.

31

*Offender Profiling Series: IV - **Profiling Property Crimes***
Edited by D. Canter and L. Alison. © 2000 Ashgate Publishing, Aldershot. pp 31-56

Louise Harsent gained a 1st Class BSc (Hons) degree in Experimental Psychology at Sussex, followed by the MSc in Investigative Psychology at Liverpool, concentrating on the issues of behavioural consistency and crime linking raised by the research presented in the chapter. After 3 years as a Divisional Analyst with Sussex Police she is now a research officer at the Probation Studies Unit, Centre for Criminological Research at Oxford University.

2 Intruders, Pilferers, Raiders and Invaders: The Interpersonal Dimension of Burglary

SIMON MERRY AND LOUISE HARSENT

An Interpersonal Crime?

House burglary is a crime that rarely involves face to face contact between burglar and victim. The fear generated by the crime tends to outweigh the actual threat of physical harm and yet the trauma experienced by victims is real and lasting. 'It was like being raped', described one victim in a house burglary survey (Bennet and Wright, 1984). This is a common reaction to this crime; yet, it is labelled a 'property' crime rather than an interpersonal crime. If the victim of a crime feels so traumatised then the intrinsic nature of house burglary has an added dimension beyond simple material loss and gain. As the victim loses materially what the burglar gains, does the same transaction apply in terms of psychological loss and gain? This interaction is lived out by both burglar and victim, to the point that they become 'intimate strangers' and thus, a form of interpersonal relationship is established. The interpersonality of house burglary may be difficult to measure, however, if the crime does have this quality it follows that the burglar's behaviour is an expression of his/her attitudes towards others, as a murder, rape or assault is an expression of the offender's attitude towards the victim. Canter (1989) asserts that most crimes have an explicitly or implicitly interpersonal quality. Explicit interpersonal interaction is clearly exhibited in murder and rape; however, the crime of house burglary is less easily classified. The invasion of a home is perceived by victims to be a personal attack to a greater or lesser degree and it is the behaviour within the premises that defines the level of impact.

33

The home is a very special place and it is the nature of mankind's relationship with territory and home which raises the emotiveness of the crime. The assertion that house burglary is, at least, an implicitly interpersonal crime suggests that the crime scene will reveal something of the offender's character beyond the skill level, which has been the conventional method of categorising this type of crime.

Blackburn (1993) contends that burglary is an 'instrumental crime' which is akin to tax evasion, suggesting it is simply a means to material gain. In contrast he presents sexual offences and assault as 'expressive crimes' as they are 'articulating a non-material need' (p.105). This comparison illustrates the idea that crimes can be scaled on a continuum, with highly expressive, interpersonal crimes at one extreme and instrumental crimes at the other, representing a lack of interpersonal conflict. It is argued that house burglary will feature towards the middle of the continuum, and its exact position will depend on the implicit or explicit interpersonal content of an individual crime.

The expressive nature of the crime has received fleeting consideration in recent studies (Bennet and Wright, 1984; Cromwell, Olson and Avery, 1991), however, the instrumental dimension has dominated understanding and the skill or craft aspects have remained the defining characteristics. For example, the burglar who has a high level of craft that enables him or her to enter a well protected home and steal antiques has traditionally been classified purely as a 'good class' or 'professional burglar'.

Walsh (1980), uniquely rose above the narrow adherence to craft related typologies and sought to introduce a psychological dimension. He accepted that material gain was not all that a burglar may seek from his offences and that abuse of the victim's home may even be the predominant reward. However, despite describing the intrusion and exploitation of a victim by a burglar as an 'intimate relationship of a curious kind' (p.51) quite unlike other dishonesty offences such as fraud, Walsh retreats from presenting all burglaries as inherently interpersonal. He prefers to draw the instrumental - expressive distinction and suggested six typologies, three 'dispossessive' and three 'challenge' burglaries respectively. The dispossessive typologies of 'novitiate', 'pillager' and 'breaksman' are categorised by the level of craft employed and have an emphasis on material gain. According to Walsh the victim is irrelevant to the burglar other than representing the owner of desired property. The classifications are summarised as follows:

Novitiate

An apprentice learning from a skilled burglar, who lacks detailed technical skill but is rational in approach. This burglar will make errors on entry, use techniques for the sake of it, miss valuable property and possibly panic.

Pillager

An unskilled adult burglar who is triggered into offending by need and fails to plan. He occasionally needs money for a drink or to resolve some pressing problem. He employs any entry method and is a disorganised looter.

Breaksman

A skilled artist, knowledgeable and secretive. He will plan ahead, establishing the target's value. He will select the most vulnerable entry point and the search will be neat and tidy. This burglar will be self-disciplined to the point of being obsessional about habits, employing the same methods to avoid uncertainties.

The three expressive, challenge typologies, 'feral threat', 'riddlesmith' and 'dominator', are distinctly different from any others proposed and draw attention to the significance of the victim to the burglar. Burglars committing these offences are described as satisfying a more emotional need by posing an explicit challenge or threat to the victim through damage or confrontation.

They are summarised below:

Feral threat

This burglar engages in malicious vandalism, spilling and tangling objects, urinating and defecating to destroy the home of the victim.

Riddlesmith

The burglar displays technical skill whilst setting puzzles and being destructive. Inventiveness is employed to cause damage and messages are left daubed on walls and mirrors. These offenders target individuals who represent a personal obsession, such as class, race or a particular individual.

Dominator

This offender seeks occupied premises and confronts the victim subjecting them to violence, abuse and terror.

Walsh (1980) developed this interesting classification system from the content analysis of interviews with victims and offenders. He examined the range of victim reactions and offender explanations and although, links were not made between the parties of specific crimes, he identified distinctions in craft and interpersonal focus. However, his separation of the six typologies into two groups denies that there are instrumental or expressive elements in all burglaries. In addition, there is little cross-reference to individual or sets of behaviours in terms of the relationship between behaviours and reliance is placed on generalised categorisation. Also, his inclusion of crimes which he labels 'dominator' burglaries involving intended personal contact are not only rare but are distinctly different in their nature and are more akin to the highly interpersonal crime of robbery. Walsh suggested that burglars resolve material and psychological problems in the course of committing their crime and this assumption leads to the conclusion that whilst dishonest material gain can be achieved by many forms of crime, the act of house burglary feeds particular psychological needs. He also introduces the idea that a crime scene will represent an offender's character, both in terms of craft ability and interpersonal need.

It is the invasion of the home, which elevates the position of house burglary on the 'interpersonal continuum', and it is the nature of home which is central to understanding the interpersonal quality of the crime.

The Role of the Home and the Impact of Invasion

'Home Sweet Home' and 'The Home is where the Heart is' are two of many prosaic notions that define the nostalgic view of home. It is a special place that is central to our daily lives, a place that is at the beginning and end of most of our journeys, it is chosen and personalised. John Ruskin, the Victorian artist and social commentator defined the nature of home in a polemic about the moral values of the age. He wrote:

...it is the place of peace; the shelter, not only from all injury, but from all terror, doubt, and division. In so far as the anxieties of outer life penetrate into it, [...] or hostile society of the outer world is allowed [..] to cross the threshold, it ceases to be home; it is then only a part of that world that you have roofed over.

Ruskin (1865) cited in Golby (1986, p.118)

Similarly, Walsh (1980) in his study of house burglary described the home as; 'A velvet-lined cave, a comfortable and luxurious retreat ... where the owners can relax and renew their strength. ... a refuge of a very private nature, the sanctity of which is not to be violated' (p.11).

These extracts capture the essence of home as a place of territory, security and identity, all of which are challenged by burglary to an extent defined by the offender. Following the assertion that house burglary has a unique invasive quality and this feeds the psychological needs of the burglar, it is useful to examine the nature of 'home' to better understand the burglar-victim 'interaction'.

The Home as Territory, Security and Part of Identity

The home could be regarded as an extension of the identity and personality of the occupier. Korosec-Serfaty and Bollit (1986) apply this appreciation of home to the intrusion of the burglar and argue that the process 'is not simply the theft of objects but also the defilement of and domination over the private aspects of identity' (p.340).

This statement summarises the findings of a number of studies into victims' reactions to burglary and stresses the role of the home in providing a secure anchor to which the householder can attach identity. Therefore there are two aspects to the role of the home that are violated during a burglary; the home as a place of safety and the home as 'a symbol of self' (Korosec-Serfaty et al., 1986, p.329). By transgressing both these roles, the burglar invades the victim's intimate space physically and symbolically. This induces strong emotional reactions such as anger, shock, sadness, and anxiety in almost two thirds of one sample interviewed and fear in at least 50% (Brown and Harris, 1989).

Victims are forced to reassess their assumptions of security and accept the vulnerability of their home to intruders. This perceived lack of control over one's environment is accentuated when entry is forced and security measures overcome. This increased desire to protect the home is commonly expressed by victims fitting further security devices to their home after a burglary in an attempt to reassert control over their environment. Brown et al. related this need for a secure home to 'territoriality theory' in which the home is regarded as a 'primary territory' where the occupant expects safety within and control over his environment. Therefore, uninvited intrusion threatens the victim's sense of control, challenging their ability to protect their own territory. An inability to protect the home affects the occupant's self image and thus damages their identity.

Therefore, even in the absence of property theft or malicious vandalism the burglar commits an offence that has a quite devastating effect on the victim by imposing a sense of vulnerability and of being personally violated. From the victim's perspective the crime is distinctly interpersonal. Korosec-Serfaty et al. describe the burglar as having initiated a relationship with the victim as they become curious about who it could have been, why they were chosen and whether the burglar will place the same value on the stolen items as they did. The victim's distress is further increased if property that is of sentimental value is taken. This is found to be more upsetting than financial loss alone, although the combination of sentimental items of high value is the most distressing (Brown et al.). Korosec-Serfaty et al. also highlighted the personal significance of certain property, emphasising that it is the investment in an object rather than the object itself that makes its loss distressing.

The home territory is not only a physical boundary but becomes a manifestation of the occupant's identity. How it is decorated, arranged and the objects within it all represent aspects of the occupant's tastes and experiences. The burglar becomes privy to such private areas, violating and contaminating them. Brown et al. found that victim distress reflected the extent of territorial invasion, especially when it extended to the more private rooms, confirming a prediction made by Waller and Okihiro (1978), who drew from the anthropological and ethnological work of Ardrey and Lorenz. Korosec-Serfaty et al. described a victim who was most upset by the invasion of her bathroom because of all the personal toiletries that were kept there, or the linen cupboard of another victim, which contained bedding that normally represented comfort and security. It is not uncommon for victims to describe burglary as a rape of their home especially when the burglar has disturbed personal photographs, letters and diaries, leaving the victim feeling 'touched' by the intruder

(Korosec-Serfaty et al., 1986, p.339). Their sense of violation increases with the number of rooms searched, the amount of damage caused and above all, the level of gratuitous mess, or ransacking that occurs (Brown et al., 1989).

These findings therefore suggest that crime scene behaviours can be crudely divided into those that the victim perceives as more invasive, and therefore more explicitly interpersonal (eg. breaching security measures, multi-room searches, ransacking and theft of personal items), and those that are more implicitly interpersonal or less intimate (access through an insecurity, tidy search, theft of more neutral objects such as electrical equipment).

The Burglar/Victim Interaction

The victim's reaction is a measure of the interpersonal degree of the crime. Each of the burglar's actions produces a response from the victim and it is suggested that during a burglary the offender anticipates these reactions and a cognitive interaction could be said to take place. The burglar could be compared to an author who constructs an 'imaginary reader' for whom he is writing in order to tailor his style to convey the message most effectively. Only by maintaining a consistent image of the reader can the author communicate in a consistent style (Coulthard, 1994). Similarly, a burglar should demonstrate behaviours at the crime scene consistent with the perception of the victim and the desired effect upon them.

The assumption that a burglar satisfies these needs through intimidation and abuse of the victim requires that they are capable of and engage in the proposed cognitive interaction.

It is argued that a home is not simply a warehouse containing goods, but a place where a thief can gain both materially and psychologically. From this understanding of the concept of home and the reaction of victims we can begin to understand the interpersonal dimension of the crime. This takes us towards an appreciation of the offender and his/her psychological mind set. In other words, it is an explanation of criminal behaviour.

Criminal Behaviour and the Crime of House Burglary

House burglary, like all crime is ultimately a set of behaviours, which has been defined as socially unacceptable. The crime occurs at the moment that the offender is triggered into trespassing into and stealing from another's home. It is at this point that the offender exposes his or her characteristic attitudes towards the sanctity of the home and the particular or type of person they believe lives in that place, as if the burglar was communicating some message to the occupant. In the process the burglar's skill or craft is employed to achieve the resolution of the problem, regardless of its psychological or material nature.

The nature of the crime is defined by the opportunity created by the victim in terms of the availability of the premises, its security and contents, and the psychological/material needs and craft ability of the offender. The latter, offender related factors present the potential for two scales, 'interpersonal' and 'craft', which are inextricably linked and may be useful in classifying different crimes. Therefore, it may be said that inherent levels of interpersonality and craft ability shape a burglar's style.

Canter (1994) argues that contemporary behaviour is a product of an individual's inner narrative, a compendium of story lines, which are the product of past internal and external conflicts and experiences. The narrative is goal directed and whilst aspirations are normally achieved in conventional ways a criminal will view the world in a distorted way justifying short cuts to goals (Hirschi and Gottfredson, 1990 cited in Blackburn, 1993). The short cuts normally involve a criminal act, for example rape may be a short cut to power or sexual satisfaction, whilst theft may be a short cut to material gain. From this explanation of individual behaviour, we return to the suggestion that there are two scales of behaviour wrapped up in the inner narrative and Canter defines these as 'interpersonal consistency' and 'cognitive capability consistency' relating to the interpersonal and craft dimensions respectively.

Canter argues that an offender's interpersonal consistency is indeed, derived from the individual's past experiences and will be manifested in degrees of domination or power and hostility or intimacy shown towards the victim. He develops this assertion and proposes that the victim's actual suffering 'reveals the inner narrative of the assailant' (p.285). In terms of house burglary, it is suggested that the victim's feeling of fear and vulnerability are psychological losses, which are translated into gains for the offender. Thus, the burglar gains materially and psychologically from the crime. In simple terms the burglar's goal or need is a product of his/her narrative script. But, burglars do not all behave the same way and this is because each person who is driven to burglary is living out a personalised narrative with different goals. Examining the psychological rewards of house burglary, given the explanation of the value of home, reveals a number of desires. These include; *power* - the power experienced from overcoming security and actually achieving a temporary coup d'etat, over the sovereign ruler of that place; *intimacy/hostility* - the intimacy of searching through private places and touching private things belonging to another or hostility through malicious damage; *revenge* - revenge against a specific individual or representative of a social group by invading the sanctity of the home; *excitement* - the excitement of simply being in a forbidden place; and *curiosity* - the opportunity to see what is in that personal and forbidden place.

These psychological rewards may be sought singularly or in combination; however, the unique circumstances and narrative of the individual burglar will produce different behaviours. From this explanation it is possible to see that the victim has a particular role to play, whether it be the sovereign who loses power, the keeper of private things who loses privacy or simply the owner of a forbidden place who has created curiosity. These are subtly different roles, but, different all the same.

The burglar's ability to realise the desired interpersonal focus will demand a commensurate level of 'cognitive capability consistency', which in itself will be constrained by a predictable pattern of development, intimating elements of the individual's background. For example, the ability of offenders to plan their burglaries in advance requires 'means-end thinking' and 'consequential thinking' and would be manifest in the level of organisation shown (Spivack, Platt and Shure, 1976, cited in Maguire and Priestley, 1985). Similarly, intellect and manual dexterity are revealed in the sophistication and success of the entry and search. The nature of the property taken reflects the scope of the burglar's distribution network, a network dependent on his/her ability to successfully negotiate a complex social minefield of co-operation and deceit, drawing upon their 'interpersonal cognitive problem-solving skills' (Spivack et al., op cit., p.157). They presented five cognitive skills necessary for effective social interaction such as the identification and appreciation of interpersonal conflicts, generation of alternative solutions, formulation of necessary steps to resolve issues and the ability to adopt another person's perspective. Individual differences in these abilities account for the levels of social integration, and hence burglary expertise those offenders demonstrate. These cognitive skills provide a holistic explanation of an offender's level of expertise, however, craft may be assessed more practically by considering the amount of planning involved, the level of intelligence demonstrated, the manual skills exhibited and the nature of the offender's social/criminal network. Each behaviour and set of behaviours can be examined in relation to these criteria and thus, a classification may be applied to a particular crime and criminal.

This explanation of behaviour suggests that an individual's actions are a product of earlier experiences of resolving presented problems of both an instrumental and expressive nature. The 'interpersonal' and 'craft' aspects are two facets of house burglary, indeed, of all interpersonal crime. They are bound up in the individuality of the offender and therefore potentially reflect his or her character. The two aspects are subject to development, but their complexity and experience based origin mean that they are likely to change slowly. This developmental aspect suggests that individuals are not types of person but that their narratives and subsequent behaviour are subject to themes.

Thus, criminal behaviour results from a quest to achieve narrative related goals, and house burglary offers a number of unique opportunities to achieve these psychological and material rewards. It is proposed that house burglary is an interpersonal crime and concerns the expression of the offender's attitude towards the victim as well as the pursuit of material gain. Walsh (1980) concludes, 'It is highly doubtful that the psychology of the individual burglar can be ignored in trying to assess why burglars in general burgle'.

Crime Scene Actions - The Facets of Interpersonal Script and Craft

Thus far, the hypothesis suggests that an offender's narrative directed behaviour would be exhibited in the form of actions at the crime scene. The range of potential rewards have been alluded to, however, it is only from the disturbance at the crime scene that evidence is available to infer an offender's narrative in terms of interpersonality and craft.

The hypothesis proposes that each behaviour will have an inherent interpersonal and craft element. It is the degree or level of each which defines the nature of the crime and the narrative theme and role of the victim.

Each behaviour may be assessed in relation to a scale of implicit to explicit interpersonal script or theme and a scale of low to high craft ability. Table 2.1 sets out a selection of crime scene actions together with an assessment of their inherent level of the interpersonal script and craft. (An explanation of each behaviour is detailed in the content dictionary at Appendix A. The content dictionary reference number is included in parenthesis.)

Table 2.1: Hypothesised Quality of Crime Scene Behaviours

Behaviour	Interpersonal Script	Craft
occupied (7)	high	low
insecurity exploited (6)	low	low
climbing (9)	high	low
no search made (8)	low	low
objects strewn (31)	high	low
malicious damage (11)	high	low
facilities used (12)	high	low
doors wedged shut (26)	high	high
curtains drawn (27)	high	high

In each case the behaviour has been assessed in terms of the offender's interpersonal gain and victim impact together with the level of craft employed. For example, trespassing into an occupied home by climbing, and eating food or using the toilet are all considered to be particularly invasive and therefore explicitly interpersonal, however, none of these actions requires the cognitive skills of consequential thinking and thus they are considered to be low in craft. Conversely, wedging shut doors and thus temporarily barring the owner's entry and stealing personal jewellery are explicitly interpersonal and high craft.

These examples also serve to suggest that certain behaviours will be expected to consistently co-occur. This assertion reflects the hypothesis that individuals behave in accordance with their narrative and this is likely to produce consistent behaviour, thus, it is expected that high craft behaviours will be broadly exhibited with other high craft behaviours and the same in relation to particular levels of interpersonal behaviours. Thus, within each of the facets there is an ordering of the behaviours in accordance with their inherent qualities.

Finally, it is through the crime, and particularly the individual and sets of actions, that the offender communicates with the victim. Therefore the exhibition of specific behaviours will allow a crime to be classified in relation to the two facets.

Testing the Hypothesis

Methodology

It is hypothesised that house burglary has an interpersonal quality and that the role of the victim is relevant to the offender's goal. It is proposed that there are two facets, which define the crime, and these relate to the interpersonal narrative or script and the craft ability of the offender. These proposals are tested by analysing a sample of burglaries to identify thematic patterns of behaviour exhibited at crime scenes.

Sixty house burglaries, each committed by a different offender in a large coastal town in Southern England in 1993, were content analysed according to the list of 35 variables detailed in Appendix A. A sample of crimes committed by different offenders presents a pure data set, which is not biased by the inclusion of variously sized sub-sets of actions committed by the same offender(s). Only completed crimes involving activity at entry, within and exit were used. Offender identity or character did not guide selection other than to exclude crimes committed by offenders already in the sample. Data was drawn from prosecution files; however, it is necessary to point out that crime scene information had been recorded for the purpose of prosecuting the offender rather than to contribute to empirical study. In most cases there were no witnesses and the data reflects disturbances at the scene. Useful data such as the attractiveness of the dwelling, sentimental value of property stolen, items ignored and relationship between offender and victim were not consistently recorded and therefore a longer list of possible attributes was reduced to a list of 35 reliable variables.

The 60 sets of behaviours underwent Smallest Space Analysis to test the predicted thematic grouping of behaviours according to craft and script.

The analysis is designed to test the hypothesised facets and themes. Each variable or behaviour is correlated with every other and relationships are represented on a spatial plot. Thus, in this case it is hypothesised, for example, those low craft behaviours will correlate closely and they will feature as near neighbours on the spatial plot. In this way each of the different behavioural themes; Implicit Interpersonality, Explicit Interpersonality, Low Craft and High Craft, should be grouped in contiguous regions. It should be noted that the complexities of studying real world phenomena comprising multivariate data will incur stresses and variables will be pushed and pulled in accordance with co-relationships. This may have an impact on the clarity of the hypothesised facets represented in the analytical output.

Analysis

The results are presented in the form of two interpretations of the spatial representation. The first depicting the frequency of behaviours and the second indicating the presence of the hypothesised facets.

Figure 2.1, represents the modulating nature of the behaviours with the most frequently occurring actions being located together in the centre and those less common radiating outwards.

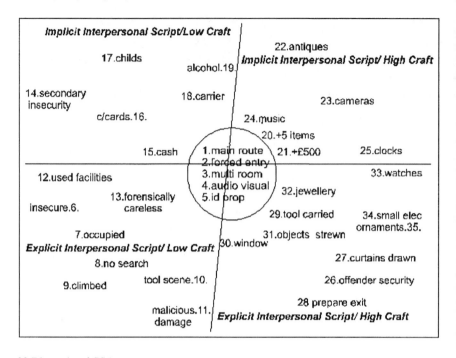

03 Dimensional SSA
Vector 1/Vector 2
Jaccard index similarity coefficient
Guttman-Lingoes coefficient of alienation = 0.18582

Figure 2.1: SSA of House Burglary Behaviours (Frequencies)

The activities that occur in over 60% of the sample are grouped together in the centre of the spatial plot and it will be seen that these are the defining behaviours of the crime. Thus, a burglary of a house situated on or near a main thoroughfare involving a forced entry, multi-room search and identifiable and audio-visual property being stolen are common features of most crimes. Behaviours that accompany these defining actions radiate out from the centre according to their frequency and co-occurrence with other actions.

The same representation is depicted in figure 2.2, however, this time the plot has been interpreted in accordance with the hypothesised facets of Interpersonal Script and Craft.

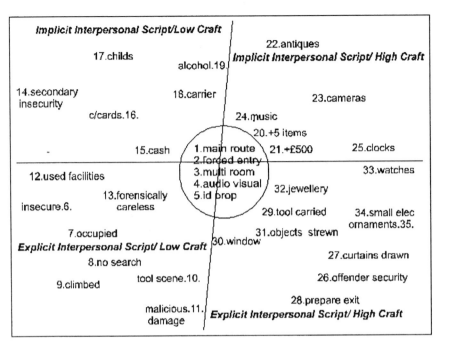

3 Dimensional SSA
Vector 1/Vector 2
Jaccard index similarity coefficient
Guttman-Lingoes coefficient of alienation = 0.18582
Numbers refer to list in Appendix A

Figure 2.2: SSA of House Burglary Behaviours (Interpersonal Script and Craft Facets)

The Interpersonal Script Facet of House Burglary

The Script Facet is similarly represented in the form of a continuum ranging from implicit to explicit interpersonal behaviours and progresses from the top to the bottom of the spatial plot.

Implicitly interpersonal behaviours are regionalised towards the top of the plot and are defined by entry via vulnerable security and theft of material items with less emphasis on emotional gain.   The implicit interpersonality is forged through the trespass into another's home. It is aggravating behaviour following trespass which defines a more explicit interpersonal theme.

Explicitly interpersonal behaviours are contiguously grouped towards the bottom of the plot. Risking entry whilst the occupants are present, using facilities and causing gratuitous damage in the form of scrawled messages or smearing food is one aspect. A second is bound up in the instrumental element, but strikes at the victim. This is manifested by temporarily displacing the occupant from their own home by blocking access points, assuming rights of privacy by drawing curtains, rearranging the interior by strewing objects and stealing items more likely to be of sentimental value such as jewellery.

The Craft Facet of House Burglary

The concept that craft is exhibited at crime scenes in a consistent way is portrayed by an ordering of behaviours from left to right, which reflects a progression from low to high craft. Indeed, the order progresses through low, middle to high craft, however, for parsimony, the low and high distinction is maintained.

Low craft is exhibited in the form of a comparative lack of planning, knowledge and skills together with a tendency of reactiveness rather than proactiveness. The scenarios presented revolve around the reaction to an opportune insecurity, climbing to gain entry despite the risk of occupancy and having entered, using facilities, stealing easily carried items without a search and being forensically careless. A second theme involves the abuse of weak security of a known victim and possibly the theft of children's belongings by juveniles. Lastly, the offender causing gratuitous damage as perhaps the primary objective exhibits low burglary craft and thus, instrumental burglary skills are of secondary importance.

Conversely, high craft behaviours featured to the right of the representation indicate cognitive capability and are proactive rather than reactive in quality. Here the scenarios comprise skilled entry with a carried tool, securing the premises from returning occupants, concealing activity by drawing curtains and stealing more numerous and higher value property such as jewellery, clocks and antiques.

This interpretation allows a crime scene and the burglar to be classified in a meaningful way. For example, if the burglar entered an occupied house by climbing to an insecure window, carried out a minimal search, stealing and eating food, the crime and criminal may be categorised as 'high interpersonal script/low craft'.

The Interpersonal Roles of Offender and Victim

Identifying the craft and interpersonal dimensions of the crime is a first step to an interpretation of the meaning of the crime for the offender. It has been argued that the burglar seeks more than material gain and this added quality will differ depending on the needs of the individual offender. The four regions created by the orthogonal relationship of the two facets reflect different interpersonal narrative themes of the offender. The regions have been reinterpreted using labels synonymous with the character of the offender and the implied role of the victim.

The representation classifies house burglars as 'Intruders', 'Pilferers', 'Raiders' and 'Invaders'.

Intruders (Explicitly Interpersonal Script/Low Craft Region)

The intruder region represents the 'explicitly interpersonal/low craft region. These correlated behaviours include offending as a result of a presented opportunity from insecurity. This style of entry may necessitate climbing and is accompanied by a risk of occupancy, the use of facilities, no search and no strong correlation with the theft of particular items of property. However, whilst there is less concern with theft there is an association with causing damage not related to entry or theft.

The offender is triggered to act through a desire to intrude and violate another's home in a cruder manner than the other themes. Causing malicious damage, using facilities, determination to climb and a preparedness to encounter victims adds an invasive and disturbing quality beyond material theft. The forensically, careless attribute underlines the lack of planning and emphasis on short lived fulfilment of desire. The potential for victim contact and impact is thus high. The aggravated interaction imposed by gratuitous damage manifests itself in a fear of being stalked or targeted out of malice by an unknown or possibly known, but not identified attacker. The offender exhibits aspects of power, hostility, excitement and revenge. The theme is highly expressive, whereby the role of the victim is that of a significant host to the unwanted visitor.

Pilferers (Implicitly Interpersonal/Low Craft Region)

The Pilferer region coincides with the 'implicitly interpersonal/low craft' region and may be considered the least impacting style of burglary. The pilferer has gained entry following a desire to intrude, possibly by knowledge of weak security. Having entered, the offender creates little disturbance and steals portable and impersonal items, such as cash and children's belongings. The offender expresses low levels of dominance and hostility, whilst there is a suggestion of curiosity and excitement. The theme is not highly expressive; however, there is little evidence of substantial material gain. The victim is irrelevant and is simply the owner of property that is attractive and available.

Raiders (Implicitly Interpersonal/High Craft Region)

This region is confined to the earlier defined 'implicitly interpersonal/ high craft' theme. To raid is to trespass and to steal material things and violate the sanctity associated with the home. The theme comprises an instrumental intrusion and theft, including the prolific theft of watches, clocks, antiques and cameras. There are no actions that are extraneous to theft and the theme is perhaps the most respectful towards the victim who may be regarded as a person who is no more than the keeper of coveted things. Here, the offender exhibits a higher level of power or dominance and less hostility. The role of the offender is that of a raider and appropriator of those same possessions.

Invaders (Explicitly Interpersonal/High Script Region)

The invader theme largely occupies the 'explicitly interpersonal/high craft' region. Here the offender employs behaviours that have a dual expressive and instrumental dimension. The combination of trespass, reconfiguring the home by barring entry, drawing curtains, strewing objects as well as stealing sentimental items such as jewellery, has all the hallmarks of invasion and plunder. The desecration or at least, the rearrangement of the personally established home represents extreme violation. There is explicit evidence of power, hostility, revenge, and excitement. In this theme the role of the victim is that of a displaced and significant host to the invading and plundering offender.

Conclusion

It has been argued that criminal behaviour is the product of a quest to achieve psychological and material goals. House burglary has been explained as a criminal behaviour, which is uniquely defined by the quality and value of home. The conventional understanding of house burglary as a property crime and committed by offenders making rational choices for material gain is accepted, however, an inextricably linked interpersonal dimension is added to the model.

This explanation adopts and extends Walsh's proposal that there is an interpersonal 'challenge' made by the burglar in some particular forms of burglary, however, it is argued that the interpersonal dimension is implicitly or explicitly inherent in every house burglary. The assertion made by Spivak et al. that offenders engage in problem solving through criminal behaviour employing 'means end thinking' and 'consequential thinking' applies to resolving both material and psychological needs. They propose that individual aptitude is constrained by ability to negotiate specific interpersonal cognitive problems and therefore, it follows that individual differences in crime scene behaviour can be expected and this behaviour is likely to be consistent over time. Canter's hypothesis that the crime scene and indeed the victim's reaction will reflect the inner narrative of the offender is consistent and extends these proposals. Applying these assertions to the crime of house burglary is more attractive in light of the explanation of home as part of personal identity.

Pursuing these explanations has lead to the hypothesis that house burglary is an interpersonal crime and that the nature of the problem to be solved and the narrative theme of the offender will be reflected in the crime scene. Analysing crime scene behaviours has supported the hypothesis that interpersonal script and craft ability will be reflected in each behaviour to a consistent degree, and the co-occurrence of these sets of behaviours presents four behavioural themes.

Further questions arise concerning the consistency of behaviour from crime to crime. Certainly, the proposal that behaviour is a product of a slowly evolving interpersonal narrative suggests that behaviour will evolve at the same rate. Some behaviour will be situationally specific and is likely to encourage altered crime scene activity. However, activity relating to search, the making of mess and damage, items stolen and particularly items that are left behind are more likely to remain consistent over longer periods. A linked question concerns how often offenders engage in hybrid thematic behaviour and is this consistent from crime to crime? Other issues surround the consistency of behaviour of offenders who commit crime whilst influenced by drink or drugs and similarly, the impact of associates needs to be explored. Another question arises over the background characteristics of offenders who consistently behave within specific behavioural themes. It is hypothesised that youngsters who have undeveloped cognitive capability will be 'pilferers' whilst older more experienced offenders will become 'raiders' and 'invaders'. Intruders are likely to be older with less dishonesty in their criminal histories. Future research employing larger data sets collected specifically for scientific study will enhance these findings. For example, data indicating different search styles will be particularly revealing. Additionally, data from alternative environmental settings, such as rural and urban will present useful comparisons.

This research has found support for the argument that a home is an intimate psychological construct rather than simply a roof over the victim's head and a warehouse for the offender. The interpersonal dimension has presented an insight, which allows a new classification based on the offender's interpersonal script and craft. The interpersonality ranges from implicit to explicit and craft from low to high consistent with the perpetrators focus as an 'Intruder', 'Pilferer', 'Raider' or 'Invader', each of which involve a subtly different significance for the victim.

References

Bennet, T. and Wright, R. (1984), *Burglars on Burglary*, Aldershot: Gower.
Blackburn, R. (1993), *The Psychology of Criminal Conduct: Theory, Research and Practice*, Chichester: Wiley.

Brown, B.B. and Harris, P.B. (1989), 'Residential Burglary Victimisation: Reactions to the Invasion of a Primary Territory', *Journal of Environmental Psychology*, 9, 119-132.

Canter, D.V. (1989), 'Offender Profiles', *The Psychologist*, Jan. 2, 12-16.

Canter, D.V. (1994), *Criminal Shadows*, London: Harper Collins.

Coulthard, M. (1994), *Advances in Written Text Analysis,* London: Routledge.

Cromwell, P.F., Olson, J. and Avery, D.W. (1991), *Breaking and Entering: An Ethnographic Analysis of Burglary*, London: Sage.

Golby, J.M. (1986), *Culture and Society in Britain 1850 – 1890*, Oxford: Oxford University Press.

Korosec-Serfaty, P. and Bolitt, D. (1986), 'Dwelling and the Experience of Burglary', *Journal of Environmental Psychology*, 6, 329-344.

Maguire, J. and Priestley, P. (1985), *Offending behaviour: Skills and Stratagems for Going Straight*, London: Batsford.

Waller, I. and Okihiri, N. (1978), *Burglary: The Victim and the Public*, Toronto: University of Toronto Press.

Walsh, D. (1980), *Break-Ins: Burglary From Private Houses*, London: Constable.

Appendix A: Content Dictionary of the 35 Crime Scene Variables

1. *Main Thoroughfare:* Where the target premises are located on or within two turnings of a main thoroughfare.

2. *Forced Entry:* Where any form of physical force is employed to breach a secured premise.

3. *Multi-Rooms Searched:* Where more than one room has been entered and searched.

4. *Audio-Visual:* All valuable electrical equipment such as televisions, video recorders/cameras, hi-fi music systems and computer equipment.

5. *Identifiable Property Stolen:* Where the property stolen includes items that the thief is likely to perceive as identifiable by the loser. For example, electrical items with serial number or inscribed jewellery.

6. *Insecurity:* Entry gained by exploiting obvious insecurity. For example, a window or door left ajar. The weakness is essentially created by the householder not the burglar.

7.   *Occupied:* Where the offender entered premises whilst one or more residents were present but unaware of the intrusion.

8.   *No Search:* No broad search was carried out. Either i) property at specific sites within the premises was targeted (eg. cheque book and cards/cash removed from drawer, no other items or areas searched) or ii) burglar removing only property immediately available at point of entry.

9.   *Climbed:* Where access to the premises was achieved by climbing to the entry point either using a ladder or existing fixtures. Usually indicated by entry point above ground level.

10.   *Scene Tool:* Instrument used to gain entry was improvised from the burglary scene.

11.   *Malicious Damage:* Overt acts of vandalism unnecessary for the commission of property theft such as; damage to property with or without extensive mess, written messages aimed at the householder or smearing the walls.

12.   *Facility Use/Abuse:* Behaviours not directly concerned with execution of the burglary that are more comparable to the occupant's use of the dwelling. Examples: drinking and eating the householder's food in situ; using the toilet.

13.   *Forensically Careless:* Leaving any identifying evidence at the scene, typically finger or foot prints.

14.   *Secondary Insecurity Exploited:* Where the householder has created an unobvious weakness in security. For example, by shutting but not locking a door or window, by concealing a key or leaving the key with an untrustworthy agent.

15.   *Cash:* Theft of any value of currency, notes or coins.

16.   *Credit Cards:* Theft of cash instruments such as credit/charge cards, benefit/pension books, cheque books and cheque/debit cards.

17.   *Children's:* Theft of property obviously belonging to a child or any items removed from a child's room.

18. *Carrier Taken:* Removal of any low value item to carry stolen goods. For example, a bag, holdall or pillow-slip.

19. *Alcohol:* Removal of any alcoholic liquor.

20. *Over 5 Items Stolen:* Where total separate items stolen exceeds 5.

21. *Value Stolen Over 500 Pounds:* Where the victim's estimation of property stolen exceeds this total.

22. *Antiques/Furniture:* Anything classed as 'antique' except jewellery. All furniture and paintings.

23. *Camera:* Theft of camera equipment (not video cameras) including automatic cameras, lenses, camera cases. Also, theft of optical equipment such as binoculars.

24. *Music:* Theft of audio and video cassettes, compact discs and records.

25. *Clocks:* excluding wristwatches.

26. *Offender Security:* Premises secured by the offender to exclude occupants should they return, by wedging or locking internal/external doors closed.

27. *Curtains Drawn:* Curtains drawn by the burglar to conceal activity.

28. *Prepared Exit:* Point of escape prepared in advance.

29. *Tool Carried:* Where evidence suggested any use of a tool by the offender and that the implement was brought to the scene by the burglar. A 'tool' is defined as any instrument used, specialised or not. For example, glass-cutters to remove a window, a jemmy or plastic card are all 'tools'.

30. *Window:* Where access was gained via a window by force or insecurity.

31. *Objects Strewn:* Property within the dwelling scattered either in pursuance of a search or gratuitously. Despite scattering, property essentially intact and undamaged.

32. *Jewellery:* Removal of one or more items of jewellery, antique or modern.

33. *Watches:* Removal of one or more watches.

34.   *Small Electrical:* Any low - medium value, small electrical equipment such as a shaver.

35.   *Ornaments:* Removal of decorative or novelty ornaments not considered antique.

3 The Criminal Range of Small-Town Burglars

MARY BARKER

An offender's patterns of travel around his home, and his familiarity with the area may explain his choice of offence locations (Brantingham and Brantingham, 1980). The hypothesis that offences will tend to be distributed in a circle around the offender's home was tested on 32 series of burglaries carried out in small towns in the south of England. Home fell in the offence area in the majority of offence series (29 out of 32, p < 0.005), and within the area described by the first five offences in 22 of the 32 series (p < 0.05). The mean distance travelled from home to offend in the whole series is 3.87 km and in the first five offences is 3.67 km, suggesting that distances travelled in committing the first five offences are indicative of the spread of the whole series. This data demonstrates the validity of the circle hypothesis in accounting for individual patterns of burglary.

Mary Barker has a degree in psychology from the University of Southampton and an MSc in Environmental Psychology from Surrey University. After leaving Surrey in 1988, she went to work for the Home Office Research and Planning Unit in central London, in their Crime Prevention Unit. There she investigated ways of preventing vandalism and street robbery, and evaluated an initiative to reduce crime on a run-down estate in Manchester. She went to the University of Bristol in 1991 to work on a project assessing the value of sex offender treatment programmes, and to evaluate a programme developed to divert mentally disordered offenders from inappropriate imprisonment. She now works for the Medical Research Council's Environmental Epidemiology Unit in Southampton.

*Offender Profiling Series: IV – **Profiling Property Crimes***
Edited by D. Canter and L. Alison. © 2000 Ashgate Publishing, Aldershot. pp 57-73

3 The Criminal Range of Small-Town Burglars

MARY BARKER

The Problem

The crime of burglary lends itself to study by environmental psychologists. Strong features of a burglary are the time and place of its occurrence. The location is itself part of the legal definition of the offence, and in committing a series of burglaries, the burglar leaves a trail of geographical, physical and temporal information.[1] The piece of work reported in this chapter uses this information and takes as its focus the spatial patterning of burglary offences, with particular emphasis on the geographical and psychological relationship between the offender's home and his offences.

The Background

The study of crime and its geography is an old one. Recent work has tried to synthesise what is known about criminal spatial behaviour, and use it to explain well-documented disparities in the geographical distribution of crime. Historically, different schools of thought have provided different explanations. The ecological tradition pointed out the geographical coincidence between areas of high crime and concentrations of social deprivation (eg. Shaw and McKay, 1969). More recently, it has been proposed that individual patterns of criminal mobility and knowledge about the opportunity structure of the environment can explain larger crime patterns. Building on these explanations, the Brantinghams offer an

---

[1] The offenders referred to in this chapter are all male. Therefore the male pronoun will be used throughout.

explanation based on a specifically spatial model of criminal behaviour, and have proposed that as its simplest, the area of activity for an offender can be encompassed by a circle, with the offender's home at its centre and with radius the offender's maximum journey to offend (Brantingham and Brantingham, 1981). As they point out, this model assumes an even distribution of offending opportunities around the offender's home, and takes no account of the topography of an area, or the offender's specific knowledge and use of that area. At the heart of the Brantingham's model of offending is the well established finding that offenders of all types tend to commit offences within a few kilometres of their homes (Philips, 1980; Brantingham and Brantingham, 1981; Baker and Donnelly, 1986). Baker and Donnelly (1986), in particular, found that 70% of all the crimes in the neighbourhoods they studied were committed by residents. Two related explanations have been offered for this phenomenon. The first proposes that the offender's familiarity with the area in which he resides would necessarily influence his knowledge of offence opportunities. As the Brantinghams put it 'information flows should bias search behaviour toward previously known areas' (Brantingham and Brantingham, 1981). The second related explanation of why offenders should offend so near home proposes that crime sites be located on and around pathways and routes that offenders habitually use in their non-criminal activities. Rengert and Wasilchick (1985) applied this notion to the particular context of burglary, and describe the burglar's 'journey to crime' as it relates to his journeys to routine activities and destinations.

The contributions of criminal mobility and familiarity to the shape and size of an individual's offence pattern are clearly overlapping, and can be explained with reference to two psychological concepts. The first of these is 'home range', this being a complex of those objects and places that provide the everyday necessities and everyday experiences of living (Buttimer and Seamon, 1980). Thus, as well as being a way of describing people's lives and habits in a geographical way, the concept of home range implies that it must have a symbolic or mental existence. The second of the psychological concepts that can be brought to bear is the 'cognitive map' (Canter, 1984). The individual is assumed to carry a mental image of the physical area, an image that would change with his experience and which is likely to be reflection of the purposes of that individual. The burglar will have a range of purposes, his cognitive map being shaped by his need for opportunities for offending, as well as for shopping, living and socialising.

As his experience of carrying out these activities in the area grows, so will his cognitive map adapt. His familiarity with the area, and the sense of security that comes from being in known territory, are both features that might bias the distribution of his offences towards this area around his home.

What is known from the study of non-criminal space use suggests that a burglar's offences are likely to fall within the area around his home. Thus the simplest geometric description of the offender's offence pattern is the circle, with his home location at the centre and with radius the longest home to offence journey. The study reported here was conducted to test the 'circle' hypothesis against the known locations of series of burglaries, bearing in mind that the ability to pin-point an offender's home location from an analysis of his offence pattern could be a valuable aid to detection.

The Study

The study used the geographical location of the homes and offences of a sample of 31 burglars, convicted of burglary offences carried out between 1981 and 1987 in a number of small towns in the south of England.

Burglars were aged between 19 and 48 years, the mean age being 27. They were identified from lists kept by the police of known burglars. The first 31 serial burglars were selected. For the purposes of this study, a series of burglaries was defined as a sequence of at least five such crimes committed by the offender prior to arrest. Five was considered to be the minimum number necessary for the construction of a meaningful offence map. To fit within this definition of a series, offences 'taken into consideration' (TIC) at the time of conviction had sometimes to be included. Appreciating the unreliability of such information, TICs were kept to a minimum.

The burglars displayed a wide range of approaches to the business of burglary. Six of them might be described as 'professional', in as far as they appear to have selected their targets for the value of their contents, and have committed the burglary in such a way to minimise the risk of being caught. These features distinguish them from the casual or 'opportunist' offender, who made up the rest of the group under study. This latter group took cash and items of little value from the premises they burgled, though some appeared to have had specialisms, an example being burglar no.18 who committed a series of 70 burglaries of garden sheds and domestic garages.

Three of the burglars had been convicted of series of offences consisting almost entirely of breaking into domestic gas and electricity coin-operated meters. Data on these burglaries were extracted from police crime reports. The dates and locations of the offences and the address given by each offender as his home address formed the basis of the data collected. This was supplemented wherever possible by information on the nature of the burglaries committed and the mode of transport to burglary locations. Offence patterns were mapped onto Ordnance Survey maps of the areas in which offenders were working, producing a map for each of the 33 series. Patterns were then broken down into straight-line distances between offence locations and between offence and home locations, as measured from these maps. The hypothesis under test did not require the 'real' distances or routes travelled to offend. The 31 burglars who made up the sample had been convicted of a total of 33 series of burglaries, in which the number of offences ranged from five to 70. The mean number in a series was 15, the median being eight and reflecting the fact that the majority of the series were between five and 20 offences long. The length of time over which the series of burglaries were committed varied from two months to five years, with a mean length of 8.9 months.

The Burglar's Home and Home Range

Examination of police records established that the burglars in the study did indeed have home addresses at the time of their offences, and in every case except one, their home addresses were in the same town or suburb as their offence locations. Burglary activity in this small town environment appeared to be the prerogative of local burglars. The one individual who lived outside the area in which he burgled was known to have lived in the area previously.

Criminal mobility research has demonstrated that property offenders, like burglars, tend to select targets within one or two miles of home (Philips, 1980; Baker and Donnelly, 1986). When the offence patterns of our current burglars were analysed, and the straight-line distances between offences and home locations were calculated, the mean distance travelled to offend was found to be 5.19 kilometres or 3.23 miles (SD 5.28 km or 3.12 m). An early decision was taken to exclude the offences of Offender no.10 from the analysis. He appeared to have travelled between 40 and 60 km or 25 and 37 miles to offend, a distance uncharacteristic of the distances being travelled by others in the sample. After his exclusion, re-analysis showed the mean to have been brought down to 3.87 km or 2.41 miles (SD 2.53 km or 1.57 miles) - still somewhat greater than that found in previous studies. White (1932) found a mean distance of 1.66 miles between home and offences, Pyle (1974) 1.77 miles for all offences, and Repetto (1974) 1.5 miles for 93% of offences

One possible explanation for the slightly longer distances to offend found in this study, may well lie in the small town context of the study. Previous research tends to have focused on property offending in large cities, such as White's 1932 study of Indianapolis. It might reasonably be supposed that opportunities for offending would be more concentrated in a big city environment, and as a consequence, offenders would need to travel shorter distances to offend. The current study included six offenders who appeared to offend in the rural areas around small towns, and another seven whose series included some offences in rural areas. Analysed separately, the mean distance to offend of the rural and mixed rural/urban burglars was found to be greater than that of the burglars operating in a purely urban setting (4.65 km as against 3.22 km). Though it seems likely that rural burglars operating in less densely populated areas would have to travel further than urban burglars to find burglary opportunities, it would take a larger study than this to demonstrate the phenomenon conclusively. However, the conclusion that can be drawn is that burglars in this study were travelling short distances to offend. They were for the most part offending within what might be called their own home territory.

Home Range and the Offence Pattern

The fact that these burglars were committing offences close to home suggests that home location may well have been functional in determining the geographical pattern of their offending. The Brantingham's circular model of offence distribution was tested on the 32 burglary series of our 30 burglars. (Offender no.10 was again excluded from analysis on the grounds that the pattern and method of his offending were atypical of the rest of the sample.) Having reduced to the same scale maps of each offence pattern, a series of analyses was undertaken.

An initial test of this hypothesis was to calculate how often the offender's home fell within the area described by his offences. The offence area was defined by a circle, the diameter of which was the distance between the two offences most distant from one another. Visual examination of the maps confirmed that home fell in the offence area in the great majority of the series (29 out of 32). Using a binomial test, with the null hypothesis that homes are equally likely to be outside as inside the offence area, it was confirmed that 29 out of 32 represents significantly more homes within the offence area than would be expected by chance ($p < 0.005$).

In order to pinpoint more accurately the location of the burglars' homes within their offence areas, a smaller circle of half the diameter of the previous one was drawn on each map. The resulting inner circle therefore covered an area half the diameter of that which defined the whole offence area. The offender's home fell within the smaller, central region in 10 of the 32 series. Given that no area contains a uniform distribution of burglary opportunities, the fact that nearly a third of the burglars' homes were in the centre of their offence areas is strong indication that the location of home is exerting an influence on their offence patterns.

A number of facts emerge from this analysis. First, that an offender's home is very likely to be located within his offence area. This suggests that criminal spatial behaviour exhibit the same characteristics as non-criminal spatial behaviour in as much as activity is concentrated in the area around the home. The habitual home range appears to influence criminal spatial behaviour as it does other sorts of spatial behaviour. The 'circle hypothesis' is largely supported by the data, and warrants closer examination.

The First Five Offences

Further analysis was conducted using only the first five offences in each series. This was done both to reduce the burglary series to comparable units for analysis, and more importantly, visual inspection had suggested that the locations of the first five offences relative to home might be modelling the pattern of offending for the whole series. The characteristic distances travelled by offenders to burgle appeared to be exhibited in the first five offences. The same seemed to be true of the geographical distribution of offences around the home. In those series, where burglars had gone on to commit more than five offences, the pattern created by the whole series looked to be much the same as that created by the first five offences.

The analysis already conducted on each of the full series of burglaries was then repeated using the locations of only the first five. New maps were drawn up and the offence area was again defined by drawing a circle around it with diameter the distance between the two most distant offences. This time the home fell inside the offence area in 22 of the 32 series, again significantly more often than not ($p < 0.05$), and in 10 of the 32 series, home fell within the central quarter of the area of the circle. This indeed suggests that the first five offences in these series of burglaries were showing the spatial characteristics of the whole series.

To explore further the extent to which the offender's first five offences were indeed modelling his general pattern of offending, the geographical distribution of offences was looked at over time.

Offence Patterns Over Time

The ability to date offences in the series meant that it was possible to look at the development of offence patterns over time as well simply their spatial relationship to one another. The development of an individual's pattern over time presumably reflects his use and increasing experience of the opportunity structure his environment offers.

The most obvious development that might be expected would be for the distance from home to offence sites to increase between early and late offences in the series, offenders seeking offence sites further afield as the series progresses. If differences were to exist between the distance travelled to offend at each stage of the series, then looking at the relationships between offences representing different stages of the series should make this apparent. The mean distances between home and the first, middle and last offences, and offence to offence distances for the first, middle and last offences were calculated. The mean home to offence distances suggested that, in general, offenders were travelling further to offend in the latter stages of their series than they were at the beginning. The mean home to first offence distance was 2.16 km, the mean distance from home to the middle offence in the series was 3.57 km and the mean distance from home to the last offence in the series was 5.62 km.

Correlations between the distances travelled by each offender allowed a more detailed interpretation. The distances between the first and last offences and home and the last offence were particularly highly correlated (Pearsons P.M. coefficient, $r = 0.79$). Other high correlations were seen in the distances between home and the last offence and the middle and last offence ($r = 0.76$), and between the first and last offence and the middle and last offence ($r = 0.95$). The fact that the last offence figures prominently in these relationships hints at its importance as an indicator of the scale of the distances travelled in the whole series. That is to say, if an individual has travelled a great distance from home to his last offence, then it is likely his offences too will be a great distance from one another. The distance travelled to offend and the geographical spread of offences in these series appears to be of a scale characteristic to each offender and indicated by the distance travelled to the final offence.

A useful visual representation of the relationships between these distances is provided by a multi-dimensional scaling technique, smallest space analysis. Smallest space analysis (SSA) plots similarity data such as a matrix of correlations as points in a geometrical space, where the similarity between items is represented by proximity on the plot. A group of items with some factor in common would therefore form a region on the plot. The SSA produces a representation of relationships in the data in a number of different dimensions, specified at the outset of analysis. Figure 3.1 is an SSA plot of the correlations of distances between home and the first, middle and last offence and between these offences. The picture is visual confirmation of the pattern suggested by the correlations. It shows all the distances involving the last offence grouped together forming one region of the plot based on their similarity to one another. There is roughly the same distance between home and last offence, and between first and last and middle and last offences within each series.

The choice of location for the last offence appears to be an indicator of the size of the whole area victimised during these series of burglaries. A second region of the plot show the other distances (home to first offence, home to middle offence and first to middle offence) to be less similar to one another but closely related enough to form a distinct group. The mean distances travelled between home and these offences, and between these offences, suggest that the sites of these offences may represent intermediate stages in a progressive exploration of the offence area.

Reducing the analysis to distances involving only the first five offences in each series reinforces this interpretation and illuminates more closely the process of exploration. Earlier analysis has already shown that locations of the first five offences suggest a pattern and scale for the whole series. The mean distance between the first five offences and between these offences and home is 3.67 km (SD 1.18 km). The mean distance travelled in the whole series is 3.87 km, indicating that offenders are travelling as far afield as they are likely to whilst committing the first five offences.

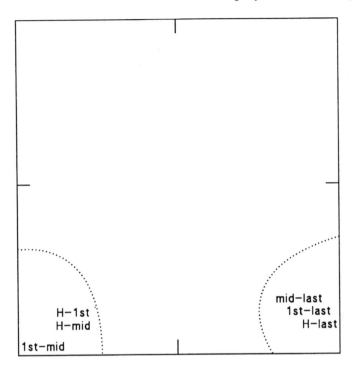

Figure 3.1: Showing the SSA Plot of the Correlations between the Distances From Home to the First, Middle and Last Offences in Each Series, and between these Offences

Table 3.1: Showing Mean Distances between the First Five Offences and between Those Offences and Home (km)

	Distances		
	Mean	**Range**	**SD**
Home to 1st Offence	2.82	0.1 - 13.0	(3.17)
Home to 2nd Offence	3.96	0.1 - 23.0	(5.14)
Home to 3rd Offence	4.05	0.1 - 21.0	(4.50)
Home to 4th Offence	3.26	0.2 - 11.9	(3.09)
Home to 5th Offence	3.59	0.1 - 21.0	(4.31)
1st to 2nd Offence	4.81	0.0 - 23.0	(5.38)
1st to 3rd Offence	4.03	0.1 - 19.0	(4.52)
1st to 4th Offence	3.10	0.1 - 10.2	(3.01)
1st to 5th Offence	3.51	0.2 - 16.0	(3.37)
2nd to 3rd Offence	4.47	0.1 - 23.0	(5.05)
2nd to 4th Offence	4.15	0.0 - 23.0	(5.03)
2nd to 5th Offence	5.10	0.1 - 24.0	(6.10)
3rd to 4th Offence	3.15	0.0 - 18.0	(4.03)
3rd to 5th Offence	5.01	0.1 - 27.0	(5.53)
4th to 5th Offence	3.72	0.0 - 27.0	(5.24)
Totals:	**3.67**	**0.0 - 27.0**	**(1.18)**

However, journeys from home to offend (mean distance 3.54 km) are in general shorter than the distances between offence sites (mean distance 4.11 km - see table 3.1). What this suggests is that the first five offences tend to be spread out around the home location producing rather longer offence to offence distance in relation to distances travelled from home to offend. It may be that these burglars are attempting to put some distance between their offences.

This interpretation is supported by the fact that there is little variation in the mean distances travelled between home and the first five offences. Home to first offence distances are slightly shorter than the other home to offence distances which vary over a range of 0.8 km. This indicates that the second, third, fourth and fifth offences in a series are being committed at roughly the same distance from home, with the offence to offence distances suggesting that they are at regular intervals around home.

The Model

A model of the developing offence pattern emerges. Between the commission of his first and fifth offence, the burglar explores a self-defined offence area. He travels similar distances from his home base each time he offends, but appears to set off in different directions, thereby putting the maximum possible distance between his offence locations. This is no doubt a dramatic generalisation of a process that must be subject to all sorts of distorting influences, the location of opportunities for burglary being one such; however, it is consistent with the circular model observed earlier, and explains how a burglar might create such an offence pattern.

The process of creating this circular offence pattern with home at the centre is illustrated vividly by the output of a smallest space analysis of the offence to offence and home to offence distances for the first five offences. In this instance, the analysis was based on dissimilarity data, working with the actual distances travelled rather than a correlation matrix. Figure 3.2 shows the plot.

The location of points on the plot look precisely as they would had they been produced by the process of exploration that has been described. Home is at the centre of the plot, with the offence locations arranged around it. The first offence is committed nearest to home, with the second at a greater distance and in the opposite direction from home. The third offence is again committed at a similar distance from home as the second and is in the opposite direction to the second offence. By the fourth offence, it might be supposed that he is becoming more confident of going undetected, and offends closer to home. For the fifth offence in the series, he travels in the remaining, unexplored direction and offends at a similar distance from home as he did in the second and third offences. By the time he has committed five burglaries, the offender has ringed his home with his offences.

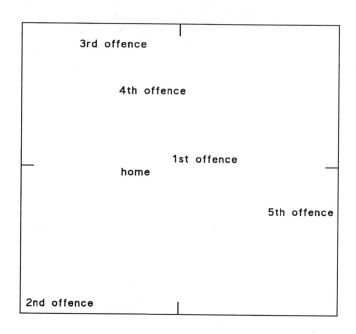

Figure 3.2: **Showing the SSA Plot based on Mean Distances between Home and the First Five Offences in each Series, and between these Offences**

The Implications

The data demonstrate the validity of the circle hypothesis in accounting for individual patterns of burglary. Offenders tend to live within their offence areas, often close to the centre of the area, and they travel relatively short distances from their homes to offend. Assuming a circular offence pattern with offences evenly spread around the home location is a useful starting point. Most significantly, the pattern and scale of further offences is clear from the positions of the first five offences in many cases. Given the small sample size in this study, the clarity of results is remarkable.

Applying the psychological concept of home range to patterns of burglary or, as Canter and Larkin (1993) have it, assuming that a burglar's criminal behaviour is as 'domocentric' as his non-criminal behaviour, is the key to understanding these patterns and possibly predicting the locations of further offences. The influence of home as a geographical location and as psychological entity is unsurprising. Since the majority of an individual's journeys are likely to begin and end at the place he is resident, this place - his home - will be central to his understanding of the area. His journeys to and from home will bring him into contact with opportunities for offending, and are bound to inform his choice of offence venue. His sense of security at being on home ground must also make a contribution. Though the literature on offenders' selection of their targets makes no explicit reference to the role of home, it is clear that familiarity with an area biases decisions towards these areas (Cornish and Clarke, 1986).

Mapping the first five offences from each series revealed that these first five were indicative of the locations and distances from home of subsequent offences. This period early on in the series is obviously significant. To find out why this is the case would probably require closer study of offenders' motives. However, the pattern of offences illustrated in figure 3.2 does allow some speculation. The development of the offence pattern can be explained in terms of the offender's changing mental representation of the area. The first offence is committed relatively close to home. He is not venturing far and has the security of knowing he can get home quickly. When he commits the second offence, he has the first offence to take into account, and consciously or unconsciously elects to travel in the opposite direction to, and a relatively large distance from, the site of his first offence. He may be trying to disassociate himself psychologically as well as physically from the first offence. As he commits his burglaries, the burglar's mental 'map' has to accommodate the new meanings that the burgled sites now have. With the commission of each new offence, there is a new feature to be drawn in. The third offence is then committed at a distance from both the first and second offences and is again at some distance from home. His confidence in himself as a burglar and his growing familiarity with area and the opportunities it provides for burglary might explain why he returns closer to home to commit his fourth offence. The fifth offence site is on the other side of the circular offence area and may represent later offences in the series in as far as the offender is moving away from the home location. This account of the offender's reasoning is purely speculative, but what is certain is that the offence pattern betrays 'a more than random association between environmental image and behaviour' (Carter and Hill, 1980).

Since carrying out this study, other work has been done in modelling offence patterns. Notably, Canter and Larkin (1993) report the application of two models to patterns of rape. Working with 45 rapists, they found that the majority were committing offences close to their homes and were producing offence patterns consistent with a 'marauder hypothesis'. The marauder hypothesis is a relative of the simple circle hypothesis, and proposes that offenders operate from a home base and commit offences within their home range. However, the offence patterns did not pass the test of circularity, termed the 'range hypothesis', wherein it is proposed that were the offence area a circle then the distances between offences would correlate directly with the distance those offences are from home. Rapists' homes were not found to be in the centre of their offence areas. The researchers suggest that what they may have been looking at the series early in their development, where offenders had not yet explored the whole area around the home, and propose further work to test the effect of criminal experience on the shape of the offence pattern.

Canter and Larkin end their paper by reporting that research on refining models of offender spatial behaviour has been successful in improving their ability to predict the offender's home location, and that they have been able to contribute valuable information to police investigations as a consequence. The results of the study reported in this chapter suggest that they might be equally successful in applying the model to burglary investigations.

References

Baker, D. and Donnelly, P.G. (1986), 'Neighbourhood Criminals and Outsiders in Two Communities: Indications that Criminal Localism Varies', *Sociology and Social Research*, **71**, 59-65.

Brantingham, P.J. and Brantingham, P.L. (eds) (1981), *Environmental Criminology*, London: Sage.

Buttimer, A. and Seamon, D. (eds) (1980), *The Human Experience of Space and Place*, New, York: St. Martins Press.

Canter, D.V. (1984), 'Putting Situations in their Place: Foundations for a Bridge between Social and Environmental Psychology' in A. Furnham (ed.), *Social Behaviour in Context*, Allyn and Bacon.

Canter, D.V. and Larkin, P. (1993), 'The Environmental Range of Serial Rapists', *Journal of Environmental Psychology*, **13**, 63-69.

Carter, R.L. and Hill, K.Q. (1980), 'Area Images and Behaviour: An Alternative Perspective for understanding Urban Crime', in D.E. Georges-Abeyie and K.D. Harris (eds), *Crime: a Spatial Perspective*, New York: Columbia University Press.

Constanzo, C.M., Halperin, W.C. and Gale, N. (1986), 'Spatial Patterns in Criminal Behaviour' in R.M. Figlio, S.M. Hakim and G. Rengert (eds), *Metropolitan Crime Patterns*, Willow Tree Press.

Cornish, D.B. and Clarke, R.V.G. (1986), *The Reasoning Criminal: Rational Choice Perspectives on Offending*, New York: Springer-Verlag.

Philips, P. (1980), 'Characteristics and Typology of the Journey to Crime', in D.E. Georges-Abeyie and K.D. Harris (eds), *Crime: A Spatial Perspective*, New York: Columbia University Press.

Pyle, G.F. et al. (1974), 'The Spatial Dynamics of Crime', *Department of Geography Research Monograph*, **159**, Chicago: University of Chicago.

Rengert, G. and Wasilchick, J. (1985), *Suburban Burglary: a Time and a Place for Everything*, Springfield, Il.: C.C. Thomas Publishing.

Repetto, T.A. (1974), *Residential Crime*, Cambridge, MA.: Ballinger.

Shaw, C.R. and McKay, H.D. (1969), *Juvenile Delinquency and Urban Areas*, Chicago: Chicago University Press.

White, R.C. (1932), 'The Relation of Felonies to Environmental Factors in Indianapolis', *Social Forces*, **10**, 439-467.

4   Bandits, Cowboys and Robin's Men: The Facets of Armed Robbery

LAURENCE ALISON, WARREN ROCKETT, STEVEN DEPREZ
AND STEVEN WATTS

This chapter identifies variations in robbery behaviour as a function of narrative role. We argue that this is related to the degree of impulsivity and planning as manifest in the crime scene behaviours. 144 British robberies were pooled from two pilot study data sets. Three dominant roles were identified. These reflect the qualities of planned/non impulsive professionalism, planned/impulsive terrorism and unplanned/impulsive aggression. The fourth possible category of unplanned/non impulsive did not exist illustrating that non-impulsive behaviour can only occur if the robbery is planned - i.e. planning is a necessary condition for reducing impulsivity. We then consider that planning and impulsivity are related to a labelling system adopted within a framework well known within criminal circles. We outline the behavioural structure of these roles and the importance of their symbolic meaning to the robbers themselves. We conclude that the narrative structure of these roles is directly reflected in the degree of planning and the ability to remain calm and rational during the offence.

Laurence Alison is currently employed as a lecturer at the Centre for Investigative Psychology at the University of Liverpool. Dr Alison is developing models to explain the processes of manipulation, influence and deception that are features of criminal investigations. His research interests focus upon developing rhetorical perspectives in relation to the investigative process and he has presented many lectures both nationally

Offender Profiling Series: IV - Profiling Property Crimes
Edited by D. Canter and L. Alison. © 2000 Ashgate Publishing, Aldershot. pp 75-106

and internationally to a range of academics and police officers on the problems associated with offender profiling. He is affiliated with The Psychologists at Law Group - a forensic service specialising in providing advice to the courts, legal professions, police service, charities and public bodies.

Steven Deprez has been a research assistant for the Centre for Investigative Psychology, at the University of Liverpool. He has recently completed a BSc in Psychology at University of Surrey.

Warren Rockett has been a Surrey Police Officer for 24 years. During that time he worked as a uniform 'bobby', as a divisional detective, and at Headquarters. In 1987, he pioneered the use of screens to protect child witnesses at court following a sexual abuse investigation. As a Detective Sergeant with the Drug Squad, he was the second in command of an investigation that uncovered Europe's first Cocaine Factory. In 1993 he was awarded a MSc in Investigative Psychology at the University of Surrey. His dissertation was titled, 'Understanding the Variations between Robbers: The First Stage in a Behavioural Approach to Robbery Investigation'. This was a unique piece of research not previously undertaken. Currently he is a Detective Chief Inspector with responsibility for specialist crime operations. He leads murders and other serious crime investigations, and has 12 Commendations for outstanding police work to his credit.

Steven Watts is a Police Officer with 22 years of service in the Hampshire Constabulary in Southern England. The vast majority of his service has been within the Criminal Investigation Department, during which time he has been an operational Detective, except for a period of one year when he studied for and achieved the Masters Degree in Investigative Psychology. Steve is currently a Detective Superintendent, Crime Co-Ordinator, and responsible for major crime investigation in the east of Hampshire including the area surrounding Portsmouth and for the Isle of Wight.

4 Bandits, Cowboys and Robin's Men: The Facets of Armed Robbery

LAURENCE ALISON, WARREN ROCKETT, STEVEN DEPREZ AND STEVEN WATTS

An Argument for Narrative Roles

Armed robbery is a serious criminal offence. There is a psychological significance in the use of a firearm by the offender and a pragmatic imperative to facilitate the investigation of the crime. In England and Wales, a person is guilty of robbery if he/she 'Steals property belonging to another and immediately before or at the time of doing so, and in order to do so, uses force or puts or seeks to put another in fear of then and there being subjected to force' (Theft Act 1968).

Hitherto, studies of armed robbery have restricted themselves to a rehearsal of descriptive statistics (McClintock and Gibson, 1961; Gabor et al., 1987). Whilst these studies examine the investigation of the offence, they are little more than reviews designed to search for best practice (Banton, 1985), or to reinforce the predominantly experiential and heuristic approach to criminal investigation. Though this has provided information that has some utility in preventive terms, a number of studies have concentrated upon the prevention of robbery in terms of target hardening strategies, or strategies aimed at minimising risk to victims. There has been a limited number of typologies of robbers reported in the literature, (Conklin, 1972; Walsh, 1986; Gabor et al., 1987). Most studies simply outline the degree of skill employed in the offence, but rarely note any psychological reason for this variation or outline what the variation is a function of. For example Walsh's (1986) typology classed robbers as either 'planners' or 'opportunists'. Whilst a useful starting point, as Letkemann (1973) points out robbery involves skilful management of a highly charged social situation, requiring social skills and self confidence. Thus, whilst skill has constantly been a consideration there are few empirical studies on the second related component - i.e. social skills and self-confidence.

This chapter argues that the central aspect of the offence is the consideration that robbers have strong and relatively consistent self-adopted roles or narrative self-images that are part of their everyday functioning. These may become especially relevant within the context of the offence. We argue that the behavioural expression of these roles is manifest in two essential and related features of the offence - namely the degree of planning (proactive-reactive) and the level of impulsivity (impulsive-rational).

Narrative Studies

In contrast to the broad based descriptive studies; in a development of narrative theory as it applies to criminal offenders, Canter (1994) saw the work of McAdams (1988) and others as fruitful in providing an explanation of the storylines by which offenders enact their lives and in particular in the narrative that they bring to an offence. Further, the narrative approach suggests a rationale for a consistency between behaviour of the offender during a crime and the way the offender may behave in other areas of his/her life. That is, an individual with a strong 'power' theme, described by McAdams (1988) as a recurrent disposition for experiences of strength and impact in relation to others, running through his/her narrative, may behave in a way during the crime which reflects that theme in the storyline. The hypothesis postulates that he/she will continue to display behaviour that is consistent with that narrative in the way he/she deals with others in everyday life.

Whilst several authors have pointed to the existence of distinct robbers' narratives, particularly in the work of Conklin (1972), Walsh (1986) and Feeney (1986), none involve any empirical analysis of they ways in which these roles are reflected during offence behaviour. Moreover, they fail to examine the extent to which variations in behaviour may be reflective of variations on the robber storyline. Instead the majority of the work is somewhat anecdotal and discursive. Katz (1988), for example in his thought provoking text on the 'Seductions of Crime' sees the career robber as a 'predator' for whom the thrill of confrontation with the victim is an important motivation for the crime. He describes the career robber as one who finds it important to maintain a self-image that conveys success and conspicuous consumption whilst projecting an illicit, dangerous impression to others. Similarly, Toch (1992) found that armed robbers took pride in their status particularly within their criminal sub-culture. Thus, whilst these impressions of the armed robber as having a very particular self image abound, there has been no systematic research of either (i) how such self images are manifest in the offence or, (ii) whether there are variations within the robbery narrative.

Despite this it seems sensible to suggest that one of the initial reasons for committing robbery is monetary gain, and that there are certain behaviours that can be performed to increase the likelihood of this gain, such as planning the robbery. However, as suggested, different styles of robbery or robber may or may not elicit these behaviours.

This chapter is designed to marry the benefits of the empirical hard line descriptive evaluations and the enriched discussion of the theorists' approaches to the constructed roles that robbers enact. We examine the narrative accounts of convicted robbers and argue that roles are manifest in the level of planning and impulsivity during the commission of the offence and that these features are borne of the type of self-image that robbers possess. In essence then an individual who promotes and lives by the image of cool professionalism should plan meticulously and remain calm under stress; an individual with a less coherent, more aggressive self-image in contrast should display less planning and be less concerned with maintaining a rational approach. Finally individuals with an aggressive self image but who are also concerned with professionalism - whilst potentially volatile should be concerned with planning - i.e. their aggression and terror tactics are designed for effective control. We are therefore concerned with two potentially related features that may relate to the expression of these images. The capacity to plan (proactive vs. reactive behaviour) and the capacity to maintain self-control (rational vs. impulsive).

Proactive and Reactive Behaviour

The general psychological definitions for proactivity and reactivity are as follows:

- *Proactive* - descriptive of any event, stimulus, or process that has an effect upon events, stimuli, or processes that occur subsequently.

- *Reactive* - characterises an action that is equal to a reaction; not internally motivated but due to a response to another's actions or a particular stimulus.

(from Penguin Psychological Dictionary)

In general terms, reactive behaviours are those that are shaped by events while proactive ones impact upon the environment.

Walsh (1986) is more explicit in his relationship of proactive and reactive behaviours:

- *Planned.* Involves victims with large amounts of non-personal money; terror used in place of violence unless violence is necessary for commission; characteristics of the individuals are ruthless, tough, isolated outside small circle; strong commitment to culture of theft and robbery; violence is avoided and weapon is instrumental.

- *Opportunist.* Desperate and chaotic lifestyle; often a precipitating factor (alcohol, drug taking, fear of capture); disorganised, engage in little or no planning; rapidly process decision to act when situation presents itself.

These studies and their relevance to underlying themes of proactive and reactive behaviours may be examined against a body of literature that lends support to four distinct themes in other areas of research. These are briefly discussed below.

Seeking Opportunity vs. Available Opportunity

Petersilia (1977) composed two profiles of a criminal career termed: *intensive* and *intermittent*. Intensives pursue criminal activity with considerably more persistence and skill and commit more offences whilst intermittent offenders are represented by occasional periods of criminal activity; offences are seen as less sophisticated and somewhat mindless.

The intensive offender seeks out opportunities to offend, may scout potential targets, and may travel further for the specific purpose of offending. The intermittent offender can be viewed as someone who reacts to available opportunities as they come across them in their own environment.

Situational Control vs. Lack of Situational Control

Einstadter (1969) determined that robberies fail if partnership co-ordination is poor, the victim is not surprised and the scene is not completely dominated. The extent to which these elements are present can be interpreted as the offender's management of the situation. A proactive robber will act to contain the situation and will neutralise developing problems. A reactive robber is more likely to respond to unexpected situations by losing focus of the goal and responding with violence or abandoning the attempt.

Random Risk-taking vs. Intentional Risk-taking

Risk-taking is most commonly examined as a personal predisposition to engage in dangerous behaviours. It is rarely differentiated into two separate categories. However, because this paper is examining it as a behavioural approach, it is possible to distinguish two types - intentional and random. Intentional risk-taking; risk behaviour is engaged in only after the weighing up of the odds carefully beforehand, and the individual has consciously decided that the risk is worth taking. Random risk-taking involves impulsive risk-taking, acting without thought of the risk. McGuire and Priestly (1985) put forth this distinction in the form of two different behavioural patterns. Firstly, individuals could be said to be impulsive, tend to act utterly, or almost utterly, without thinking, and plunge themselves into difficulties as a result. In contrast others take risks because they want to. Though perfectly aware of the chances involved they are seduced by the uncertainty itself and find any temptation to gamble more or less irresistible.

Another way to conceptualise this variation is to see the random risk-taker as someone who engages in risky behaviour because they simply are not aware of the risk and don't engage in any assessment of it before they act. The intentional risk-taker engages in only those risks that he has evaluated to be worth his desired outcome. This category is also a clear representation of the behavioural form the different thinking patterns applied in this study - i.e. the rational/impulsive decision-making processes can take.

In sum, typical characteristics of more proactive offence behaviour is manifest in:

- seeking opportunities/preparedness;
- being in control of situations;
- taking weighed risks to achieve goals.

Whilst more reactive behaviour is manifest by:

- responding to available opportunities;
- displaying a lack of control over life situations;
- taking risks without considering their consequences.

Impulsivity and Rationality

Clearly related to the proactive-reactive qualities of offence behaviour is the extent to which individuals are impulsive or rational during the offence. In other words whilst proactivity-reactivity is related to the extent of planning prior to the offence, the degree of impulsivity relates directly to reactions to events during the offence. It is possible that these features may overlap. Theoretically if an individual has predicted likely external events and planned for them the actions in response to those events have a certain sense of predictability and therefore less immediacy. However, impulsivity could still arise as a volatile over-reaction to events whether predicted or not. Let us clarify some of these issues in relation to the rational impulsive qualities. In relation to this concept the following definitions apply:

Rationality: decision-making process displaying awareness of best interests and working toward achieving goals.

Impulsivity: decision-making process displaying chaotic thinking and a lack of focus and direction.

These qualities relate to thought processes in response to stimuli. There is empirical support for differentiating offenders on the basis of their general thought patterns.   In 1984, Yochelson and Samenow conducted a study which distinguished 'hard-core' criminals from 'non-core' criminals in terms of thinking patterns, including emotions and attitudes as well as styles of information processing.   'Hard-core' criminals engaged in more systematic decision-making and displayed less emotion during their offences.   'Non-core' criminals displayed more chaotic thinking patterns and responded more emotionally during the offence.   The current study focuses on this sort of distinction along decision-making processes. Further, McGuire and Priestley (1985) identify five interpersonal cognitive problem-solving skills that influence behaviour.

Problem Awareness and Social Cause/Effect Thinking

Failure to develop social skills has long been viewed as a factor in criminal development (Eysenck, 1969; Walsh, 1986).   Kaplan states (1980, cf. Blackburn, 1993), 'Self-esteem derives from competence and confidence in achievements, and acceptance in social relationships. Failures in these areas lead to self-derogation which motivates alternatives to conventional behaviour'.   Blackburn (1993) indicates the potential for variations within the criminal population along a scale of self-regulation.

Failure of socialisation reflects a failure to develop self-controlling responses (eg. delinquents need for immediate gratification found in study by Mischel, Shoda and Rodriguez, 1989).   Delinquency and psychopathy are thus seen in terms of a deficient self-regulatory system, which facilitates susceptibility to deviant influences and the emergence of antisocial responses, but which is under the control of selective discriminative stimuli.

Blackburn (1993)

This implies that individuals who lack social skills also lack self-control, and the control they do exercise is limited by what they choose to attend to in their environment. Spivak, Platt and Shure (1976) propose that impersonal problem solving is dependent on IQ, but interpersonal problem solving is more a function of acquired skills. Therefore, socialisation is learned behaviour and can be limited by the range of experiences an individual is exposed to during development. In 1973, Chandler performed an experiment with delinquents and non-delinquents and found that the delinquents were significantly more egocentric in a test used to measure their ability to see situations from a perspective other than their own.

This egocentrism leads to a lack of awareness about the effect one's actions have on others and difficulty interacting in a social environment. In terms of criminal decision-making, a lack of these skills will be displayed by decisions, which show a failure to consider the victim's reaction during planning.

Alternative Thinking

Problem-solving is a cognitive-behavioural process which:

- makes available response alternatives for dealing with problem situations, such as interpersonal conflict or loss of reinforcers;

- increases the probability of selecting the most effective response from those alternatives (D'Zurilla/Goldfried, 1971).

This definition of problem solving assumes that the cognitive process of decision-making will be relatively complex and will generate a range of possible behaviours. However, the size of this range is more likely to vary within individuals at different levels of complexity.

Kagen (1965) recognises this range in decision-making complexity. Impulsiveness - tendency to initiate a reasoning sequence suggested by the first hypothesis that occurs; 'Reflexivity - tendency to reflect over the adequacy of a several solution hypothesis and to consider the quality of an about to be reported answer'.

Under these definitions, impulsive behaviour can be viewed as haphazard, whilst reflexive decision-making would tend to be more analytic. The role of others in an individual's decision-making process is covered under the next variable - problem awareness and social cause/effect thinking.

- *Means-End Thinking:* Means-end thinking refers to one's ability to determine the necessary steps towards reaching a goal - systematic decision-making aimed at a certain purpose. Baron (1985) equates 'thinking with a search to remove doubt'. This search process moves in stages from:

- *Possibilities - various resolutions to doubt* (This stage relates back to the first variable, *alternative thinking* - regarding the generation of possible solutions).

- *Goals* - criteria used to evaluate the possible solutions generated.

- *Evidence* - any object which helps to determine the extent to which it is possible to achieve a goal.

The last two stages relate to the offender's cognitive ability to systematically decide on the best course of action in his behavioural repertoire. Under this conceptual framework, rational decision-making will help fulfil goals by selecting the best possibilities generated. Impulsive decisions will arise when there is an insufficient search for possibilities and the goal is very unfocused. Rather than systematic, this is haphazard decision-making.

- *Consequential Thinking:* Consequential thinking involves the ability to anticipate the consequences of one's actions or to have foresight. Mischel (1984, cf. Blackburn, 1993) found that consistent delay of gratification 'Is associated with sustained attention, higher intelligence and cognitive development, and resistance to temptation; preference for immediate reward is related to a present-oriented focus, lower socio-economic status and membership in groups in which achievement needs are low'. One may reasonably hypothesise that impulsive offenders have short-term or immediate goals that are unclearly formed and evolve in a limited cognitive fashion. Offences will not be committed for any long-term goal such as financial stability but are more likely to occur in the context of obtaining money for drugs or some other short-term reason.

In sum the research has shown that more rational offenders:

- generate several possible courses of action for a problem;
- display interpersonal awareness and social skills;
- form steps towards achieving clear goals;
- show foresight concerning the consequences of their actions.

And that more impulsive offenders:

- generate a limited range of behavioural options for any problem;
- are involved in dysfunctional relationships and will display a lack of social skills;
- have short-term goals and a disorganised idea of how to achieve them;
- fail to consider the consequences of their actions.

Having discussed the literature that relates to these two themes and the indication that there may be some differences that may manifest themselves within the offence we postulate that three robber typologies will become apparent from the data obtained.

Robin's Men

> *It was business. No buzz at all. I suppose all the money might be a buzz, buying your wife a ring, some shoes. But if I want to get a buzz, I'd rather have my son sat on my lap and watch a video. We just did it for the money.*
>
> fr. Alison and Maruna (1997)

The term Robin's Men is derived from the legend of Robin Hood and was a term known within the criminal fraternity. It refers to 'professional thieves eg. bank robbers' (obs. 1890 gen. use Crime Book Archives). Katz (1988) notes a similar type of robber in his research, called the 'hardman', these robbers display an adopted self image, that may be based on media interpretations of the typical armed robber, the cool, calm and collected individual. Robin's Men are often career criminals, inducted into crime at an early age and progressing from petty theft through to robbery. The typical Robin's Man is able to react to situations that may arise within the offence, they meticulously plan their crime, possibly acting in groups with roles defined for each member. In terms of the evidence above, Robin's Men can be seen as rational proactive robbers.

In sum this region is associated with behavioural indices of consideration of how to perform the act in advance in some detail and the ability to deal with contingencies that arise during the course of the offence. Of course to some extent the degree of planning must afford better opportunities to predict in advance possible outcomes thus limiting the need for unpredictable response to those conditions. This theme and its associated role structure is heavily influenced by attitudes of the desire to be professional, to learn the trade and form experience, and not to fall prey to merely image related gratuitous violence to establish dominion over victims.

Bandits

Now we used to go to work with a nail gun. With a nail gun if you run up and put it on the window and fire it, it fires a nail straight through the glass which gives you a hole which is big enough to get the barrel of a gun in and then you just tell them to open up. Obviously you don't shoot them to kill 'em - its one in the leg or something and they'll open up.

fr. Alison and Maruna (1997)

The term 'Bandit' refers to outlaws or individuals that terrorise victims (underworld use - Criminal Book Archives). The theme is dominated by behaviours that display a degree of planning and yet tactics that are extremely aggressive. Whilst bandits will show an element of preplanning, they will rarely consider events that may unfold during the offence; this may lead to outbursts of extreme violence as they realise they are no longer in control of the situation they have created and try to regain it.

The role manifests itself in behaviours that display a degree of proactive behaviour - there is little room for reactions from any witnesses and clearly the tactics are 'designed' for a reason. However, the gross acts of violence may come as a result of this planning strategy and in fact may lead the robber - in his heightened state - to performing more impulsive and gratuitously violent behaviour. Thus in this case the strategy may in part be designed to satisfy the need for a 'buzz' or 'hit'. In other words though the behaviour is planned it may in part be planned in order for spontaneity to occur - that is partly the legitimisation for more impulsive acts.

Cowboys

I've been drinking more and more and taking more and more drugs and so at this point I am getting very unstable. I then just had this idea of robbing this prostitute - I had sex with her and kidnapped her and stole £30 off her ... I just cracked under pressure.

fr. Alison and Maruna *(1997)*

A 'Cowboy job' is considered by other robbers as discriminating the 'professionals' from the 'losers' - it refers to a 'robbery committed recklessly or by beginners' where individuals 'needlessly brandish weapons and attack their victims' (Crime Book Archives). As stated the cowboy robber is often in contrast to the professional Robin's Man, many commit their robbery to fund a drug habit.

Rather than having a strong view of the self this region may be associated with those who are living from day to day with no clear self identity, ability to act proactively or maintain a degree of control over their behaviour. Therefore at the most extreme end of the scale such individuals may actually be acting on 'remote' simply to obtain money for drugs. Alternatively they may be so intoxicated that their actions become volatile, somewhat random and dictated seemingly chaotically by the situation that the robber finds himself in.

The region is clearly more indicative of more reactive behaviours and a higher degree of impulsivity.

Table 4.1: Offence Variables

No.	Variable
1	Confidence Approach
2	Surprise Attack
3	Blitz Attack
4	Enters Private Area, Control
5	Enters Private Area, Later
6	Weapon Indicated
7	Weapon, Other
8	Weapon, Firearm
9	Spontaneous Verbal Threat
10	Responsive Verbal Threat
11	Hostage Taken
12	Response Violence
13	Gratuitous Violence
14	Resistance, Undeterred
15	Resistance, Deterred
16	Precautions
17	Floor
18	Victim Security
19	Demeaning Language
20	Reassuring Language
21	Apologetic Language
22	Made Disguise
23	Improvised Disguise
24	Non-Personal Property Taken
25	Personal Property Taken
26	Victim Participation
27	Implied Knowledge
28	Target, Dwelling
29	Target, Financial
30	Target, Business
32	Verbal Instructions
33	No Disguise
34	Offender(s)

Descriptive Details

Before moving on to an examination of the relationships between the variables, it is instructive to explore other features of the data set.

Time of robbery. The findings from this data set concurred with a previous British study (McClintock and Gibson, 1961) and a United States of America study (Block, 1986), in identifying that robbery is primarily an after dark event (over 70%). Darkness perhaps providing a certain degree of physical and psychological cover for criminal activity. This particular study also showed that robbery was more likely to occur at weekends (80%), which was not the case in the two aforementioned studies.

Locations. Moreover, in this sample the robberies tended to occur in one of three locations, dwelling houses (5%), financial premises (20%), or other business premises (47%).

Type of gain for the robber. At those locations victims are attacked for either:

- *personal property*: bicycles, handbags, watches, wallets: primarily these attacks tend to occur in public places, or for

- *non-personal property*: moneys and goods connected to a business: perhaps not surprisingly these occur most frequently inside commercial type establishments.

Lone victims were at greatest risk of attack for personal property, whereas groups of people were more likely targets for non-personal property.

Robber Tactics. If the management of the victim(s) and the scene is important to the successful outcome of a robbery, then psychological domination of the victim(s) by creating terror and control, rather than physical assault or contact, may be indicative of the more professional intelligent approach. Lethal weapons, such as firearms, have been considered as terror weapons that help robbers psychologically dominate crime scenes (Conklin 1972); with robbers viewing them in instrumental terms. Such weapons provide them with the ability to control groups of people, employees and bystanders, and tackle harder and more lucrative targets with less chance of resistance, such that property is more readily given up.

It appears that firearms are a feature of robbery, with 67% of robbers carrying guns of some description. Targets such as financial institutions, appear to require quick effective control to be established, which perhaps can best be maintained by terror caused by the presence of lethal weapons.

Skogan (1978) commented, for example, that attacking multi-person premises, such as businesses, with a firearm, required a degree of skill and confidence by robbers if dominance and control were to be maintained.

This data set revealed that firearms are strongly related to stealing non-personal property, the type of property found in such institutions, and at businesses. Few robbers engaged in stealing this type of property without some form of weapon, for business premises firearms were used in 85% of cases, and financial institutions 79%. The use of firearms in robbing a dwelling is considerably lower, 14%. With the firearm acting as a buffer zone between the robbers and victims, and the use of instructional language, victims were more likely to assist firearm carrying robbers (71%) by passing property being stolen to them rather than risk the perceived consequences of non-co-operation. This is effective robber, crime scene management in action. Homans (1974) viewed such behaviour as robbers and victims working together to maximise benefits and minimise the potentially lethal costs of the crime, particularly in cases where the victims had no strong personal attachment to the property concerned.

We should however emphasise that the employment of firearms does not mean decreased potential for lethal actions. In fact it could be that more minor refusals may result in considerably more damage where the robber has the threat of such weapons. For example, Toch (1992) suggested there are two general categories of interpersonal violence 'self preserving strategies' and 'approaches that dehumanise others'. Should a robber's demands be refused, that robber may be in a 'put up or shut up' situation, such that to remove the pressure and maintain credibility the robber may need to resort to aggression. If this is the case in a firearm situation obviously the robber has far greater potential for inflicting severe and potentially lethal damage.

Resistance and Violence. Where attempts to steal personal property occur, the robber is often met with resistance (52%). Resistance can take many forms, including verbal refusal, shouting out for help, pressing alarm buttons or fighting back. Most frequently resistance comes from victims attacked in public place, such as street muggings. This is supported by Karman (1984) who found that resistance was less likely in robberies at businesses than against individuals.

Disguise. Certain fictional and historical accounts might lead many to believe that wearing a disguise in the commission of the offence was the norm. For example Charlie Peace in the 1870's wore numerous disguises, including wigs and make-up in his career as a burglary robber (Ward, 1989). In more recent times, books, films and articles have been made about robber gangs most of whom are depicted in balaclavas, crash helmets or other disguises. More recently there have even been photographs in National newspapers of masked robbers. For example 'The Daily Express' showed a member of the George Davies gang both masked and carrying a sawn-off shotgun in the moments immediately before attempting a robbery on a security vehicle (Kelland 1987). However within this dataset, nearly half (46%) wore no disguise, whilst a third (32%) wore an improvised disguise, such as glasses, hats or a wig, whilst only 20% chose to wear a made disguise such as a balaclava. It has been suggested that mask and balaclava wearing is a crime tool that adversely effects control by diminishing the persona of the wearer, together with limiting vision and hearing (Walsh, 1986). However, examination of this sample does not support that view, but rather shows that disguise wearing is a control tool like the firearm. Indeed there is a strong relationship between wearing a made disguise and carrying a firearm. In addition disguises conceal and alter identity, helping to prevent later identification. In 21% of the cases some form of overt security was present, 73% of robbers wore some disguise when robbing such locations. In only seven of the disguise cases did the robbers use physical violence. In fact disguised robbers seemed to use tactics that effected better control over their victims' movements. In 87% of cases where the victims were secured in some way, then the robbers wore some form of disguise.

Language. In 30% of the cases robbers conducted their crimes without making any verbal demand for goods from their victims. This might perhaps have been an expected finding for public place personal property robbery where force rather than verbal skills would arguably be more in demand. Yet interestingly verbal demands were reported as absent in almost as many personal property cases. It seems in the latter there was an implicit understanding by the victims of what the robbers were seeking.

Instructional language was associated with control, being used by robbers in almost half the cases. It was also present where victims assisted robbers (70%).

In sum, robbers who know their business carry firearms, give clear instructional demands, and some may, depending upon their targets, wear disguises. It is the joint action of control and management capabilities delivered by psychological domination tactics that are the successful keys to robbery.

Results

Having constructed the new data set the 144 robberies were subject to a Smallest Space Analysis or SSA (Lingoes 1973 - see introduction). The SSA can be divided into a three-way classification. The output of this geometric representation is outlined in figure 4.1 below. In addition to describing the three regions, examples of robbers who fit each of the classifications will be given from the interviews carried out by the University of Liverpool. Apart from these three classifications of robbers there is also some evidence of a modulating temporal facet inherent in the SSA, expanding concentrically out from the core variables. However there are several instances where this temporal facet appears to falter and so it is not included in the final analysis.

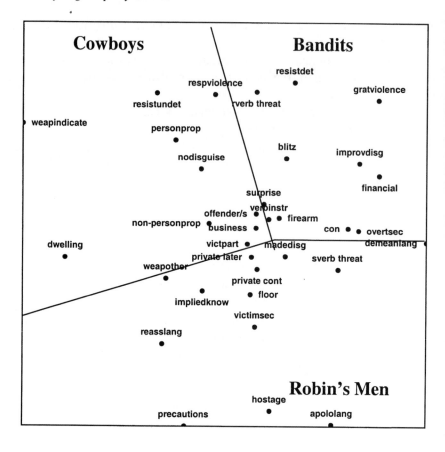

Figure 4.1: SSA of 144 British Armed Robbers Illustrating Three-way Classification System

Let us now consider the implications and details of these three themes:

Robin's Men

I teamed up with this guy Carl. Carl was a professional thief. He was out there reading books and getting smart. He bought his wife a three-piece suite and was living very nice. The rest of us we'd spend it all on a piss up, while he is saving and investing.

To me the old school armed robbers were the ultimate criminals, in that they were calculated, had loads of balls and were completely two faced. You know they were lovely to your face but don't cross them. They'll sit there and compliment your wife, then stab you in the back later that night.

fr. Alison and Maruna (1997)

The behaviours in this region are a clear indicator of non-impulsive, well planned, tactical attacks on establishments with high yields. Initially there is evidence of pre-planning, the robbers are likely to use made disguises and are likely to have some knowledge of the premises they are attacking. This may on some occasion mean that they have contacts within the establishment that they are trying to rob or have been on surveillance of the building for some time. Individuals gain access to private areas of the target, and are able to manipulate staff into complying with their demands. In fact, they are able to involve staff or other witnesses in participating in the robbery - i.e. filling bags for them. Other behaviours associated with the region involve forcing witnesses to the floor and tying them up. This theme is also associated with keeping victims calm rather than agitating them or provoking anxious responses. To achieve this there is rarely any violence and reassuring language and on occasions apologies. Moreover on occasion they will take a hostage as a form of security and to maintain control, occasionally precautions are taken - such as drawing down blinds, securing doors in the event of detection and possible police interception. These behaviours under stress are indicative of (a) planning and (b) the ability to remain calm. Thus the intention appears less to terrorise staff, to indulge in violence or to provoke a reaction but rather to keep clientele and witnesses calm in order to achieve non-combative or stressful interaction. There is therefore a preoccupation with professionalism, methodical planning and coolness. In fact this latter quality was commented upon by some of the armed robbers interviewed by researchers at the University of Liverpool:

When your system is hormones and endorphins running around like riot its knowing these and being able to know how to use them .... you take a robbery - its like - um - you plan a robbery and you can sense, can know its going to come off OK .... so you see something weaker than yourself that you can actually draw off.

I've never been one of these people that goes in and starts shouting and all that sort of stuff - you know. Whenever I do a bit of work its like, 'Come on - you know the score' and I calm them right down, 'Go on fill it up' and I just sort of leave them alone - but what you don't want to do is frighten them on a bit of work cos when they're frightened they make decisions that they wouldn't normally make and get a bit nervous they drop the money.

fr. Alison and Maruna (1997)

Harry can be seen as a typical example of a Robin's Man. He gradually progressed, under the tutelage from an older more experienced criminal, from stealing cars through burglary and eventually armed robbery.

I'd almost become like a disciple and he'd led me through burglary and I suppose from like 17 it was robbery, it was try an off license the first time and eventually up to a Securicor van.

I was like initiated into armed robbery.

fr. Alison and Maruna (1997)

Despite having a philosophical outlook on life there are times when his account - especially when talking of his crimes and the money he earned - he displays signs of adopting roles, what Katz calls the 'hardman'.

I've had holidays everywhere.... and going to a dog track and spending a couple of grand and that.

fr. Alison and Maruna (1997)

He discusses doing 'a bit of work' with close associates and implies that in jobs each person was assigned a role, and that their 'cut' was related to the role they were given. Although role assignment was not a variable in this study it has been found to be associated with more planned and sophisticated crimes (Watts 1994). Again, the expected yield of these robberies is higher, as exemplified by Harry.

Eventually I was doing some quite prominent things, you know. It was like three million pound bit of work, and four and a half million pound bit of work.

fr. Alison and Maruna (1997)

Bandits

> *I mean obviously in that type of crime I mean when you're on the*
> *pavement and your - you got a gun, you're not - you're not - you*
> *haven't got the gun to wave about. It's there for a purpose.*

> *Ant was an extremely tough man. Always violent, No matter where in*
> *the country he was always violent ... Ant was always breaking*
> *peoples' jaws or cutting peoples' hands off and that sort of thing.*

fr. Alison and Maruna (1997)

The Bandit region is characterised by a much more haphazard approach to the offence than the Robin's Men. Whilst there is still some evidence of planning the robbery, such as the use of improvised disguises, the robbery is subject to the reactive side of the robbers' behaviour. Firearms and a blitz attack are used to instil fear and needless demeaning language and acts of gratuitous violence are situated within this region. These sometimes involve acts such as shooting staff or witnesses or sadistic acts, in one case hacking a security guard's leg off. Despite this rash use of violence Bandits may be likely to be deterred by resistance from victims or witnesses. This is possibly due to their lack of planning and proactive ability. Clearly, individuals displaying these behaviours seem to enjoy the violence and the adrenaline rush that is associated with such blitz attacks. Thus part of the symbolic role of the robber is as one who terrorises and commands a situation through brute force and fear.

Frank displays several characteristics concurrent with being a Bandit robber. In his interview he re-affirms this in several places, when discussing his robberies he states:

> *They weren't set to a clock or a timetable but certain things had to*
> *happen at certain times to make the robbery successful.*

Whilst Frank is obviously not the spontaneous robber characteristic of Cowboys, he is also not the meticulous planner of the Robin's Men. It becomes apparent from reading Frank's narrative that whilst his crimes are planned he is also impulsive in his decisions to rob establishments.

But as we approached the bank there was a woman going in with a child in a buggy, and I said just walk by, y'know.

This theme of impulsivity can be seen to run through his life, making snap decisions to do certain acts and can be seen to feature in his early violent episodes.

I got into armed robbery through somebody I met - I mean that's what got me into that.

It was over this bloke's dog barking at me – that's what it was all about - uhm - and I ended up I mean I freaked right out and I did and I could remember nothing about it.

fr. Alison and Maruna (1997)

During the latter incident Frank bit two of the dog owner's fingers off. Whereas many armed robbers, particularly Robin's Men, are career thieves who work their way up to armed robbery, Frank simply decided to start robbing with a friend.

Cowboys

The junkies will stick together just to get gear, but that's all. I don't give a fuck about the junkie robbers. When I was on the outside I'd give a junkie drugs and say, 'Here you go, take this it will kill you.' Good. Another dead junkie.

I was spending all my money on drink. I got done for robbery. I didn't care - I just wanted the money so I gave her a kick.

I were just a robot going back to what I know.

fr. Alison and Maruna (1997)

Whilst the Bandit region may be haphazard the Cowboy region is somewhat chaotic. Their behaviours are indeed indicative of little planning, of spontaneity and opportunistic violence and abuse of victims. Initially they do not bother to disguise themselves, and during the offence may steal personal property from victims. Any resistance from victims is met with violence or verbal threats of violence. In fact it is significant that this is the only region met with any form of resistance from the victim. Apart from carrying firearms they may also indicate they are carrying a weapon whether or not they then show it. This could indicate that they are in fact unarmed and they have robbed on impulse. Despite resistance they are unlikely to be deterred from completing the robbery. It is also significant that the target of the robbery may be a dwelling of some kind, this type of target is unlikely to yield any significant reward, again highlighting the spontaneity of the crime. If as suggested, the initial reason for committing robbery is monetary gain then the lack of planning and the spontaneous nature of the crime is perhaps indicative of the target of the robbery, in this case the presence of dwellings. The Cowboy robbery is a far cry from the 'professional' Robin's Man.

The Commonalties between Robberies

In conclusion there is some evidence that there are broadly three thematic developments in robberies. What they share in common are many of the features in the core of the plot - i.e. a surprise attack, bringing a firearm to the offence, using verbal instructions, and attack business properties. These are all actions that are indicative of the initial sequence of the offence.

Therefore a 'pure' 'Robin's Man' will display these core behaviours but then move to establishing control in a private area of the target site, secure the victims, then reassure them that they will come to no harm. They then may ensure necessary precautions, take hostages if necessary and apologise before leaving. In contrast, after the initial attack 'Bandits' will employ a blitz attack, use demeaning language, respond with verbal threats and may conclude with some act of gratuitous violence. Finally 'Cowboys' will steal non-personal and personal property, respond to resistance with violence and verbal threats and may indicate that they have a weapon.

If this is a replicable structure - i.e. that there are three broad themes that correspond to levels of planning and impulsivity as a function of self adopted roles, and that robbery may be understood as an offence that becomes increasingly discriminate across the offence. There is then potential for target-hardening strategies to be formed. For example the longer the offence continues the more the robber has to maintain control and be able to have a contingency plan for any external stimuli (including of course the actions of victims). That 'Robin's Men' see themselves as professional means that they are prepared for sequences across the offence and remain stable throughout - not responding with violence but in extreme cases even apologising before they leave, in essence they display rational, proactive behaviour. In contrast 'Bandits' may become increasingly impulsive and with increasing time may in extreme cases respond with brutish violence. Similarly 'Cowboys' may become increasingly chaotic by responding to the victim's resistance with verbal and physical violence and threatening them with a weapon, i.e. they are displaying impulsive reactive behaviour. In this way the later an action occurs the more influenced it is by the qualities of planning (or lack thereof) and self control (or lack thereof) and that to some extent the former effects the latter. In other words, the extent of planning can be used to prevent loss of control or, as in the Bandits actively encourage it, or in the case of Cowboys lead imminently to loss of self control. These, we have argued may relate to the images that robbers cast for themselves - i.e. whether they see it as a 'buzz' a 'profession' or simply a 'reaction to the state they are in'. It is clear that within groups of armed robbers these distinctions are made - it remains to be seen whether such structural relationships are maintained in other samples and whether indeed these qualities may be related to a variety of features outside of the robbery that accord with the proposed roles. For example, is an individual who sees himself as a Bandit more brash in other areas of his life - displaying his wealth and dominance in flagrant and egocentric ways? Does the 'Robin's Man' see his self image as rational and controlled and are his actions similarly controlled in non-offence behaviour? Finally does the 'Cowboy' merely see himself as a responding entity - without direction or control and is his life expressive of this chaos? Whilst these self promoted roles may come across as trite and even inappropriate given the seriousness of the offence they appear to be apparent driving forces in many robbers that have been interviewed. Supportive work for the threefold classification and for its impact on behaviour may be gleaned from focusing on this threefold classification in studies designed specifically to elicit narrative accounts. Further investigation into the classification may eventually result in a method of target hardening that reduces the risk of violence and danger within the situation.

References

Alison, L. and Maruna, S. (1997), Unpublished interviews conducted at a Maximum Security prison in the UK.

Banton, M. (1985), *Investigating Robbery*, Aldershot: Gower.

Baron, J. (1985), *Rationality and Intelligence*, Cambridge: Cambridge University Press.

Blackburn, R. (1993), *The Psychology of Criminal Conduct: Theory, Research and Practice*, Chichester: Wiley.

Block, R. (1977), *Violent Crime: Environment, Interaction and Death*, Lexington: Lexington Books.

Borg, I. and Lingoes, J. (1987), *Multidimensional Similarity Analysis*, New York: Springer-Verlag.

Canter, D.V. (1985), *Facet Theory: Approaches to Social Research*, New York: Springer-Verlag.

Canter, D.V. (1989), 'Offender Profiling', *The Psychologist*, **2**, 12-16.

Canter, D.V. (1994), Criminal Shadows: Inside the Mind of the Serial Killer, London: Harper Collins.

Canter, D.V. and Heritage, R. (1990), 'A Multivariate Model of Sexual Offence Behaviour: Developments in "Offender Profiling"', *The Journal of Forensic Psychiatry*, **1(2)**, 185-212.

Conklin, J.E. (1972), *Robbery and the Criminal Justice System*, Philadelphia: J.B. Lippincott.

Crail, M. and Patrick, A. (1994), 'Linking Serial Offenders', *Policing*, **10(3)**, 181-187.

Debaun, E. (1950), 'The Heist: The Theory and Practice of Armed Robbery', *Harpers,* **200**, 69.

Donald, I. (1985), 'The Cylindrex of Place Evaluation', in D.V. Canter (ed.), *Facet Theory: Approaches to Social Research*, New York: Springer-Verlag.

D'Zurilla, D.G. and Goldfried, J.J. (1971), 'Problem Solving and Behaviour Modification', *Journal of Abnormal Psychology*, **78**, 107-126.

Einstadter, W.J. (1969), 'The Social Organisation of Armed Robbery', *Social Problems*, **17(1)**, 64-83.

Eysenck, H.J. (1964), *Crime and Personality*, London: Routledge & Kegan Paul.

Feeney, F. (1986), 'Robbers as Decision Makers', in D.B. Cornish and R.A. Clarke (eds), *The Reasoning Criminal: Rational Choice Perspectives on Offending*, pp. 53-71, New York: Springer Verlag.

Feshbach, S. (1964), 'The Function of Aggression and the Regulation of Aggressive Drive', *Psychological Review*, **71**, 257-272.

Gabor, T., Baril, M., Cusson, M., Elie, D., LeBlanc, M. and Normandeau, A. (1987), *Armed Robbery: Cops, Robbers and Victims*, Springfield: Charles C. Thomas.

Gabor, T. and Normandeau, A. (1989), 'Armed Robbery: Highlights of a Canadian Study', *Canadian Police College Journal*, **13**, 273-282.

Gudjonsson, G. (1992), *The Psychology of Interrogations, Confessions and Testimony*, Chichester: John Wiley & Sons.

Guttman, L. (1968), 'A General Nonmetric Technique for Finding the Smallest Co-ordinated Space for a Configuration Point', *Psychometrika*, **33(3)**, 469-506.

Hammond, S. (1989), 'Multivariate Data Analysis on Psychometric Data Sets', *Psychometric Analysis Package*, University of Surrey.

Homans, G. (1974), *Social Behaviour: It's Elemental Forms*, New York: Harcourt, Brace, Jovanovich.

Kagan, J., Rosman, B.L., Day, D., Albert, J. and Phillips, W. (1964), 'Information Processing in the Child: Signature of Analytic and Reflective Attitude', *Psychological Monographs*, **78(1)**, 578.

Kaplan, H.B. (1980), *Deviant Behaviour in Defence of Self*, New York: Academic Press.

Karman, A. (1984), *Crime Victims: An Introduction to Victimology*, Monterey: Brooks Cole.

Katz, J. (1988), *The Seductions of Crime: Moral and Sensual Attractions in doing Evil*, New York: Basic Books.

Kelland, G. (1987), *Crime in London: From Postwar Soho to Present-Day 'Supergrasses'*, London: Grafton.

Korn, R.R. and McCorkle, L.W. (1959), *Criminology and Penology*, New York: Holt, Reinhart & Winston.

Letkemann, P. (1973), *Crime as Work*, Englewood Cliffs: Prentice Hall.

Levy, S. (1985), 'Lawful Roles of Facets in Social Theories', in D.V. Canter (ed.), *Facet Theory: Approaches to Social Research*, New York: Springer-Verlag.

Lingoes, J. (1973), *The Guttman-Lingoes Non-Metric Program Series*, MA Thesis: University of Michigan.

McAdams, D.P. (1988), *Power, Intimacy and the Life Story: Personalogical Inquiries into Identity*, New York: Springer.

McClintock, F.H. and Gibson, E. (1961), *Robbery in London*, London: MacMillan.

McGuire, J. and Priestley, P. (1985), *Offending Behaviour: Skills and Stratagems for going Straight*, London: Batsford Academic and Educational.

Mischel, W. (1984), 'Convergences and Challenges in the Search for Consistency', *American Psychologist*, **39**, 351-364.

Petersilia, J., Greenwood, P.W. and Lavin, M. (1977), *Criminal Careers of Habitual Felons*, Santa Monica, CA.: Rand.

Read, P.P. (1979), *The Train Robbers: Their Story*, London: W H Allen.

Reber, A.S. (1985), *Dictionary of Psychology*, London: Penguin Books.

Roebeck, J.B. (1967), *Criminal Typology*, Springfield: Thomas.

Shye, S. (1978), *Theory Construction and Data Analysis in the Behavioural Sciences*, San Francisco: Jossey Bass.

Skogan, W.G. (1977), 'Dimensions of the Dark Figure of Unreported Crime', *Crime and Delinquency*, **23**, 41-50.

Spivak, G., Platt and Shure, M. (1976), *The Problem Solving Approach to Adjustment*, San Francisco, CA.: Jossey Boss.

Theft Act (1968), *An Act of Parliament*, HMSO: London.

Toch, H. (1992), 'Violent Men: An Enquiry into the Psychology of Violence', *American Psychological Association*.

Walsh, D. (1986), *Heavy Buisness: Commercial Burglary and Robbery*, London: Routledge & Kegan Paul.

Ward, D. (1989), 'King of the Lags: The Story of Charles Peace', *Classic Crime Series*, London: Souvenir Press Ltd.

Watts, S. (1994), *Robbers and Robberies: Behavioural Consistencies in Armed Robbers, and their Interpersonal Narrative Constructs*, Unpublished MSc dissertation, University of Liverpool.

Willmer, M.A. (1970), 'The Measurement of Information in the Field of Criminal Detection', *Operational Research Society Quarterly*, December.

Yochelson, S. and Samenow, S. (1976), *The Criminal Personality. Volume 1 of Profile for Change*, New York: Jason Aronson.

Appendix

1.   *Confidence Approach*: Style of approach involves contact with the victim/s in order to give the false impression of legitimacy, by means including, a false story, asking for directions or posing as a customer.   Encoded dichotomously.

2.   *Surprise Attack*: An attack by the offender/s on the victim/s, whether preceded by a confidence approach or not. The attack is sudden, and characterised by the use of verbal threats and threats of harm, including with a weapon, verbal abuse but not physical violence. Encoded dichotomously.

3.   *Blitz Attack*: An attack that is either sudden or preceded by a confidence approach in which there is an immediate use of physical force or an assault, that permanently or temporarily incapacitates the victim. Encoded dichotomously.

4.   *Enters Private Area, Control*: The offender/s enter a private area of the premises in order to assert control over the victims, this includes entry by

confidence trick, jumping over a payment counter. Encoded dichotomously.

5. *Enters Private Area, Later*: The offender/s enter a private area having gained control, in order to search, or for any other reason. Encoded dichotomously.

6. *Weapon Indicated*: Those offender/s who are prepared to indicate or imply that they are armed, whether they later produce a weapon or not. Encoded dichotomously.

7. *Weapon, Other*: The offender/s carry weapons during the offence that are not firearms, for example, knives, baseball bat, noxious sprays etc. Encoded dichotomously.

8. *Weapon, Firearm*: The offender/s carry a weapon that can be classified as a firearm, for example, handgun, shotgun, these can be imitations or real weapons. Encoded dichotomously.

9. *Spontaneous Verbal Threat*: Any verbal threat that the offender/s use that implies harm to the victim/s to control them, and is not a response to victim resistance. Encoded dichotomously.

10. *Responsive Verbal Threat*: Any verbal threat or intimidating language that the offender/s use as a result of non-co-operation by the victim/s. Encoded dichotomously.

11. *Hostage Taken*: This variable determines those cases where the offender/s take a hostage to enforce control over the victim. This includes customers held whilst demands are made, or other persons, not directly involved with the target, such as relatives held at other locations. Encoded dichotomously.

12. *Response Violence*: The offender/s are prepared to use physical violence including use of a weapon in response to resistance or non-co-operation; or perceived resistance or non-co-operation by the victim. Encoded dichotomously.

13. *Gratuitous Violence*: An assault by the offender/s which is more than necessary to assert or maintain control over the victim. In some cases apparently for its own sake. Encoded dichotomously.

14. *Resistance, Undeterred*: Offender/s actions or intentions are not changed by victim resistance or intervention whether it is physical or verbal. Encoded dichotomously.

15. *Resistance, Deterred*: The offender/s actions or intentions change in some way due to victim resistance or intervention. Encoded dichotomously.

16. *Precautions*: The offender/s take precautions to ensure that they are not detected whilst committing the offence, eg. pulling down blinds, disconnecting phones and locking doors. Encoded dichotomously.

17. *Floor*: As a part of the offence the offender/s force the victim/s to lie or sit on the floor. Encoded dichotomously.

18. *Victim Security*: The offender/s take action to secure the victim/s or other persons present by physical means, including binding, locking them in a room. Encoded dichotomously.

19. *Verbal Instructions*: Language used by the offender/s which instruct/s the victim/s to do or not to do an act, and includes demands for goods or money. Encoded dichotomously.

20. *Demeaning Language*: Language used by the offender/s that is demeaning or insulting to the victim, this is above the general use of profanities used whilst giving instructions. Encoded dichotomously.

21. *Reassuring Language*: Those offenders who use reassuring/comforting language both spontaneously or accompanying a threat to comply with instructions. Encoded dichotomously.

22. *Apologetic Language*: Language used by the offender/s at any stage that is directed at the victim/s and is apologetic in its nature. Encoded dichotomously.

23. *Made Disguise*: An item used by the offender/s to disguise their appearance which has been made or altered specifically for that purpose, including stockings, woollen sleeves with eyeholes cut. Encoded dichotomously.

24. *Improvised Disguise*: An item used to disguise the offender/s appearance that is an everyday item, for example, glasses, hood or hat. Encoded dichotomously.

25. *No Disguise*: The offender/s make no attempt to disguise their features. Encoded dichotomously.

26. *Non-Personal Property Stolen*: The type of property stolen by the offender/s is of a non-personal nature, such as valuable securities, business cash/cheques or commercial goods. Encoded dichotomously.

27. *Personal Property Stolen*: As above but the property stolen is personal items such as jewellery, wallets, bicycles. Encoded dichotomously.

28. *Victim Participation*: The offender/s instruct the victim/s to perform a task for them such as opening safes, indicating alarms, and putting moneys into bags, or within reach of the offender. Encoded dichotomously.

29. *Implied Knowledge*: Attacks where the offender/s appear to know something about the target, whether they are a person or business. Such as personal details, or knowledge of the alarm systems. Encoded dichotomously.

30. *Target, Dwelling*: The target is an individual or property in a particular dwelling. Encoded dichotomously.

31. *Target, Financial*: The target is a premises which provides a public financial service, eg. banks, building societies. Encoded dichotomously.

32. *Target, Business*: The target is a business, whether commercial or otherwise, including supermarkets, filling stations, and industrial premises. Encoded dichotomously.

33. *Overt Security*: The target has clearly visible protection, or is well known to be protected in some way, eg. by alarms, bandit glass, security personnel. Encoded dichotomously.

34. *Offenders*: Whether the offender worked alone or in groups of 2 or more. Encoded dichotomously.

5 Criminal Weapon Use in Brazil: A Psychological Analysis

ALINE LOBATO

This study sought to find a link between the meaning of the weapon, offending behaviour, and offenders' personality characteristics. The study was based on responses to 120 questionnaires completed by offenders in three prisons in Northeast Brazil. The data was analysed using Smallest Space Analysis (SSA).

The results indicated that both offending behaviour and offenders' personality characteristics were expressed by the role the offenders assigned to the weapon they used. The weapon was an object that had meaning for the criminal and the criminal's attitude towards this object reflected aspects of their general characteristics. The findings suggest that offenders will differ in the way they interpret the meaning of their weapons. This helps to distinguish them and consequently to identify them.

The present investigation concludes that to ignore the meaning of the weapon for a criminal and the weapon's role at the scene of the crime is to ignore an important factor, which may help to access an offender's characteristics.

Aline Lobato graduated in Clinical Psychology from the State University of Paraiba, N.E. Brazil. She was appointed a lecturer in psychology at the Lutheran University of Brazil in Manaus where she was also a clinical psychologist at the Military College. She has undertaken research on Brazilian criminal behaviour particularly on the psychological meaning of

Offender Profiling Series: IV- Profiling Property Crimes
Edited by D. Canter and L. Alison. © 2000 Ashgate Publishing, Aldershot. pp 107-145

the criminal's weapon, collecting her data from various prisons in the Northeast of the country. She has a Masters Degree in Investigative Psychology from the University of Liverpool where she is currently developing her research into Brazilian criminal behaviour as part of her PhD studies.

5 Criminal Weapon Use in Brazil: A Psychological Analysis

ALINE LOBATO

The Research Problem

The weapon is an object that is used by the criminal to engage in his criminal actions, it is therefore a tool or object of his criminal activity. To ignore the meaning of this object in relation to a criminal act is to lose important aspects of the criminal's behaviour. If the use of a weapon is a regular feature of criminal activity the presence of this object cannot be separated from the offender's pattern of behaviour.

The accomplished use of a tool will reflect the professional activity of the person who is manipulating it and consequently this can hint at certain psychological traits. In others words, because the object is used by a person to engage in actions, it may therefore reflect the psychological characteristics involved in the act. Pollio (1974) stated that 'What a person "knows" about an object or event ... does not reside in the object itself, but rather in the person'. In the case of a criminal, the type of weapon chosen can be hypothesised to relate to his experience and thus the interaction between the criminal and the weapon may reflect his psychological characteristics.

When the individual is gaining experience with the object he will give meaning to the object and this process will involve the individual's psychological traits. Human beings will therefore act towards things and objects on the basis of the meaning that the object has for them. Blumer (1969) also pointed out that 'The meaning of a thing is but the expression of the given psychological elements that are brought into play in connection with the perception of the thing'. He concluded that objects are impregnated with psychological elements such as sensations, feelings, ideas, memories, motives and attitudes. Thus for example a weapon can carry the sensation of power or a feeling of hate. According to this concept the relationship between people and objects represents a symbolic interaction in which psychological characteristics are being expressed.

The weapon is the immediate object between the offender and his victim. Thus, it can also be supposed that the weapon, as an object of criminal activity, can also play a specific role in the interpersonal transaction involved in crimes since its presence can interfere in the offender's behaviour, in the victim's behaviour and in the progress of the crime.

The aim of the current investigation is to establish whether weapons used by criminals express the offending behavioural style and psychological characteristics of the criminal. It will be recognised here that to understand the role and the meaning of the weapon in offending behaviour can help to identify offenders' characteristics. From this perspective, the present study investigates what the use and the presence of the weapon can say about the offenders' general characteristics. The main assumption here is that the role the criminal assigns to himself during a criminal act may be related to the meaning that a weapon has for him. In order to make this possible, some consideration will be given to understanding the relationship between the meaning of weapons and the offender's personality. The issues to be considered are:

1)   The weapon is an object that has meaning for the criminal.

2)   The criminal's attitude towards this object (weapon) is based on the meaning it has for him.

3)   The way the relationship between the criminal and the weapon can lead to the expression of important personality traits.

4)   How the meaning of the weapon for the criminal is related to offending behavioural style, and how this may reflect the offender's characteristics.

The Meaning of the Objects: The Psychological Significance

The attempt to link the meaning of criminal weapons to offending behavioural style and offenders' characteristics is supported by philosophies such as the one emphasised by Csikszentmihalyi and Rochberg-Halton (1981). They stated that 'Man is not only *homo sapiens* or *homo ludens*, he is also *homo faber*, the maker and user of objects, his self to a large extent a reflection of things with which he interacts'. Indeed scientists have concluded that studying the relationship between people and objects can help in the understanding of human life, particularly because the things people use reflect aspects of the owner's personality (Csikszentmihalyi and Rochberg-Halton, 1978; Turner, 1967).

However, it is not simple to understand how people relate to objects. The meaning of an object is also formed from the way in which others act towards that object. Indeed people are initially prepared to act towards an object based on the meaning that the object has for their specific group. For example a weapon can represent power for a criminal group who use it to achieve their criminal goal. In contrast a weapon can represent an object of entertainment to a group which practises target practice or knife throwing.

Different groups come to develop different behaviour towards an object, which consequently will have different meanings. Blumer (1969) stated that 'To identify and understand the life of a group it is necessary to identify its world of objects; this identification has to be in terms of the meanings objects have for the members of the group'. Thus, it can be said that the meaning of a weapon can at first sight distinguish criminal groups from other groups, and secondly the different meanings that a weapon can have may help to distinguish behaviour patterns between sub-sets of criminal groups. For example, a weapon can have different meaning for sexual offenders than for dishonest offenders. Thus, an understanding of what meaning the weapon has for a specific type of criminal can help to distinguish him from other types of criminals.

There is a passage in the book of Csikszentmihalyi and Rochberg-Halton (1981, p.108) about the relationship between a policeman and a brace of handguns which illustrates very well how closely the identity of a person can be linked to an object:

Well, they are my working tools, they save my life, you know, at least give me the feelings that they will. I like to take real good care of them, keep them up, keep them oiled, and so on. They are my living to an extent (without them) that would mean that I wouldn't be able to work... They would be a matter of survival and guns to a policeman are like a horse to a jockey, you got to get used to them, work them a lot, know what they are capable of, know their strength and weakness, how it does what it does, every gun is different. A gun is not just something that makes a loud noise. The policeman who knows his job, he knows his gun too, so with a new gun it takes a lot of breaking in. So I would sure hate to have to break in a bunch of new guns. It would be a lot of trouble if I didn't have my guns, the ones I know.

Indeed the objects that people use appear to express themselves, their behaviour towards others and also the environment in which they live. Csikszentmihalyi and Rochberg-Halton (1981) stated that, 'Objects are chosen to represent the power of the bearer' more than any other traits. They quote an example from Evans-Pritchard, (1956, p.233) of how a particular object can act as a central symbol of power:

A man's fighting spear (mut) is constantly in his hand, forming almost part of him and he is never tired of sharpening or polishing it, for a Nuer is very proud of his spear. In a sense it is animate, for it is an extension and external symbol which stands for the strength, vitality and virtue of the person. It is a projection of the self.

Analysing this quotation, Csikszentmihalyi and Rochberg-Halton concluded that the spear in this case is more than a sign. It is a set of inner needs or desires, this weapon 'conveys to the man the power he lacks'. Thus this weapon is reflecting the person's needs and desires and this will express his personality traits, his own image. In the same way a weapon may carry this meaning of power for the criminal, it may reflect his needs and his personality. Csikszentmihalyi and Rochberg-Halton (1981) were very confident about the relationship between objects and the desires for power. They emphasised that 'Objects reflect, or create, a sense of power in those who use them'.

To understand the relationship between the meaning of an object and peoples' psychic activity it makes sense to pull together all the main issues discussed previously and summarise them as follows. There is an object which has a meaning, this meaning comes from the process of interpretation of the individual, which involves symbolic representations given to the object. This process demands psychic energy being spent to direct attention to a specific object related to a specific action. This psychic energy spent in the process of interpretation deposits elements representative of the individual's self in the object, which from now on carries characteristics of the self. Thus to interpret the meaning of the object and consequently the role of the object in the individual's actions, is to interpret the characteristics of the individual's personality.

The Weapon as a Tool of Criminal Activity

Diener and Kerber (1979) when exploring the reasons behind gun ownership found that gun-owners had personalities characterised by low sociability and a high need for power. They emphasised that the explanation for why people use weapons is linked to their need for a feeling of power and virility. They believed that 'The most celebrated explanation has come from the psychoanalytic tradition in which guns are seen as phallic symbols which represent masculine power'. They also stated that 'A gun asserts to a person's strength and invulnerability'. Perhaps these results might also be applied to the criminal community. Conklin (1972) concluded that a weapon gives to the offender a sense of omnipotence in dominating his victims. He interpreted the weapon as an expressive psychological support to the offender.

Others scientists emphasised different reasons in using a weapon in a criminal act. Block (1991) stated that the prime aim in using a weapon is to immobilise the victims. Similarly, Macdonald (1975) suggested that weapons are used by the criminal to intimidate victims, to obtain co-operation and prevent resistance. Skogan (1977) and Hindelang (1972) stated that the use of a weapon increases the offender's security by extending their control over the scene of the crime. The offender who uses a weapon in a crime is in reality trying to protect himself from the possible consequences of the victim's reactions. Indeed the use of a weapon puts fear into the victims who will be intimidated and this may prevent acts of resistance.

Studies have shown that in a majority of cases which involved the use of weapons the offender's intention is not to harm the victim but to avoid resistance and consequently to gain control over the victim and the crime scene (Haran, 1984; Gabor et al., 1987). The offenders will hurt the victim if they meet resistance, and this reactive violence arises to guarantee the success of the crime.

Perhaps the more important point to consider when discussing the use of weapons is that the lethal nature of the weapon may decrease the amount of violence (Skogan, 1977). More specifically, studies concluded that there is a strong negative correlation between the presence of firearms and the use of force (Block, 1991; Haran, 1984; Conklin, 1972). The absence of firearms seems to increase the risk of injury because the victim's resistance is unlikely to occur in the presence of a more lethal weapon. Gabor et al. (1987) observed that one of an offender's greatest fears was the unpredictable need to use a gun. Watts (1994) stated that this factor 'appears to challenge the police viewpoint that firearm-wielding robbers are more dangerous than those without firearms'.

Expressive and Instrumental: Aspects of Offending Behaviour

Several researchers have adopted a typological classification of offenders in an attempt to identify their different behavioural styles. The underlying proposal is that different types of offending behaviour are a product of different personalities. There are a number of studies which have focused on patterns of offending behaviour in relation to different personalities however, the most relevant are those which have tried to link types of offending behaviour to different types of aggression.

Feshbach's study (1964) concluded that aggression is the basic component in crimes and suggested two types of aggression, namely Hostile (expressive), and Instrumental aggression. These types of aggression are related to the goals or rewards that they offer to the perpetrator. The hostile type of aggression relates to 'anger-inducing conditions' and the goal is to make the victim suffer, thus this type of aggression is shown by people who feel some form of gratification from inflicting harm on others. The Instrumental type of aggression is related to the desire for objects or status possessed by another person, thus aggressive acts are used to achieve some desired object or thing.

According to Feshbach's theory each individual develops characteristic levels of aggressiveness which remain stable into adulthood. This may suggest that offenders will act consistently during their crime based on the level of aggression that characterises them, and this may be linked to offenders' background characteristics.

Feshbach's theory, which emphasises Hostile (expressive) and Instrumental types of aggression, has motivated several important studies. In this present study Feshbach's framework will be used in an attempt to link the meaning of the weapon to types of offending behaviour.

Personality Dimensions and Individuals' Characteristics

In order to examine if there is a correlation between the meaning of the weapon for the criminal and the criminal's personality characteristics, two approaches to personality dimensions will be considered. The Fundamental Interpersonal Relations Orientation Theory - FIRO (Schutz, 1958) emphasises that personality dimensions may vary based on the interpersonal tendencies of individuals, namely: Control and Inclusion (Schutz, 1958). Control refers to the need for power and authority over others, and Inclusion refers to the need for contact and the attention of others. The present investigation will examine the relationship these dimensions of personality have to the meaning that the weapon has for the criminal. Eysenck's Dimensions of Personality (Eysenck, 1977) was also utilised. In the present study, Eysenk's Extroversion-Introversion dimension will be considered, as this dimension was more consistently emphasised.

Eysenck observed that extroverts had a lower threshold of arousability than introverts, and they formed conditioned responses less readily, requiring more intense stimulation to maintain pleasurable states of consciousness. In general, Eysenck believed that conscience is a conditioned reflex and socialisation involves the avoidance of punishment, which is aroused by a conditioned anxiety response. Thus because extroverts show conditioned responses more slowly they will be less socialised than introverts. This slow conditioned response in extrovert personality is linked to impulsive components of an extrovert's behaviour and this impulsiveness implies 'acting' without moderation.

In summary, the present investigation will verify if there is a meaning of the weapon for the criminal, and if this hypothesis is supported, then an attempt will be made to identify if the meaning of the weapon can be related to the offending behavioural style and the offenders' characteristics, in accordance with dimensions of personality. The aim will be to distinguish criminal offending behaviour and personality characteristics from the role they assign for their weapon.

Methods

Data Collection

The data used in this study were collected in prisons in the Northeast of Brazil. The prisons which collaborated in this research were; Presídio do Serrotão, in the city of Campina Grande, Paraíba; Presídio João Chaves, in the city of Natal, Rio Grande do Norte; and the Instituto Penal Olavo Oliveira, in the city of Fortaleza, Ceará. The data was collected by using an anonymous questionnaire completed by prisoners, who freely agreed to collaborate with the project.

Sample

The offenders in this sample were all post-sentence, that is they were not on remand. The sample included offenders who had committed various types of crimes, from embezzlement to serial murder. The sample contained 120 subjects, all males, aged between 18 to 70 years old.

Procedure

A questionnaire (Appendix I) containing seventeen questions relating to the meaning of the weapon for the criminal was used. These questions were developed after listening during informal interviews, to what the offenders considered were the most relevant issues on the subject of the meaning of the weapon for criminals. A further eighteen questions referring to the offenders' personality were also asked. The questions required 'yes' or 'no' answers from the respondents. The questionnaire also contained information about the offenders' convictions. The convictions were used as variables in the statistical analysis linking the meaning of the weapon and the offending behavioural style.

Data Analysis

Smallest Space Analysis (SSA) was used in this present research to examine the relationship between variables. It is a non-metric multidimensional scaling procedure, which examines the relationship between each variable and every other variable and represents the relationships in a geometric space.

SSA represents the correlation between variables as a distance in geometric space. It computes correlation coefficients between all variables creating a triangular matrix consisting of correlation coefficients for each variable as correlated with every other variable. The computer algorithm achieves the best fit feasible between the rank order of these correlations and the inverse rank order of the distances in the space.

The more highly correlated two variables are, the closer will be the points which represent these variables in the SSA space. Thus, the patterns of points that represent regions can be examined by looking at the contiguity of the points. If the variables, which are hypothesised to share the same facet elements appear together in the multidimensional space this is taken as evidence for those facets. Variables which have low interrelation will appear in different regions of the plot (see Canter and Heritage, 1990). SSA provides the possibility of identifying elements of the same facet by looking at the position of the points in the plot. The aim then is to search the regions of the space to identify themes within identifiably similar variables.

As a first step in this study seventeen variables which reflected the meaning of the weapon for the criminal were selected from the questionnaire (The variables are described in Appendix II).

These seventeen variables were analysed using the Smallest Space Analysis procedure (SSA). Since the SSA represents the relationship between variables in a geometric space, the aim of this first analysis was to search for groups of variables which could represent themes related to the meaning of the weapon to test the hypothesis that there is meaning of the weapon for the criminals.

With coherent groups of variables co-occurring together forming patterns related to the meaning of the weapon a second analysis could be performed which includes an additional nine variables related to the offenders' convictions. Thus a second SSA analysis was carried out containing the original seventeen variables referring to the meaning of the weapon and nine additional variables related to offenders' convictions.

The first aim in running a second SSA including the offenders' convictions, was to examine if the variables relating to the meaning of the weapon could still form coherent patterns despite the presence of the additional nine convictions variables (these nine variables referring to the convictions are described in Appendix I). The second aim in running the second SSA was to verify which themes of the meaning of the weapon could be related to which of the themes of crime (i.e. *Instrumental* or *Expressive* crime). The SSA plots were therefore examined for regions common to the themes involved in the analyses. Thus, a total of twenty-six variables were considered in this second SSA, seventeen variables relating to the meaning of the weapon and nine variables referring to the offenders' convictions.

In order to test the hypothesis that there is a correlation between the meaning of the weapon and the offenders' personality characteristics, two more SSA's were produced.

The third SSA was produced to test for a relationship between the themes of the meaning of the weapon and the FIRO Inclusion and Control dimensions of personality. This SSA contained the ten selected variables referring to the meaning of the weapon and ten variables related to Inclusion and Control dimensions of personality. The variables included in this third SSA are described in Appendix II.

The fourth and final SSA plot was then produced to establish whether there were some relationships between the selected variables of the meaning of the weapon and Eysenck's Introvert/Extrovert dimensions of personality. This fourth SSA contained the ten selected variables of the meaning of the weapon plus eight variables related to extroversion and introversion. The eight additional variables referring to Eysenck's Introvert and Extrovert dimension of personality are described in Appendix II.

Results

The SSA data analysis (figure 5.1) showed that it was possible to find distinct regions on the plot, which could be related to themes of the meaning of the weapon for the criminal.

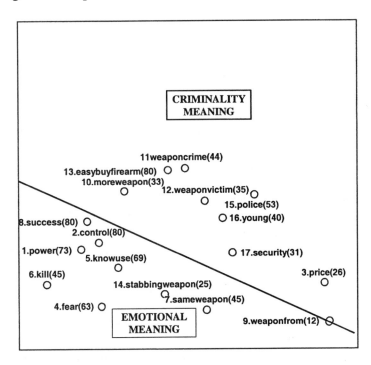

CRIMINALITY
MEANING

11weaponcrime(44)

13.easybuyfirearm(80) O O

10.moreweapon(33)
O   12.weaponvictim(35) O

O   15.police(53)

8.success(80) O   O 16.young(40)

2.control(80)
O

1.power(73) O   O 17.security(31)

5.knowuse(69)

6.kill(45)   O   3.price(26)
O   O

14.stabbingweapon(25)

4.fear(63) O   7.sameweapon(45)
O

EMOTIONAL
MEANING   9.weaponfrom(12) O

Coefficient of alienation = 0.15, Yule's Q the measure of association.

Figure 5.1: **SSA of Seventeen Variables Referring to the Meaning of the Weapon in Relation to the Themes: Criminality Meaning and Emotional Meaning**

The variables 'weapon crime', 'easy to buy a firearm', 'more than one weapon', 'weapon victim', 'police', 'young', 'security', and 'price' were found in the top right-side of the SSA plot (see also Appendix II for details of the variables). This region was consequently named *Criminality*

Meaning, since the variables in this region seemed to reflect the offenders' interpretations of the weapon from a criminal perspective. The crime itself seemed to be the target for these offenders linked to the theme of *Criminality Meaning,* and the weapon is interpreted as a tool to facilitate the crime.

Those offenders who were linked to the theme *Criminality Meaning* are more likely to use firearms to commit their crimes since the variable 'young' that appeared in this region of the plot relates to the use of firearms from an early age. The variable 'security' also appeared in this region. This variable refers to offenders' concerns about the security the weapon could provide for them during the crime. This may reflect a less impulsive style of thinking, which is usually associated with older and more experienced criminals. According to the literature the lack of concern about risks is linked more closely to younger and less experienced offenders (Walters, 1990).

The variable 'easy to buy a firearm' was found in the *Criminality Meaning* region. This may reinforce the suggestion that the offenders linked to this theme will be the more experienced ones since it is more likely that the experienced offender will have had easier access to more sophisticated weapons because of their established criminal contacts. The interpretation of the meaning of the weapon in relation to a criminal perspective also leads the offenders to be more concerned with facts such as the 'price' of the weapon.

The offenders who can be related to the theme *Criminality Meaning* are also likely to change the type of weapon used depending on the type of crime they will commit, and the type of victim to be attacked. The variables 'weapon crime' and 'weapon victim', which refers to when the offenders may change the type of weapon used, appeared in the region *Criminality Meaning.* However, because of the high percentage of criminals found in this study who use firearms, it is more likely that they will always use firearms as their weapon of choice.

In summary, for the interpretation of the weapon in relation to the theme *Criminality Meaning,* the weapon is a tool of criminal activity, which provides security during crimes. This interpretation of the meaning of the weapon, linked to the criminal perspective, can be seen as a rational focus. It emphasises facts such as the price of the weapon, and the security that it can provide. The weapon is an object that can help to achieve a criminal objective, which for these offenders seems to be the execution of the crime itself.

A contrasting interpretation is of the meaning of the weapon in a more emotional way. In the bottom left-side of the same SSA plot (figure 5.1) a region reflecting coherent patterns of variables was identified and named in this study as the *Emotional Meaning* theme. The group of variables that appeared in this region reflected emotional characteristics relating to the meaning of the weapon for the criminal.

The variables 'power', 'control', 'kill', 'fear', 'success', 'stabbing weapons', 'same weapon', and 'weapon from' appeared in the region relating to the theme of *Emotional Meaning*. For this theme the weapon is used to provide 'power', to gain 'control', to cause 'fear' to the victim, and to 'kill'. The weapon in this case is not interpreted as an instrument to facilitate the crime, but as an instrument to cause psychological and physical injuries to others. For this theme, the victim seems to be the target and the weapon is a helpful object in achieving the desired aim of causing injury to the victims.

Offenders who interpret the meaning of the weapon in a more emotional way are unlikely to change the type of weapon used since the variable 'same weapon' appeared in the *Emotional Meaning* region. This may reflect a more faithful emotional relationship between these offenders and a specific type of weapon which is likely to be a stabbing weapon since the variable 'stabbing weapons' appeared in this region very close to the variable 'same weapon'.

The variable 'stabbing weapons' appeared in the *Emotional Meaning* region together with the variables 'power', 'control', 'fear', and 'kill'. This reflects a correlation between these variables, which suggests that the use of a stabbing weapon is likely to be concerned with power and control over the victim. This theme relates also to killing the victim, since the variable 'kill' appeared in this region. This agrees with some of the findings in the literature which report that the use of firearms is less related to the offenders' desires to kill than other weapons (Block, 1991; Skogan, 1977; Conklin, 1972), as for example the use of stabbing weapons here. The criminal who uses stabbing weapons when the weapon has an emotional meaning, is also likely to use a weapon taken from the scene of the crime, since the variable 'weapon from' appeared in this region as well.

The results of this study on stabbing weapons allow some inferences to be made about the meaning of the weapon in relation to offenders' characteristics. For example, when a stabbing weapon is used, the search may be for someone who has expressive desires for power and control, who has used the same type of weapon in previous crimes, and who usually uses a weapon taken from the scene of the crime.

The *Emotional Meaning* theme may also express the optimistic idea that the weapon can always guarantee the success of the crime since the variable 'success' appeared in this region. From this perspective it may be hypothesised that this theme is characteristic of not spending much time planning the crime, since it implies that the mere possession of a weapon can guarantee the success of the crime.

The findings of the study showed that it was possible to identify themes referring to the meaning of the weapon by observing the correlation between the variables, which reflected the characteristics of these themes. The division in the SSA plot (figure 5.1), which defined the two themes of *Criminality Meaning* and *Emotional Meaning* supported the principal hypothesis of this study that the weapon has a meaning for the criminal. The coherent patterns within the variables that provided the means of identifying these themes also lend support to the concept that the criminals' attitude towards weapons is linked to the meaning the weapons have for them.

The Relationship between the Meaning of the Weapon and Expressive/Instrumental Offending Behaviour

After identifying the themes referring to the meaning of the weapon an attempt was made to link these themes to Expressive and Instrumental types of crimes in relation to offending behaviour. A second SSA (figure 5.2), was produced using the variables of the meaning of the weapon plus nine additional variables relating to offenders' convictions to examine if there was a relationship between these two sets of variables (see Appendix II).

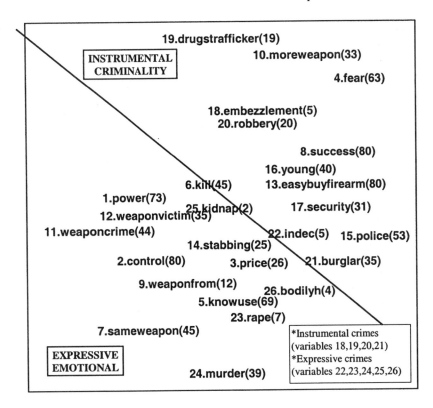

Coefficient of alienation = 0.36, Yule's Q.

Figure 5.2: SSA of Seventeen Variables Referring to the Meaning of the Weapon and Nine Additional Variables Referring to Convictions

It can be seen in the second SSA plot (figure 5.2) that the variables related to the meaning of the weapon still formed coherent patterns despite the presence of the nine additional convictions variables. Almost the exact same groupings of variables found in the first SSA (figure 5.1) related to the themes of the meaning of the weapon were found in the second SSA (figure 5.2).

The variables 'more than one weapon', 'easy to buy a firearm', 'security', 'police', and 'young' relating to the original theme *Criminality Meaning* of the weapon were found in the top right-side of the second

SSA plot (figure 5.2). In this same region the variables 'embezzlement', 'drugs trafficker', 'robbery', and 'burglary' referring to the offenders' convictions were also found. Since these types of convictions refer to instrumental crimes, and because this region also contained the variables relating to the Criminality Meaning of the weapon this region was assigned the name *Instrumental Criminality*.

The variables 'power', 'control', 'kill', 'same weapon', 'know to use', and 'stabbing weapons' relating to the *Emotional Meaning* of the weapon (see figure 5.1), were found in the bottom left-side of the second SSA plot (figure 5.2). The variables were found in the same region as the variables 'indecent assault', 'bodily harm', 'rape', 'murder', and 'kidnap', which are related to Expressive types of crime. This region was named *Expressive Emotional* because it contained the variables associated with the Emotional Meaning of the weapon and those variables related to Expressive types of crime.

Thus in the second SSA plot (figure 5.2), which included the variables related to both the meaning of the weapon and offenders' convictions, the distinct themes, *Instrumental Criminality* and *Expressive Emotional,* were identified.

The SSA represents the rank of the correlations as the inverse rank of distances, and therefore it is possible to reveal meaningful patterns in weak associations. Thus, given the practical implications of these results, it is of value to consider some of the actual correlations on which the SSA is based. Table 5.1 presents some major correlation coefficients for the key variables.

Table 5.1: Yules' Q Correlations between Selected Crimes and Meanings of Weapons Variables

Meaning of Weapons	Crimes			
	Expressive		Instrumental	
	Indecent	Body Harm	Embezz	Robbery
Expressive Variables				
Know use	1.00	1.00	-0.28	0.24
Weapon from	1.00	1.00	-0.38	-0.32
Instrumental Variables				
More weapon	0.18	-1.00	0.59	0.36
Easy buy	0.59	0.48	0.30	-0.22

Table 5.1 shows that in the expressive region of the space, there are remarkably strong correlations, but in the other regions, these are weaker and less consistent. This is probably due to the rather general instrumental definitions of the crimes, and the meanings of the weapons, leading to ambiguity in individual items. The SSA structure therefore is best considered as an indication of the trends running throughout the data that goes beyond the ambiguity of any individual item.

The division in the second SSA plot (figure 5.2), defining the new themes of *Instrumental Criminality* and *Expressive Emotional,* does support certain assumptions. The interpretation of weapon, based on a criminal perspective, does relate to instrumental types of crimes. This lends support to the feasibility that there is a class of crimes associated with instrumental offending behaviour. This may be seen as a broadening of Feshbach's (1964) perspective on aggressive crimes to crimes in general.

Instrumental types of crime imply an instrumental offending behaviour style, which refers to the search for goals or the rewards that the crime offers to the perpetrator. The desire is for objects or status possessed by another person, and the aim in committing the crime is to possess the desired object or thing. In instrumental types of crimes the weapon is likely to be interpreted from a criminal perspective, with the use of the weapon to facilitate the crimes and to provide security for the offender.

The priority in these instrumental crimes is not to hurt or kill others. Indeed in the second SSA plot (figure 5.2) the variable 'security' which referred to the offender's concern about the security the weapon can provide for him was found in the region *Instrumental Criminality,* and the variable 'kill' was not related to this region.

In this study the offenders who committed instrumental types of crime were also more likely to use firearms to commit their crimes since the variable 'young' which refers to the use of firearms from a young age was found in the *Instrumental Criminality* region. These instrumental offenders are interested in the victims' possessions, and because in this study it was found that they usually used firearms, it may be hypothesised that these offenders are less likely to hurt their victims since other studies have shown that strong violence towards the victim is not usually related to the use of firearms (Skogan, 1977).

The variables 'more than one weapon' and 'easy to buy a firearm' which appeared in the *Criminality Meaning* region of the first SSA plot (figure 5.1) are, in the second SSA plot (figure 5.2), related to instrumental types of crime and appeared in the *Instrumental Criminality* region. This might suggest that these offenders who reported that they used more than one weapon in their crimes, and for whom it was easy to buy a firearm, may be the ones who commit instrumental types of crime. From this, perhaps it can be hypothesised that the offenders who commit instrumental crimes, have established contacts with the criminal community since it was easy for these offenders to buy firearms and this may explain why they possessed more than one weapon.

The variables 'fear' and 'success', which originally were found in the first SSA plot (figure 5.1) relating to the theme *Emotional Meaning* of the weapon, now appear in the second SSA plot (figure 5.2) in the region *Instrumental Criminality.* This may be explained by the high frequency of these variables reflecting their common meanings in association with weapons. This explanation is supported by the fact that in the first SSA plot (figure 5.1), the variable 'success', for example, appeared very close to the boundary between the themes *Emotional Meaning* and *Criminality Meaning,* implying a relationship between the variable 'success' and both themes. The only other very high frequency variable 'easy buy' is also close to that boundary.

The variable 'fear' appeared in the first SSA plot (figure 5.1) close to the bottom of the plot, and in the second SSA plot (figure 5.2), close to the top. Thus, it is clear that fear is an aspect of weapons that can take on rather different emphasis in different contexts. Further research would therefore be of value to distinguish between instrumental and expressive functions of 'fear' for criminals.

The results in the second SSA plot (figure 5.2) also revealed a distinct region, which was named *Expressive Emotional*. In this region the original variables relating to the *Emotional Meaning* of the weapon (see figure 5.1) and the Expressive types of crime were found. This suggests that the offenders who interpret the meaning of the weapon in an emotional way are more likely to be the ones who commit expressive types of crimes such as murder, rape, indecent assault, and bodily harm.

The literature concludes (Feshbach, 1964) that the offenders who commit expressive types of crime are associated with the Expressive Offending Behaviour style, which refers to the fact that for the offenders the goal in a crime is to make the victim suffer. The objective of these offenders is not the committing of the crime itself, but their desire is to cause injury since these offenders feel some gratification from inflicting harm on others. This is supported by the nature of the variables 'power', 'control' and 'kill', which appeared in the *Expressive Emotional* region, and which refer to the power and control given to the offender by the possession of a weapon and the possibility to kill which it provides.

The results from this study suggest that offenders for whom the weapon carries an Emotional Meaning and who commit these Expressive crimes, are also more likely to be the ones who use stabbing weapon, since the variable 'stabbing weapon' appeared in the region *Expressive Emotional*. These offenders also are likely to use the same type of weapon in their crimes, and are more likely to use a weapon taken from the scene of the crime, since the variables 'same weapon' and 'weapon from' were found in this *Expressive Emotional* region.

The variables 'weapon victim' and 'weapon crime', which in the first SSA plot (figure 5.1) were found in the region *Criminality Meaning* in the second SSA plot (figure 5.2), appeared associated with the *Expressive Emotional* region. It was expected that these variables should have appeared in the opposite region. However, on closer consideration of the plot (figure 5.2), it can be observed that these variables are close to the variable 'kidnap'. The relationship with the variable 'kidnap' may explain the way these variables were 'pulled' into the *Expressive Emotional* region. This is because the variable 'kidnap' seemed to be related to both *Expressive Emotional* and *Instrumental Criminality* themes since this variable is close to the boundary between them. Indeed it is known that the crime of kidnap can be associated with different aims (Wilson et al., 1995). Kidnapping may be based on both instrumental, eg. for financial gain, and/or a desire to attack people.

In summary, the results in this present study revealed that for those offenders who are associated with the Expressive Offending Behaviour style, the weapon carries an *Emotional Meaning*. The *Expressive Emotional* (figure 5.2) region predominantly contained the Expressive types of crime and the variables associated with the *Emotional Meaning* of the weapon (figure 5.1). Thus it was possible from the findings of this study to support the argument that the expressive offending behaviour style is characteristic of those offenders for whom the weapon carries an emotional meaning. The weapon is interpreted in an emotional way, which is an expression of the offender's desire to inflict pain and cause injury to others.

The Relationship between the Meaning of the Weapon and Personality Dimensions

Two more SSAs were carried out in order to test for a relationship between the themes comprising the meaning of the weapon for the criminal, and personality dimensions. One of these SSA plots was produced to examine the relationship between the meaning of the weapon and Inclusion and Control dimensions of personality - FIRO. The other SSA was produced to establish if there was a relationship between the meaning of the weapon and Extrovert and Introvert Eysenck dimensions of personality.

Inclusion

The first of these new SSA plots (figure 5.3) contains ten selected relevant variables of the meaning of the weapon and ten variables related to FIRO dimensions of personality, where five variables refer to the Inclusion dimension and the other five to the Control dimension (see Appendix II). Because of the ambiguity of some of the weapon meaning items, those used here were selected to have least ambiguity. On the left-side of the SSA plot (figure 5.3) are the variables referring to the *Criminality Meaning* of the weapon and the variables of Inclusion dimension. This region was named *Criminality Inclusion.* On the right-side of the same SSA plot were found the variables related to the *Emotional Meaning* of the weapon and the variables referring to Control dimension of personality. This region was called *Emotional Control.*

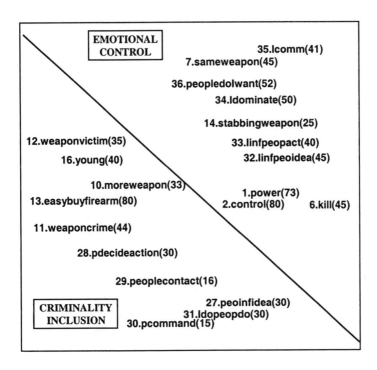

Coefficient of alienation = 0.16, Yule's Q.

Figure 5.3: SSA of Ten Selected Variables Referring to the Meaning of the Weapon and Ten Variables Referring to FIRO Inclusion/Control Dimensions of Personality

The results in this SSA plot (figure 5.3) revealed that there was a relationship between the Criminality Meaning of the weapon and the Inclusion dimension of personality. The relationship between the variables in the *Criminality Inclusion* region suggested that offenders who interpret the meaning of the weapon based on a criminal perspective are likely to be the ones who express characteristics associated with the Inclusion dimension of personality. Since the Inclusion dimension reflects the individual's need for affection from others (Schutz, 1958), the personality characteristics of these offenders are an expression of their need for contact and attention from others. The behaviour of offenders associated with Inclusion dimension of personality in their daily life will be driven by their need for human affection and attention. Thus, it may be hypothesised that they will be a submissive type of individual, since to gain people's affection it may be necessary to allow people to control the events in their lives.

This third SSA plot (figure 5.3) allowed some assumptions to be made about the personality characteristics of these offenders. One of the characteristics of the offenders associated with the Inclusion dimension of personality is their desire for the attention of others, and maybe the weapon is used to achieve this aim. For example, the variable which refers to the use of 'more than one weapon' appears together in the plot with the variables of the Inclusion dimension of personality. This may suggest that the possession of more than one weapon may be a way for the offender to gain the victim's attention. Thus, it might be hypothesised that the use of additional weapons by the offender may reflect his attempt to show a certain 'status', which he expects the victim to recognise.

The variables 'weapon crime' and 'weapon victim' related to the theme Criminality Meaning of the weapon were also found in the region *Criminality Inclusion*. These variables referred to the offender's report that they chose the type of weapon according to the type of crime they intended to commit, and the kind of victim they would attack. This may suggest that these offenders who changed the type of weapon used, are more likely to be the ones who in their daily life express personality characteristics related to the Inclusion dimension of personality.

Despite the offenders associated with the *Criminality Inclusion* region reporting that they changed the type of weapon they used, it can nevertheless be suggested that these weapons will probably always be a kind of firearm. The variable 'young', which refers to the use of firearms from an early age, was also found in this region. The presence of the variable 'easy to buy a firearm' in this same region also reinforces the assumption that these offenders will use firearms because they are easy to obtain. Thus the offenders who use firearms are more likely to be those who are expressive in their lifestyles, showing behaviours linked to a need for affection and attention from others. This lends support to the hypothesis put forward previously that those offenders for whom the weapon carries a meaning, the objective for the offender does not seem to be one of hurting the victim. Since the Inclusion dimension of personality is related to the need for people's affection and attention, the incident where the offender hurts or kills the victim destroys this possibility.

In the bottom right-side of this same SSA plot (figure 5.3) the *Emotional Control* region contains variables relating to the previous theme of the Emotional Meaning of the weapon (see figure 5.1) and the variables referring to the Control Dimension of Personality (FIRO). The variables referring to the Control Dimension of Personality were 'I influence people's ideas', 'I influence people's actions', 'I command', 'I dominate', and 'people do what I want', which referred to the need to exert power and authority over others. The *Emotional Meaning* of the weapon variables 'power', 'control', and 'kill' were the ones also found in this region.

Those offenders who interpreted the meaning of the weapon in an emotional way were likely to use the same type of weapon to commit all their crimes since the variable 'same weapon' appeared in the Emotional Meaning region of the SSA plot of figure 5.1. In the SSA plot of figure 5.3, the variable 'same weapon' was found in close proximity to the control characteristics of personality. It can therefore be deduced that those offenders who do not change their type of weapon are likely be the ones who show in their daily life a need to exert power, control and authority over others.

One of the findings from this study was that offenders associated with the *Emotional Control* theme were those who used stabbing weapons to commit their crimes, since the variable 'stabbing weapons' was found in this region. It might be suggested therefore that if a stabbing weapon was used in a crime, the search should be for someone who in his daily life shows behavioural characteristics related to a strong desire for power and control over others. The offender who uses a stabbing weapon may also wish to have close contact with his victim when inflicting pain and perhaps this close contact increases their gratification.

In summary, the FIRO Control variables and some of the variables referring to the Emotional Meaning of the weapon combined to express the offender's strong desire for power and control over others. An offender's desire for power and authority over others is achieved by, and expressed in his relationship with the weapon. This suggests here that the offenders who have a relationship with their weapon based on the Emotional Meaning it has for them, will be the ones who show strong desires for control in their lifestyle and in their general relationships with others. Their behaviour will be driven by their need to exert power and control over others.

Extroversion

In order to verify if there was some relationship between the meaning of the weapon, and Eysenck's Introvert and Extrovert Dimensions of Personality, a new SSA plot (figure 5.4) was produced.

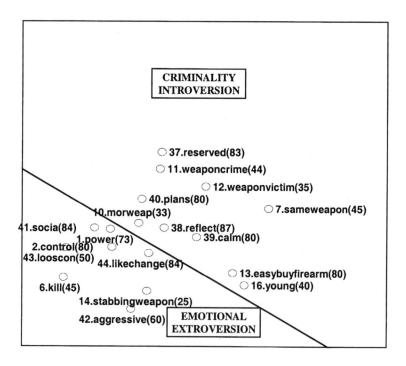

Coefficient of alienation = 0.15, Yule's Q.

Figure 5.4: SSA of Ten Selected Variables Referring to the Meaning of the Weapon and Eight Variables Referring to Eysenk's Introvert/Extrovert Dimension of Personality

In the top right-side of this SSA plot (figure 5.4) are the variables referring to the theme Criminality Meaning of the weapon (see also figure 5.1), and the variables which reflected the Introversion dimension of personality. Thus this region was named *Criminality Introversion*. In the bottom left-side of this SSA plot (figure 5.4) are the variables referring to the theme Emotional Meaning of the weapon and the variables relating to the Extrovert dimension of personality. Consequently this region was called *Emotional Extroversion*. Thus in this SSA plot (figure 5.4) two distinct regions were found namely *Criminality Introversion* and *Emotional Extroversion*.

In the *Criminality Introversion* region of the SSA plot are the variables 'reserved', 'reflective', 'calm', and 'plans' which according to Eysenck's theory (1977) reflect characteristics of introverted individuals. Also found in the same region of the plot were the variables 'weapon crime', 'weapon victim', 'easy to buy a firearm', and 'young', which related to the theme Criminality Meaning of the weapon. Thus, this suggests that the offenders who interpret the weapon in a criminal perspective are likely be introverted individuals.

Eysenck (1977) stated that introverted individuals are expected to show superior conditioning under conditions of partial reinforcement. Eysenck concluded that conscience and socialisation are conditioned reflexes that are not linked with impulsivity. Thus from the analysis of the region *Criminality Introversion* (figure 5.4), it may be hypothesised that the offenders for whom the weapon carries a criminal perspective are likely be those who are more conscientious, more socialised but less impulsive.

It may also be suggested that the offenders who showed characteristics associated with the Criminality Meaning of the weapon such as the use of firearms from an early age, will express in their daily lives characteristics related to introversion. Therefore the use of firearms rather than stabbing weapons will be related to less impulsive, reserved, calm, introverted individuals who will also show a tendency to plan their lives.

The offenders associated with the theme Criminality Meaning of the weapon (see figure 5.1), changed the type of weapon used according to the type of crime to be committed, and the type of victim to be attacked. The SSA plot (figure 5.4), showed that these offenders were also the ones who expressed introverted characteristics. This was supported by the presence of the variables 'reflective', 'reserved', 'calm', and 'makes plans', co-occurring together with the variables 'weapon crime' and 'weapon victim' in the region *Criminality Introversion*.

The variable 'more weapon' which referred to the use of more than one weapon to commit the crime, and the variable 'makes plans' that referred to an introversion characteristic, were found very close together in the same plot (figure 5.4). This suggested that the offenders who reported that they used more than one weapon to commit their crimes may also be the individuals who express the typical introvert tendency of making plans for every event in their lives.

In summary, by observing the relationship between the variables in the region *Criminality Introversion* it was possible to hypothesise that the offenders who interpret the weapon in a criminal perspective are likely to be the ones who show introvert characteristics in their daily lives.

In the bottom left-side of the same SSA plot (figure 5.4) the region *Emotional Extroversion* was found. This contained the variables referring to the Emotional Meaning of the weapon (previously identified in figure 5.1), and the variables that express the characteristics of Extrovert individuals. The co-occurrence of these variables in this *Emotional Extroversion* region of the plot (figure 5.4) suggests that the offenders who interpreted the weapon in an emotional way will be the extroverted individuals.

According to Eysenck's theory, the extrovert individuals will have low arousal, weak conditionability and a deficient conscience. Consequently, Eysenck (1977) pointed out that these extrovert individuals will be the impulsive ones who will act without moderation. He also concluded that the relationship between extroversion and low arousal is linked to a strong tendency to under-socialisation and expressive criminal behaviour.

Thus, from an analysis of the *Emotional Extrovert* region, it may be suggested that the offenders who interpret the weapon in an emotional way and thus reported that they use the weapon to exert power and control over the victim, will show characteristics linked to extroversion, such as aggression and loss of control. This assumption was supported by the presence of the variables 'power' and 'control' (related to the *Emotional Meaning* of the weapon) and the variables 'aggressive' and 'lose control easily' (relating to Extroversion) in the same region of the plot.

The variable 'stabbing weapon' also appeared together with the Extroversion variables in this region of *Emotional Extroversion* in figure 5.4. This lends support to the suggestion that the offenders who use stabbing weapons are likely to show characteristics of extroversion such as impulsivity, aggressivity, and loss of control. Thus extrovert offenders are also likely to be sociable people who like change in their lives.

The variable 'kill' (which referred to the *Emotional Meaning* of the weapon), was also found in the *Emotional Extroversion* region of the plot presented in figure 5.4. This variable referred to offenders who were concerned with the opportunity for killing the victim, which the weapon could provide. Thus it may be suggested that these offenders, who seemed to be more likely to kill the victim, would probably show behaviour characteristics such as impulsivity which are linked to the extroversion dimension of personality.

As was mentioned before, for those offenders who interpreted the role of the weapon in an emotional way, the victim seemed to be the target and not the crime itself. For these offenders the objective seemed to be to hurt and cause injury to the victim and thus it may be hypothesised that these offenders who desire to hurt others will be extrovert, impulsive, and aggressive individuals who lose control easily.

This study revealed that there was a relationship between the meaning of the weapon and Eysenck's Extroversion/Introversion dimensions of personality. It showed that the *Emotional Meaning* of the weapon seemed to be related to Extroversion while the *Criminality Meaning* of the weapon appeared to be linked with Introversion. Thus, it was possible to show that the meaning the offenders' assign to the weapon they use, may reflect their personality characteristics.

Discussion

This study addressed the following issues: a) Is there a meaning of the weapon for criminals? b) Does the meaning of the weapon reflect the type of crime committed and criminals' offending behavioural style? c) Is it possible to link the meaning of the weapon to personality characteristics?

a) Is there a Meaning of the Weapon for Criminals? The results in this study reveal that there is a meaning of the weapon for criminals. More specifically, the results indicate that there are two themes related to the meaning of the weapon. One refers to the *Criminality Meaning* of the weapon where the criminal seems to interpret the role of the weapon from a criminal perspective. The other theme refers to the *Emotional Meaning* of the weapon where the weapon seems to carry emotional characteristics.

The nature of the *Criminality Meaning* of the weapon suggests that for these offenders the crime itself is the target, and the weapon is interpreted as a tool to facilitate the crime. This suggests that these offenders interpret the crime in a more 'rational' way and also suggests that they are more likely to use firearms to commit their crimes.

In contrast, this study reveals that for those offenders who interpret the weapon in an emotional way, the target is the victim and not the crime itself. The weapon in this case is not interpreted as an instrument to facilitate the crime, but as an instrument to cause psychological and physical injury to others. The results show that the offenders for whom the weapon carries an *Emotional Meaning* are likely to use stabbing weapons. The results also suggest that these offenders are also more likely to kill the victim. This finding is in accordance with the results of other studies in the literature, namely that the absence of firearms seems to increase the risk of injury, and thus when the lethal nature of the weapon decreases, the violence tends to increase (Skogan, 1977).

b) Does the Meaning of the Weapon Reflect the Type of Crime Committed and Criminals' Offending Behavioural Style? The results in this study show that the meaning of the weapon may be linked to the type of crime committed which in turn reflects the criminal's offending behaviour. It seems that these offenders for whom the weapon carries a *Criminality Meaning* commit Instrumental types of crime such as embezzlement, drugs trafficking, robbery, and burglary.

Feshbach (1964) proposed that an instrumental offending behavioural style was one in which the crime was part of a search for goals or rewards. The aim in committing these crimes is to obtain desired objects or things possessed by another person. This agrees with the findings in this present study that the *Criminality Meaning* of the weapon relates to an Instrumental offending behaviour style.

The present study also reveals there is a relationship between the *Emotional Meaning* of the weapon and Expressive types of crime, such as murder, rape, indecent assault, and bodily harm. This Expressive Offending Behavioural Style according to Feshbach, (1964) refers to the fact that for these offenders the goal is to make the victim suffer. The desire is to cause injury to the victim since the offender feels some gratification from inflicting harm on others. The results here show that for these offenders, who can be linked to the *Emotional Meaning* of the weapon, the target similarly seems to be the victim. The objective in using a weapon is to hurt the victim.

Therefore the findings presented here indicate that it is possible to link the meaning of the weapon to the types of crime committed and consequently to the criminals' offending behavioural style. Thus the role that the offenders assign to the weapon may also be an expression of their offending behaviour.

c) Is it Possible to Link the Meaning of the Weapon to Personality Characteristics? This current research shows that there is a link between the meaning that offenders assign to their weapons and their personality characteristics. The results reveal that there is a relationship between the meaning of the weapon and the FIRO Inclusion/Control Dimensions of Personality. The way in which the Inclusion Dimension of Personality operates seems to be related to the characteristics of the offenders who interpret the weapon from a criminal perspective.

The Inclusion Dimension of Personality reflects the individual's need for affection and contact with others (Schutz, 1958). Thus, since the results in this present study show that the offenders who assign a criminality meaning to the weapon are likely related to Inclusion, then these offenders will express a need for affection and contact with others in their daily lives.

This investigation supports the existence of a relationship between the characteristics of the FIRO Control Dimension of Personality and the *Emotional Meaning* of the weapon. Since the Control Dimension refers to the need for power and authority over others, the offenders for whom the weapon carries an Emotional Meaning are therefore likely to show characteristics of personalities that reflect their desire for power and authority. The nature of the *Emotional Meaning* of the weapon reveals that the role of the weapon in this case is linked to a strong desire for power and control. This is very similar to the characteristics relating to the Control Dimension of Personality.

This research also showed that there is a link between the Meaning of the weapon and Eysenck's Introvert/Extrovert Dimension of Personality. The findings demonstrated that there is some relationship between the *Criminality Meaning* of the weapon and the Introvert individual's characteristics, and another link between the *Emotional Meaning* of the weapon and the characteristics of the Extrovert type of personality.

The results in this research show another relationship between the characteristics of the offenders who interpret the meaning of the weapon in an emotional way and Extrovert personality. According to Eysenck's theory, extroverted individuals will show weak conditionability and deficient conscience, which are related to impulsivity and expressive criminal behaviour. Thus the findings presented here suggest that the offenders for whom the weapon carries an *Emotional Meaning* and therefore who reportedly use the weapon to exert power and control over the victim, will show personality characteristics linked to Extroversion, such as impulsivity, aggressivity and loss of control. The results here also show that the *Emotional Meaning* of the weapon is related to the use of stabbing weapons. Thus because of the relationship between the *Emotional Meaning* of the weapon and Extroversion this finding suggests that those offenders who use stabbing weapons are more likely to express extrovert characteristics.

Conclusions

It might be concluded therefore that the weapon is an object that may carry and reflect characteristics of the self. From this perspective, the understanding of the meaning of the weapon for the criminal may help to access some of the offender's behavioural style, which can help in predicting his personality tendencies, characteristics, and identity.

In showing that the meaning of the weapon may be a reflection of the criminals' offending behaviour style, and consequently their personality characteristics, it has potential implications for police investigations.

The findings of this study also have implications for the interpersonal perspective on crime, since the identified themes of the weapon seem to be directly dependent upon the offender's interpersonal relationships with the victim and with others. The results also lend support to the concept that the study of the role of the weapon at the scene of the crime and what it represents to the offender, may be useful in helping to make inferences about the offender's characteristics.

It is necessary to emphasise that the results in this study need to be considered carefully since the field of study of the role of the weapon is in its infancy and there is still little published work in this area. However this does not decrease the importance of this field or of this present research. On the contrary, the lack of studies in this field demonstrates a need to fill the present gap in knowledge on the role of the weapon and the present investigation may motivate further research in this area.

References

Block, C.R. and van Der Werff, C. (1991), *Initiation and Continuation of a Criminal Career*, Deventer, Klewer Law and Taxation Publishers.

Blumer, H. (1969), *Symbolic Interactionism. Perspective and Method*, Prentice-Hall Press, U.S.A.

Canter, D.V. and Heritage, R. (1990), 'A Multivariate Model of Sexual Offence Behaviour: Development in "Offender Profiling"', *The Journal of Forensic Psychiatry*, **1 (2)**, 185-212.

Conklin, J. (1972), *Robbery and the Criminal Justice System*, Philadelphia, PA: Loppincot.

Csikszentmihalyi, M. and Rochberg-Halton, E. (1978), 'People and Things: Reflections on Materialism', *The University of Chicago Magazine*, **70 (3)**, 6-15.

Csikszentmihalyi, M. and Rochberg-Halton, E. (1981), *The Meaning of Things. Domestic Symbols and the Self*, Cambridge: Cambridge University Press.

Diener, E. and Kerber, W. (1979), 'Personality Characteristics of American Gun-Owners', *The Journal of Social Psychology*, **107**, 227-238.

Evans, P. (1956), *E.E. Nuer Religion*, Oxford: Oxford University Press.

Eysenck, H.J. (1977), *Crime and Personality*, London: Routledge & Kegan Paul.

Feshbach, S. (1964), 'The Function of Aggression and the Regulation of Aggressive Drive', *Psychological Review*, **71**, 257-272.

Gabor, T., Bamil, M., Cusson, M., Elie, D., Leblanc, M. and Normandeau, A. (1987), *Armed Robbery, Cops, Robbers, and Victims*, Springfield: Charles C. Thomas Publishers.

Haran, J.F. and Martin, J.M. (1984), 'The Armed Urban Robber: A Profile', *Federal Probation*, 48-73.

Hindelang, M.J. and Weis, J. (1972), 'The Bc-Try Cluster and Factor Analysis System: Personality and Self-Reported Delinquency', *Criminology*, **10**, 268-294.

Macdonald, J.M. (1975), *Armed Robbery: Offenders and their Victims*, Springfield: Charles C. Thomas Publishers.

Pollio, H.R. (1974), *The Psychology of Symbolic Activity*, Reading, Mass.: Addison-Wesley Press.

Schutz, W. (1958), *FIRO: A Three Dimensional Theory of Interpersonal Behaviour*, New York: Rinehart.

Skogan, W.G. (1977), 'Dimensions of the Dark Figure of Unreported Crime', *Crime and Delinquency*, **23**, 41-50.

Turner, V. (1967), *The Forest of Symbols*, Ithaca, N.Y.: Cornell University Press.

Walter, G.D. (1990), *The Criminal Lifestyle. Patterns of Serious Criminal Conduct*, Sage Publications Press, U.S.A.

Watts, S.A. (1994), *Robbers and Robberies: Behavioural Consistencies in Armed Robbery and their Interpersonal Narrative Constructs*. Unpublished Dissertation in Investigative Psychology, University of Surrey.

Wilson, M.A., Canter, D.V. and Smith, A. (1995), 'Modelling Terrorist Behaviour', *Final Report to the U.S. Army Research Institute*, Alexandria, USA: ARI.

Appendix I

Questionnaire (directly translated from Portugese)

Part 1 - These questions are about the weapon you use.

1. Do you use a weapon because you think this gives you more power over the victim?

☐ Yes ☐ No

2. Do you use a weapon because you think about using it to control the victim?

☐ Yes ☐ No

3. Are you concerned about the price of the weapon?

☐ Yes ☐ No

4. Do you use a weapon thinking about the fear it can cause the victim?

☐ Yes ☐ No

5. Do you use only a specific type of weapon that you know how to use?

☐ Yes ☐ No

6. Do you use a weapon because you are thinking of the potential to kill, which the weapon provides?

☐ Yes ☐ No

7. Did you always use the same type of weapon?

☐   Yes   ☐   No

8. Do you use a weapon when committing a crime because you think it can guarantee the success of your actions?

☐   Yes   ☐   No

9. Do you often go to commit a crime without a weapon because you think it is easier to take a weapon from the scene of the crime?

☐   Yes   ☐   No

10. Do you often carry more than one weapon when going to commit a crime?

☐   Yes   ☐   No

11. Do you change the type of weapon according to the type of crime?

☐   Yes   ☐   No

12. Do you change the type of weapon according to the type of victim?

☐   Yes   ☐   No

13. Do you think it is easy to buy a firearm?

☐   Yes   ☐   No

14. Do you usually use stabbing weapons?

☐   Yes   ☐   No

15. When you have a weapon are you less worried about the police?

☐   Yes   ☐   No

16. Have you used a firearm from an early age?

☐   Yes   ☐   No

17. Do you use a weapon during the crime because you think it gives you more security?

☐   Yes   ☐   No

Part 2 - This part of the questionnaire is designed to give me some information about you

General Details

18. How old are you? Please write your age in the box.   ☐

19. How old were you when you were first found guilty of a crime by a court?

☐

20. How many convictions do you have and what are these for?

☐

Part 3 - Here are a number of personality characteristics that may or may not apply to you. Please tick the box 'Yes' when you agree that a statement reflects your personality characteristic and 'No' when you disagree.

	Yes	**No**
21. People influence my ideas	☐	☐
22. People decide my actions	☐	☐
23. People control my actions	☐	☐
24. People command	☐	☐
25. I do what people do	☐	☐
26. I influence people's ideas	☐	☐
27. I influence people's actions	☐	☐
28. I dominate	☐	☐
29. I command	☐	☐
30. People do what I want	☐	☐

I see myself as someone:

31. Reserved	☐	☐
32. Reflective	☐	☐
33. Calm	☐	☐
34. Who make plans	☐	☐

35. Sociable

36. Aggressive

37. Who loses control easily

38. Who likes change

Appendix II

Description of Variables Used in This Study

Variables referring to the meaning of the weapon

1. *Power*: The offender used the weapon to exert power over the victim.
2. *Control*: The offender used the weapon to control the victim.
3. *Price*: The offender was concerned about the price of the weapon.
4. *Fear*: The offender thought about the fear caused to the victim by the presence of the weapon.
5. *Know to Use*: The offender reported that he only used a weapon that he knew how to use.
6. *Kill*: The offender was concerned about the potential to kill that the weapon provided.
7. *Same Weapon*: The offender always used the same type of weapon.
8. *Success*: The offender believed that guaranteed success in the crime was linked with the fact that he was carrying a weapon.
9. *Weapon From*: The offender used a weapon taken from the scene of the crime.
10. *More Weapon*: The offender often used more than one weapon to commit the crime.
11. *Weapon Crime*: The offender changed the type of weapon used according to the type of crime.
12. *Weapon Victim*: The offender changed the type of weapon used according to the type of victim.
13. *Easy to Buy a Firearm*: The offender thought it was easy for him to buy a firearm.
14. *Stabbing Weapons*: The offender usually used stabbing weapons.
15. *Weapon Police*: The offender was less worried about the police because he had a weapon in his possession.
16. *Young*: The offender had used firearms from an early age.

17. Security: The offender used a weapon because he was concerned about the security it gave him.

Variables referring to the offenders' convictions

18. Embezzlement
19. Drug Trafficker
20. Robbery
21. Burglary
22. Indecent Assault
23. Rape
24. Murder
25. Kidnap
26. Bodily Harm

Variables referring to inclusion

27. People influence my ideas
28. People decide my actions
29. People control my actions
30. People command
31. I do what people do

Variables referring to control

32. I influence people's ideas
33. I influence people's actions
34. I dominate
35. I command
36. People do what I want

Variables referring to introversion

37. Reserved
38. Reflective
39. Calm
40. Who make plans

Variables referring to extroversion

41. Sociable
42. Aggressive

43. Who loses control easily
44. Who likes change

6 The Contribution of Psychological Research to Arson Investigation

KATARINA FRITZON

Most recent research on arson is aimed at identifying the various motivations underlying the act. This work can be classified into three general groupings. The first category of research looks at the characteristics of people who set fires. The second has sought to create typologies of their motives. A third approach has developed that has been termed a 'functional analytic' model of firesetting behaviour.

In terms of the practical investigation of arson, relatively little has been done to understand the relationships between the different types of arson and the characteristics of the individuals who are likely to be involved. What has been done has generally evolved out of the FBI work on what has been termed 'offender profiling'. Rather than focusing on what is actually available to an arson investigator, i.e. aspects of the arson crime-scene itself, these attempts generally classify individuals in terms of the supposed underlying motive and then create a 'profile' of that individual based on this inference.

The current chapter firstly examines the two main ways that current psychological research on firesetters can contribute to the investigation of arson. Firstly, the literature on the characteristics of people who set fires allows the identification of the key features of such individuals that distinguish them from people, including other criminals, who do not set fires. Secondly the typologies of motives of firesetters allows the possibility of distinguishing between arsonists themselves. In conclusion, a new approach to arson research is outlined which focuses on the meaning of the firesetting act to the offender and what this can tell us about his or her other likely characteristics.

147

*Offender Profiling Series: IV- **Profiling Property Crimes***
Edited by D. Canter and L. Alison. © 2000, Ashgate Publishing, Aldershot. pp 147-184

Katarina Fritzon has a first degree in Psychology from the University of Aberdeen, a Masters in Investigative Psychology from Surrey University, and a PhD from Liverpool University. The title of her PhD thesis was 'Differentiating Arsonists: Fire as a Destructive Action System' and she has also written several papers on arson. The main focus of her work to date has been to develop a classification of styles of firesetting based on the source and target of the act. She has also lectured to Fire Brigades and academic audiences and has assisted police and defence solicitors on arson cases. She is currently a lecturer at the University of Surrey where her other research interests include intrafamilial homicide and offender spatial behaviour.

6 The Contribution of Psychological Research to Arson Investigation

KATARINA FRITZON

Introduction: A Brief History of Arson

In the early half of this century, Freud wrote an article entitled 'The Acquisition of Power over Fire', in which he said that firesetting resulted from a fixation or regression to the phallic-urethral stage of libidinal development. Freud (1932) based his theory of firesetting on the Greek legend of Prometheus who stole fire from the Gods. The fact that Prometheus carried the fire in a hollow fennel stalk was interpreted by Freud as symbolic of the penis, and he went on to say that 'The warmth radiated by fire evokes the same kind of glow as accompanies the state of sexual excitation, and the form and motion of the flame suggests the phallus in action' (p.407). Although an emphasis on the sexual symbolism of fire continued into the 1950's, new perspectives began to question these urethral-erotic interpretations and firesetting behaviour became increasingly to be viewed as more complex in its root causes.

For the last 20 years the original psychoanalytic formulation has been under severe criticism. For example, in what still remains the largest study of arson of its kind, Lewis and Yarnell (1951) identified only 40 among a sample of 1,145 adult male firesetters who appeared to derive sexual pleasure from setting or watching fires. Although some more recent studies (eg. Lange and Kirsche, 1989) continue to find support for the sexual arousal motivation in fire-raising, there are many more that do not. For example, Rice and Harris (1991) identified only six out of their sample of 243 male firesetters who were recorded as having had sexual arousal to fire as a motive for their offence(s). Other work at the same institution (Quinsey, Chaplin and Upfold, 1989) reported no differences between normal subjects' and firesetters' sexual arousal patterns to fire-related stimuli.

Unfortunately, although this sexual aspect to firesetting has been discredited by most empirical scientifically valid research, it is a view that some writers find hard to dispel. For example, Macdonald (1977) states that 'the majority of pyromaniacs, both male and female, describe sexual excitements while watching the blaze, and some masturbate at the scene' (p.191). He goes on to offer advice to those investigating suspected cases of arson: 'The investigator will want to talk to anyone seen masturbating in the area of the fire' (p.223). Barracato (1979), a respected fire investigator who clearly took Macdonald's advice to heart, went further in suggesting that investigators should follow suspects to the bathroom because 'Urination is a psychological form of sexual gratification for the pyromaniac, and it is impossible for him to function in front of other people' (p.4).

The term 'pyromania' dates back to the nineteenth century when it became a very popular topic in the scientific literature. It was simply defined at that time as an irresistible impulse to set fires and anyone who fitted that description was regarded as legally 'insane'. People were frequently diagnosed as pyromaniacs based on the single clinical criteria of repeatedly setting fires.

Today, more comprehensive medical definitions of pyromania are being used to clarify this phenomenon. According to the most recent edition of the Diagnostic and Statistical Manual of Mental Disorders (American Psychiatric Association, 1994), pyromania is defined as repeated deliberate and purposeful firesetting associated with tension or affective arousal before the act, followed by intense pleasure or relief when setting the fires or witnessing/participating in its aftermath. DSM-IV lists several behavioural traits that characterise the pyromaniac, such as making elaborate preparations before starting a fire, being a regular observer at fires, setting off false alarms, and showing interest in fire-fighting paraphernalia. Onset is usually in childhood and may continue through adolescence into adulthood. Thus whilst it has been suggested that the term 'pyromania' has no psychiatric meaning and is merely a catch-all term which is used by 'lazy psychiatrists' (Robbins & Robbins, 1967), its use nevertheless persists and continues to have an impact on modern psychiatric treatment of firesetters.

In fact, pyromania is the diagnosis *least* frequently used for firesetters, as they are more likely to be viewed by mental health practitioners as suffering from either a conduct disorder (in children), an antisocial personality disorder, schizophrenia, mental retardation, organic psychosis or a mood disorder (Barnett and Spitzer, 1994).

In order to understand the etiology of firesetting behaviour in individuals who are not classified as pyromaniacs, and who have not carried out the act for 'rational' reasons such as crime-concealment or profit, the bulk of the current research on arson is aimed at identifying the various motivations underlying the act. This work can be classified into three general groupings. The first category of research looks at the characteristics of people who set fires. The second has sought to create typologies of their motives. A third relatively recent approach has developed what has been termed a 'functional analytic' model of firesetting behaviour.

In terms of the practical investigation of arson, relatively little has been done to understand the relationships between the different types of arson and the characteristics of the individuals who are likely to be involved. What has been done has generally evolved out of the FBI work on what has been termed 'offender profiling'. Rather than focusing on what is actually available to an arson investigator, i.e. aspects of the arson crime-scene itself, these attempts generally classify individuals in terms of the supposed underlying motive and then create a 'profile' of that individual based on this inference.

This chapter firstly examines the two main ways that current psychological research on firesetters can contribute to the investigation of arson. The literature on the characteristics of people who set fires allows the identification of the key features of such individuals that distinguish them from people, including other criminals, who do not set fires. Additionally, the typology of motives of firesetters allows the possibility of distinguishing between arsonists themselves. Of greater investigative value, however, is a new approach to arson research that not only describes differences in the characteristics of arsonists, but relates this to directly observable crime-scene features.

Arsonists and Non-Arsonists

The first step in providing a psychological contribution to arson investigation is to identify those characteristics that distinguish firesetters from individuals who do not commit arson. An American psychologist, Ken Fineman (1991, 1995) has stated that while few child arsonists grow up to be adult arsonists, most adult arsonists start setting fires in childhood. It may therefore be useful to begin a discussion of modern theories of firesetting by focusing firstly on those that have attempted to explain the etiology of arson behaviour in children.

Characteristics of Juvenile Firesetters

Work by Kafrey (1978, 1980) has shown that most young children experiment with fire. Fascination with matches, lighters and fire may be a normal investigative part of growing up, and not necessarily a prelude to firesetting behaviour. However, other research has suggested that although some firesetting by children is motivated simply by curiosity, habitual firesetting from an early age may be a way of expressing anger or frustration with aspects of the child's family circumstances (Kolko and Kazdin, 1991a, 1991b). Fineman (1991) recently outlined the need to distinguish between 'curiosity' and 'psychological' firesetting, stating that 'curiosity' was responsible for 60% of all arson committed by children. The only difference in the characteristics of these two groups that Fineman identified, however, was that the first was mainly represented by children under five years of age, while the latter consisted of 5-10 year olds. The question therefore arises as to how one can determine when a child's act of firesetting arises out of mere curiosity and when it is indicative of more deep-rooted behavioural problems.

Some studies of child firesetters have found that certain psychological characteristics differentiate these children from other non-firesetters. For example, Rothstein (1963) studied the Rorschach responses of eight firesetting boys ranging in age from six years to 12. He found two distinct groups in this sample which he described as borderline psychotics and impulsive neurotics. The first group demonstrated weak egos which Rothstein said collapsed under the need to discharge tension. In contrast, the second group of children was described as over-controlled and since neurotic personalities blocked the expression of daily tension, their anxiety mounted until it resulted in a sudden breakdown of control accompanied by acting-out behaviour. It is difficult to imagine how the results of this study could be used by arson investigators, however, as the administration and interpretation of the Rorschach test is something which requires a considerable level of psychological expertise, and its results are largely subjective. Therefore, although these findings may be useful from a clinical perspective, it is difficult to know how they could be refuted. Research highlighting differences in directly observable characteristics would be more helpful.

In the largest study of juvenile firesetters to date, Wooden and Berkey (1984) compared the characteristics, as reported by their parents, of 69 young arsonists apprehended in Southern California with a control group of 78 non-firesetters. The aim of the study was both to identify those characteristics which differentiate the firesetters from the non-firesetters, and also to discern those behaviours that distinguish the more serious and recidivist firesetting delinquents from the less serious and infrequent firesetters.

Of the 84 possible behavioural problems examined in the study, 33 items statistically differentiated the two juvenile groups. The two most distinguishing characteristics of the 33 problem areas were stealing and truancy. As shown in figure 6.1, the parents of the firesetters reported that their children both stole and were truant significantly more often than did the parents of non-firesetters (47% versus 13% for sometimes or frequent stealing and 37% versus 6% for occasional or frequent school truancy). These differences were both significant at the $p \leq 0.001$ level.

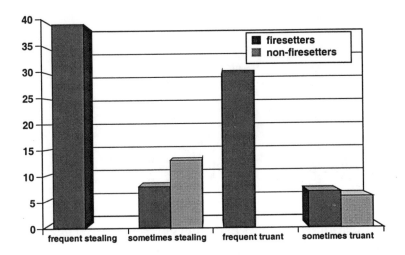

Figure 6.1: Behavioural Problems of Firesetters and Non-Firesetters

The firesetters also exhibited more behavioural problems and learning difficulties than the non-firesetters, many of which have been documented in other studies. These include lying, playing alone, impulsiveness, fighting with siblings or peers, impatience, being out of touch with reality, jealousy, shyness, hyperactivity, stuttering, expressing anger, violence, and being a poor loser (eg. Kolko and Kazdin, 1991; 1991b). Kafry (1978) has explained the link between setting fires, hyperactivity and aggression in the young by suggesting that a child, unable to control impulses, may attempt to discharge tension through external means such as firesetting.

The above findings all relate to differences in personality characteristics between firesetters and non-firesetters, however Wooden and Berkey also discuss aspects of the two groups' social and family environments. For example, the parents of the firesetters reported over twice the number of recent disruptive changes in the family than did the parents of non-firesetters (61% versus 28%). As depicted in figure 6.2, these changes included, in descending order, a recent divorce and/or remarriage (20%), the death of a relative (13%), some other type of major change (13%), and the presence of a new baby (8%).

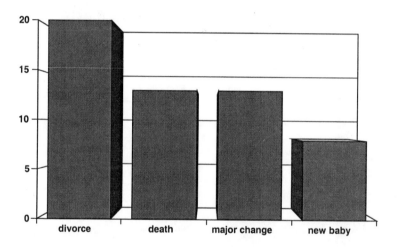

Figure 6.2: Disruptive Changes in Families of Young Firesetters

Whereas 82% of the non-firesetters group lived with both natural parents, only 51% of the firesetters lived with both parents. Other research has also consistently noted significant family disturbances in the background of firesetters. For example, in Bradford and Dimock's (1986) comparison of 57 adult arsonists and 46 adolescent arsonists, both groups came from disrupted family backgrounds. As shown in figure 6.3, seven (15%) of the adolescents, and seven (12%) of the adults were illegitimate and 10% in

total were adopted. Nearly 40% of the adolescents were in a single parent
family home with their mother.

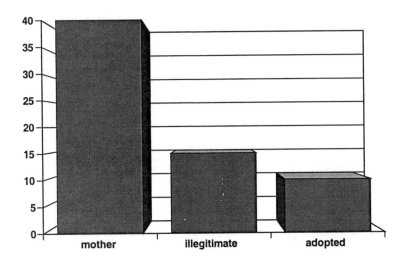

Figure 6.3: Family Backgrounds of Adolescent Firesetters

Additionally, DeSalvatore and Hornstein (1991) found that in more
than half of their sample of 52 juvenile firesetters the parents had received
a psychiatric diagnosis (54%), and a smaller number has a history of
alcohol or drug abuse (23%).

Another difference observed in the Wooden and Berkey study was in
the method of discipline chosen by the parents of the two groups. Figure
6.4 shows that the parents of the non-firesetters employed withdrawing of
privileges more frequently than the other group (36% versus 12%). The
parents of the firesetters, on the other hand, employed corporal
punishment more frequently than those of the non-firesetters (12% versus
4%).

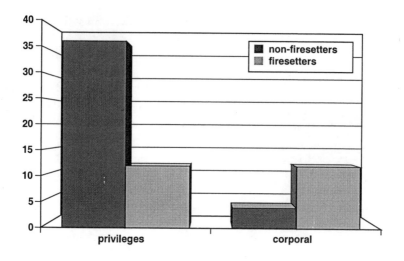

Figure 6.4: Method of Discipline Employed by Parents of Firesetters and Non-Firesetters

The authors point out that these slight differences in punishment methods may in fact be indicative of some socio-economic differences between the two sample groups. As past research has shown, the parents of lower socio-economic strata more frequently use corporal punishment than parents from the middle socio-economic strata. Other research has examined this link between socio-economic factors and firesetting, suggesting that arson is sometimes used by lower-class individuals who lack persuasive skills (eg. Pettiway, 1987). This perspective is discussed further in the section on characteristics of adult firesetters.

Wooden and Berkey also explored those behaviours that characterised the severity of the firesetters themselves. They found that as the children got older the number of behavioural problems shared by the more serious firesetters in each age group increased (from 15 shared by the four to eight year-olds, to 23 for the pre-teenagers, to 44 for the teenage group). The older the juvenile, the more varied and complex the problem areas became. There were also subtle distinctions in terms of the behavioural problems shared by each of the three age groups.

The younger firesetters were more likely to express their anger and frustration by striking out at things close to them, such as the family pets, their own toys, and their siblings, as well as themselves. The pre-teenage firesetters displaced this hostility onto others by fighting with their peers.

In the teenage firesetters, frustration and aggression were expressed through such means as strange thought patterns, bizarre speech, and severe depression. What characterises all of these groups, is the inability to express anger either directly, or through more appropriate means. The use of arson as a means of expression is described by Geller (1992) as the most common presentation of pathological firesetting in adults, where the behaviour is neither a primary symptom of a psychiatric disorder, nor attributable to pyromania, but is used as means of communicating a desire, wish or need.

An important question arising from the above set of behavioural problems associated with youngsters' firesetting activity, is whether firesetting is, as some researchers have argued, simply an extreme form of antisocial behaviour (Patterson, 1982), or whether the antisocial behaviours associated with firesetting differ from those associated with Conduct Disorder in general. Addressing this question, a study by Forehand et al. (1991) has found that it is the severity of behavioural problems, rather than their uniqueness that is associated with young firesetters. In their sample of 36 male juvenile delinquents, the 12 firesetters reported significantly more conduct disorder symptoms, than the non-firesetters.

This section has presented two apparently conflicting views of firesetting by children. On the one hand some researchers have argued that firesetting is a natural consequence of a difficult progression through a developmental stage, whereas others have emphasised the role of the family situation as an environmental stressor. Inevitably, however, there is a proportion of young firesetters whose behaviour cannot directly be explained by either of these theories. These are individuals who neither appear to have disrupted family lives, nor significant psychological problems who nevertheless set fires. Similarly, there are children who do not set fires despite a variety of emotional and environmental disturbances. Therefore, additional factors must be considered in formulating a unifying approach to understanding firesetting behaviour.

Characteristics of Adult Firesetters

Firesetting behaviour in adults has generally been addressed from a psychiatric perspective and has focused on the identification of clinical features, which are commonly found for this group of individuals.

Like the studies of child firesetters, research has shown that the family histories of adult arsonists were characterised by disturbances of some kind. For example, Hurley and Monahan (1969) found that firesetters reported high incidences of early parental separation (20%), illegitimacy (16%), death of close relatives (24%) and being adopted or brought up in children's homes (28%). However, none of these results differed significantly from a control group of non-arsonists. What did differentiate them was their high level of relationship and other social problems. Fifty-four percent reported sexual maladjustments, 62% reported difficulties in relationships with the opposite sex; of those that had married, two-thirds were divorced.

This suggestion that arsonists experience particular social and relationship problems has also been picked up by later studies. For example, Harris and Rice (1984) found that firesetters were less assertive than other patients in situations requiring the verbal expression of negative feelings, and they described themselves and were described by others as more shy and withdrawn. Based on this they hypothesised that assertion deficits and social isolation play a large contributing role in the etiology of firesetting behaviour. This was supported by a later study by the same researchers (Rice and Harris, 1991) using a larger sample of 243 male firesetters. Comparing these individuals with 100 other patients in the same hospital, they found that the firesetters were more socially isolated (as indicated by variables such as hobbies, marital status, living arrangements, etc.), less likely to be physically aggressive, less intelligent, younger, less physically attractive and had more extensive psychiatric histories than other mentally disordered offenders. Multiple discriminant analysis further indicated that the firesetters were more likely to have suffered childhood abuse. Their families were more likely to have reported unusual interest in fire, the number of such fire-related misbehaviours as false fire alarms was higher and they were significantly less likely to have previous non-fire and violent charges. This latter finding appears to contrast with the results of Hurley and Monahan (1969) who found that arsonists had almost eight times as many previous property convictions as non-arsonists (52% versus 7%). However, this result is contaminated by the fact that the category of property convictions included previous convictions for arson.

In summary, then, these results were consistent with the hypothesis that firesetters are more socially isolated, less likely to be physically aggressive, and have more extensive psychiatric histories than other mentally disordered offenders. Together, the earlier results of Harris and Rice (1984) and the later study (Rice and Harris, 1991) lend considerable support to the idea that social skills in general and assertiveness in particular represent important clinical characteristics of firesetters. This again points to the possibility that arson may be used as a method of communication by such individuals (Geller, 1992).

The second way in which the current psychological literature on arson can contribute to police investigations is in examining aspects of firesetters' characteristics that differ according to the particular type of arson that they commit.

Differentiation between Groups of Arsonists

In addition to studies which give characteristics that differentiate between firesetters and non-firesetters, a few studies have also examined differences between sub-groups of arsonists. For example, Rice and Harris (1991) compared one-off arsonists with known repeat offenders. They found, interestingly, that repeat offenders were younger but had more extensive criminal histories than the first-time firesetters. Also, first-time offenders were more likely to have victimised a person they knew and for reasons that were psychotic. Finally, repeat offenders were less likely to have a history of interpersonal aggression, were more likely to be diagnosed as personality disordered, and were more likely to have set fires in extreme excitement or as a release of tension. This last result suggested that some of the repeat offenders may have been pyromanicas, however, closer examination of their clinical fires indicated that anger and revenge were more important precursors of the firesetting activity.

A study by Sakheim, Osborn and Abrams (1991) focusing on juvenile firesetters also provides a number of variables that can be used to discriminate between subgroups of these offenders. The authors identify four categories of firesetters based on levels of risk for recidivism. Minor risk is attached to young firesetters who play with matches out of curiosity as increased parental supervision can usually combat this habit. When a child sets a fire as a 'cry for help' there is a moderate risk of recidivism as they will probably continue to set fires until their emotional needs are recognised. A definite-risk firesetter is usually a conduct-disordered, more anti-social child who is chronically angry and rebellious, and uses fire repeatedly in power-struggles with adults. Finally an extreme risk for future firesetting is attached to children or adolescents who belong to the category of 'pyromaniac', or who are psychotically disturbed. Their behaviour is unpredictable and therefore dangerous. For this study, the first two groups were called minor firesetters, and the latter two were called major or severe firesetters.

Using psychological test data, psychiatric evaluations and social histories of the 50 firesetters examined, the authors found that 10 of the 35 variables significantly discriminated between the two categories. Inadequate superego functioning, sexual excitement, poor social anticipation and awareness, rage at insults or humiliation, and cruelty to children or animals were found to be more frequent in the severe group than in the minor group, with a high degree of statistical significance ($p < 0.001$). Also, intense anger at maternal rejection, neglect or abandonment; poor social comprehension and judgement; and attraction to or pre-occupation with fire were found more frequently in the severe than in the minor firesetting group, with a statistical significance of $p < .05$. In contrast, the presence of obsessive-compulsive defences against impulsivity was observed more often among the minor firesetters than severe firesetters at the $p < 0.005$ level of significance. Also, there was a tendency for the presence of guilt or remorse over previous firesetting episodes, separation anxiety, and a wish for reunion with a paternal figure to be found more frequently among the minor than the major group ($p < 0.10$). The authors claim that using these variables correctly classified the minor firesetters in all cases, and the severe firesetters in 88% of cases.

Although this study focuses on child firesetters, the motives used, with the possible exception of the 'playing with matches' group, can also be applied to adults in order to distinguish their risk of recidivism. However, while the results of this study may be useful as a clinical tool for identifying those firesetters who remain seriously at risk for future firesetting in the community, a criticism is that the majority of the variables used were somewhat psychodynamic in nature. It would not be readily observable at an arson crime scene, for example; or during the course of non-psychoanalytic therapy sessions; or in judicial proceedings considering the appropriate dispersal of arsonists.

A more useful set of variables from an investigative point of view would be those relating to previous criminal records. To date, few studies of arsonists have attempted to gather past criminal histories. This may be a function of the fact that most studies have been from a psychiatric perspective, concentrating on pathological aspects of the act of firesetting. A study by Hill et al. (1982), however, performed a discriminant analysis of a group of arsonists' criminal histories and found that 70% were property offenders and 30% were violent offenders. Similarly, a study by Leong (1992) found that of a total of 29 arsonists in his sample, the number having committed only property offences was nine, whereas those having committed only violent crimes, was five. A further four had committed both.

Another area of research with important investigative implications is the relationship between aspects of an arson, and the residence of the offender. A study by Pettiway (1987) examined the relationship between demographic variables (age, race and sex) along with environmental characteristics of the offender's residence, and the motivation for arson. This study differentiated between arson which was retaliatory (revenge) in motivation and that which was non-retaliatory (eg. playing with matches, crime concealment).

The results for age and race showed a reversal of the pattern for retaliation for whites and blacks in different age categories. For white offenders, the youngest age group (below 18) was most likely to use arson as a means of retaliation, with odds increasing from the main effect value of 0.681 to 0.859 (for non-whites the odds decrease to 0.54). On the other hand, non-whites were more likely to commit retaliatory arson if they were over 18. Blacks in the age bracket 19-30 were 1.52 times more likely to commit this type of arson (main effect odds of 1.262) and the equivalent figure for those over 30 was 1.21 (main effect of 1.164). Pettiway suggested that the explanation was related to the demographic and structural characteristics of the offenders' place of residence. Individuals residing in type six neighbourhoods, so-called 'natural areas' for crime, were more likely to commit retaliatory arson. These areas consist of predominantly black female-headed households, a large proportion of separated males and divorced females, living in single-unit detached properties, often with inadequate kitchen and bathroom facilities. Pettiway found that those individuals who are most likely to retaliate (whites under 18 and blacks over 18) are more often residents of type six environments than those who do not commit retaliatory arson. This study suggests, therefore, that environment is a more important determinant of the likelihood of committing arson for revenge, than are characteristics such as age and race. Whilst it may be controversial to suggest that individuals in lower socio-economic strata may be more likely to use aggressive non-verbal means of retaliation because of lack of persuasive skills, this study can be seen to provide general support for the hypothesis that arson may be used by certain individuals as a means of communication (Geller, 1992).

In this way arson is seen as a way of achieving goals. This brings us to the variety of other goals, or motives, which various studies have offered as causes of firesetting. This is one of the main bodies of research that differentiates between groups of arsonists.

The Motives of Arsonists

The majority of the studies reported in the previous section relied on the identification of motive as a way of differentiating between sub-groups of firesetters. In the current arson literature the focus has been on producing lists of motives, rather than attempting to tie these into a meaningful psychological framework for exploring ways in which firesetters differ from each other. In order to be of greater explanatory value, it is useful to discuss the motives for arson within the general framework of motivational theory. The factor that has received the most attention from motivational theorists is the concept of human needs as these determine what people want from the environment. Theories of human needs have been termed 'content theories' of motivation, as distinct from 'process theories', which address the issue of how motivation operates (Steers and Porter, 1991).

Operating within this framework, firesetting behaviour can be seen as an attempt to address an individual's needs; therefore the motives of arsonists can be discussed within the terms of need theories. Two of the most important of these are Maslow's need hierarchy and McClelland's learned needs (Steers and Porter, 1991).

Maslow's theory explains human behaviour in terms of a hierarchy of five general needs. The most basic of these are physiological needs, including food, water, oxygen, etc. In Geller's (1992) typology of motives for arson he mentions a category of firesetter described as vagrants. In some cases, serious fires can result from these individuals' efforts to stay warm when unsheltered. Lewis and Yarnell (1951) described them as wanderers and hobos; these days they would probably comprise a proportion of the homeless population. Certainly the desire to stay warm can be categorised as a physiological need. Another motive for firesetting that could be similarly classified has been the subject of some controversy, and that is the sexual arousal that allegedly accompanies some individuals' firesetting activities. Again, Lewis and Yarnell (1951) describe one of their groups of firesetters as an erotic group, made up of pyromaniacs and firesetters who derive direct sexual pleasure from setting and watching fires. As previously mentioned, however, more recent research (Rice and

Harris, 1984; Quinsey et al., 1989) has minimised the importance of such a motive.

Finally, fires which are set for financial gain could also be said to be motivated by physiological need in that food and shelter are usually dependent on financial considerations. Most typologies of motives for arson include this category (Geller, 1992; Douglas et al., 1992; Icove and Estepp, 1987).

The second level of Maslow's hierarchy of needs is Safety and Security needs. These include a desire for security, stability and protection. In terms of arson, firesetting, which is motivated by crime-concealment, fulfils the need for protection from the undesirable consequences of being caught and convicted of the primary crime, eg. murder, burglary, etc.

The next level of the hierarchy concerns Social needs such as the need for love, affection and a sense of belonging. Maslow states that individuals who are unable to satisfy this need will feel lonely, ostracised and rejected. Whilst arson that is motivated by rage, hatred, unrequited or rejected love and jealousy (Barnett, 1992) may not actually achieve the social needs of the firesetter, their behaviour can be seen as resulting from the frustration and dissatisfaction of these needs. It may be a way (albeit a dysfunctional one) of restoring the disequilibrium that such frustration causes.

The desire to achieve a sense of social belonging may also be what motivates vandalism firesetters who usually form part of a group of like-minded juvenile delinquents. Similarly, firesetting by younger children has been categorised as being motivated by either curiosity or anger (Wooden and Berkey, 1984; Kolko and Kazdin, 1991). Whilst the former probably only involves 'fire play' rather than deliberately setting fires, the latter group may be seen as attempting to draw attention to social needs that are being neglected or ignored within a disruptive home environment. Kolko and Kazdin (1991) examined the firesetting risk (measured by factors such as eliciting greater community complaints about their contact with fire, and engaging in more fire-related activities) of these two types of child firesetter, and found that children motivated by anger may be more deliberate or purposive in their use of fire to resolve particular individual problems.

The fourth level of Maslow's hierarchy concerns ego and esteem needs, which can be focused either internally or externally. When focused internally, the esteem needs include a desire for strength, achievement and independence. When focused externally this need consists of a desire for reputation, status, fame and glory, attention and importance. According to several typologies of arsonists' motives (Prins et al., 1985; Home Office, 1988; Rice and Harris, 1990) the most common single reason behind acts of firesetting is revenge, either against an individual or against society. This category of arson can be seen as an attempt to redress self-esteem by someone who feels they have been wronged. Other categories of arson which can be viewed as attempts to enhance esteem include arson because of jealousy (Rider, 1980) and vanity or recognition firesetting (Geller, 1992).

The final stage of the need hierarchy is the need for self-actualisation, which refers to the process of developing our true potential as individuals to the fullest extent. This would include the development of a personal ideology and membership of groups, which support that ideology. Arson that is committed by political and extremist groups, such as the Animal Liberation Front, therefore, can be viewed as being motivated by the need for actualisation of the particular goals and ideals propagated by that group.

Another well-known need theory is the learned needs theory developed by David McClelland. This theory is closely associated with learning theory since he believed that needs were learned or acquired by the kinds of events people experienced in their culture. Taken together with reinforcement approaches to motivation which argue that present behaviour is shaped by the consequences of past behaviour, the motivation to commit arson can be viewed as an interaction between social, psychological and environmental factors. This is the approach taken by Jackson, Glass and Hope (1987) who present a functional analytic view of recidivistic arson.

Cognitive Behavioural Model of Firesetting

An analysis of behaviour based on this model requires the identification of both antecedent events which are considered important for the initiation of the behaviour, and the consequences of that behaviour which maintain and direct its developmental course. Functional analysis allows for the same behaviour to serve different functions and be a function of different antecedents across time and situations. Thus, the model is particularly suited to analyses that stress the developmental aspects of a particular behaviour. Arson can be seen as a type of behaviour that has such dynamic qualities.

Jackson et al. consider recidivistic arson to serve a number of functions and represent a number of motives. Central to their model is the notion that a fascination and experimentation with fire is a widespread feature of normal child development and that the responses of parents, other authority figures and peers to the firesetting behaviour are important factors in the development to more pathological arson. As previously mentioned, Kafrey (1978) has found almost universal fire interest in five to ten year-old children, therefore it is important to identify those factors which maintain and exaggerate this interest. The antecedent events proposed by Jackson et al. are of these types: *general setting conditions, specific psycho-social stimuli* and *triggering events.*

The first, general-setting conditions, includes psycho-social disadvantage, general dissatisfaction with life and the self, and ineffective social interaction. That arsonists are dissatisfied with themselves is indicated by findings suggesting a high incidence of depression and suicidal inclination. A study of firesetters in psychiatric institutions in Ireland (O'Sullivan et al., 1987) found that there was a consistent proclivity for individuals of all diagnostic types to engage in self-destructive behaviour. Lewis and Yarnell (1951) also pointed out that some of the arsonists in their sample acted out heroic roles. With regard to ineffective social interaction, Vreeland and Levin (1980) suggested that firesetting along with anti-social behaviours, sexual, marital and occupational maladjustment and alcoholism (which have been found to have a high incidence among arsonists) may be considered as indicators of a general lack of social skills and self-esteem.

The second type of antecedent event, specific psycho-social stimuli, may explain why the arsonist 'chooses' firesetting behaviour rather than socially acceptable responses, or even other forms of deviant behaviour. The literature suggests that arsonists avoid interpersonal conflict, however, it is unclear why they do so. The specific factors that direct arsonists towards the use of fire will vary according to the individual experiences of the firesetter. They may include some early experience with a fire. Some studies have found that fathers of arsonists have some work involvement with fire.

The third factor is a triggering stimulus, which evokes the firesetting. Again, this will vary amongst individuals, but may include rejection by others and abuse. A common feature suggested by Jackson et al. is that the event induces an undesired situation over which the arsonist is powerless. An important area of research, therefore, would be to examine the emotions preceding firesetting or the temporal relationship between the triggering event, the emotional antecedents and the firesetting.

The behaviour of firesetting itself is also considered an important factor in the model. The targeting of specific property types by particular arsonists indicates that this may form an intrinsic part of the overall arson behaviour. Following the firesetting, many arsonists stay at the scene of the crime, allowing them to achieve some of the aims that were initially responsible for them setting the fire, such as control. Arsonists may become progressively more involved in the aftermath of fire, such as raising the alarm, staying at the scene, helping to fight the fire, etc.

The consequences of firesetting have important implications for the continuance of the behaviour. Where young firesetters feel isolated and rejected with little alternative avenues to improve their situation, firesetting may provoke greater contact with parents and peers, thereby positively reinforcing the behaviour. With repetitive firesetting the child may also gain the interest of a number of professionals. Negative reinforcement may also occur, where the child firesetter is recognised as suffering from emotional problems and is therefore protected from stressful situations. In contrast, adopting a punitive approach to the behaviour is likely to encourage secretiveness, which in turn diminishes the positive consequences of the act. This may be a factor in the individual increasing his involvement in the aftermath of the firesetting.

Finally, the dramatic consequences of the fire itself (eg. fire engines, crowds, praise and recognition) together with the effect of this in light of a history of social inadequacy may be classically paired with fire. Additionally, if the offender is apprehended, enforced avoidance of fire and firesetting materials may prevent the development of appropriate behaviour towards fire.

Admittedly, the hypotheses outlined in the Jackson et al. paper suffer from a lack of empirical testing, being based on the cumulative clinical experiences of the authors, however a number of avenues for future research are suggested, such as examining the developmental aspects of firesetting behaviour.

Cognitive-behavioural evaluations of firesetting emphasise the need to understand the different motivations underlying the act. For example, Fineman (1995) states that a fire set out of jealousy with an *accompanying* feeling of anger must be regarded as different from one which is *motivated* by anger itself. Similarly the role of alcohol can play a different role depending on the individual firesetter. To the opportunistic arsonist the consumption of alcohol might act as a catalyst for setting a fire, whereas to a more serious arsonist it might simply act as a disinhibitor.

A later study by the same authors (Jackson et al., 1987) developed the idea that individuals use arson where they feel they do not possess a repertoire of alternative behaviours for dealing with given situations. The study tested the 'displaced aggression hypothesis' of arson, which suggests that feelings of hostility may be redirected away from people targets and onto property targets. The results showed that arsonists rated themselves as significantly less assertive that either violent offenders or control groups. This suggests that arsonists experience considerable difficulty in resolving interpersonal conflict in an interpersonal manner - which may promote the redirection of hostility onto property. Secondly, arsonists were found to have less stable or less well-defined constructs of the seriousness of person versus property offences compared to the other groups. There was no significant bias towards rating person offences as being more serious than property offences. This may reflect a psychological conflict regarding the seriousness of property and person crimes which is responsible for the displacement of hostility provoked by an individual onto property.

The theories outlined offer various explanations for why people set fires, ranging from environmental and social factors such as poor parenting and poverty, to individual psychological characteristics such as mental illness and lack of social skills. There does not appear to be any cohesion amongst these numerous theories, until it is considered that what they could represent are various explanations for different forms of arson, rather than conflicting explanations of a single phenomena. For example, the types of firesetting behaviour studied by Kafrey (1978; 1980) primarily concerned 'experimental' match play by children that involved setting fire to small household items. In contrast, other research has focused on arson committed by individuals housed in psychiatric institutions and special hospitals (eg. Jackson et al., 1987; Harris and Rice, 1984). These authors are very often dealing with prolonged pathological firesetting by adults where both the nature of the behaviour and its consequences - in terms of extensive destruction of property and potential loss of life - are much more serious.

In order to be of real investigative value, any explanation of arson must take into account variations in firesetting behaviour, offering alternative explanations for each category. It has been almost two decades since Vreeland and Waller (1979) wrote, 'The lack of an adequate system of classification is a major contributory factor to our lack of understanding of firesetting behaviour'. To date there have been several attempts to create typologies of arsonists, most of which are based on classifications of motive (eg. Inciardi, 1970, Vreeland and Waller, 1979, Prins, 1994). This reliance on uncovering the supposed 'motives' for firesetting as the basis of a classification system suffers from serious problems of validity and reliability. As Durkheim (1897) warned, 'Human intention is too intimate a thing to be more than approximately interpreted by another person'. More recently, Geller (1992a) also criticises motivational classifications on the grounds that they focus on possible explanations for the firesetting behaviour, rather than describing variations in the behaviour itself.

Unfortunately, however, a major focus in classifications of arsonists has been on the development of motivational typologies. The most comprehensive of these, at least in terms of the sheer number of motivational categories, is the framework put forward by the FBI in Douglas et al.'s (1992) Crime Classification Manual. Despite the criticism levied against this work, the results retain investigative value in that they describe the different offender characteristics associated with various forms of arson behaviour.

Characteristics of Arsonists Corresponding to Motives

The FBI approach involves extrapolating from crime-scene evidence what the likely motives are, and then (by an unknown process) inferring the typical characteristics of the offender with each of those motives.

Aside from the reliance on motives, there are also methodological concerns regarding this work in that the classifications were based on 'A review of arson research literature and actual arson cases and interviews of [*an unspecified number of*] incarcerated arsonists across the country'. This does not clarify the empirical basis, if any exists, of the classification system. According to the FBI classification, the defining characteristics of arson are described as being determined by the type of victim selected and crime scene indicators, which they categorise in terms of the level of organisation shown by the offender. They describe the organised arsonist as typically using elaborate incendiary devices, leaving less physical evidence and using a methodical approach. The disorganised arsonist uses whatever materials he has to hand (eg. matches to ignite and cigarette lighter fluid to accelerate the fire) and leaves behind more physical evidence such as footprints and fingerprints.

The seven main groups of motives for arson described in the manual are: *vandalism, excitement, revenge, crime concealment, profit, extremist* and *serial offences*. A number of corresponding offender characteristics are given for each of the motive types. *Vandalism* arsonists tend to be juveniles from a lower-class background. They usually live with their parents less than a mile away from the crime scene. Additionally, they will probably be known to the police. Alcohol and drug use are generally not associated with this type of firesetting. Properties likely to be targeted include educational facilities, residential areas and vegetation.

Where the arson is committed for *excitement* motives, the typical offender is an unemployed single juvenile or adult male from a middle-class family living with both parents. This offender often has a history of police contact and is likely to be socially inadequate. Serial offending is common in this group and alcohol or drugs may be used by the older offenders. The type of property likely to be targeted include; bins, skips, vegetation, building sites and residential property.

Where the motive for arson is *revenge*, the offender will most likely be someone known to the victim and may have previous convictions for burglary, theft or vandalism. Any relationships will be unstable and short-term. The use of alcohol during the offence is common to this type. The property which is targeted will be something of significance to the victim, such as a vehicle or bed. If the revenge is directed at society, then a public building, such as a library, may be targeted.

Less clear offender characteristics are given in the case of *crime-concealment* motivated arson. One reason for this may be that the main determinant of the type of perpetrator is the particular crime that is being concealed. If the fire is started for the purpose of concealing murder, for example, then the characteristics of the offender may depend on the nature of the relationship with the victim, eg. a domestic murder may involve an entirely different type of offender from one who commits a stranger-murder. Some suggestions, however, are that the offender is likely to be a young adult living in the surrounding area with a history of police involvement, and alcohol and drug use are common.

If the arson is committed for *profit purposes*, i.e. in order to claim insurance on the property, there may be two separate offenders involved. The primary offender is the businessman whose property is to be burned, and the secondary offender may be a known 'torch' who is hired to commit the arson. There can be several indications that the primary offender has planned the fire, eg. valuable furniture may have been substituted with less expensive furniture, and there may be indicators of financial difficulties or recent changes in insurance policies.

Extremist motivated arson is usually indicated by the perpetrators themselves. They will often inform the media, or leave spray-painted slogans on the walls of the targeted property. The property itself will also give clues, as it will usually represent the antithesis of the offender(s) beliefs.

Finally, the *serial arsonist* targets unoccupied properties usually at night. The typical offender is usually an unemployed, or erratically employed male and possibly a juvenile with a history of substance abuse and police involvement for minor nuisance offences. He will be minimally educated and will have been an under-achiever at school. He will have poor interpersonal relationships, and be socially inadequate. He generally lives within a mile of the crime scene, and may often remain at or return to the scene to watch the fire.

As with FBI classifications of other offences, many of the most salient points made are ones which are drawn from unreferenced previous literature. Perhaps nowhere is this as clear as with their typology of rape. Here the labels produced by the FBI are almost identical to those used by Knight and Prentky (1987) and because of the theoretical and empirical basis to the latter work, there is some external validity to those similar concepts used by the FBI. However, where the connection to previous literature is not so clear, where the links between motives and characteristics appear to be based on mere conjecture, the arguments made by the FBI lack any substantive basis. In referring simply to mental conditions or drives towards behaviour there is no adequate explanation as to why other individuals in the same mental state or with the same needs do not engage in firesetting. For example, with the revenge motive that is commonly cited as one of the most frequent motives for firesetting, merely identifying it as a category of arson does not explain why individuals use this particular form of revenge.

Another behavioural classification of arson that is also related to motives, but has the advantage of employing an empirical approach is by Pisani (1982). This study developed a typology of arson based on correlations among variables. The sample for this study was 138 randomly selected cases of persons arrested for arson in New York City. The largest group of arsonists (53%) were described as using fire as a weapon for revenge. These fires were usually set at night in occupied buildings and were started by flammable liquid. These arsonists often threatened to set fires before doing so and usually had not set fires previously. Three other groups of firesetters with instrumental motives - insurance and welfare fraud as well as crime concealment - together made up a total of 16% of the arson arrests. Vandal firesetters comprised 12% of the sample. These individuals rarely used accelerants in setting fire and usually set fire to only one spot at the scene. Another group with similar offence characteristics to the vandals were called 'pyros' by Pisani and made up 10% of the sample. The difference with this group was that they were said to derive emotional relief or sexual gratification from the fires. A final 9% of the sample were made up of a group who Pisani called 'psychos' who usually had some form of psychiatric history and set fire to occupied buildings, frequently their own apartments. These fires were set by taking a match to bedding and did not usually involve accelerants.

Finally, a recent study by Harris and Rice (1996) classified mentally disordered arsonists by employing multivariate statistical techniques (cluster analysis) to identify four subtypes of firesetters. These four groups were called psychotics, unassertives, multi-firesetters and criminals. The first of these groups made up a third of the sample for the study. Compared to the rates of mental illness cited by previous research (eg. Bradford, 1982) this seems high, but as stated the sample was defined by being mentally disordered. These individuals were usually diagnosed as schizophrenic and had set few fires in their lives, nor had they a history of criminal or aggressive behaviour. They were less likely than members of other clusters to have used accelerants and their rate of recidivism was not particularly high for any further violent, non-violent and firesetting offences.

The next largest group (28%), were called 'unassertives'. These did not tend to have a history of aggression, or criminal activity, were more intelligent and had better employment histories. They were the least assertive of all the four types and were most likely to set fires out of anger or a desire for revenge.

The 'multi-firesetters' accounted for 23% of the total sample. They had the worst childhood histories and had high levels of aggression. Although they had little criminal history generally, they had previously set many fires. They were least intelligent and were most likely to have been institutionalised as children, and they had parents with psychiatric problems. They were also very unassertive, but were least likely to have been diagnosed as schizophrenic. In terms of the characteristics of their fires, they were most likely to have fired institutions and to have confessed. They were also most likely to commit their offences during the day and had a high rate of recidivism for all crime types.

Finally, the smallest subgroup were the 'criminals', making up 16% of the sample. These individuals had extensive criminal histories and poor childhood backgrounds marked by abusive parents. They were most likely to have been diagnosed as personality disordered. In terms of the fires they set, they were least likely to have known the victim of the fire, were most likely to set fire at night-time and were least likely to report the fire or confess. These offenders were the most assertive and were most likely to commit further fire and violent offences when released.

Harris and Rice (1996) also attempted to develop a typology of the characteristics of the fires themselves, and to relate this to the four subgroups of offender. However, the only association they identified; was that more serious fires were set by younger offenders with more extensive histories of firesetting.

One possible reason for this failure of the identification of more substantial links between offence and offender characteristics, is the absence of a theoretical framework underpinning the study. Without such a basis to guide hypotheses about expected differences in the characteristics of the fires set by each of the four groups of arsonists, it would be difficult to know what aspects of the fires to include in the analysis.

While it can be shown that certain studies share at least some of the same terminology in their approach to classifying arsonists, even the short review above has revealed many inconsistencies in the exact composition of equivalent categories.

Also, there are many studies that list categories that are not readily comparable with other frameworks. For example, the 'playing with matches' group of children described by Sakheim et al. (1991) does not readily fit into any of the categories described by the FBI. Conversely, this otherwise comprehensive classification system does not contain all of the categories found elsewhere, eg. arsonists suffering from mental disorder.

For this reason an alternative classification is required which will not only consolidate all of the categories of arson that previous research has already mentioned, but also be flexible enough to incorporate other forms of arson which may not yet have been identified. Canter and Fritzon (1998) adopted a framework such as this in a recent study. This study overcomes many of the flaws in existing work by focusing purely on the observable aspects of crime-scene actions rather than attempting to infer specific motivations. As such this research represents the only example of a combined theoretical and empirical classification of arson which also identifies links between firesetting behaviour and offender characteristics.

From Actions to Characteristics

The objective of the study was to identify observable differences in the behaviour of arsonists that would be characteristic of particular styles of firesetting. The framework for this study was arrived at by considering arson as a process of destructive interactions with the environment, therefore the important elements of the framework are the source of the impulse to set fires and the locus of its effect. The existing literature on the motives for arson draws attention to the causes of the behaviour. In terms of the more specific causes of particular crimes, a common distinction is made in relation to acts of aggression, between instrumental and expressive motivations (Fesbach, 1964, Rosenberg and Knight, 1988). Although this distinction has not yet been applied to acts of arson, researchers with a clinical frame of mind such as Geller (1992b, 1992c) and Sakheim et al. (1991) have looked at other potential sources of arson within the individual, for example, psychiatric or psychological problems.

Other researchers, particularly those involved in the insurance industry (eg. Wood, 1995; Arson Prevention Bureau, 1995), draw attention to the targets that are selected by arsonists. While these writers are primarily concerned with property targets, a significant proportion of arsons can be seen as being directed at people, i.e. the owners of the fired properties. This distinction between person and property targets of arson is potentially very significant and suggests another dimension on which a general classification model could be based.

Therefore, a combination of these perspectives leads to the consideration of the whole process of arson as being, on the one hand derived from a variety of sources and, on the other, having the possibility for different types of target.

The Canter and Fritzon (1998) study tested whether consistencies could be found in firesetting behaviour that distinguish four styles of arson, namely:

1)   An arson that is instrumentally motivated and directed at an object is an attempt to change aspects of the object where the change will be of direct benefit to the firesetter. A burglar who sets fire to a residence to hide clues to his theft, or the car thief who burns a

stolen car for similar reasons are both examples of this type of firesetting. The person who sets fire to a building for insurance purposes, referred to by Vreeland and Levin (1980) as 'arson for profit' can be seen as a more extreme version of this form of arson.

2)   Arson, which is expressive and directed at an object, involves the demonstration of aspects of the arsonist on the external world. This accords with Geller's (1992) description of firesetting as a means of emotional acting out, but the desire to make an impact on the environment also draws attention to forms of arson in which the target has some symbolic, emotional significance to the fire setter.

3)   Expressive arson which is directed at a person often involves emotional distress is being turned inwards to lead to the disintegration of the fire setter him/herself. Suicide by arson will usually be dealt with in a therapeutic context as a form of depressive acting out, so this is also an aspect of arson that is usually not dealt with as such in publications on arson.

4)   The final form of arson can be seen as a reaction to frustration by another person, which the firesetter wishes to hurt or remove. In this sense the offence has some direct instrumental objective but that objective is focused on changing the emotional state of the fire setter. It is thus a more directed form of revenge from that when the target has a symbolic significance. That act, for example against an institution, is thus more appropriately considered as expressive, whereas the retaliatory act against an individual has a more directly instrumental consequence.

Analysing 175 solved arson cases from across England tested the hypothesis that these four themes would differentiate arsonists. The case files were content analysed to produce 42 behavioural variables taken from both the crime reports and witness statements. In order to test the hypotheses of differentiation a Smallest Space Analysis was carried out. The central task of the analysis was to identify themes relating to the four suggested styles of firesetting, within the co-occurance of the actions. This involved, in effect, the comparison of every one of the 42 offence variables with every other, across the 175 cases. The function of the SSA is to test the relationship each of the variables has to every other variable. This is achieved by creating an association matrix from which a geometric representation of the relationships between variables is generated, as with other Multi-dimensional scaling procedures.

A 3-dimensional SSA solution was found to have the reasonable Guttman-Lingoes coefficient of alienation of 0.13 in 10 iterations. Figure 6.5 below shows the projection of the first two vectors of the 3 dimensional space. In this figure each point represents an aspect of the arson derived from the content analysis as listed in appendix A. So the closer together any two variables are in figure 6.5 the more likely when one occurs in an offence that the other will also occur. By contrast, for illustration, it is very unlikely that when a public building is the target that a suicide note will be left. These two variables are on opposite sides of the space.

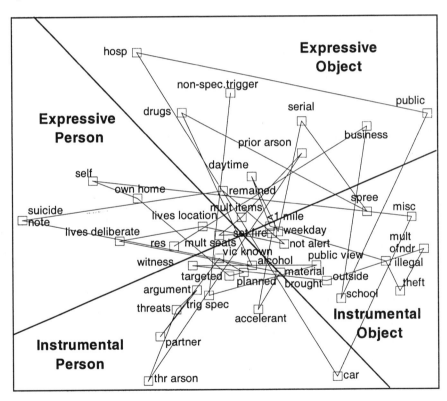

Figure 6.5: SSA Outlining the Characteristics of Arsonists

The results supported the hypothesised framework giving rise to four distinct themes to arson. These four themes and the actions that define them are presented in table 6.1 below.

Table 6.1: Scales of Actions

Instrumental Person	Instrumental Object	Expressive Person	Expressive Object
accelerant	illegal entry	lives endangered	drug use
Alcohol	uninhabited	deliberately	hospital/
argument	property	lives endangered	institution
car	multiple	by location	prior arson
planned	offenders	multiple seats of	public
targeted	did not alert	fire	building
threats	outside	own home	remained
threat of arson	public view	remained	serial
trigger specific	spree	residential	non-specific
to victim	theft	self	trigger
victim partner		suicide note	
victim known			
witness			

Instrumental Person

These arsons often occur as a direct result of some sort of dispute between the offender and another person, usually an ex-partner, or sometimes an ex-employer. This external event causes anger and a sense of injustice within the individual, which he may attempt to redress by retaliative arson.

Thus this form of arson is the instrumental aspect of the person-oriented region. The arson behaviour was directed externally, in other words at another individual. These fires often involved prior threats and violence towards the victim, and there was usually some specific discernible trigger that occurred immediately prior to the firesetting indicating the reactive nature of this type of behaviour. These arsons are classified as instrumental because they served a specific purpose, usually revenge.

Instrumental Object

This type of arson can be seen as opportunistic in that the decision to commit the crime may only be arrived at when the individual recognises the environmental possibilities. It suggests a form of criminal sophistication in which arson is part of the repertoire for achieving criminal goals. This type of firesetting activity is often committed by groups of youngsters where the choice of target is opportunistic rather than selective. It is not so much personally meaningful as just available. The variables illegal entry and theft from premises were found in this region, also indicating instrumentality, where the firesetting can be seen as an externally-generated (perhaps by peer pressure) part of the overall activity of breaking into properties.

Expressive Person

This form of arson behaviour may be an attempt to restore emotional equilibrium, or alleviate distress by seeking attention from family or the authorities. The desire to set fires emerges internally, and coupled with the need for attention, results in the actualisation of the firesetting also being directed internally.

Within the person-oriented offences, there was a sub-group of 'cases where the individual either set fire to him/herself, or to objects placed around them, in what would appear to be an act of suicide. However, in the few cases classified as this type of arson, none of the individuals actually died. In one case, the arsonist attempted to set fire to himself in front of his partner and attending fire officers, and in others the time of day chosen was such that neighbours were alerted by smoke before any serious damage could be done. These cases, therefore are probably better viewed as para-suicides or cries for help.

Expressive Object

These fires tended to be of a serial nature with the arsonist often targeting particular types of public buildings. The fact that these individuals commit serial offences suggests that there is some type of intrinsic fascination for fire that relates to the internal emergence of the behaviour. The targeting of particular buildings that, in their perception, cause a lot of attention to be focused on the individual may also reinforce the firesetting tendencies. These fires were often preceded by some kind of emotionally charged event as indicated by the variable 'non-specific trigger'. This reinforces the notion that the firesetting in these cases acted as a way of obtaining emotional relief. There is some suggestion in the psychiatric literature that some individuals use arson as a means of communication emotional states (eg. Geller, 1992). Such individuals may commit this type of firesetting.

These fires tended to involve repetition over time and prior arson by the offender. The target in these cases was often a public building or hospital, which may have held some meaning for the individual, for example, he may feel anger against authority figures or the symbol that a hospital represents. Another reason for targeting these types of buildings may be that they usually attract a number of fire engines and crowds thus creating vicarious attention for the arsonist. This hypothesis is supported by the fact that the arsonists often remained or returned to the scene of the fire in order to observe or participate in its aftermath.

The finding that the behaviour of arsonists can be differentiated in this way is in itself of considerable practical importance. On the basis of relatively few crime-scene variables arson investigators can gain important insight into the psychological process by which the perpetrator came to set the fire.

However, the additional advantage of this classification scheme over those previously outlined (eg. Harris and Rice, 1998) was that Canter and Fritzon (1998) were also successful at matching the four styles of firesetting with equivalent themes in offender characteristics. These arsonists and the characteristics that define them are listed in table 6.2 below.

Table 6.2: Scales of Arsonists' Characteristics

Failed Relationship	Psychiatric History	Repeat Arsonist	Young Offender
alcoholism	depression	AWOL	caution
cohabiting	psychosis	false alarms	living with
married	psychiatric	personality	parents
qualifications	institution	disorder	school pupil
separated	suicide attempts	prior arson	social services
unskilled	suicide threats	social services	

Young Offender

As hypothesised there is a set of offenders who have been cautioned previously for criminal activities and have come to the attention of the social services. These tended to be the younger offenders who as a consequence were living at home and were of school age (mean age = 16 years). There was a statistically significant correlation between these characteristics and the instrumental object group of actions ($\psi = 0.44$, $p < 0.001$).

Repeat Arsonist

The expressive object theme was proposed to reflect the person for whom arson was a significant aspect of their ways of dealing with others and as a consequence would be reflected in their specifically absenting themselves to set fires, as well as making fire alarm telephone calls. Thus it was found that the variables of the individual having a history of setting fires are close to that of making false alarm calls as well as having usually come to the attention of police and social services, often for arson related matters. Although the SSA was run with the gender variable 'male' rather than 'female' in fact most of the arsonists in this group were women (63%). The mean age of the offenders in this group was 25 years which is also the mean for the sample as a whole. The youngest offender in this group was 12 and the oldest was 60 years. The characteristics of these arsonists correlated with the expressive object group of actions ($\psi = 0.56$, $p < 0.001$).

Psychiatric History

This theme is seen as fundamentally disintegrative, in which arson emerges out of the person's self-destructive emotions; suicide attempts and a history of mental illness are therefore strongly hypothesised to intercorrelate if this theme is to be identifiable. The region with all the variables together that relate to these aspects is therefore a strong indicator of the validity of this theme. Looking at the individuals who had some form of psychiatric history ($n = 51$) it was found that most (84%) usually received a psychiatric diagnosis of either depression (51%) or psychosis (33%) and had made suicide threats (57%) and attempts (43%) prior to setting a fire. In order to have accumulated such a history it is usually necessary for such arsonists to be slightly older (mean age = 29). There were statistically significant correlations between this group of characteristics and two of the actions themes: expressive person ($\psi = 0.38$, $p < 0.001$) and expressive object ($\psi = 0.42$, $p < 0.001$).

Failed Relationship

Here the arson is seen as a direct means of affecting a person who is significant to the arsonist, and as a device the offender uses to achieve focused revenge. These offenders were the oldest in the sample (mean = 31 years) which is not surprising given that most had been married or had had at least one long term partner. Again, these characteristics correlated with two of the arson styles: expressive person ($\psi = 0.21$, $p < 0.005$) and instrumental person ($\psi = 0.49$, $p < 0.001$).

Overall, then, this system of correlations between actions and characteristics provides strong support for the suggestion that the way an arsonist sets fires is a reflection of his characteristics as a person.

Conclusion

The model proposed by Canter and Fritzon (1998) is consistent with the view that arson has a number of very different psychological origins. Some arsons may be the consequence of a deviant life style, being used as a criminal tool, for people who have little other intellectual or physical resource. Other forms of arson may derive directly from the person's own self-destructive tendencies. For others it is a product of their inherently limited way of dealing with other people. A fourth group for whom setting fires is a dominant means of expressing anger and frustration can also be identified. Different treatment programmes would be appropriate for the different forms of arson, for example by dealing with the self-destructive urges, or by addressing directly the mode of anger expression.

The implications of this study extend to the actual investigation of fires. For example, the finding that object-oriented arsons are associated with repetition, coupled with the fact that the offenders tend not to travel far from home, suggests the importance of implementing surveillance in areas recently subjected to arson attacks. It is also likely that offenders responsible for arsons to public properties, including schools and hospitals, will be known to police for previous firesetting. Another implication is that where an arson is relatively serious, showing evidence of planning and the use of materials such as accelerants, it is likely that it represents a targeted attack and that the victim will know the perpetrator.

The model proposed here does provide a framework within which a diversity of perspectives in the literature can be shown to complement one another, rather than being in conflict. It also shows that hypotheses about the relationships between the details of the offence and the characteristics of the offender can be elaborated and tested. It is therefore plausible that the model will also be relevant to other forms of criminal activity.

References

American Psychiatric Association (1994), *Diagnostic and Statistical Manual for Mental Disorders*, 4th edn., Washington DC.

Barnett, W. (1992), 'Psychology and Psychopathology of Firesetting 1955-1991 - A review', *Fortschritte der Neurologie-Psychiatrie*, **60(7)**, 274-286.

Barnett, W. and Spitzer, M. (1994), 'Pathological Firesetting 1955-1991: A Review', *Medicine, Science and Law*, **34(1)**, 4-20.

Barracato (1979), *Fire... Is it Arson?*, Hartford, Ct.: Aetna Casualty and Surety Company.

Bradford, J. and Dimock, J. (1986), 'A Comparative Study of Adolescents and Adults who Wilfully Set Fires', *Psychiatric Journal of the University of Ottawa*, **11(4)**, 228-234.

Canter, D.V. and Fritzon, K. (1998), 'Differentiating Arsonists: A model of Firesetting Actions and Characteristics', *Legal and Criminological Psychology*, **3**, 73-96.

Clare, I.C., Murphy, G.H., Cox, D. and Chaplin, E.H. (1992), 'Assessment and Treatment of Firesetting: A Single Case Investigation using a Cognitive-Behavioural Model', *Criminal Behaviour and Mental Health*, **2(3)**, 253-268.

DeSalvatore, G. and Hornstein, R. (1991), 'Juvenile Firesetting: Assessment and Treatment in Psychiatric Hospitalisation and Residential Placement', *Child and Youth Care Forum*, **20(2)**, 103-114.

Douglas, J.E., Burgess, A.W., Burgess, A.G. and Ressler, R.K. (1992). *Crime Classification Manual*, New York: Lexington Books.

Durkheim, E. (1952), *Suicide: A Study in Sociology*, (trans. by J.A. Spaulding), G. Simpson (ed.), London: Routledge & Kegan Paul.

Fesbach, S. (1964), 'The Function of Aggression and the Regulation of Aggressive Drive', *Psychological Review*, **71**, 257-272.

Fineman, K.R. (1991), *Firesetting by Children and Adolescents*, Paper given at CFPA - Europe conference on Juvenile Arson, Luxembourg.

Fineman, K.R. (1995), 'A Model for the Qualitative Analysis of Child and Adult Fire Deviant Behaviour', *American Journal of Forensic Psychology*, **13(1)**, 31-60.

Forehand, R., Wierson, M., Frame, C.L., Kempton, T. and Armistead, L. (1991), 'Juvenile Firesetting: A Unique Syndrome or an Advanced Level of Antisocial Behaviour?', *Behavioural Research Therapy*, **29(2)**, 125-128.

Freud, S. (1932), 'The Acquisition of Power over Fire', *International Journal of Psychoanalysis*, **13**, 405-410.

Geller, J.L. (1992a), 'Arson in Review: From Profit to Pathology', *Clinical Forensic Psychiatry*, **15(3)**, 623-645.

Geller, J.L. (1992b), 'Communicative Arson', *Hospital and Community Psychiatry*, **43(1)**, 76-77.

Geller, J.L. (1992c), 'Pathological Firesetting in Adults', *International Journal of Law and Psychiatry*, **15**, 283-302.

Harris, G.T. and Rice, M.E. (1984), 'Mentally Disordered Firesetters: Psychodynamic versus Empirical Approaches', *International Journal of Law and Psychiatry*, **7**, 19-34.

Hill, R., Langevin, R., Paitich, D., Handy, L., Russon, A. and Wilkinson, L. (1982), 'Is Arson an Aggressive Act or a Property Offence? A Controlled Study of Psychiatric Referrals', *Canadian Journal of Psychiatry*, **27**, 648-654.

Holmes, R.M. and Holmes, S.T. (1996), 'Arson and Psychological Profiling', in *Profiling Violent Crimes: An Investigative Tool*, Thousand Oaks, CA.: Sage Publications.

Home Office (1988), *Standing Conference on Crime Prevention: Report of the Working Group on the Prevention of Arson*, London.

Hurley, W. and Monahan, T.M. (1969), 'Arson: The Criminal and the Crime', *The British Journal of Criminology*, **9**, 4-21.

Icove, D.J. and Estepp, M.H. (1987), 'Motive-Based Offender Profiles of Arson and Fire-Related Crimes', *FBI Law Enforcement Bulletin*, **56**, 175-185.

Incardi, J.A. (1970), 'The Adult Firesetter – A Typology', *Criminology*, **8**, 145-155.

Jackson, H.F., Glass, C. and Hope, S. (1987), 'A Functional Analysis of Recidivistic Arson', *British Journal of Clinical Psychology*, **26**, 175-185.

Jackson, H.F., Hope, S. and Glass, C. (1987), 'Why are Arsonists not Violent Offenders?', *International Journal of Offender Therapy and Comparative Criminology*, **31(2)**, 143-151.

Kafrey, D. (1978), 'Fire Survival Skills: Who Plays with Matches?', in W.S. Wooden and M.L. Berkey (1984), *Children and Arson: America's Middle-Class Nightmare*, New York: Plenum Press.

Kafrey, D. (1980), 'Playing with Matches: Children and Fire', in D.V. Canter (ed.), *Fires and Human Behaviour*, 1st edn., London: David Fulton.

Knight, R.A. and Prentky, R.A. (1987), 'The Development Antecedents and Adult Adaptions of Racist Stereotypes', *Criminal Justice and Behaviour*, **14**, 403-426.

Kolko, D.J. and Kazdin, A.E. (1991), 'Aggression and Psychopathology in Matchplaying and Firesetting Children: A Replication and Extension', *Journal of Clinical Child Psychology*, **20(2)**, 191-201.

Kolko, D.J. and Kazdin, A.E. (1991), 'Motives of Childhood Firesetters: Firesetting Characteristics and Psychological Correlates', *Journal of Child Psychology and Psychiatry*, **32(3)**, 535-550.

Lange, E. and Kirsch, M. (1989), 'Sexually Motivated Fire-Raisers', *Psychiatrie Neurologie und Medizinische Psychologie*, **41**, 361-366.

Leong, G.B. (1992), 'A Psychiatric Study of Persons Charged with Arson', *Journal of Forensic Sciences*, **37(5)**, 1319-1326.

Lewis, N.D.C. and Yarnell, H. (1951), 'Pathological Firesetting (pyromania)', in R.G. Vreeland and M.B. Waller (1978), *The Psychology of Firesetting: A Review and Appraisal*, grant no. 7-9021, Washington, D.C.: U.S. Government Printing Office (National Bureau of Standards, 1980).

MacDonald, J.M. (1977), *Bombers and Firesetters*, Springfield, Il., Charles C. Thomas.

McKerracher, D.W. and Dacre, A.J.I. (1966), 'A Study of Arsonists in a Special Security Hospital', *British Journal of Psychiatry*, **112**, 1151-1154.

O'Sullivan, G.H. and Kelleher, M.J. (1987), 'A Study of Firesetters in the South-West of Ireland', *British Journal of Psychiatry*, **151**, 818-823.

Patterson, G.R. (1982), *Coercive Family Process*, Eugene, Ore., Casteliz.

Pettiway, L.E. (1987), 'Arson for Revenge: The Role of Environmental Situation, Age, Sex and Race', *Journal of Quantitative Criminology*, **3(2)**, 169-184.

Pisani (1982), 'Identifying Arson Motives', *Fire and Arson Investigation*, **32**, 18-25.

Prins, H. (1994), *Fire-Raising: Its Motivation and Management*, London: Routledge.

Prins, H., Tennent, G. and Trick, K. (1985), 'Motives for Arson', *Medicine Science and the Law*, **25(4)**, 275-278.

Quinsey, V.L., Chaplin, T.C. and Upfold, D. (1989), 'Arsonists and Sexual Arousal to Firesetting: Correlation Unsupported', *Journal of Behaviour Therapy and Experimental Psychiatry*, **20(3)**, 203-209.

Rice, M.E. and Chaplin, T.C. (1979), 'Social Skills Training for Hospitalised Male Arsonists', *Journal of Behaviour Therapy and Experimental Psychiatry*, **10**, 105-108.

Rice, M.E. and Harris, G.T. (1991), 'Firesetters Admitted to a Maximum Security Psychiatric Institution. Offenders and Offences', *Journal of Interpersonal Violence*, **6(4)**, 461-475.

Rider, A. (1980), 'The Firesetter: A Psychological Profile', *FBI Law Enforcement Bulletin*, **49**, 7-17.

Robbins, E. and Robbins, L. (1967), 'Arson with Special reference to Pyromania', *New York State Journal of Medicine*, **67**, 795-798.

Rosenburg, R. and Knight, R.A. (1988), 'Determining Male Sexual Offender Subtypes using Cluster Analysis', *Journal of Qualitative Criminology*, **4(4)**, 385-410.

Rothstein, R. (1963), 'Exploration of Ego Structures of Firesetting Children', *Archives of General Psychiatry*, **9**, 246-253.

Sakheim, G.A. and Osborn, E. (1986), 'A Psychological Profile of Juvenile Firesetters in Residential Treatment: A Replication Study', *Child Welfare*, **65(5)**, 495-503.

Sakheim, G.A., Osborn, E. and Abrams, D. (1991), 'Toward a Clearer Differentiation of High-Risk from Low-Risk Firesetters', *Child Welfare*, **70(4)**, 489-503.

Steers, R.M. and Porter, L.W. (1991), *Motivation and Work Behaviour*, 5th edn., New York: McGraw-Hill.

Vreeland, R.G. and Levin, B.M. (1980), 'Psychological Aspects of Firesetting', in D.V. Canter (ed.), *Fires and Human Behaviour*, 1st edn., London: David Fulton.

Vreeland, R.G. and Waller, M.B. (1978), 'The Psychology of Firesetting: A Review and Appraisal', *National Bureau of Standards*, grant no.7-9021, Washington, D.C.: U.S. Government Printing Office.

Wood, B. (1995), 'Children's Firesetting Behaviour', *Fire Engineers Journal*, Nov., 31-35.

Wooden, W.S. and Berkey, M.L. (1984), *Children and Arson: America's Middle-Class Nightmare*, New York: Plenum Press.

7   Theft at Work

ADRIAN ROBERTSON

This chapter positions crime at work as presenting a set of investigative problems that are similar to those of 'public' crime, although there may be a narrower range of behavioural or crime scene clues. Studies using survey and content analysis of archives, do however, support the general Investigative Psychology hypothesis that across a sample of offenders, there will be systematic co-variance between characteristics of the offender and characteristics of the offence. By extrapolating these co-variances, the resources available to the detective can be enhanced, and more importantly, criminal behaviour at work can be perceived as a systems phenomenon. This offers the possibility of cross-organisational crime prevention strategies where crime can be designed out by greater sensitivity to the risks that individuals may present when they find themselves in tempting environments. By viewing crime as a sub-system of the organisation, and by seeing employee crime as an accumulating developmental path of deviance, intervention methods which are more discerning, more long term, and behaviourally based than those based on physical security alone are suggested.

Adrian Robertson has over ten years' experience as a police officer and a company detective. He has a particular interest in behavioural and system dimensions of employee crime, and is a graduate of the MSc course in Investigative Psychology at the University of Surrey. He now works as an internal consultant within a major UK Corporation, where he has continued to develop a wider systemic perspective on workplace deviancy and performance failure, focusing on deviant activities as an essential part of building diagnostic evidence in quality improvement programmes. More recently he has begun to look at the possibility of

*Offender Profiling Series: IV- **Profiling Property Crimes***
Edited by D. Canter and L. Alison. © 2000, Ashgate Publishing, Aldershot. pp 185-207

working on employee crime at a cultural level, creating a spirit of participation and inquiry around preventing failure and peer challenge of inappropriate workplace behaviours. Adrian believes that most companies could adopt much more sophisticated approaches to tackling employee crime, and that in general, company detectives and managers have a limited view of the problem. This in turn, hampers their capacity to deal with the problem in ways which are systematic, engage the genuine support of a workforce, and will have a lasting rather than a temporary effect. He currently works in a virtual team, and has recently explored ways in which deviancy may be permitted and sustained in virtual workplaces.

7   Theft at Work

ADRIAN ROBERTSON

Introduction

The investigation of theft at work shares two key concerns with other kinds of criminal investigation. Firstly, the need to identify one individual from a larger population. Secondly, the likelihood that there are common patterns and themes in the psychology of the crime. The situation is made more difficult because there is not a 'conventional' crime scene rich in behavioural clues. Enquiry tactics used by company detectives include matching loss data to employee attendance patterns, surveillance, 'negotiated' access to public criminal records, the use of informants and interviewing, and searching people and their property with consent.

This chapter questions the extent to which available information is fully used by organisations, particularly psychological information. It proposes that an Investigative Psychology approach may help develop an account of the common patterns and themes that characterise the underlying behavioural structure of the crime in both individual and organisational terms. By developing a social science based vocabulary of concepts and analysis, investigations can focus on the *problem* in broader systemic terms, applying a more penetrating range of skills to catching the criminals and producing crime prevention reports that executives can act on.

Social Science and Workplace Crime

Social science research offers useful insights to companies in dealing with employee crime. Two approaches are found in the literature. Individualist approaches view workplace crime as a continuity in a life history characterised by delinquency and crime proneness. Socio-cultural approaches see the workplace as the creator of its own criminal cultures, styles and methods.

Individualist

Individualist views hold that people who steal from their employers do not confine their offending to theft of property, but also offend against the conduct and reliability standards of the company more often than honest employees. It is the individual who imports the problem into the workplace. Workplace crime is intrinsic to the individual, not the workplace.

These approaches stem from North American human resource consultancies, who sponsor psychological research into the psychological characteristics of employee offenders. Findings of research are used to develop recruitment screening questionnaires. The two reviews that follow refer to approaches that stem from this industry and show how researchers have sought to establish empirically based behavioural correlates of crime at work.

Hogan and Hogan (1989), designed a questionnaire based around the California Personality Inventory, intended to test for the presence of personality attributes likely to be associated with dishonesty in job applicants, such as hostility towards authority, thrill seeking, impulsiveness, lack of conscientiousness, confused vocational identity and social insensitivity. They suggest a multifaceted characterisation, consisting of alternatives to theft as an index of dishonesty:

> *A first step towards understanding employee deviancy is to identify the key underlying construct. In our view, counter-productive acts such as theft, drug and alcohol abuse, lying, insubordination, vandalism, sabotage, absenteeism and assaultive actions are elements of a larger syndrome that we call organisational delinquency.*

Hogan and Hogan (1989) locate the root of the organisational delinquency problem in poor community socialisation. Employee thieves are not necessarily delinquent in public, but lack the personal resources to deal properly with a responsible job. The thieves are superficially rule-compliant, but passively hostile to external controls. They are not necessarily identifiable solely in terms of interactive style, as they may be popular with peers and supervisors.

Jones and Terris (1983) developed a psychological questionnaire designed to gauge theft-prone attitudes by asking respondents direct questions about their honesty, as distinct from making inferences from wider personality response items. In a 1983 study, they administered an honesty attitude test to 86 current employees of a home improvement chain in the USA. Following the administration of the test to each individual, the progress of each employee was followed over an eight-month period in three ways:

(i)   Managerial ratings of individuals.

(ii)   Frequency of internal investigations at each of the company's retail outlets.

(iii)   Shrinkage levels at each of the stores.

Those with higher dishonesty scale scores were more likely in the following eight months to be involved in one of the following:

- Disciplined for mishandling company cash.
- Committed intentional damage to company property.
- Rated as a poor worker.
- More often late for work.
- Had higher absence rate.
- Had more unauthorised extensions of work breaks.

On the basis that those employees who had higher dishonesty scores were more likely to work at stores with higher losses, a 'prediction' could be made about the kinds of individuals involved in theft.

A key problem identified in both studies is low base rates of apprehended employees upon which to assess studies, although the finding of individualist approaches are very suggestive of a likely relationship between crime and broader measures of counter-productive behaviour at work. Also, by focusing only on the individual, the issue is only addressed on one aspect of the problem.

Socio-Cultural Approaches

Socio-cultural approaches view workplace crime as intrinsic to the workplace, arising out of situational determinants such as poor labour relations, exploitation, negative employee sub-cultures, marginal employment conditions, low morale, poor management and badly run work systems. These approaches face the investigator with the question as to what is driving the problem along in systemic terms, rather than focusing only on individualist 'bad apple' theories.

Ditton (1977), in a participant observer study of 'fiddling' by delivery drivers in a wholesale bakery characterised the workplace thief in marked contrast to the individualist approaches.

> *The pilferer is usually explained away by the 'rotten apple' thesis; a morally defective individual, unable to resist temptation, liable to infect others ... In fact, employee thieves rarely match the stereotype of the pitifully inadequate petty thief. Ironically, employee offenders (apart from their dishonesty) often resemble the stereotypically perfect employee, generally filling trusted positions, working hard (for nefarious purposes), coming early and leaving late, and when the occasion demands virtuously offering to remain behind to do the yearly inventory.*

The Delivery Drivers (who were also salesmen) were responsible for collecting money from customers. They had to ensure a sufficient amount of takings to cover the retail value of each consignment delivered. However, poor stock control and despatching procedures obliged drivers to overcharge customers to ensure they did not finish the week short on takings. If they did, the company may question their own integrity, they may be dismissed, or required to make up the shortfall from their own pockets.

The system of loading-up vans before they went out on delivery was frantic and haphazard. Too many vanloads were loaded with too little time and space. Consignments were not properly counted and checked, often resulting in the delivery driver signing for more than he had actually received. However, as he was obliged to accept responsibility for 'errors', so it became established to overcharge the customer to cover the risk.

In short, whilst learning the job, the recruit is gradually made aware of the fact that 'mistakes' and thus 'shortages' are inevitable. Once low pay and long hours have become a reality for him, he is considered to be morally and technically ready for a demonstration that both problems may be solved by overcharging customers. For most men, the relief at finding a solution dilutes any moral qualms, and many go on to from here to make money for themselves in ways not explicitly accepted by the firm.

Ditton (1997)

Ditton considers that the company management were well aware of the deficiencies of the system, but allowed the 'fiddling solution' to continue because it guaranteed profits and low wages without the expense of upgrading systems and improving work conditions. Moreover, because it coerced staff into illicit activity, without making it official policy, it held them in a kind of moral blackmail.

Rather than import crime into the workplace, Ditton shows how new recruits were manoeuvred into participating in it by a process of insidious moral entrapment. He illustrates how he was 'recruited':

During my first week, when a supervisor and I ate an apple pie from the van, he said, 'remind me to declare it as "waste" at the end of the week'.

Ditton's notion of intimidatory socialisation raises serious questions for approaches that focus only on individuals. He suggests a wider organisational dimension, challenging the idea that crime levels in organisations can be understood only as the aggregate activity of individuals.

Mars (1982), using an anthropological framework, proposed that jobs could be modelled as having different structures of technical and social opportunities. He argued that by viewing a workplace as a culture, or set of sub-cultures, which shape the possibilities and freedoms open to individuals, crime in the workplace would fall into discernible patterns, and systematic predictions could be made about the types of crime that are possible to commit.

He proposed that workplace cultures differed in the extent to which they regulate the behaviour of individuals. In some, roles are heavily codified and constrained; in others there is more autonomy for individuals. Workplaces also differ in the way workgroups influence and control the behaviour of individuals. In some, the survival of the group is more important than the survival of the individual, and the interests of the individual are subordinate to those of the group. In other cultures, groups may exist, but may be less pervasive, and may exert less over-riding control over individuals.

Mars' focus is on the informal social structures of workplaces, and does not necessarily relate to the 'official' organisational perception of how an industrial operation is organised, or to any approved corporate notions of mission or culture. This is reflected in the psychological literature:

> *We must distinguish between the groups that appear on organisation charts, and the actual groupings of people who interact with one another with some frequency, like one another, or feel that they have something in common. There are people who interact who are not supposed to, and people who do not interact who are supposed to.*
>
> Argyle (1989)

Mars proposed four types of workplace culture.

1. Workplaces with tight informal hierarchies where crime is a carefully engineered social endeavour. Examples include dustcart crews, baggage handlers and dockers.

2. Workplaces where people are tied to fixed monotonous routines, affording nil or minimal contact with co-workers, and where crime is more likely to be the repetitive theft of one type of item or merchandise, but without any informal social controls on frequency levels. Examples include production line workers.

3. Workplaces where people have greatest social mobility with little accountability, minimal constraint or peer supervision. Crime in these jobs is the least definable and most re-interpretable, and is likely to involve borderline expenses or perks. Examples are organisational specialists or the self-employed.

4.	Workplaces where people work ostensibly in formal groups, but against a backdrop of perpetual tension between competitive and co-operative activity within the work-group. The group control in these jobs is loose and the group configuration permanently unstable, unlike the tighter workgroups. Examples include Ditton's bakery, and service industry. In practice, Mars proposed that his typology should be viewed as a way of assessing the biases of a workplace, and not imply a rigid model.

Socio-cultural approaches alert us to the compulsions and seductions of group norms in social settings. They suggest that workplaces may present hazards to immature and novice individuals, and challenge the idea that bad faith must already be an established characteristic of the person involved.

Bridging the Gap between Approaches

In reporting the results of an extensive study of crime at work, Hollinger and Clark (1983) attempted to provide an account of the characteristics of likely offenders in the context of the kinds of setting they may operate. In one key sense, this agrees with the findings of individualist approaches:

Perhaps we have limited for too long our view of employee deviance to the theft of tangible property and assets. Instead, the theft of property should be considered as the criminally illegal proportion of a much broader continuum that includes all deviant acts occurring within the work organisation.

Their research was conducted using an anonymous survey and interview methodology. Nine thousand questionnaires representing employees from 47 firms across three industries and three cities were examined. A sample of 500 employees of all grades was also interviewed. Direct questions were put to respondents about their involvement in counter-productivity and theft at work. For example, how often over the previous year they had been involved in illicit activities such as fraudulent sick absence, theft of merchandise or supplies, unauthorised meal break extensions, deliberately overcharging or undercharging customers and unauthorised discounting? Responses were classified in terms of admissions to property deviance or production deviance. Within each sector (retail, hospital and manufacturing) about a third admitted involvement in various kinds of property deviance. The most common for retail employees was misusing store discount privileges; for hospital employees, was taking hospital supplies such as linens and bandages; for manufacturing employees, it was the taking of production raw materials. The three most common forms of production deviance were taking a long meal-break without approval, coming to work late or leaving early and using sick leave when not sick. This order held across the three sectors.

Combining these results, Hollinger and Clark derived three key correlations, around which they suggested theft and counter-productivity at work, were related phenomena.

Table 7.1: Pearson Product Moment Correlations of Property Deviance with Production Deviance (P < 0 .0001)

Property Deviance		
Retail	**Hospital**	**Manufacturing**
0.48	0.45	0.39

*(row label: **Production Deviance**)*

Hollinger and Clark reported that key personal characteristics positively associated with crime at work include being a young male, unmarried, of short tenure and in temporary employment. They questioned a number of popular notions about crime at work, for example, the idea that theft at work is mainly carried out by individuals trying to resolve a personal financial problem brought about by gambling, alcoholism or an extra-marital affair. This casts doubt on an earlier notion put forward by Cressey (1953) as the typical workplace thief being a lonely cash embezzler with a 'non-shareable' problem. They found no significant statistical relationships between self-reported deviancy and community indices of economic deprivation and crime, suggesting that the two are not necessarily correlated. The idea that 'everyone does it given the chance' is also not supported. In fact, the opposite is suggested, that most (two thirds) of employees have no involvement in such activity.

In common with Mars and Ditton, they proposed that temporary or casual labour arrangements provides a background setting of low morale, lack of identification with the company, and lack of concern about its assets or property. Their data across all sectors supported the general idea that low job satisfaction co-exists with higher levels of employee deviance.

Within manufacturing, there were some counter-intuitive findings. The highest self-reported theft did not occur amongst low status assembly personnel, but amongst higher status engineering and technical personnel. Having access to goods seemed not to be the key issue here, but more importantly knowledge of what the finished product can be used for the pilferer has the skill to 'finish' it. Hollinger and Clark suggested that security monitoring in factories tended to be focused on assembly line staff, with no consideration given to the expertise required to benefit from pilfered technical tools and semi-manufactured components. This is a case where it is more productive to take Mars' approach and consider the structures of accountability and control, rather than the activities of individuals.

In the hospital sector, highest self-reported theft levels were found amongst higher status nursing staff and those with direct access to patient care ward services. However, the production deviance levels were lower amongst these staff, and did not yield a high theft/high counter-productivity relationship. The face-to-face interview data suggested that hospital ward staff tended only to target property belonging to the institution, taking care not to jeopardise patient welfare either by stealing essential supplies or by engaging in counter-productive behaviour. The hospital data shows the flaws in only focusing on staff with poor conduct histories.

Hollinger and Clarke suggest how the individualist and socio-cultural approaches may complement each other by providing an account of how the vulnerabilities and intentions of individuals may interact with aspects of the setting.

The Relationship Between Actions and Characteristics

In a study carried out in a courier and distribution company, Robertson (1993) examined how criminal behaviours and offender characteristics vary with different kinds of workplace crime, using the archived files of 93 blue-collar workers dismissed (and in some cases prosecuted) for theft and other offences. Most offenders were males (n = 88). The youngest 75% of employees concerned were aged 32 years or less; the shortest serving 75% had less than four years' service. Available personnel data revealed 42 of the individuals (60%), *before* being caught, had one or more formal conduct warnings for matters such as excessive absenteeism, poor timekeeping and negligence with merchandise. A wider random trawl of 2000 employee records found that 23% had one or more conduct warnings. Although a relationship between theft and counter-productive workplace behaviour was revealed, pre-employment data was less revealing. Virtually all the sample had minimal industrial skills and educational qualifications, but of itself this did not distinguish them from the wider workforce. Most had favourable pre-employment references. Very few had formal criminal records (n = 15), and most of those were from one sub-group who were mainly stealing courier traffic from banks and other financial institutions. Most of the pre-convictions (nine out of 13) were for dishonesty. Within the sample, there were some distinct variations between behaviours seen in the crimes and the individuals involved.

Offenders Classified into Three Broad Groups

Criminality Group (n = 41)

This sub-group was close to the notion of a deviant career. These offenders were caught stealing courier traffic despatched by banks, which had the highest chance of containing items such as credit cards. They left no debris or torn packaging in the workplace, and smuggled intact items from the factory floor. Their behaviours in and around the crime suggested more focus and determination in criminal style, with a cluster of other activities such as; having stolen property unlawfully at home or in cars, having criminal links on the outside, working with staff accomplices, using convenience addresses, obtaining employment by deception and fraudulently using stolen plastic cards. Nine of this group had pre-convictions prior to joining the company. They were mostly between their early twenties and early thirties, with offending almost entirely confined to the first six years of service. More were unmarried than married.

The interview responses of these offenders indicate that about half made total denials even when faced with good circumstantial or unequivocal evidence, and about a quarter requested the presence of a solicitor, reflecting a greater degree of acquired notions and repertoires of what to do when captured.

Opportunity Group (n = 22)

These were individuals stealing small amounts of cash or low value goods such as pens, watches, cheap jewellery and small electrical items. This criminal style appeared more opportunistic and not distinguished by any particular sophistication or experience. None had pre-convictions. This criminal style typically involved selecting items from the courier traffic and opening them at the workstation and removing the contents. Offenders tended to return debris and torn open items into the traffic stream, or leave them in corners and alcoves. This is in effect a crime scene and over time can build up a pattern enabling the source to be traced. It also suggests lack of criminal shrewdness ('forensic naiveté').

This group had a wider age range (mid-twenties to mid-fifties), with a service range from two to 14 years, although more commonly over five. These individuals were likely to be married, and to have settled lifestyles. They were less likely to have evidence of their crimes at home. Most made at least partial admissions to their crimes when interviewed.

Three of the nine offenders expressed bitter remorse about what had happened, with a further five having 'personal' difficulties (for example, depression, involvement with psychiatrists). This may be within the scope of what Cressey (1953) referred to as a 'non-shareable problem'.

Responsibility Group (n = 12)

These were individuals who were abandoning consignments of courier traffic in wasteland, or taking it home and hiding it. There was neither financial gain nor evidence of theft in any of these cases, and the offending style appears more linked to capability and coping under pressure. Their actions were always traceable.

This group had the highest concentration of young employees, some were teenagers, and most were under 25 years of age. All had less than four years' service. None had pre-convictions and none were married. The prevalence rate of serious conduct problems was the highest across the sample.

Eighteen of the individuals were classified as multiple thieves or uncertain theft, for example, where they had been found in possession of several types of stolen property, or where they had been caught with damaged packaging but the detectives could not ascertain what the item had originally contained.

This group is difficult because it is hard to know what their priorities are, although in general, the theft of several classes of merchandise implied less specialism and criminal experience.

This study was not explicitly about group or setting factors although 24 of the individuals were caught up in staff accomplice enquiries (mostly from the criminality group) including some thefts that were facilitated by group activity. These occurred more commonly in group-based shiftwork tasks. They suggest how the social and technical structure of work relationships provides a different set of criminal possibilities than where employees work alone.

The five case studies that follow were drawn from the sample:

'Bill' - Male, Aged 26 Years with Two Years' Tenure

Caught trying to smuggle out traffic items containing credit cards. He had an outside receiver for items he stole, and could cite current street prices for credit cards.

His work history indicated only one previous job (lasting two months), although five years' worth of information was missing on his application form. His conduct history indicated good training reports, although within 18 months he had received an informal warning regarding his attendance. This was followed up by a formal warning several months later, as the situation did not improve.

The report indicated that he was not married, lived a shiftless and disorganised lifestyle. He lived in a squalid one bedroom flat. No pre-convictions were known.

'Den' - Male, Aged 27 with Two Years' Tenure

Caught stealing small items of low value from courier packets, after large numbers of torn open items were traced back to him as the only logical source point. He worked alone on a fixed task, doing a job that resembled a production line. The repetitive and invariant method of his crimes is reminiscent of Mars' notion of isolated subordination

Den opened courier items by sliding in his finger in the bottom one of a hand-held pile, sometimes whilst having a conversation with a supervisor or colleague standing next to him. He was sociable and well liked by peers and supervisors. Apart from his crimes, his work appeared to be efficient and accurate, although he sometimes took long meal breaks.

He had an unsettled existence, alternating between several addresses, and had no contact with the children of his broken marriage.

He had been employed although had been dismissed previously by the company, for having a chronic absence record. He was given another chance a year later and was re-employed. Within six months, he was warned for excessive absence. There was some improvement but the problem nonetheless continued. His recruitment reports on both occasions indicated satisfactory performance on training tasks with no indication of future problems.

Having left school at 16 with no educational qualifications or marketable skills, he had a history of blue-collar industrial work with good references. He had no police record.

'John' - Male, Aged 28 with Three Years' Tenure

Caught stealing plastic bankcards and music CDs.

During the course of enquiries and interviews, John told the investigators that he had spent large amounts of money on gambling, and that he was an addict. At one point said he was glad to have been caught, as he would otherwise have been unable to stop himself. He was emotionally distraught during interview. Later he said he was suicidal, and pleaded for his job back.

One supervisor held John in high esteem, describing him as, 'A generally hard and efficient worker'. This comment appeared when John was the subject of internal discipline for deciding of his own volition to delay urgent traffic, take it home overnight, and deliver it the next day.

The supervisor fended off a dismissal action. At around the same time, he received a warning for excessive absence in early service. References from several manual jobs indicated no attendance or reliability problems, and no problems reported with his attitude or behaviour with the courier company.

He married some time after starting with the courier company, and appeared to have a settled home life.

He received a police caution as a juvenile for theft (shoplifting). This had not been disclosed on his application form.

'Joe' - Male, Aged 59 with Five Years' Tenure

Caught stealing small valuables from items being carried by the delivery company.

The matter came to light when empty, torn-open transit packs were found in a public rubbish bin. These were handed into a police station. The company was alerted. Investigators interviewed Joe the next day when Joe outlined some difficulties in his life. His mother had recently died and his wife was unwell. He said that he felt life was getting on top of him, and because of his age, was frightened of losing his job. The company management accepted a recommendation that Joe was clinically depressed, and did not press charges.

His work conduct record was exemplary, with virtually no sick absence, and no managerial warnings. His training period had passed without problems, and his personnel file indicated that his immediate supervisors thought well of him. To all appearances, Joe was the model employee.

He had neither formal qualifications nor industrial skills. His previous employment had been for twelve years as a messenger, from which he was provided with a good reference.

There was nothing in Joe's background to suggest any criminal experience. His offences were clumsily committed.

'Tim' - Male, Aged 18 Years with 17 Months' Service

He forgot to hand in items he was unable to deliver because the customer had changed address, and subsequently hid them in his locker. Some two months passed, when he became worried and abandoned them in the depot, where they were found and handed in. Their routing and handling history was traced, and Tim identified. A search of his home address revealed one sealed item, which he seemed to have taken home in a satchel and forgotten about. The investigators accepted his protestations of not being involved in theft.

His personnel record indicated a warning for poor attendance had been recorded within his first few months of service. The investigator's report indicates he was somewhat immature, and failed to grasp the significance of his actions. He had no police record.

This study indicates that pre-employment data does not predict involvement in employee crime in direct ways. However, it does suggest that the nature of the crimes may suggest the characteristics of the individuals likely to be involved.

Cognitive and Motivational Issues

There is some agreement in the literature that employees find it psychologically difficult to steal from their employers, which Ditton points out in his study. Bartol (1991) makes a succinct summary of the issues:

> *Regardless of the explanation, blue-collar crime seems to require some subjective justification on the part of the worker. He or she does not perceive his or her conduct as illegal or even unethical, either because the behaviour is in line with group norms, in line with internal standards, or both.*

Cressey (1953) identifies 'vocabularies of adjustment', where, for example, people stealing money will tell themselves they are only 'borrowing' it. Whilst Hollinger (1991), in a review of cognitive techniques for neutralising crime, suggested two key rationalisations were most commonly adopted by employee offenders. These are Denial of Injury and Denial of Victim.

Denial of Injury

This suggests the perception that the offence is seen as not doing any real harm or causing any real loss. Smigel (1970) reported that questionnaire responses indicated people saw big business and government as much more able to absorb losses than small businesses. Similarly, Horning's (1970) study into blue collar theft at a North American electronics plant indicated that rather than steal property that was distinctly owned by individuals or by the company, 91% of workers admitted to stealing property of 'uncertain ownership'. This meant that whilst personal clothing and tools, or expensive company equipment was normally off-limits, items such as scrap parts, screws, nails, nuts and bolts were seen as fair game.

Denial of Victim

This is where the offender sees the victim as the offenders getting their just deserts, putting themselves in the role of moral avenger. Tucker (1987) puts the issue in a workplace crime context:

> *Employees, thus, pursue justice in a number of ways. Indeed, an entire 'justice system' can be envisioned where strikes, sabotage, work slowdowns, absenteeism, turnover, etc. are possible penalties awaiting employers 'convicted' of deviant conduct. Theft is one possible sentence.*

Hollinger suggested that these were more likely to be found in those over 25 than those under 25. This may be because younger employees were more prone to peer pressures, and perceived fewer deterrents or adverse consequences than older employees.

In addition to behavioural correlates, Jones (1991) puts forward a psychodynamic and motivational psychological profile. He argues that employee thieves typically rate themselves lower in honesty and integrity; believe or suspect that most employees steal; often fantasise about successful theft; make many more theft-related admissions and accept many of the common rationalisations for theft.

The problem of motive within workplace crime is that it is a highly speculative basis from which to work. However, psychological self-justification processes within the individual may be triggered by the way the organisation is perceived to behave. These are important crime prevention issues and will be mentioned again in the next two sections.

Implications for Investigations

This chapter has shown that there is scope to improve the way investigative information is structured and organised in workplace crime enquiries. However, the case studies, and the findings of Hollinger and Clarke (1983) show that a positive relationship between employee misconduct and crime will not necessarily be found in all cases.

Drawing the issues in this chapter together, investigators could usefully focus on a number of key questions in live investigations.

What are the Likely Antecedents of Criminal Behaviour in this Setting?

Investigators need to look critically at the behavioural style that is likely to characterise the individual committing crimes. This can be done systematically by examining the archives of previous investigations, and should not depend on experience or intuition.

Each investigation at a particular site should explore the hypothesis that conduct history may be related to offending, and that there may be a developmental path from conduct offending to crime. Once the nature of the crime is clearly known, and a prolific and repetitive crime pattern has been established, the investigation problem may be structured on the basis of the likely characteristics of the offender, for example, age, service, conduct history, marital status and ethnic origin. If the parameters of likely characteristics can be stated in relation to the crimes, although they will not be definitive, they will provide a basis upon which to examine staff lists.

Cognitive factors should also alert the investigator to the possibility that employee thieves may be psychologically troubled, may lack criminal history or experience, and will not necessarily be identifiable from criminal record checks and reports of antisocial behaviour. The theories of immediate supervisors may be misleading. Awkward employees are not necessarily thieves, and those liked by supervisors are not necessarily above suspicion.

How Do Technical Processes and Normal Work Procedures Facilitate Crime in this Setting?

The investigator needs to focus on how technical aspects of an operation may facilitate crime. This means looking critically at what might be viewed as 'normal'. For example, leaving merchandise for long periods in one place, or without protection, or without robust hand-over procedures, may be taken to imply that its loss would not matter to anyone. This kind of organisational behaviour may provide a link between operational practices and cognitive rationalisations.

Taking Ditton's example, 'normal' ways of working may hide a sub-world of coping practices that are illegal or dubious, yet essential to do the job.

Shiftwork patterns, with minimal supervision, access to valuables, or knowledge of how to use specialist parts, may also create a structure of opportunities for orchestrated or systematic crimes.

How Can Groups Facilitate Crime in this Setting?

Commercial investigators need to consider the role of informal groups in workplace crime. As indicated by Mars' research, high volume thefts of similar merchandise are likely to suggest lower skilled offenders operating in isolation, although not necessarily without the knowledge of peers. Where theft appears more targeted, especially with high value goods or bulky goods with a criminal market potential, then it is likely that a group effort is involved. There may also be tacit consent of management.

There is further scope here for the use of archives to assemble a history of offending. The investigator needs to consider when and in what circumstances past cases indicate group theft is likely to be the norm, as distinct from solo activity.

Intelligence gathering and operations planning needs to be informed by information about the likely characteristics of offenders and how their criminal style is deployed. For example, an individual operating alone may not be counselled or supported by others, and may be more amenable to firm investigative interviewing. However, someone who is part of a group endeavour may be highly motivated to stay silent. Selecting interviewees suspected to be part of group endeavours and subjecting them to ill-prepared and pressurised interviewing in the absence of corroborating evidence is likely to fail.

To get the most out of social science approaches, the investigator needs to bear in mind the strong possibility that workplace thieves may have continuities in their life histories that indicate poor behaviour standards in or out of work. However, the workplace itself may also be a strong agent of socialisation, and detectives should be sensitive to issues that arise in groups, and how a novice can be sucked into a web of deviant practices. This will mean being able to observe problems at several levels. In particular, interviewing and listening skills are vital to pick up indications of adverse employee sub-cultures or despondent attitude climates that may be deeply entrenched in the 'factory floor' workplace culture.

In the report, the investigator will make a more enduring contribution to crime prevention if s/he can not only deal with the immediate investigative issues, but on what is driving the problem along in systemic and human terms.

Implications for Executives

Executives need to be well placed to receive reports of this nature and act on them. They need to view crime as linked to a range of cross-organisational issues, and not as an isolated dark corner. The idea that the organisation *behaves*, as well as the individuals within it, is a key issue. Senior management can only establish business ethics and acceptable practices. People will feel less restraint at victimising an employer they believe to be lacking in integrity.

The kinds of behaviours tolerated in the company will set the tone for the socio-cultural environment. For example, total quality policies must be practised both in and out of direct customer gaze. Aspirations will be merely rhetorical to employees who are used to dirty work conditions, poor systems, rough treatment of customers' merchandise and uncaring supervision.   Similarly, the toleration of harassment, bullying and discrimination will communicate negative messages to employees about their employer. High levels of absenteeism should be examined closely, as this may indicate a deeper malaise.

A fractious industrial relations climate or adverse employee sub-cultures may indicate that rather than being the actions of 'bad apple' individuals, crime thrives in a supportive niche. Criminal nurturance can be implied rather than explicit, and a lack of positive consensus about the company may provide the space for negative attitudes to grow. Damaging sub-cultures are more likely where there is significant use of marginal labour with poor wages and work conditions.

Recruitment and training policies need to reflect a policy of care for company property and the safety and security of the working environment. Low-grade blue-collar jobs may require considerable maturity and personal resilience from employees, and recruiting casual staff with a lack of appropriate training and supervision may lead to unnecessary risks. Cheapest is not necessarily the least expensive.

Executives cannot afford to assume that it is the job of the school system to prepare people for responsible employment. Many young people arrive at their first job poorly equipped to deal with responsibility. Employers gain nothing by merely complaining about the quality of human material available.

All workplaces socialise new members into particular ways of thinking, and executives need to consider the kind of learning that is available to new employees. This is particularly the case with young and immature employees, who may be more easily swayed into illicit activities. Employers need to understand that some employees are more vulnerable or at risk to criminal socialisation than others, and that policies need to be designed to address this. Clear messages need to be given to the workforce about what activities are regarded as crime and how they will be dealt with. This is essential if people are to be discouraged from latching onto the common rationalisations for crime.

Employees who fall short of required conduct standards (which must be clearly published) should be confronted with their behaviour without delay, and given clear improvement targets within a context of caring supervision. There should also be clear consequences and time frames for failing to improve.

Concluding Remarks

Crime at work is often seen as a chance act of random malice without rational explanation. This chapter challenges that view, and calls for a cross-organisational approach on the part of companies who wish to reduce their theft losses. Such an approach would cease to view the security departments of companies as operating in a different world from any other department. Crime and deviancy levels are as much a valid measure of performance as the more mainstream issues chosen for measurement in factories and workplaces. High levels of deviant behaviour may indicate a company with a poor emotional environment in which to work. Security and investigation departments can develop the capacity to report on these issues, as well as catch offenders. Likewise, company managers should be prepared to respond to well-founded criticism, and reform degenerate work systems.

References

Argyle, M. (1989), *The Social Psychology of Work*, London: Penguin Books.

Bartol, C.R. (1991), *Criminal Behaviour: A Psychosocial Approach*, New Jersey: Prentice Hall.

Cressey, D.R. (1953), *Other People's Money, A Study in the Social Psychology of Embezzlement*, Belmont, California: Wadsworth Publishing.

Ditton, J. (1977), *Part-Time Crime: An Ethnography of Fiddling and Pilferage*, London: MacMillan.

Hogan, J. and Hogan, R. (1989), 'How to Measure Employee Reliability', *Journal of Applied Psychology*, **74**, No **2**, 273-279.

Hollinger, R.C. (1991), 'Neutralising in the Workplace: An Empirical Analysis of Property Theft and Production Deviance', *Deviant Behaviour*, **12**, 169-202.

Hollinger, R.C. and Clark, J.P. (1983), *Theft by Employees*, Massachussetts: Lexington Books.

Horning, D.N.M. (1970), 'Blue Collar Theft: Conceptions of Property, Attitudes towards Pilfering, and Work Group Norms in a Modern Industrial Plant', in E.O. Smigel and H.L. Ross (eds), *Crimes Against Bureaucracy*, New York: Van Nostrand Reinhold.

Jones, J.W. and Terris, W. (1983), 'Predicting Employees' Theft in Home Improvement Centres', *Psychological Reports*, **52**, 187-201.

Jones, J.W. (1991), *Pre Employment Honesty Testing: Current Research and Future Directions*, New York: Quorum Books.

Mars, G. (1982), *Cheats at Work: An Anthropology of Workplace Crime*, London: Allen and Unwin.

Smigel, E.O. (1970), 'Public Attitudes towards Stealing as Related to the Size of the Victim Organisation', in E.O Smigel And H.L. Ross (eds) *Crimes Against Bureaucracy*, New York: Van Nostrand Reinhold.

Tucker, J. (1987), 'Employee Theft as Social Control', *Deviant Behaviour*, **10**, 319-334.

8   The Psychology of Fraud

NICK J. DODD

*Fraud has not been the subject of concerted behavioural research.
Similarly, it is suggested, that it is not a high priority in terms of police
and organisational resources.   This chapter proposes that an
understanding of the psychological issues that serve to formulate and
mediate fraudulent behaviour is crucial to its investigation and
prevention. These issues are drawn from the psychological literature and
include risk taking, attitudes towards targets and money, self-perception
and the perceived seriousness of the crime. It is hypothesised that greater
knowledge of these issues, as a result of behavioural research, will
provide organisations with the means to effectively identify fraudsters in
their systems.   It will also provide them with the ability to influence the
deviant perceptions and beliefs of the offender in order to prevent him/her
from making the decision to defraud in the first place.   Finally, it is
suggested that early detection of the fraudster may prevent him/her from
going on to commit more 'serious' crimes, as research has revealed that
robbers, burglars and juvenile delinquents invariably have previous
histories which include deception and fraud.*

Nick J. Dodd was awarded a BA (Hons) Psychology from University
College, Swansea, University of Wales and a PhD from The University of
Liverpool.   A keen interest in the application of psychology to
investigating and preventing crime led to him being awarded an MSc in
Investigative Psychology by the University of Surrey.   A specialised
interest in the psychological aspects of fraud developed during this period.
This received support from the insurance industry in an examination of
the behavioural aspects of insurance claim fraud.   A more recent interest
has been exploring the psychological aspects of   pilfering and its

Offender Profiling Series: IV- Profiling Property Crimes
Edited by D. Canter and L. Alison. © 2000, Ashgate Publishing, Aldershot. pp 209-231

relationship to organisational culture and employee variables.   This attracted the support of the Economic and Social Research Council and an international parcel delivery company. Concurrently, advisory roles have been undertaken on projects exploring compliance, control and security issues in the working environment.

8   The Psychology of Fraud

NICK J. DODD

Fraud involves greater losses than those arising from theft, robbery and burglary put together. However, it is virtually ignored by researchers both in terms of the psychology of the crime and methods for its investigation. This is all the more surprising when it is realised that fraud and deception are crimes committed by the majority of criminals at some point in their 'career' whether they are robbers, burglars or juvenile delinquents. This lack of research is accompanied by a lack of prioritisation by the police in terms of investigation and resources. This chapter hypothesises that the application of psychological research to fraud will have major investigative and preventative value. Account is taken of fraud investigators' beliefs that, generally, there are two types of fraudster in operation that can be distinguished in terms of their criminal sophistication. However, such experiential definitions take no direct account of psychological factors affecting fraudulent behaviour. Thus, this simple dichotomy is assessed and hypothesised that psychological processes have an important function in formulating and mediating fraudulent behaviour, and that these should be addressed by researchers and investigators. Suggestions are made as to how a richer understanding of the psychology of fraud can be achieved through behavioural research. The practical issue of applying the findings of such research to the detection and prevention of fraud is discussed as a natural conclusion to this chapter.

The Variety of Fraud

There are a vast number of ways for describing different types of fraud. Simple categories can be defined by *target* as in banking fraud, benefit fraud and insurance fraud. In addition, *legal* definitions could also be employed. For example, fraud and related offences (forgery, counterfeiting, deception, corruption, bigamy, smuggling, copyright

211

offences, embezzlement etc.) are detailed in at least 35 parliamentary Acts ranging from Common Law to the more specific Tele-communications Act (1984). In fact, fraudulent offences number at least 150 on the statute books. For this reason alone the use of the terms 'fraud', 'dishonesty' and 'deception' throughout this chapter will be used interchangeably and only as general descriptors of the whole arena of fraudulent offences referred to above unless it is specified otherwise.

The Frequency of Fraud

Research has shown that the majority of criminals, from bank robbers to juvenile delinquents, have a previous criminal history of deception (Gibbons, 1975; Hindelang, 1972). Whilst these and almost the whole family of 'serious' crimes have been the subject of concerted psychological research efforts, fraud has remained a neglected cousin. This lack of research may well be due to the sidelining of fraud investigation by police forces, as well as the acceptance by many commercial concerns that being the target of a certain amount of fraud is part of their everyday functioning. However, plastic card fraud losses in 1992 reached £165 million and Narula (1993), a forensic accountant, reports that, 'Mortgage fraud is estimated to be costing lending institutions well in excess of £3bn'. Furthermore, the Association of British Insurers (ABI), with 450 UK members, estimates that losses through fraudulent insurance claims in 1994 totalled £600 million (Wagstaff, 1996).

Clearly, the value of these losses is not a minor matter. This, as well as the fact that committing fraud appears to be a common link between persistent offenders' criminal histories, is a cause for some concern. This concern is heightened when it is realised that investigators and researchers alike are relatively ignorant of the psychological processes mediating fraudulent behaviour. A richer understanding of the psychology of this all-pervading element of criminality has important implications not only for the prevention and detection of fraud but also for investigating other crimes.

Investigative Concerns

According to Home Office statistics there was an increase of 64% in the number of notifiable fraudulent offences between 1981 and 1991, from 106,671 to 174,742. A drop of 15% in the clear-up rate accompanied this increase in occurrence from 70 to 55% in 1991 (Home Office Criminal Statistics, England and Wales, 1991). These figures attest to the growing difficulties faced by fraud investigators. The main problem that confronts investigators appears to be proving, in the eyes of the law, that a crime has been committed. This is especially true in the insurance industry (see Clarke, 1989) though all types of fraud investigations are hampered by a serious lack of reliable information due to modern business practice. Perceptions of police officers, jurors and legal representatives are also likely to vary on whether a crime has actually been committed (Deffenbacher and Loftus, 1982). Indeed, there is evidence to suggest that the nature of many commercial fraud trials is beyond the understanding of the lay juror (see Fraud Trials Committee Report, 1986; Binning, 1996). This can often result in the accused being acquitted because the prosecution fails to prove that the accused *knew* that they were misappropriating funds. Thus, there is an absolute need to define exactly what constitutes fraud and what does not. In itself, this poses serious problems for fraud investigators during the course of their enquiries.

Types of Fraudster

Informal discussions with fraud investigators (police and commercial) reveal anecdotal information which suggest that two general types of fraudster operate against the interests of the commercial concern that they represent or are assisting.

Opportunist Fraudster

It is suggested that the *Opportunist* does not initially intend to defraud. They are believed to be individuals who are already embroiled in a criminal lifestyle but have not previously come to police attention. For example, they may be burglars, car thieves, joyriders etc. who steal a chequebook supplementary to the original offence and then use it to defraud. In this context, these offenders are seen as being non-routine in their approach and, as such, are difficult to detect. Insurance Link (1993) states that, in the insurance industry, the 'opportunist' constitutes the largest group of insurance fraudsters. He/she initially exaggerates a claim and, if this is successful, is likely to defraud again. Insurance Link goes on to say that the 'opportunist' insurance fraudster is unlikely to have any previous record of dishonesty and this renders them difficult to detect. *Opportunist* fraudsters are seen only to try to secure small amounts from their targets and are believed to be in financial difficulty.

Sophisticated Fraudster

This offender is seen to know his/her way around the system that they are defrauding and, therefore, creates his/her own opportunities rather than abusing those already in existence. Some of these fraudsters are described as running their frauds like legitimate businesses (commonly known as long firm fraud), utilising their knowledge of their target to great advantage. By implication these offenders should be routine in their approach and should pose less of a problem in investigative terms. Whether they are more routine has not been established but they certainly do not pose less of a problem in investigative terms and often succeed in defrauding their targets out of vast sums of money. These fraudsters are always seen to try to defraud large amounts of money.

Although these generalised accounts contain some useful information, there are no objective grounds for a distinction of this kind. The dichotomy tends to be dictated by the difficulty of the investigation of the fraudster and the size of the 'prize' as opposed to the behaviours he or she exhibits. As such, there is actually no reliable method for measuring the level of sophistication of these two types. Thus, investigators merely suggest that there are '*opportunist*' and '*sophisticated*' fraudsters who exist at opposite ends of the scale of investigative difficulty, and who target small or large amounts of money.

On the surface, such subjective definitions of these types of fraudsters are of little use to the investigator as they provide no consistent basis upon which to pursue the criminal. However, when looked at more closely, it is possible to hypothesise, from these anecdotal observations, that psychological processes such as attitudes and risk taking play a central role in formulating, and mediating, fraudulent behaviour. It is suggested that a fuller understanding of these processes can provide investigators and researchers with the consistent basis required to assist in their detection, investigation and prevention of fraud.

The Psychological Processes of Fraud

Like most crimes fraud consists of a variety of actions determined by the attitudes and experiences of the perpetrator. Many psychological factors come into play when the fraudster commits his or her crime (see Dodd, 1993). The task of the remainder of this chapter is to explore the potential effect of these and how they affect fraudulent behaviour.

Economic Behaviour

In the majority of fraudulent crimes money, or gaining pecuniary advantage over another individual or organisation, is the aim of the offender. Thus, money would appear to hold great significance for the fraudster (though attitudes towards the target may be more important in succeeding in the crime). This significance is likely to vary between offenders as it does between non-offenders. As Firth (1963) states: 'Money is a symbol. It represents in some measurable way some command over goods and services'. In other words money involves multiple symbolisations. Furnham (1984), using factor analysis in a study of attitudes towards money, revealed six factors, including *power*, *obsession with money* and *money retention*. In themselves these findings highlight differences in the meanings of money to various individuals and are likely to be just as relevant to offenders as non-offenders. In fact, Furnham and Lewis (1986) point out that, 'The dangers of money are manifold: it creates a false sense of independence and invulnerability' (attitudes in themselves) and that, 'It can most easily be acquired immorally and hence encourages bad habits'. The clearest manifestation of these *bad habits* is fraud.

Intuitively, defrauding large amounts of money should be a different attitude to defrauding small amounts of money (Lewis, 1979) though the two values may have different meanings to different individuals. However, it would be unwise to assume that an individual's attitude towards money is the single root cause of dishonesty and deception because any attitude towards obtaining money dishonestly will be tempered by knowledge of the target, risk taking and other attitudes towards criminality. For this reason, it is unlikely that the fraudster's attitudes towards money on their own, significantly differ to the non-fraudster's attitudes towards money. It is hypothesised that the concentration and strength of such attitudes, and the deviant way that the fraudster goes about gaining money, is where the greatest variation occurs.

Entrepreneurial Behaviour

Some fraudsters go to great lengths to succeed in their crime. This appears to be the case, in particular, where large amounts of money are at stake and where more elaborate methods of deception are inevitably employed. Levi (1981) indicates that in long firm fraud the offenders run a bogus business as though it were legitimate. They maintain up-to-date accounts, retain receipts etc. all of which present an image of legitimacy. Whilst this is necessary to remain undiscovered it also reflects a need to achieve and succeed. 'Achievement motivation' (*n Ach*) (McClelland, 1961) has been positively correlated with entrepreneurial behaviour (Crockett, 1962). Thus, entrepreneurial behaviour appears to have an important role to play in the make up of the long firm fraudster at least. Whilst long firm fraud may be the clearest example of this behaviour, clinical literature suggests that elements of entrepreneurship are relevant to fraud in general. Person (1986) states that entrepreneurs utilise manipulation in order to achieve wealth, prestige and power. For some offenders this is likely to be an important facet of their identity, which is reflected in their offence behaviour.

Tax Evasion

Furnham and Lewis (1986) hypothesise that evasion is a function of opportunity, probability of detection and size of punishment, the influence of which is mediated through the attitudes, perceptions and beliefs of the perpetrator. Support for this theory comes from Warneryd and Walerud (1982) who revealed that people admitting to tax evasion had more realistic perceptions of the probability of being detected. Aitken and Bonneville (1980) provide further support for this, albeit from the point of view of those not evading, in their finding that non-offenders tended to overestimate the number of audits and investigations that takes place. This implies that if their perceptions were more realistic this type of fraud could be more common. This finding has major preventative implications, which will be discussed subsequently.

Attitudes of the Fraudster Towards His/Her Victim/Target

Fraud is not usually classified as a crime against the person. Whilst no *direct* attack on an individual/individuals occurs the cost of fraud against banks and insurance companies, for example, can be indirectly passed on to customers who suffer high bank charges and premiums as a result. This, of course, may be meaningless to the fraudster in that the positive objective of self-enrichment completely outweighs the loss to others as this latter point is not considered. Festinger's (1957) theory of cognitive dissonance is relevant here in that negative aspects of the rejected alternative (non-fraud) or positive aspects of the chosen alternative (fraud and enrichment) allow the individual to reduce dissonance.

Tax evasion has been described as not as serious as other crimes (robbery, burglary etc.) because it is directed against a government body or large organisation rather than other individuals (Henry, 1978). Fraud investigators put this down to these organisations being perceived as able to afford the losses that fraud incurs. In addition, such institutions are seen as an easy source of very rich pickings which fraudsters believe deserve the losses that they suffer. Financial institutions seen as deserving fraudulent attacks are often those who receive money for what can be perceived as inactive services (eg. Inland Revenue, insurance companies). In the case of an insurance company it can be perceived as completely inert in an agreement if the policyholder never has cause to make a claim. Thus, for what can be a relatively large sum of money the policyholder is provided with only a piece of paper that acts as a certificate of insurance. The utility of this certificate is only realised when the individual does need to make a claim. Most people accept this situation as the normal state of affairs between customer and company. However, investigators and researchers (eg. Gill, 1995) suggest that certain fraudulent individuals decide that it is about time that they received money back from the organisation to which they have been paying. In this context, it is likely that the insurance company is seen as benefiting from the individual's money whilst the individual sees no immediate benefit from the money that they have paid out.

Attitudes Towards the Crime of Fraud

Research shows that fraud such as tax evasion of small amounts of money, whilst still considered wrong by the majority, is seen as only about as serious as stealing a bicycle (Song and Yarbrough, 1978). Indeed, Vogel's (1974), as reported in Lea, Tarpy and Webley, (1987) survey indicates that, 'House-breakers, drunken drivers, car thieves and embezzlers should all be punished more severely than tax evaders'. In this case there are different attitudes towards the severity of different types of fraud. Moreover, evasion of small amounts is viewed quite differently from evasion of large amounts (Lewis, 1979). British and American research (Walker, 1978; Schrager and Short, 1980) into the perceived seriousness of different crimes has indicated that commercial frauds are regarded more seriously than any other non-violent property crimes.

Whilst these findings do not exclusively represent the attitudes of the fraudster towards his/her crime it is expected that for some fraudsters there must be a shared opinion that fraud is not a particularly serious crime in order for them to carry it out in the first place. At the same time they are no doubt of the opinion that it is more sophisticated and, to some extent, a more intelligent crime than burglary and theft. The extent to which the offender shares these opinions is bound to be determined by his/her own self-perception and social identity.

Self-Perception, the Self Concept and Social Identity of the Fraudster

The culture in which the individual is embroiled is likely to affect his/her perceptions of whether the activity that they are carrying out is actually criminal or not. Many investigators hold the view that fraudsters (of both small and large amounts) do not perceive themselves as criminals. The fact that fraudsters do this is likely to be related to the functioning of the self. There is a wealth of social psychological literature on the formation of personal and social identities and how these might affect behaviour (eg. Zavalloni, 1983; Breakwell, 1987) with the majority of these acknowledging that the central role of the self is as a mediator between the environment and an individual's actions (Markus and Wurf, 1987).

Thus, identities, as formulated through self-evaluation and self-perception, of the potential fraudster, can serve a mediating function between his/her situation and resulting actions. A thorough examination of the fraudster's situation prior to the offence is required to explore this theory in this context.

Group membership has 'emotional significance' for individuals according to Tajfel (1978). However, individuals who are members of specific categories do not necessarily define themselves as such, and this may explain why fraudsters do not see themselves as criminals. This is borne out in the findings of Ethier and Deaux (1990) and Dion (1989) that between 15 and 50% of their respective samples did not list specific group membership (parent, adult etc.) as one of their psychological identities. Realising that social psychological identities have specific personal meaning for fraudsters who do not see themselves as a criminal is important. Comparisons with specific ingroups and outgroups by the fraudster may lead them to a self-description as 'intelligent' (because they succeeded in their crime) but not as 'criminal' because, as far as the fraudster is concerned, this is not an ingroup definition.

Kaplan (1980) undertook a study that looked at the relationship between self-attitudes and deviant behaviour. His general theory postulated that, 'A broad range of deviant patterns served as responses to self attitudes and as antecedents of changes in self attitudes, given theoretically specified intervening and conditional circumstances'. Thus, in this context, the deviant responses defined above served a self-protective function. The important point here is that the direct influence of self protective patterns upon self attitudes diminishes the experience of negative self-feeling (such as feeling criminal) by removing it from consciousness or by evoking a counter-balancing effect. Perhaps more indirectly, the self-protective response patterns may permit the subject to distort his perceptions of expressed attitudes towards him. Thus, the fraudster may protect him/herself from a 'criminal' label via this process of distortion because they do not feel that they possess disvalued attributes, that they have not performed disvalued behaviours or that valued others have not expressed negative attitudes towards them.

The degree to which fraudsters perceive themselves as 'criminal' is likely to vary dramatically between individuals, depending upon the nature of the crime. Frauds involving a great deal of deceit and manipulation can easily be seen as more criminal or deviant than ones which may just involve an inflated insurance claim for household goods though, technically, they both break the law to the same extent. The degree to which the fraudster describes him/herself as a member of a specific category is seen to be psychologically important in this light. For example, perceiving oneself as 'criminal' is likely to imply different degrees of emotional significance for various individuals. To illustrate this we can look to the previous discussion of the entrepreneurial individual, who utilises manipulation and interpersonal skill, and is more likely to be elaborate in his/her approach to fraud. The fact that this individual has successfully carried out an elaborate crime, which involved a certain degree of risk, no doubt enables them to perceive themselves as skilful in this area of their lives. Such a perceived 'skill' will not be in line with a negative social identity of 'criminal'. Thus, the 'criminal' act is distorted into a 'skilful' act. The fraudster's *self-deception* is paramount here.

Risk Taking and Decision-Making

Successfully receiving financial rewards, whether they are high or low, is the key element in the decision to commit fraud. Actually receiving the financial reward is the ultimate aim whether it is for self-enrichment or to 'get one over' on a target company or individual. But what factors and processes are likely to come to bear upon the decision to undertake a plan of action that involves the potentially high levels of risk which fraud incurs? The offender's potential losses and gains are obvious in this respect but more specific factors, and the way that these are processed, are equally relevant to the decisions that the fraudster makes.

Risk taking is an integral part of all economic behaviour in that choices between actions inevitably involves a degree of uncertainty. To solve this problem between choices, 'The individual needs some means of taking into account the chance that the benefit will be obtained or the penalty really incurred' (Lea et al., 1987), when the cost or value of any desired state is estimated. This is particularly relevant in the decision to commit fraud where the probability of success is almost always unknown. Several theories of risk taking/decision-making under uncertainty (including expected value analysis, subjective probability and subjective expected utility) have been proposed, but all of them assume that the behaviour under question is rational. It is highly debatable whether the decisions leading to any crime, let alone fraud, are entirely rational. The fraudster may rationalise the crime to himself or herself but to the spectator it will usually appear irrational. Thus, 'Irrationality at one level can serve rationality at another' (Robinson, 1996, p.327).

There is a general economic assumption that individuals act so as to maximise utility i.e. to maximise gains from any plan of action they pursue (Bernoulli, 1938, 1954). However, the presence of other facets outside of this rational explanation, which will affect the risky choice, has led many authors to seek accounts of risk taking which do not assume rationality. For example, Friedman and Savage (1952) talk of a loss of self-esteem if the wrong action is chosen under uncertainty whereas Margolis (1981) discusses the idea that each person has two utility functions, one selfish in nature and the other showing consideration for others. These extra facets are equally relevant in the decision to commit fraud. Failure in the crime may lead to loss of self-esteem. In addition, the fraudster acts selfishly towards the target but some may be committing the crime in order to provide for a family, for example. Thus, for the fraudster, risky choice may be influenced by what is to the individual's economic advantage, but it could also be strongly influenced by social norms such as the need to give proper care to one's children (Lea, 1992). These are merely hypotheses but these extra facets detract from the assumption that risky choice in this context is a rational behaviour. Indeed, Lea et al. (1987) concludes that risky choice offers no empirical support for rationality as a general description of human behaviour.

Gambling

The decision to commit fraud is a gamble. All gambling behaviour involves making a decision between two or more choices, and deciding to follow one course of action automatically removes the opportunity to follow another (Lea et al., 1987). It is likely that certain factors influencing the individual to gamble will also have an effect that influences the individual to commit fraud. Both economic behaviours are similar in that they involve a certain amount of risk taking and both result in potentially high payoffs.

Furnham (1984) states that people in the lower economic strata gamble more than those in the higher strata and in more diverse forms. He cites examples of bingo, dog racing and slot machines for those in the lower strata whilst those who are 'better educated' tend to bet on horses. Cornish (1978) has already pointed out that those in the lower socio-economic strata report less satisfaction with their jobs and a stronger belief that winning something like a lottery will provide them with the economic solution that they require. However, this is a major generalisation and may only apply to such gambling behaviour as football pools and the National Lottery where the discrepancy between cost and potential payoff is enormous. The vast majorities in the lower socio-economic strata have no legal way of gaining large amounts of money regardless of how hard they work and how intelligent they are. As such, gambling appears to be a sensible legal alternative. In contrast, fraud is an illegal alternative.

Economic and sociological factors are as likely to affect the fraudster as much as the gambler. Support for this comes from Pearline et al. (1967) who noted that lying, cheating and stealing increase as people strive for important objectives with great pressure on them to achieve and with limited opportunity or ability to attain their goals. Nettler (1982) claims that this is the most well travelled route to fraud as the struggle to survive generates deceit. Indeed, Redden (1939) reported that people at risk of becoming embezzlers were suffering less property ownership, more job changes, lower monthly incomes than their lawful counterparts and higher indebtedness. However, Robertson [7][1] reports, counter-intuitively, that in the related area of workplace crime there was little evidence of his offending employees facing indebtedness or financial difficulty. Certain elements of society, possibly those in the lower socio-economic strata, are likely to view the potential gains of fraud as a means to gaining otherwise unattainable large amounts of money. However, their experience of the systems that they are defrauding is most probably dictated by the limited amount of money they have been able to invest in such organisations. Consequently, the probability of detection of this group is high.

Situational Factors Influencing the Decision to Commit Fraud

Betting shops are a familiar sight in most towns, and thus the opportunity to gamble is presented as convenient to the gambler. Similarly, some

---

[1] A number in [ ] suggests a chapter in this volume.

individuals are provided with a greater opportunity to commit fraud than others are. Hartshorne and May (1928), Briar and Pillavin (1965), Cornish and Clarke (1975) and Mayhew, Clarke, Sturman and Hough (1976) have all stressed how situational inducements and behavioural adaptations to the environment, rather than internal predisposition or personality, are key elements in the decision to commit an offence. The emphasis in Cornish and Clarke's (1975) approach was on the stimuli presented by the situation in which the action occurs and on the individual's previous experience of similar situations. These situational factors are seen as *inducements to criminality* which are moderated by the perceived risks involved in carrying out such a crime. Clearly, if an ideal opportunity is provided for the potential fraudster there will be few, or no, perceived risks. Indeed, fraud investigators have talked of a 'weak control environment' and poor management providing the opportunity for internal fraudsters to offend.

Many investigators suggest that successful fraudsters have a good knowledge of the system that they are defrauding. Without doubt, this is likely to reduce the individual's perceived probability of detection. This is just one element, in this context, of what Mayhew et al. (1976) describe as the *opportunity factor*. This factor is likely to have a major effect on any risky choice that is made between criminality and legality in an individual's actions. Many authors cite situational factors leading to specific crimes (eg. Morris and Hawkins, 1970) but Baldwin (1974) made a point very relevant to fraud that carelessness on behalf of the victims can help explain patterns of crime. Cohen and Felson (1979) took stock of the above findings but pointed out that, 'An important coming together of events which affects crime is the convergence in space and time of likely offenders, suitable targets and the absence of capable guardians against crime'.

Bias in the Decision to Commit Fraud

Research has highlighted how people suffer bias when deciding the probability of a possible outcome. Tversky and Kahneman (1974) undertook a discussion of problems inherent in estimating the probabilities of certain outcomes. Because probability cannot be directly measured these authors proposed that people adopt three strategies for assessing the probability of events occurring. They also pointed out that these three strategies, or heuristics, each have sources of serious error. The first heuristic involved the use of representativeness of an event whereby the individual ignores prior probabilities and sample sizes. The second heuristic depended on the availability of a similar event in recent memory. If this was readily available there is a tendency to think of outcomes as being highly probable if an example of the outcome could be brought to mind relatively easily. Amongst other things, the major source of bias here is the individual's tendency to forget. Furthermore, some events may be highly salient and yet improbable. The third and final heuristic looks at the judgement of the probability of future events in terms of anchor points. By finding an instance appropriately similar to the one in question the individual adjusts his/her estimation of the probability of an outcome in light of the probability of the identified anchor point. The bias here is introduced by the individual's tendency to stay near the anchor point when judging the probability of a certain outcome. Thus, there is an underestimation of the difference between the anchor point and the new instance.

As Lea et al. (1987) point out, 'These ideas suggest that all of us, gamblers or not, are prone to commit errors of judgement when estimating the probability of uncertain outcomes'. Like gamblers, fraudsters will suffer from bias in their decision-making. Errors of judgement, in terms of the number of audits and investigations carried out by organisations, were discussed earlier. These, and other biases, can be utilised to alter the attitudes and perceptions of the potential fraudster and thus have a major preventative role to play.

Implications for the Future

This review indicates that a number of psychological processes may mediate and formulate fraudulent behaviour. However, a mere knowledge of these issues has little utility if it is not effectively examined by researchers and then applied by companies and investigators in the fight against fraud.

Research

Several psychological processes appear to have a role to play in fraudulent behaviour. Unfortunately, it is unlikely that any one element of the psychology of fraud provides the key to an individual's decision to commit the crime or the approach that a particular offender takes to the perpetration of the offence. As a result, research in this area would need to be broad enough to assess the influence of all the processes and procedures discussed in this chapter.

Sets of hypotheses can be generated that are open to direct empirical testing. For example, variations in offenders' attitudes towards money, their targets and their crime can be assessed and relationships between these and other elements such as perceived risk of detection and committing other, more serious crimes can be explored. In other words, more generally, it is hypothesised that particular issues will correlate with offence behaviours. It is also hypothesised that there are consistencies and variations in the occurrence of these between subgroups of offenders. If this was shown to be the case then it may lead to the establishment of a psychological categorisation of fraudsters, which would have direct preventative and investigative benefit.

A comparative assessment of non-offenders' attitudes in these areas would also have great utility because it would serve to indicate differences between the offender and non-offender. Similarly, one may examine circumstances that result in, or mitigate against, fraud. Such an understanding would have preventative value in terms of biasing an informed decision to commit fraud without apprehension.

Prevention

Knowledge of the attitudes and perceptions of the fraudster provides the targets of fraud with the opportunity to control its occurrence proactively. Fraudsters' attitudes towards their targets will be closely linked to their knowledge of the procedures of the target system and their perceived probability of being detected. Spotting a weakness in the preventative armour of the company is no use to an offender if they have no strategy for successfully exploiting the weakness. Potential targets need to identify both the weakness and the strategies *before* the fraudster as well as making a clear statement as to what is fraud and what is not. They also need to emphasise that fraud will not be tolerated and, if detected, will be treated very seriously.

Unfortunately, this ideal faces two stumbling blocks: the judiciary and profit making. For the former, fraud is not taken seriously in terms of sentencing and juries are ill equipped to deal with fraud trials effectively. In addition, fraudsters are rarely required to pay back dishonestly attained funds. For the fraudster, the message from this is that the cost of fraud is minimal whereas the payoff is potentially very high. This is a distorted rationale that serves to forge the attitudes of the fraudster. These are further tempered by the fact that profit-making organisations are loathe to admit to a fraud problem (Clarke, 1989). Investors and customers are perceived as unlikely to support a company with a fraud problem. Understandably, this is a delicate issue which, in many cases, is best tackled through an industry-wide initiative of which one of the only examples is the insurance industry's Claims and Underwriting Exchange (CUE) database of insurance claims. Thus, a second message is relayed to the fraudster that organisations do not see fraud as a priority and are prepared to accept a certain amount of deception (which is not investigated) as long as they remain profitable. In some cases, it is likely that in order to maximise profit margins organisational systems actually facilitate a low level of fraud. Put together, these perceptions are likely to produce the attitude that fraud is not treated as a criminal offence, and will not be regarded as such by the judiciary and that organisations are 'soft' targets.

Altering offenders' attitudes so that their decision to commit fraud is biased through minimal or ambiguous information should make moves towards the prevention of fraud. This reduces offenders' abilities to make a rational and accurate decision about the probability of success and increases both their chance of detection and the probability of them deciding against the crime in the first place.

Investigation

Invariably, there are no witnesses to fraud and there is no crime scene. Thus, there is very little information, in the traditional investigative sense, upon which to form the beginnings of an enquiry. Any details that are available are usually the function of an existing contract between the fraudster and the target, often in the form of computer records.

Furthermore, due to the nature of the crime the majority of information will be false. Organisations need to seize upon the opportunity to gather and process accurate details about their customers or else they will be perceived as 'soft' targets by potential offenders. The streamlining of latter day banking and insurance procedures already fuels offenders' perceptions in this context. In both instances visual contact with the customer is rarely required and most business can be carried out over the telephone. Application forms have been designed for speed and maximum turnover rather than the provision of reliable, relevant, information. Checks on the legitimacy of customers usually only occur once suspicion has been aroused. Thus, whilst there are obvious preventative implications of strengthening this poor control environment, investigative implications also exist. Quite simply, the investigator has minimal information upon which to base an enquiry and, consequently, is provided with little opportunity to increase the amount of information available. Maximal, effective provision of information is necessary in order for the investigator to make informed decisions and pursue relevant lines of enquiry. It is also necessary so that empirical psychological research can make its fullest contribution. Without information there is no feasible way of assessing any psychological factors which have mediated the fraudulent behaviour under investigation.

If this contribution is made then certain implications for investigators follow. Firstly, identifying consistent features that always occur in subgroups of fraud allows for the opportunity to focus on subsequent lines of enquiry. This aids the investigator's decision-making process and prioritises specific areas of the investigation. It is likely that these will be different for specific targets i.e. fraud against banks will have different consistent features to those against the Benefit Agency, though they may share the same psychological meaning or function. Focusing on elements of the investigation, such as interviewing, which otherwise would have shared equal importance with all the other aspects of the enquiry, will lead to a faster and more efficient retrieval of information. It will also concentrate resources rather than spreading them thinly - a factor which is of utmost importance to profit-making organisations.

Secondly, consistent features of an offence that strongly relate to the consistent features of other offences may lead to the conclusion that these are committed by a common offender. This will not only increase the amount of information available about a single offender but it will contribute towards detection. In this case the apprehension of one offender will increase the clear-up rate of fraud for the police and will reduce the losses suffered by the target. Multiple fraud of this kind appears to be a common practice according to investigators. Thus, the ability to identify other offences committed by the same offender will serve as a complementary tool to other investigative initiatives that are in operation.

Thirdly, focusing enquiries and linking offences in this way increases the possibility of detecting offenders earlier in their 'criminal career'. Individuals already recorded in the investigative system are easier to identify and prioritise. As previously mentioned fraud and deception are crimes which usually appear earlier in the careers of other types of offender. If these earlier instances are detected then investigations of later offences will be assisted by readily available information about these offenders who have already come to police notice (for dishonesty). Not only will this increase the detection rate of fraud but also that of other crimes.

Conclusions

Relating the psychological issues under discussion in this chapter to offence behaviour is the key to a richer understanding of how fraudulent behaviour is formulated and mediated. Concerted empirical exploration is required in order to embrace fraud in research and investigative terms. This will provide direct guidance as to what, and how, investigative psychological skills can be effectively employed in fraud investigations. By being aware of consistencies and variations between fraudsters, investigators and researchers alike will have made the first tentative steps towards a scientific classification of fraudsters. Before this can occur, the standard of information yielded by the target organisations and the investigators must improve. Reliable investigations of the empirical and the investigative kind rely on a source of good quality information. Once this information is available the door is open to utilising research findings to assist in fraud prevention, focusing enquiries, linking offences, and apprehending other types of offenders earlier in their 'career'. An empirically derived classification of fraudsters would make a more significant contribution towards these preventative and investigative issues and research is now urgently required in this area.

Principle Source

Dodd, N.J. (1993), 'The Categorisation of Fraudulent Offenders and their Offences: Outlines for Future Psychological Research', *Unpublished MSc dissertation*, Surrey, Department of Psychology, University of Surrey.

References

Aitken, S. and Bonneville, E. (1980), *A General Taxpayer Opinion Survey*, Washington D.C.: C.S.R. Incorporated.

Baldwin, J. (1974), 'The Role of the Victim in Certain Property Offences', *Criminal Law Review*, June, 353-358.

Bernoulli, D. (1954) [1738], 'Specimen Theoriae Novae de Mensura Sortis', *Economica*, **22**, 23-36 (Trans. L. Sommer).

Binning, P. (1996), 'Are Juries Essential?', *The Times*, Tuesday September 24th.

Breakwell, G.M. (1987), 'Identity', in H. Beloff and A. Coleman (eds), *Psychology Survey*, Leicester: British Psychological Society.

Briar, S. and Pillavin, I.M. (1965), 'Delinquency, Situational Inducements of Commitment to Conformity', *Social Problems*, **13**, 35-45.

Clarke, M. (1989), 'Insurance Fraud', *The British Journal of Criminology*, **29 (1)**, 1-20.

Cohen, L.E. and Felson, M. (1979), 'Social Change and Crime Rate Trends: a Routine Activity Approach', *American Journal of Sociology* **73**, 73-83.

Cornish, D.B. (1978), *Gambling: A Review of the Literature*, Home Office Research Study, **42**, London: H.M.S.O.

Cornish, D.B. and Clarke, R.V.G. (1975), *Residential Treatment and its Effects on Delinquency*, London: H.M.S.O.

Crockett, H.J. (1962), 'The Achievement Motive and Differential Occupational Mobility in the United States', *American Sociological Review*, **27**, 191-204.

Deffenbacher, K.A. and Loftus, E.F. (1982), 'Do Jurors Share a Common Understanding Concerning Eyewitness Behaviour?', *Law and Human Behaviour*, **6**, 15-30.

Dion, K. (1989), *Gender Differences in Parental Roles*, Paper presented at Nags Head Conference on Sex and Gender, Nags Head, NC., May.

Ethier, K. and Deaux, K. (1990), 'Hispanics in Ivy: Assessing Identity and Perceived Threat', *Sex Roles*, **22**, 427-440.

Festinger, L. (1957), *A Theory Of Cognitive Dissonance*, Evanston, Ill.: Row, Peterson.

Firth, R. (1963), *Elements Of Social Organisation*, 3rd edn., Boston: MIT Press.

Fraud Trials Committee (1986), 'Improving the Presentation of Information to Juries in Fraud Trials: Four Research Studies', *The Medical Research Council Applied Psychology Research Unit for the Fraud Trials Committee* under the chairmanship of E.W. Roskill, London: H.M.S.O.

Friedman, M. and Savage, L.J. (1952), 'The Expected-Utility Hypothesis and the Measurability of Utility', *Journal of Political Economy*, **60**, 463-475.

Furnham, A. (1984), 'Many Sides of the Coin: The Psychology of Money Usage', *Personality and Individual Differences*, **5**, 95-103.

Furnham, A. and Lewis, A. (1986), *The Economic Mind*, Brighton: Harvester.

Gibbons, D.C. (1975), 'Offender Typologies - Two Decades Later', *British Journal of Criminology*, **15(2)**, 8-23.

Gill, K.M. (1995), 'Insurance Fraud and the Fraudster's Perspective', *Insurance Trends: Quarterly Statistics and Research Review*, No. **5**, April.

Hartshorne, H. and May, M.A. (1928), *Studies in Deceit: Part 1 in the Nature of Character*, New York: Macmillan.

Henry, S. (1978), *The Hidden Economy*, Oxford: Martin Robertson.

Hindelang, M.J. (1972), 'Personality and Self-Reported Delinquency. An Application of Cluster Analysis', *Criminology*, pp.260-294.

Home Office Criminal Statistics for England and Wales (1991), London: Home Office.

Insurance Link (1993), Advertisement Flyer.

Kaplan, H.B. (1980), *Deviant Behaviour in Defence of Self*, London: Academic Press.

Lea, S.E.G. (1992), 'Assessing the Psychology of Economic Behaviour and Cognition', in G.M. Breakwell (ed.), *Social Psychology of Political and Economic Cognition. Surrey Seminars in Social Psychology*, Surrey: University Press.

Lea, S.E.G., Tarpy, R.M. and Webley, P. (1987), *The Individual in the Economy*, Cambridge: University Press.

Levi, M. (1981), *The Phantom Capitalists*, London: Heineman.

Lewis, A. (1979), 'An Empirical Assessment of Tax Mentality', *Public Finance*, **2**, 245-257.

Margolis, H. (1981), 'A New Model of Rational Choice', *Ethics*, **91**, 265-279.

Markus, H. and Wurf, E. (1987), 'The Dynamic Self-Concept: A Social Psychological Perspective', *Annual Review of Psychology*, **38**, 299-337.

Mayhew, P., Clarke, R.V.G., Sturman, A. and Hough, J.M. (1976), *Crime as Opportunity*, Home Office Research Study No. **34**, London: H.M.S.O.

McClelland, D.C. (1961), *The Achieving Society*, Princeton, N.J.: Van Nostrand.

Morris, N. and Hawkins, G. (1970), *The Honest Politician's Guide to Crime Control*, Chicago: University of Chicago Press.

Narula, S. (1993), 'Unwitting but still Implicated', *Accountancy Age*, 18th February.

Nettler, G. (1982), 'Lying, Cheating and Stealing', *Criminal Careers*, **3**, Cincinnati: Anderson Publishing Company.

Pearline, L.I. et al. (1967), 'Unintended Effects of Parental Aspirations: The Case of Children's Cheating', *American Journal of Sociology*, **73**, 73-83.

Person, E.S. (1986), 'Manipulativeness in Entrepreneurs and Psychopaths', in W.H. Reid, D. Dorr, J.I. Walker and J.W. Bonner III (eds), *Unmasking the Psychopath*, pp.256-273, London: Norton.

Redden, E. (1939), *Embezzlement: A Study of One Kind of Criminal Behaviour, with Prediction Tables Based on Fidelity Insurance Records*, PhD dissertation, Chicago: Department of Sociology, University of Chicago.

Robinson, W.P. (1996), *Deceit, Delusion and Detection*, London: Sage.

Schrager, L. and Short, J. (1980), 'How Serious a Crime? Perceptions of Organisational and Common Crimes', in G. Geiss and E. Stotland (eds), *White-Collar Crime*, Beverly Hills, CA.: Sage.

Song, Y.D. and Yarbrough, T.E. (1978), 'Tax Ethics and Taxpayers' Attitudes', *Public Administration Review*, **38**, 442-452.

Tversky, A. and Kahneman, D. (1974), 'Judgement under Uncertainty: Heuristics and Biases', *Science*, **185**, 1124-1131.

Tajfel, H. (1978), *Differentiation between Social Groups: Studies in the Social Psychology of Intergroup Relations*, London: Academic Press.

Vogel, J. (1974), 'Taxation and Public Opinion in Sweden: An Interpretation of Recent Survey Data', *National Tax Journal*, **28**, 499-513.

Wagstaff, J. (1996), 'The Middle Man', *Police Review*, 12th January.

Walker, M. (1978), 'Measuring the Seriousness of Crimes', *British Journal of Criminology*, **18(4)**, 348-364.

Warneryd, K.E. and Walerud, B. (1982), 'Taxes and Economic Behaviour: Some Interview Data on Tax Evasion in Sweden', *Journal of Economic Psychology*, **2**, 187-211.

Zavalloni, M. (1983), 'Ego-Ecology: the Study of Interaction between Social and Personal Identities', in A. Jacobson-Widding (ed.), *Identity: Personal and Socio-Cultural*, Uppsala: University Press.

9 Statistical Approaches to Offender Profiling

DAVID P. FARRINGTON AND SANDRA LAMBERT

This research aimed to advance knowledge about how far it was possible to predict characteristics of offenders from characteristics of offences, characteristics of victims, and descriptions of offenders by victims and witnesses. It was based on case files of convicted offenders (345 burglary and 310 violence) in Nottinghamshire, where nobody (victim, witness or police) knew the identity of the offender at the time of the offence. Topics addressed included: (1) characteristics of offenders; (2) the reliability of police-recorded descriptions of offenders; (3) how offenders were apprehended; (4) the accuracy of victim and witness descriptions in relation to police-recorded offender characteristics; (5) how far victims and witnesses agreed in describing offenders; (6) how far characteristics of offenders could be predicted from offence and victim characteristics; (7) how far offenders repeated similar types of offences and victims; (8) the similarity of co-offenders; and (9) relationships between age/sex/ ethnicity/address offender profiles, age/sex/address victim profile and location/site/time/day offence profiles.

David P. Farrington is Professor of Psychological Criminology at the Institute of Criminology, Cambridge University. He is president of the European Association of Psychology and Law, President elect of the American Society of Criminology, and a Fellow of the British Academy. He has been President of the British Society of Criminology, Chair of the Division of Criminological and Legal Psychology of the British Psychological Society, and Vice-Chair of the US National Academy of Sciences Panel of Violence. He received his PhD in psychology from Cambridge University, and the Sellin-Glueck Award of the American

*Offender Profiling Series: IV- **Profiling Property Crimes***
Edited by D. Canter and L. Alison. © 2000, Ashgate Publishing, Aldershot. pp 233-273

Society of Criminology for international contributions to criminology. His major research interest is in the longitudinal study of delinquency and crime, and he is Director of the Cambridge Study in Delinquent Development, a prospective longitudinal survey of over 400 London males from age eight to age 40. In addition to 220 published papers on criminological and psychological topics, he has published 20 books, one of which, 'Understanding and Controlling Crime' won the prize for distinguished scholarship of the American Sociological Association Criminology Section.

Sandra Lambert is a Senior Intelligence Analyst in Hampshire Constabulary. She has been employed by the Police Foundation and by the Cambridge University Institute of Criminology as a researcher on projects directed by Professor Farrington. She has also worked as a Criminal Intelligence Analyst for the Metropolitan Police and as a Research Officer in the Home Office Police Research Group.

9 Statistical Approaches to Offender Profiling

DAVID P. FARRINGTON AND SANDRA LAMBERT

The main aim of offender profiling is to assist police in the detection of offenders and the solution of crimes, by predicting a combination of characteristics of an offender. This offender profile is predicted from characteristics of the offence, characteristics of the victim, and descriptions of the offender by victims or witnesses.

Offender profiling, as originally developed by the FBI's Behavioural Science Unit, was essentially clinical in nature (see Hazelwood and Burgess, 1987; Ressler et al., 1988). Its aim was to analyse the behaviour of the offender, understand the motive for the offence, and hence infer what type of person had committed the offence. This inference was based on the experience and expertise of the profiler. Therefore, as Grubin (1995) pointed out, it is sometimes not clear how far this type of profiling is significantly different from traditional detective work, which also relies on hunches.

In England, the clinical approach to offender profiling has been set out by Copson et al. (1997). Profilers aim to establish what happened, where, when, how, and to whom. They aim to reconstruct the events and infer the offender's motive. They search for underlying psychological influences, including the offender's emotions, moods, desires and obsessions. Based on their clinical experience and expertise, and on their knowledge of relevant literature, profilers provide advice to police about likely characteristics (a 'psychological signature') of the offender.

Canter (1995) has pioneered a more statistical approach to offender profiling. For example, he investigated the statistical relationships between characteristics of rape offences (eg. the offender forcing the victim to masturbate him, the offender binding the victim) and characteristics of offenders (eg. previous convictions for indecent exposure or indecent assault). Several researchers (Canter, 1994; Davies and Dale, 1995;

Godwin and Canter, 1997) have investigated statistical relationships between locations of offences and addresses of offenders. Aitken et al. (1995) discussed statistical problems of simultaneously predicting a number of offender variables, using the CATCHEM database of sexually oriented child homicides.

Offender profiling has attracted a great deal of attention from the mass media in Great Britain, partly because of the popular television series *Cracker* and partly because of the willingness of some profilers to star in prime-time television documentaries. Because of the mass media focus on solved crimes, several reviewers have commentated on the danger of making exaggerated claims about the usefulness of profiling, or the fact that it has been 'oversold' (Ainsworth, 1993; Grubin, 1995; Towl and Crighton, 1996; Wilson and Soothill, 1996). However, the history of profiling does not consist entirely of successes.

In the Rachel Nickell murder case, for example, Colin Stagg fitted the (clinically obtained) profile of the offender and allegedly was seen on Wimbledon Common at the time of the murder. Attempts were made, using an undercover female police officer, to trap him into admitting the murder, but he never did so. Consequently, the case against him collapsed, and the judge (Mr Justice Ognall) criticised the use of profiling as proof of the identity of the offender (Ward, 1994). Perhaps the judge was seeing some analogy between offender profiling and DNA profiling, because there has not yet been any suggestion from profilers that the fact that a person fits an offender profile might be put forward in court as evidence of guilt.

Copson (1995) carried out the most extensive review of the use of offender profiling by British police forces. He collected information on 184 cases (predominantly of murder or rape) in which profiling had been used, from 48 different police forces. He discovered an exponential increase in the use of profiling, from 25 cases in 1992 to 45 in 1993 and 75 in 1994 (the most recent year). Copson found that profiling helped to solve the case only 14% of the time and helped to identify the offender in only 3% of cases. However, it helped the police to understand the offender in 61% of cases, reassured officers about their own judgements in 52%, and was considered operationally useful in 83% of cases.

Copson found that statistical profilers were twice as likely to be rated not useful as clinical profilers (25% as opposed to 13%) were, but this was mainly a function of the particular individuals involved. For example, one profiler was thought to be carrying too heavy a workload to concentrate on the case and another was considered to be using the police to further his/her own knowledge rather than trying to help the police. Nevertheless, most officers thought that they would definitely (69%) or probably (24%) seek profiling advice again.

Offender profiling could be viewed as a special topic within the general field of research on criminological prediction (Farrington and Tarling, 1985). On the basis of classic works by Meehl (1954) and Sawyer (1966), it might be concluded that statistical prediction is generally more efficient than clinical prediction. The main aim of our research is to throw light on the feasibility of a statistical approach to offender profiling. We aim to predict characteristics of the offender from characteristics of the offence, characteristics of the victim, and reports by victims and witnesses about features of the offender. An alleged limitation of offender profiling is that it can only be used with serial murders or rapes where there are distinctive or ritualistic patterns of behaviour (Wilson and Soothill, 1996). We disagree. We believe that a statistical approach to offender profiling can and should be used with more common offences of burglary and violence.

We further believe that the time is now ripe to construct and implement a computerised offender profiling system to assist in routine police operations. For certain offences that remain undetected after 24 hours, information about characteristics of the offence, characteristics of the victim, and descriptions of the offender would be coded and entered into the system, which would then generate the most likely profile of the offender: the offender's age, sex, ethnicity, height, address, and so on. Also, the system would generate a list of names and addresses of likely offenders from those persons stored in local police records who most closely matched this likely profile. Hence, the aim of a computerised offender profiling system would be to narrow down the range of likely offenders to a feasible number who could be targeted for surveillance and questioning.

The Case of the Yorkshire Ripper

Ideally, such a system would make it easier to solve a series of crimes presumably committed by the same person. It is instructive to review the classic case of the 'Yorkshire Ripper' (Peter Sutcliffe), who was convicted of 13 murders and seven attempted murders of women during 1975-80.

Table 9.1 summarises characteristics of these 20 victims, all of whom were attacked from behind with a hammer.

Table 9.1: Characteristics of 20 Victims of Peter Sutcliffe

Off = Offence; M = Murder; AM = Attempted Murder; Eth = Ethnicity; W = White; B = Black; A = Asian; H = Mixed race; Int = Interval in days since previous offence; Dis A = Distance in miles from previous offence; Dis B = Distance in miles from Sutcliffe's home; Rla = Red light area; Y = Yes; N = No.

No	Name	Off	Age	Eth	Occupation	Date	Day
1	Anna Rogulsky	AM	34	W	Housewife	5/7/75	Sa
2	Olive Smelt	AM	46	W	Cleaner	15/8/75	Fr
3	Wilma McCann	M	27	W	Prostitute	30/10/75	Th
4	Emily Jackson	M	41	W	Prostitute	20/1/76	Tu
5	Marcella Claxton	AM	20	B	Prostitute	8/5/76	Sa
6	Irene Richardson	M	28	W	Prostitute	5/2/77	Sa
7	Patricia Atkinson	M	33	W	Prostitute	23/4/77	Sa
8	Jayne MacDonald	M	16	W	Shop Asst.	26/6/77	Su
9	Maureen Long	AM	42	W	N/A	10/7/77	Su
10	Jean Jordan	M	20	W	Prostitute	1/10/77	Sa
11	Maralyn Moore	AM	25	W	Prostitute	14/12/77	We
12	Yvonne Pearson	M	21	W	Prostitute	21/1/78	Sa
13	Helen Rytka	M	18	H	Prostitute	31/1/78	Tu
14	Vera Millward	M	40	W	Prostitute	17/5/78	We
15	Josephine Whitaker	M	19	W	Clerk	4/4/79	We
16	Barbara Leach	M	20	W	Student	2/9/79	Su
17	Marguerite Walls	M	47	W	Civil Servt.	20/8/80	We
18	Upadhya Bandara	AM	34	A	Student	24/9/80	We
19	Teresa Sykes	AM	16	W	N/A	5/11/80	We
20	Jacqueline Hill	M	20	W	Student	17/11/80	Mo

No	Name	Time	Int	Location	Dis A	Dis B	Place	Rl a
1	Anna Rogulsky	0225	-	Keighley	-	11	Alley	Y
2	Olive Smelt	2350	41	Halifax	15	7	Alley	N
3	Wilma McCann	0430	76	Leeds	23	18	School field	Y
4	Emily Jackson	2030	82	Leeds	1	18	Waste ground	Y
5	Marcella Claxton	0500	109	Leeds	4	21	Park	Y
6	Irene Richardson	2400	273	Leeds	0	21	Park	Y
7	Patricia Atkinson	2335	77	Bradford	18	4	Her flat	Y
8	Jayne MacDonald	0215	64	Leeds	15	18	Play ground	Y
9	Maureen Long	0300	14	Bradford	14	5	Waste ground	Y
10	Jean Jordan	2330	83	Mancstr	34	34	Allotmnt	Y
11	Maralyn Moore	2030	74	Leeds	40	17	Waste ground	Y
12	Yvonne Pearson	2130	38	Bradford	14	3	Waste ground	Y
13	Helen Rytka	2240	10	Hudrsfld	10	12	Wood yard	Y
14	Vera Millward	0130	106	Mancstr	24	33	Hospital ground	Y
15	Josephine Whitaker	2400	322	Halifax	24	13	Park	N
16	Barbara Leach	0100	151	Bradford	11	3	Street	N
17	Marguerite Walls	1900	353	Leeds	6	8	Street	N
18	Upadhya Bandara	2345	35	Leeds	6	14	Alley	N
19	Teresa Sykes	2000	42	Hudrsfld	14	12	Alley	N
20	Jacqueline Hill	2135	12	Leeds	16	14	Street	N

Typically, Sutcliffe persuaded his victims (who were often prostitutes) to get into his car late at night and, as they bent down to get into his car, he hit them on the back of the head with his hammer. Subsequently, he often mutilated their bodies with a knife and left the bodies in degrading positions with breasts and/or buttocks exposed. Typically, the attempted murders occurred because Sutcliffe was disturbed before he could complete the murder. The offences were usually committed in red light areas of Yorkshire cities such as Bradford, Leeds, Halifax and Huddersfield, but Sutcliffe ranged over quite a wide geographical area, as shown by the distances travelled in table 9.1.

Sutcliffe was arrested in January 1981 when two police officers in Sheffield were checking premises at about 11.00 pm. They noticed a car at the rear of a building and found him in it accompanied by a prostitute. They arrested Sutcliffe partly because the car had false number plates and partly because he resembled the photofit of the Yorkshire Ripper. Interestingly, Sutcliffe asked to urinate, and while he was doing this he threw a hammer and a knife that he had in his possession over a fence. These were recovered in a later search of the area. It emerged that Sutcliffe lived in Bradford and worked as a driver, which involved him travelling round the North of England. His wife Sonia worked as a part-time nurse on some evenings (especially Saturdays), so she did not notice his absences. The most common nights for his offences were Wednesdays and Saturdays.

After Sutcliffe was arrested, information came to light which led many people to ask why he had not been arrested sooner. At the time, the Yorkshire Ripper investigation was the largest ever carried out by a British police force, involving hundreds of detectives from different police forces and interviews with many thousands of suspects (Doney, 1990). And yet, nobody apparently noticed that Sutcliffe had been convicted in October 1969 of 'going equipped to steal' after chasing a prostitute with a hammer in a red light area (the Manningham area of Bradford). A good photograph of him, taken on 30th September 1969, was available in police files from the time of this offence. Furthermore, a month earlier, while out driving in the same area with his close friend Trevor Birdsall, Sutcliffe had stopped his car and had attacked a prostitute with a sock containing two stones. The police interviewed both men at the time, but no charges were pressed by the injured woman (Yallop, 1981, p.338).

Trevor Birdsall was also in the car with Sutcliffe before and after the attack on Olive Smelt (victim no.2) in 1975. Sutcliffe dropped him off before the attack and picked him up later, appearing very breathless. Birdsall subsequently sent an anonymous letter to the police naming Sutcliffe as the offender in this case. In the case of Jean Jordan (victim no. 10) in 1977, a brand new £5 note was discovered in her handbag. It was realised that this had almost certainly been given to her by the murderer, since £5 was the 'going rate' for prostitution in that area at that time. This particular £5 note had been released into circulation less than four days before the murder, in a batch sent out for wages by the Midland Bank at Shipley. Sutcliffe's firm was identified as one of those who received the notes and (along with 8,300 other people) he was interviewed twice at that time.

In fact, Sutcliffe was interviewed nine times by the police between 1977 and 1980, but sometimes by different officers who did not communicate effectively with each other. Also, his car appeared at least 50 times on computer checks of cars seen in red light districts. The problem was that no central computer was used to collate the mountain of information assembled on this case (Beattie, 1981, p.144). After this famous case, and after the Byford (1984) inquiry into it, the HOLMES computer system was set up to collate information about major cases from police forces all over the country.

Peter Sutcliffe had a distinctive appearance which he did not attempt to change over time, notably black hair and a full black beard. Table 9.2 summarises descriptions of the offender given by five attempted murder victims. It compares these with descriptions of Sutcliffe on police antecedent forms from October 1975 (when he was arrested, coincidentally by a D.C. Sutcliffe, for stealing five car tyres from his load) and January 1981 (when he was finally arrested). The description from Marilyn Moore (victim no. 11) in 1977, and the accompanying photofit, was particularly accurate and similar to the October 1975 antecedents form (and indeed the September 1969 photograph). However, some of the other descriptions and photofits were less accurate. Of course, it must be remembered that the attacks usually took place in poor lighting conditions, and the victims suffered head injuries that could have impaired their intellectual functioning and memory.

Table 9.2: Descriptions of the 'Yorkshire Ripper'/ Peter Sutcliffe

Source	Smelt	Police	Claxton	Moore
Date	15/8/75	17/10/75	17/10/76	14/12/77
Sex	Male	Male	Male	Male
Ethnicity	White	White	White	White
Age	30	29	30	27-28
Height	5'6''	5'8''	-	5'7-8''
Eye Colour	-	Brown	-	Brown
Hair Colour	Dark	Black	Black	Black
Hair Style	Long Sideburns	-	Centre parting	Wavy, on collar
Facial Hair	Stubble or beard	Black, full beard	Black, short beard	Black beard, moustache
Eyebrows	-	Black, bushy	-	Bushy
Build	Slight	Medium	Medium	Proportionate
Accent	-	-	-	Leeds / Liverpool
Voice	-	High pitched	-	Soft
Dress	Dark suit, not smart	Leather jacket black trousers		Dark coat, blue jeans
Occupation	-	Driver	-	-
Place of Birth	-	Shipley, Yorks	-	-
Address	-	Clayton, Bradford	-	-
Car	-	-	-	Dark red, black seats
Other	-	Pale complexion, round face	Gold ring on left hand	Swarthy complexion

Source	Bandara	Sykes	Police
Date	24/9/80	5/11/80	5/1/81
Sex	Male	Male	Male
Ethnicity	White	White	White
Age	25-35	25-33	34
Height	5'9''	5'8''-6'0''	-
Eye Colour	-	-	Brown
Hair Colour	Brown/blonde	Dark	Black
Hair Style	Short	Collar length	-
Facial Hair	Short beard	Brown short beard	-
Eyebrows	-	-	-
Build	-	Slim	Proportionate
Accent	-	-	Yorkshire
Voice	-	-	-
Dress	-	-	Camel car coat
Occupation	-	-	Driver
Place of Birth	-	-	Shipley, Yorks
Address	-	-	Heaton, Bradford
Car	Dark red, black seats	-	-
Other	Swarthy complexion	Long thin face	-

A major problem was to determine which offences were committed by the Yorkshire Ripper and which offences were not. For example, it seems very likely that Sutcliffe committed at least four and possibly more than ten other attempted murders - all using a hammer from behind - to which he did not admit. Two of these victims, Gloria Wood (11.11.74 Bradford) and Tracey Browne (27.8.75 Silsden), both gave quite good descriptions of the offender. These two attempted murders occurred before and just after Sutcliffe's first admitted offences. On the other hand, the four-page newspaper entitled 'Help us Catch the Ripper', which was distributed to 2,000,000 people by West Yorkshire Police after offence no.16, mistakenly included Joan Harrison (20.11.75 Preston) as a victim of the Ripper. As Bland (1984) pointed out, the Harrison murder clearly had a sexual motive, some semen was found in the victim's vagina. There is no corroborated evidence that Sutcliffe had sexual intercourse with any of his admitted victims, although he claimed that this was the case with Helen Rytka (victim no.13).

More seriously, the police investigation was hampered by three letters from Sunderland posted in 1978-79 and by a tape recording of a man claiming to be the Yorkshire Ripper, with a Wearside (Geordie) accent, posted in June 1979. The sender gave details of the Joan Harrison murder that had not been made public and forensic tests showed that the person who licked the envelopes had a rare blood group B (shared by 6% of the population) which was the same as that identified from semen in Harrison's body. Hence, it is not impossible that the man with the Geordie accent was the killer of Joan Harrison. However, one of the reasons why Sutcliffe had been eliminated from the investigation was because he had a Bradford rather than a Geordie accent. An important implication of this experience is that an incorrect offender profile could hinder a police investigation for many months.

We would argue that Sutcliffe would have been caught much sooner if a computerised offender profiling system had been in operation at the time. Knowing that the Yorkshire Ripper attacked prostitutes with a hammer in red light areas of Yorkshire cities, it should have been possible to search police records to find persons with convictions involving carrying a hammer in red light areas of Yorkshire cities, and persons known or suspected of attacking prostitutes in red light areas. It should have been possible to locate known Yorkshire offenders with black hair and full black beards. It was not difficult for Kind (1987), using geographical mapping, to locate the Ripper's address as most likely to be in the Manningham or Shipley areas of Bradford; actually, Sutcliffe lived in Heaton, which is situated between Manningham and Shipley. The aim of a computerised offender profiling system would be to identify types of offenders in police records with specified characteristics (eg. a full black beard), living in specified areas (eg. Bradford), who commit specified types of offences (eg. attacking with a hammer) and who choose specified victims (eg. prostitutes). Searching for a relatively small number of these types of factors would soon have narrowed down 8,300 people who received new banknotes to Peter Sutcliffe.

Aims of Our Research

Our research is described in more detail in Farrington and Lambert (1994, 1997a, 1997b). Its main aim is to assess the feasibility of statistical approaches to offender profiling. It is exploratory in nature, but we believe that it provides indications about how to design a large-scale computerised offender profiling system. The main aims of the research follow from the aims of offender profiling. As already mentioned, offender profiling aims to improve the detection of offenders and the solution of crimes, to assist in targeting offenders for surveillance and interviewing, and to assist in questioning offenders about possible crimes they might have committed. Its main aim is to predict characteristics of the offender from characteristics of the offence, characteristics of the victim, and descriptions of the offender by the victim or a witness. It also aims to narrow down the range of possible offenders and identify a limited number of likely offenders from those stored in police records; and to determine how far a series of offences and/or victims are likely to be attributable to the same offender.

Our research is based on police records of offences leading to convictions, and hence it is vulnerable to all the limitations of police records. How far convicted offenders might be similar to undetected offenders is not entirely clear, although self-report studies (eg. West and Farrington, 1973) suggest that they are similar in many respects. Therefore, it should be possible to generalise our conclusions to undetected offenders. Since our method involves comparing contemporaneous offence, victim and witness data with later-discovered information about the offender, our first question is:

1.   How reliable are police-recorded characteristics of offenders?

Information about the offender in police records is essentially the criterion against which we compare other data, so we need to know the accuracy of this offender information. For example, if Sutcliffe was recorded as 6 feet tall in one interview and 5'6'' tall in a later interview, there would be no reliable criterion of height against which to compare the victim and witness descriptions.

An offender profile is a list of values of different variables for an offender. For example, Sutcliffe's offender profile might consist of values of his sex (male), ethnicity (white), age (born 2.6.46), height (5'8"), and so on. Two important questions are:

2.   How are offender characteristics inter-related?

3.   How can offender profiles be developed?

Offender profiles are essentially typologies of offenders, so a key question centres on what are the most useful typologies for any particular detection problem.

Offender profiling clearly will not be useful for all types of offenders or offences. For example, in many cases, the victim knows the identity of the offender, so it is unnecessary to establish this. Offender profiling is likely to be especially useful in cases where nobody (victim, witness or police) knows the identity of the offender at the time of the offence, and these are the cases that we study. In order to improve the detection of offenders, an important question is:

4.   How are offenders apprehended now?

Sutcliffe was apprehended during routine police checking of premises. The following questions really lie at the heart of offender profiling:

5.   How accurate are victim descriptions of offenders in predicting offender characteristics?

6.   How accurate are witness descriptions of offenders in predicting offender characteristics?

7.   How far do victims and witnesses agree in their descriptions of offenders?

8.   How far can offender characteristics be predicted from offence characteristics?

9.   How far can offender characteristics be predicted from victim characteristics?

Offender profiling will be particularly useful to the extent that victims and witnesses are accurate.   In the Sutcliffe case, some victims and witnesses did provide reasonably accurate descriptions. Offender profiling will also be particularly useful to the extent that specific types of offenders commit specific types of offences and choose specific types of victims. Sutcliffe committed his offences in very distinctive ways, always hitting the victim on the back of the head with a hammer. However, he then varied his methods of mutilating the dead bodies, in some cases deliberately trying to confuse the police (eg. when he used a hacksaw to try to decapitate Jean Jordan, although another factor here was because he was angry that he could not find his £5 note). ·Sutcliffe always chose lone female victims, many of whom were prostitutes, but otherwise did not choose a particular type of victim. He moved out of red light areas when he became aware of extensive police activity and checking there.

Offender profiling will be useful to the extent that offenders repeat similar types of offences, choose similar types of victims, and choose similar types of co-offenders, as opposed to varying offences, victims and co-offenders randomly, opportunistically or unpredictably.   Hence, three final questions are the following:

10.   How far do offenders repeat similar types of offences?

11.   How far do offenders repeat similar types of victims?

12.   How far do offenders choose co-offenders who are similar to themselves?

Description of the Research

Our research was based on case files entering the Nottinghamshire Criminal Record Office (CRO) after conviction. These case files were extensive and voluminous. Most of the documents were destroyed after the essential information was computerised for Nottinghamshire CRO purposes, but we were able to extract data for our purposes before the CRO staff extracted data for their purposes. The information about previous offences in the files and in computerised records was not sufficiently detailed for our purposes.

Nottinghamshire, in the Midlands of England, consists of a predominantly rural county surrounding the large city of Nottingham. The populatio of Nottinghamshire in 1991 was about 1,000,000. Nottinghamshire was chosen as the site for this project because previous research had been conducted there by Farrington and Dowds (1985). In 1991, Nottinghamshire had the highest *per capita* rates of violence, sex and theft offences in England and Wales (Home Office, 1993). However, as Farrington and Dowds showed, part of the reason for this high crime rate was the assiduous recording of crimes by the Nottinghamshire police.

Information was extracted and computerised for 655 different offenders whose files reached the Nottinghamshire CRO during the 9-month period 1st March - 30th November, 1991. Our original aim was to extract data about all offences of burglary or serious violence committed in Nottinghamshire and leading to a conviction, where nobody (victim, witness or police) knew the identity of the offender at the time of the offence. Obviously, problems of detecting offenders do not arise in cases where someone knows the offender (as is true in the majority of cases of serious violence, which are between acquaintances, relatives, friends or intimate cohabitees). All the included offences involved offenders who were strangers to the victim. For statistical purposes, we needed several hundred of each type of case.

Our original design was modified in two ways. First of all, because the flow of eligible burglary cases was about twice as great as the flow of eligible violence cases, we randomly excluded up to half of the burglary cases to keep the numbers manageable. Secondly, a small number of offences committed just outside the county were included in our dataset, because they were dealt with by the Nottinghamshire police and hence eventually reached the Nottinghamshire CRO.

The offenders in our sample comprise 345 burglars and 310 violence offenders (166 convicted of causing actual bodily harm or section 47 assault, 35 convicted of wounding/causing grievous bodily harm or section 18/20 assault, 39 convicted of affray, violent disorder or common assault, and 70 convicted of robbery). Seventeen offenders were convicted of both burglary and violence during this time period; they were included in the number of violence offenders. An additional 316 burglars were excluded (271 at random and 45 because a victim or witness knew the offender). Similarly, 889 violence offenders were excluded (815 because the victim or witness knew the offender and 74 where the victim was a police officer and the violence occurred during an arrest). Hence, problems of detection occurred for only 310 out of 1199 violence offenders (26%), but for 633 out of 678 burglars (93%).

The data consists of w offenders, x offences, y victims and z witnesses for each incident. This makes the analysis very complicated. Generally, we have overcome the problems by basing analyses on n pairs. For example, in comparing victim characteristics with offender characteristics, the analysis was based on n victim-offender pairs. However, it must be realised that the same victim can appear in more than one pair, just as the same offender can appear in more than one pair.

Characteristics of Offenders

The police information on characteristics of the 655 offenders was extracted from the C10 (description and antecedent history) form, which was completed at the time of arrest. This C10 form contained information about the offender's name, date of birth, place of birth, sex, ethnic appearance, nationality, height, weight, build, accent, eye colour, voice, hair colour, hair length, facial hair, marks/scars/abnormalities, dress, address, occupation, education, marital status and children. The Nottinghamshire C10 form was similar to the national NIB74 form, which was accompanied by coding instructions and categories. For example, the coding instructions for ethnic appearance specified White European, Dark European, Afro-Caribbean, Asian, Oriental, Arab or Mixed race.

Table 9.3 summarises the characteristics of the burglary and violence offenders and offences (see also Farrington and Lambert, 1994). For example, the vast majority of offenders (95% for burglary and 91% for violence) were male. However, there were significantly more females among the violence offenders. Also, the vast majority of offenders (89%) were White, with 6% Afro-Caribbean, 4% Mixed race and 1% Asian (of Indian, Pakistani or Bangladeshi ethnic origin). Ethnicity was not significantly related to the type of offence, although more of the violence offenders were Afro-Caribbean or of Mixed race. The age of the offenders ranged from 10 to 59, but the majority of offenders (72%) were aged 14-24. Violence offenders were significantly older.

Table 9.3: Characteristics of 655 Burglary and Violence Offenders

Variable (% Recorded)	Category	N	% of 345 Burglary	% of 310 Violence	Significance
Sex (100.0)	Male	610	95.4	90.6	.017
	Female	45	4.6	9.4	
Ethnicity (97.4)	White	567	91.4	86.0	
	Black	36	3.8	7.7	N.S.
	Mixed	27	3.8	4.7	
	Asian	8	0.9	1.7	
Age (100.0)	10-13	24	3.8	3.5	
	14-16	116	23.2	11.6	.0001
	17-20	214	38.8	25.8	
	21-24	142	17.7	26.1	
	25-29	73	9.0	13.5	
	30-39	62	4.9	14.5	
	40 +	24	2.6	4.8	
Height (99.8)	<=5'	24	4.6	2.6	
	5'1-5''	68	11.3	9.4	N.S.
	5'6-8''	189	29.9	27.8	
	5'9-11''	226	32.8	36.6	
	>=6'	147	21.4	23.6	
Weight (97.1)	<=8st	75	15.1	8.1	
	8st1-9st	57	13.3	4.0	.0001
	9st1-10st	122	23.7	14.1	
	10st1-11st	146	21.9	24.2	
	11st1-12st	104	12.7	20.5	
	12st1-13st	64	5.9	14.8	
	13stones +	68	7.4	14.4	
Build (98.8)	Small/slim	343	63.9	40.8	
	Medium	216	28.4	38.9	.0001
	Large	88	7.6	20.3	
Hair colour (99.1)	Blonde	59	6.7	11.8	
	Grey	9	1.2	1.6	N.S.
	Black	91	12.5	15.7	
	Ginger	29	5.5	3.3	
	Light brown	141	23.3	19.9	
	Dark brown	305	48.1	45.8	
	Highlights	15	2.6	2.0	

Variable (% Recorded)	Category	N	% of 345 Burglary	% of 310 Violence	Significance
Hair length (91.3)	Shaved	16	0.9	4.6	.005
	Balding	13	1.6	2.8	
	Collar	449	80.4	69.1	
	Shoulder	72	11.4	12.8	
	> shoulder	17	2.5	3.2	
		31	3.2	7.4	
Hair style (50.7)	Curly/permed	109	29.0	37.2	N.S.
	Straight	110	39.8	25.6	
	Centre part	14	4.0	4.5	
	Side part	21	5.7	7.1	
	Neat	19	6.3	5.1	
	Unkept	25	8.5	6.4	
	Afro/dreads	13	2.3	5.8	
	Shaved	21	4.5	8.3	
Facial hair (98.3)	None	451	72.9	66.9	.053
	Moustache	142	21.5	22.6	
	Beard	37	4.7	6.9	
	Stubble	14	0.9	3.6	
Eye colour (98.6)	Blue/grey	286	43.2	45.4	N.S.
	Green	69	11.8	9.5	
	Brown	291	45.0	45.1	
Accent (96.5)	Notts	546	92.2	79.9	.0001
	Other English	33	3.9	6.7	
	Other British	23	2.7	4.7	
	Other	30	1.2	8.7	
Voice (82.1)	Medium	149	29.1	26.2	N.S.
	Deep	135	20.1	30.4	
	Loud/rough	28	5.4	5.0	
	Quiet/soft	222	44.6	37.7	
	Stutter	4	0.7	0.8	
Tattoo (99.2)	Yes	247	36.5	39.6	N.S.
	No	403	63.5	60.4	
Scar/ Birthmark (100.0)	None	469	70.1	73.2	N.S.
	Face/neck	79	10.7	13.5	
	Arm/hand	65	12.5	7.1	
	Body/leg	42	6.7	6.1	
Facial feature (100.0)	No	642	98.8	97.1	N.S.
	Yes	13	1.2	2.9	

Variable (% Recorded)	Category	N	% of 345 Burglary	% of 310 Violence	Significance
Dress **(98.6)**	Smart/casual	32	3.2	6.9	
	Sloppy/casual	587	93.0	88.5	N.S.
	Gaudy/garish	14	1.8	2.6	
	Sports/athletic	13	2.1	2.0	
Place of birth **(97.6)**	Nottingham	136	22.9	19.4	
	Notts	353	59.1	50.8	.003
	Other England	108	14.1	20.1	
	Other British	22	1.5	5.7	
	Other	20	2.4	4.0	
Nationality **(98.8)**	British	642	99.1	99.3	N.S.
	Other	5	0.9	.07	
Address **(97.9)**	N.central	108	17.8	15.8	
	N.suburban	243	38.6	37.2	.068
	N.county	104	15.1	17.4	
	Mansfield	79	14.2	10.2	
	Newark	24	4.2	3.3	
	Wrksop/Retfd	20	3.6	2.6	
	Other	63	6.5	13.5	
Living **Circumstance** **(91.9)**	NFA	10	2.2	1.0	
	Parents	331	54.8	55.2	N.S.
	Relatives	30	4.8	5.2	
	Friends	47	7.3	8.3	
	Spouse/cohab.	111	17.2	19.8	
	Alone	73	13.7	10.4	
Marital **Status** **(99.1)**	Single	497	79.8	73.1	
	Married	49	5.9	9.4	N.S.
	Cohabiting	66	10.0	10.4	
	Divorced/sep	37	4.4	7.1	
No. children **(100.0)***	0	502	81.4	71.3	
	1	69	9.0	12.3	.031
	2	47	4.9	9.7	
	3	25	2.9	4.8	
	4 or more	12	1.7	1.9	
Occupation **(98.9)**	Unemployed	328	60.6	39.6	
	Manual	153	11.8	36.7	.0001
	Non-manual	39	3.5	8.8	
	Education	128	24.1	14.9	

Variable (% Recorded)	Category	N	% of 345 Burglary	% of 310 Violence	Significance
	Comp/second	560	97.8	96.9	N.S.
Education (87.8)	Gram/private	15	2.2	3.1	
	Higher	-	-	-	

Absence of information assumed to be negative information; Significance based on chi-squared; N.S. = Not Significant; N. = Nottingham/Notts.; Comp. = Comprehensive; Gram. = Grammar; st = stone (14lbs.).

Most offenders (63%) were between 5'6" and 5'11" tall, and most (58%) weighed between 9 stone 1 pound and 12 stones. Violence offenders were significantly heavier. Similarly, violence offenders had a significantly larger build. Offenders tended to have dark brown (47%) or light brown (22%) hair. Regarding hair length, three-quarters of offenders (75%) had hair above the collar. Violence offenders were more likely to have deviant hair length (shaved or very long). Hair style was only recorded in about half of the cases, and most of these offenders (66%) had curly/permed or straight hair. The presence or absence of facial hair was recorded in nearly all cases, and violence offenders were more likely to have a beard, moustache or marked stubble.

Most offenders had blue/grey (44%) or brown (45%) eyes. The vast majority (86%) had a local (Nottinghamshire) accent. Only 5% had other English accents (eg. Geordie), 4% had other British accents (Welsh, Scottish or Irish) and 5% had non-British accents. Violence offenders were significantly more likely to have non-local accents. It was most common (41%) for offenders to have quiet or soft voices. Over one-third of offenders (38%) were tattooed. Scars or birthmarks were noted in 28% of cases. Unusual facial features (bulging eyes, teeth missing, gold teeth, marked acne or pitted complexion, wearing glasses) were noted in only 2% of cases. The offender's dress at the time of arrest was recorded in almost all cases, but in the vast majority of these (91%) it was only classified as sloppy/casual.

Three-quarters of offenders (77%) were born in Nottingham or Nottinghamshire. Violence offenders were significantly more likely to have been born outside Nottinghamshire. Almost all offenders had British nationality. Most offenders lived in Central Nottingham (postcodes NG1-NG3), Suburban Nottingham (postcodes NG4-NG9) or in the County (postcodes NG10-NG17). Fewer lived in the Mansfield area (postcodes NG18-NG21), the Newark area (postcodes NG22-NG25), the Worksop/Retford area (DN postcodes), or outside Nottinghamshire. There was some tendency for violence offenders to live outside the county. Over half of the offenders (55%) lived with their parents, and about three-quarters (77%) were single. More of the burglary offenders were single. About a quarter of offenders (23%) were recorded as having children, and violence offenders were significantly more likely to have children. About half (51%) were unemployed at the time of arrest. There was a significant tendency for burglary offenders to be more often unemployed or still in education. Finally, only 3% of offenders had been to grammar or private schools or in further or higher education.

Reliability of Police Descriptions of Offenders

As the C10 form was used as the criterion against which information from victims and witnesses was compared, it was important to investigate the reliability and validity of the information contained on it about characteristics of offenders. Reliability refers to the extent to which the information from different sources is concordant, whilst validity refers to the extent to which information from a particular source agrees with an external criterion. Unfortunately, it was impossible to establish validity, as there was no external criterion against which to compare the C10 data. For example, it was not possible to interview offenders within the scope of this research.

The reliability of police-recorded descriptions of offenders was assessed by studying cases where the same offender had two or more C10 forms completed independently (because of two or more separate arrests during the 9-month study period; see Farrington and Lambert, 1997b). Cases of obvious duplication of C10 forms (eg. by photocopying) were excluded. In total, 56 offenders had more than one C10 form completed, allowing a total of 177 comparisons of C10 forms. Reliability was measured using Kappa, which is a statistical measure of agreement in excess of chance expectation (Cohen, 1960). A Kappa value of 1 indicates perfect agreement, while a Kappa value of 0 indicates a level of agreement no better than chance. According to Fleiss (1981, p.218), a Kappa value of 0.40 or greater shows good agreement between sources, and a Kappa value of 0.75 or greater shows excellent agreement.

The most reliably recorded observable offender characteristics were sex (Kappa = 1), ethnicity (0.86), age (0.81) and eye colour (0.75). Other observable offender characteristics recorded with good reliability were accent (0.69), tattoos (0.68), weight (0.63), height (0.59), facial hair (0.51), hair colour (0.49) and unusual facial features (0.39). In contrast, hair length (0.26), voice (0.17) and build (Kappa = 0) had low reliability. In some cases (eg. age, height, weight) there were genuine changes between one arrest and another, so that Kappa under-estimates the true reliability. The most useful non-observable offender characteristic was address. The Kappa value of 0.60 for address indicates the relatively high mobility of these repeat offenders. This high mobility poses some problems for offender profiling, since any profiling system is likely to include predictions about the offender's address at the time of the current offence, and since the police records will only specify the offender's address at the time of the last offence.

Overall in our analyses, we concluded that the 12 most important observable characteristics of offenders in police records were sex, ethnicity, age, height, build, hair colour, hair length, facial hair, eye colour, accent, tattoos and unusual facial features. The most important non-observable characteristic of offenders was their address.

Developing an Offender Profile

As might have been expected, many of the offender characteristics were inter-related. For example, female offenders were more likely to be non-white, younger, smaller and to have black, long hair. Females were less likely than males to have facial hair or tattoos. Afro-Caribbean and Mixed-race offenders tended to be younger, to have black, long hair, to have beards, and to have brown eyes. Non-white offenders were less likely to have local accents and less likely to have tattoos, but they were more likely to have unusual facial features. Younger offenders tended to be smaller, with shorter hair, less facial hair and less tattoos, and they were more likely to have local accents. Smaller offenders tended to have shorter hair, less facial hair and less tattoos. Black-haired offenders tended to have long hair, facial hair, and brown eyes, but tended not to have tattoos. Long-haired offenders tended to have facial hair, and facial hair was also associated with brown eyes and tattoos. However, brown-eyed offenders were relatively unlikely to have tattoos.

A factor analysis was carried out on the 12 key observable features (all dichotomised) to investigate how many different underlying constructs they reflected. Three important factors were extracted, accounting for 16%, 14% and 11% of the variance, respectively. After a varimax rotation, the highest loadings on the first factor were non-White ethnicity (0.73), brown eye colour (0.77) and black/dark brown hair colour (0.69). Hence, this factor seems to reflect ethnicity. The highest loadings on the second factor were older age (0.76), facial hair (0.56), larger build (0.47) and non-local accent (0.44). This factor seems to reflect age. The highest loadings on the third factor were male sex (0.79), tall height (0.53) and short hair length (0.54). This factor seems to reflect sex. Hence, the factor analysis indicated that the three most important dimensions underlying these observable features were sex, ethnicity and age.

An offender profile is essentially a combination of values of variables for an offender. As already mentioned, Sutcliffe's profile would consist of the values of his sex, ethnicity, age, height, etc. An offender profiling system stores the profiles of offenders convicted in the past. A key issue is how to choose how many and what variables to include in this profile. In our analyses, we focused particularly on sex-ethnicity-age and sex-ethnicity-age-address profiles of offenders. For example, with sex (2 categories), ethnicity (4 categories) and age (7 categories), there were 56 possible profiles, but only 35 contained offenders in this project. The largest category comprised 177 White males aged 17-20, followed by 120 White males aged 21-24, 86 White males aged 14-16, and 62 White males aged 25-29. Eight profiles contained only one offender and of course 21 contained none (Farrington and Lambert, 1997b).

Even with a small number of offender characteristics, each measured in a small number of categories, there are a large number of possible profiles. For example, eight observable offender characteristics (sex, ethnicity, age, height, build, hair colour, hair length, facial hair) produced 141,120 possible profiles. As with DNA profiling, it would soon be possible to say that only one person in a million matched a particular offender profile.

In offender profiling, the ideal is to identify a relatively small proportion of persons stored in the system as likely offenders, and to have a high probability that the number of identified likely offenders includes the true offender. As the number of variables in the profile increases, the average number of offenders with each unique profile decreases. In general, profiles containing very few offenders in a system may be the most useful in pinpointing likely offenders. Unfortunately, however, as the number of variables in the profile increases, so also does the probability of a victim or witness getting at least one of them wrong, so that the offender would not be identified correctly. It is clearly necessary to compromise between minimising the proportion of persons identified as likely offenders and maximising the probability of identifying the true offender.

Methods of Apprehension of Offenders

In considering how to improve the detection of offenders, it is useful to determine how offenders are currently detected (see also Farrington and Lambert, 1997b). As explained before, all cases where the identity of the offender was known were excluded from our analyses. We had detailed records of a total of 742 arrests of our 655 offenders; this number is slightly less than the number of C10 forms (750) because police statements about arrest were missing in eight cases. In 694 of the 742 cases where police statements were found (94%), it was possible to establish the main reason why the offender was apprehended. Unfortunately, this information was recorded rather carelessly, and it would have been necessary to interview officers to determine the reasons accurately. Ideally, officers should complete a systematic checklist of reasons for apprehension.

The most important ways in which burglars were arrested were; they were caught in the act (14%), through an informant (12%), they were caught near to or leaving the scene of the crime (12%), they were traced through property left at the scene of the crime or through the disposal of stolen goods (10%), they were seen acting suspiciously in the area, for example carrying stolen goods (8%), they were caught for another crime and admitted this burglary (7%), or through an accurate description by a witness (7%). The most important ways in which violence offenders were arrested were; they were detained at the scene of the crime (16%), through an accurate description by a victim (15%), through an accurate description by a witness (13%), through a description of a vehicle or a number-plate (11%), because they were caught in the act (11%), or as a result of enquiries in the local area (7%). Clearly, victim and witness descriptions were far more important in apprehending violence offenders than burglars, because violence offenders were more often seen by victims and witnesses.

In view of the frequency of catching offenders at or near to the scene of the crime, it was not surprising to find that the time interval between the first report of an offence and the apprehension of the offender was typically quite short. Over half of the violence offenders (61%) were arrested straight away or within one hour, as were 43% of burglars. It is reasonable to conclude that the likelihood of an offender being arrested declines steeply with time after the commission of the offence, especially for violence offences. One of the aims of an offender profiling system would be to increase the probability of detecting the offender at least one day after the crime, when the immediate trail had gone cold.

Accuracy of Victim and Witness Descriptions

There were 652 possible comparisons of victim reports and offender characteristics for burglary, and 417 for violence. However, as very few burglary victims could provide any descriptive information about their offenders, our analysis focused on violence victims (Farrington and Lambert, 1997b). These victims were most accurate in reporting sex (Kappa = 0.91), ethnicity (0.85), hair length (0.75), facial hair (0.59) and hair colour (0.50) of the offender. They were moderately accurate in reporting accent (0.44), height (0.38), age (0.36) and build (0.33). Hence, our earlier conclusion that build was not recorded reliably, based on the low agreement between C10 forms, was incorrect. The multiple offenders who had more than one C10 form disproportionally had a small build, but this was not true of violent offenders in general, who were equally distributed over the three categories of build (small, medium and large).

As an illustration of the use of victim descriptions in an offender profiling system for violence offences, an attempt was made to predict the sex-ethnicity-age profile of the true (police-recorded) offender from the sex-ethnicity-age profile of the offender as described by the victim. Full information about the sex, ethnicity and age of both victim-described and true offenders was available for only 196 of the 417 victim-offender comparisons (47%). In the simplest analyses, sex, ethnicity and age were all dichotomised, so that there were only eight possible offender profiles. In this case, the victim's profile of the offender was correct in 71% of the cases (Kappa = 0.58).

This percentage would obviously decrease as the complexity of the profile increased. As an example, consider the sex (2 categories) - ethnicity (4 categories) - age (7 categories) profile, which had 56 categories in principle but 27 in practice (because of missing values). In this case, 46% of victim-reported offender profiles were correct. Interestingly, the accuracy of rare profiles (the 22 containing five or fewer offenders) was greater than the accuracy of more common profiles (the other five). About half (51%) of rare offender profiles were correct, compared with 44% of common offender profiles.

There were 440 possible comparisons of witness reports and offender characteristics for burglary, and 610 for violence. Burglary witnesses were most accurate in reporting sex (Kappa = 0.99) and ethnicity (0.88), followed by hair length (0.56), hair colour (0.49), age (0.45), build (0.32) and height (0.26) of the offender. Violence witnesses were similarly most accurate in reporting sex (0.89) and ethnicity (0.86), followed by facial hair (0.60), hair colour (0.53), age (0.44), hair length (0.43), build (0.41) and height (0.34).

As an illustration of the use of witness descriptions in an offender profiling system, an attempt was made to predict the sex-ethnicity-age profile of the true offender from the sex-ethnicity-age profile of the offender as described by the witness. In this analysis, sex had 2 categories, ethnicity had 4 categories, and age had 7 categories. Full information about the sex, ethnicity and age of both witness-described and true offenders was available for only 315 of the 1050 witness-offender comparisons. Burglary and violence witnesses were combined in this analysis partly to increase the numbers and partly because their accuracy was similar (55% for burglary and 53% for violence). Over all witness-offender comparisons, 54% of witness-reported offender profiles were correct. Hence, witnesses were more accurate than victims in identifying offenders, Interestingly, the accuracy of rate profiles (the 18 containing six or fewer offenders) was greater than the accuracy of more common profiles (the other nine): 57% of rare profiles were correct, compared with 53% of common profiles.

In order to investigate how far two victims of the same offender agreed on characteristics of that offender, all possible (918) offender-victim-victim triplets were constructed from cases where an offender had two or more victims. Kappa was used to measure agreement between victims in their reports of characteristics of offenders. Because few burglary victims could report characteristics of offenders, this analysis was based on 223 triplets containing two violence victims. Because of missing data (few victims reporting characteristics of offenders), each offender characteristic could only be measured in two or three categories. Two victims agreed quite well in reporting the offender's sex (Kappa = 1.00), ethnicity (0.94), facial hair (0.74), hair length (0.55), build (0.40), age (0.34), height (0.31) and hair colour (0.30). The sex-ethnicity-age profile of the offender could only be compared for 32 pairs of violence victims, but they agreed in 63% of cases (Kappa = 0.50).

In order to investigate how far two witnesses of the same offender agreed on characteristics of that offender, all possible (764) offender-witness-witness triplets were constructed from cases where an offender had two or more witnesses. Two witnesses agreed quite well in reporting the offender's facial hair (Kappa = 1.00), ethnicity (0.98), sex (0.94), age (0.60), hair length (0.55), hair colour (0.54), height (0.44) and build (0.42). In general, agreement between two witnesses was greater than between two victims. The sex-ethnicity-age profile of the offender could be compared for 158 pairs of witnesses, and they agreed in 75% of cases (Kappa = 0.67).

In order to investigate how far a victim and a witness agreed on characteristics of an offender, all possible (1867) offender-victim-witness triplets were constructed from cases where an offender had at least one victim and at least one witness. Because few burglary victims could report characteristics of offenders, the analysis was based on 938 triplets containing violence victims and witnesses. Victims and witnesses agreed quite well in reporting the offender's ethnicity (Kappa = 0.99), sex (0.98), hair colour (0.71), age (0.62), hair length (0.61), facial hair (0.58), build (0.50) and height (0.38). The sex-ethnicity-age profile of the offender could be compared for 187 victim-witness pairs, and they agreed in 78% of cases (Kappa = 0.72).

The major practical problem in increasing the number of variables in an offender profile is missing data. There was unsystematic coverage of offender characteristics in questions to victims and witnesses. For example, it is likely that much of the missing data on sex and ethnicity involved reports of males and Whites, and that police officers sometimes did not bother to specify such common categories in the records of witness (and indeed victim) statements. Some statements included sentences such as 'the youth ran off' without specifying the youth's sex, but there was probably the implicit assumption in virtually all cases that the youth was male. More systematic coverage of offender characteristics, preferably using simple checklists, is needed.

Predicting Offenders from Offence and Victim Characteristics

The records indicated that the 655 offenders had committed a total of 1017 offences. Because of the phenomenon of co-offending (Reiss and Farrington, 1991), there were not 1017 separate incidents but 1017 offence-offender pairs. The offence and the offender could be compared in 1017 cases, 650 involving burglary and 367 involving violence. Farrington and Lambert (1994) systematically compared characteristics of burglary and violence offences. For example, most burglaries were committed in Suburban Nottingham (38%) or Central Nottingham (22%), while most violence offences were committed in Central Nottingham (40%) or Suburban Nottingham (24%).

There were numerous regularities between characteristics of offences and characteristics of offenders (focusing especially on eight key observable characteristics: sex, ethnicity, age, height, build, hair colour, hair length and facial hair; see Farrington and Lambert, 1997a). For example, in regard to the location of the offence, burglary offences in the city of Nottingham were significantly more likely to be committed by non-White offenders than burglary offences elsewhere. This result may reflect the geographical distribution of ethnic minorities in Nottinghamshire. Violence offences in the city of Nottingham were also more likely to be committed by non-White offenders than violence offences elsewhere, and relatively more likely to be committed by female offenders than violence offences elsewhere. Burglary and violence offences in the city of Nottingham were also more likely to be committed by relatively small offenders, by those with black or dark brown hair, and by those with relatively short hair.

Residential burglaries significantly tended to be committed by male offenders, while there was some tendency for burglaries of shops and business premises to be committed by female offenders. Violence in pubs or entertainment places was significantly likely to be committed by older offenders, while violence in streets or shops was more likely to be committed by younger offenders. Violence in shops was also more likely to be committed by non-White offenders, while violence in transport places (eg. bus stations) was more likely to be committed by White offenders. Burglaries of residential, education or pub/entertainment premises tended to be committed by relatively small offenders with short hair and no facial hair. Burglaries of business and transport places tended to be committed by offenders with black or dark brown hair. Violence in transport and pub/entertainment places tended to be committed by relatively large offenders.

Most burglary (69%) and violence (55%) offenders lived within one mile of the scene of the crime. Only 8% of burglars and 15% of violence offenders lived more than five miles away from the scene of the crime. Hence, the location of the offence was an important clue to the address of the offender, as found in numerous other studies (eg. Canter, 1994; Davies and Dale, (1995). In the case of burglary, relatively older and larger offenders tended to live far away from the scene of the crime. In the case of violence, female, non-White, younger and smaller offenders tended to live close to the scene of the crime.

In their burglaries, younger offenders entered buildings disproportionally through the roof, whilst females tended to enter through the front. Older offenders tended to smash windows, whilst non-Whites tended to force open doors or windows. In burglary, female, non-White, and younger offenders tended to use no instrument (pliers, screwdrivers, bricks, etc.). Similarly, in violence, female and younger offenders tended to use no weapons (knives, sticks, etc.). After committing their offences, female and younger offenders were disproportionally likely to escape on foot as opposed to in a vehicle. Male, White, older and larger offenders were disproportionally likely to be under the influence of alcohol at the time of their offending.

These results relating offence features to offender characteristics were quite intriguing. There were repeated suggestions that male, White and older offenders committed offences in a rather different way from female, non-White and younger ones. Ideally, it would be desirable to develop a criminological theory to explain these kinds of results. This might require the supplementation of records by interviews with offenders asking them about their choice of offences and victims.

Factor analyses were carried out on features of burglary and violence offences (all dichotomised) to investigate how many underlying constructs they reflected. The offence features included in the analyses were: location, site, time, day, season, escape method, alcohol influence and reason (for burglary and violence), entry area, access method, instruments used (for burglary only), and disguise, clear intention and weapon use (for violence only).

For burglary, four important factors were extracted, accounting for 51% of the variance. After a varimax rotation, the highest loadings on the first factor were residential site (0.76), day time (0.63) and entry from the rear

(0.67); on the second factor were winter season (0.56), entry by smashing windows (0.72) and alcohol influence (0.64); on the third factor were monetary gain reason (0.73), escape not on foot (0.61) and weekday offence (0.34); and on the fourth factor were city of Nottingham location (0.54) and no instrument (0.72). For violence, similarly, four important factors were extracted, accounting for 52% of the variance. After a varimax rotation, the highest loadings on the first factor were night time (0.84), alcohol influence (0.80) and clear intention (0.45); on the second factor were street site (0.74), no weapon (0.65) and no disguise (0.44); on the third factor were city of Nottingham location (0.57), escape on foot (0.70) and reason not anger (0.58); and on the fourth factor were weekend offence (0.73) and summer season (0.52).

These factor analyses suggest that the basic and easily measured offence variables of location, site, time, day and season are key features of the fundamental dimensions underlying offence variables. Other offence variables were associated with at least one of these basic variables. Hence, these basic offence variables were used to develop offence profiles. Specifically, the extent to which the offence profile of location-site-time-day predicted the offender profile of address-age-sex-ethnicity was investigated. The sample was divided at random into two halves, one used as a construction sample and the other as a validation sample. Offence profiles were related to offender profiles in the construction sample; to determine which offender profile was most commonly associated with each offence profile. The success of this prediction was then investigated in the validation sample. However, the analysis of burglary profiles was rather uninteresting, because in almost all cases the predicted offender profile was a young White male, living in the same area (city or county) as the offence.

Interesting regularities between offence and offender profiles were discovered for violence. For example, violence offences in the city of Nottingham, not in the street, committed in the daytime and at the weekend, the offender most commonly lived in the city of Nottingham, was young (under 21), female and non-White. For violence offences committed in the county, in the street, at night-time and at the weekend, the offender most commonly lived in the county, was older (21 or over), male and White. In the validation sample for violence, 48% of predictions of offender profiles, based on offence profiles, were correct.

In comparing victim characteristics with offender characteristics, the analysis was based on 1084 offender-victim pairs. There were 655 different offenders and 739 different victims recorded in the files. Unfortunately, it was difficult to study the characteristics of burglary victims. Burglary is a crime essentially against a household or business, not against an individual. However, characteristics of dwellings or business premises were not typically recorded in the files. In practice, the person listed as the victim of burglary (the 'injured party') was usually the person who reported the crime to the police. Hence, if a household was burgled and the husband reported the crime to the police, the husband would be listed as the victim, even though the wife and children had also been victimised. Therefore, the fact that burglary victims recorded in the files were disproportionally male (68%) was misleading.

These considerations led us to study only the characteristics of violence victims (in the 420 victim-offender pairs; see Farrington and Lambert, 1997a). There were many regularities between characteristics of the victim and characteristics of the offender. For example, nearly a third of female victims had female offenders, compared with only 2% of male victims, a highly significant difference. Hence, knowing that a victim was female helped in predicting the sex of the offender. Female victims were also associated with non-White offenders, younger offenders, smaller offenders, and offenders with no facial hair.

These analyses were limited by missing data on victim characteristics. For example, the ethnicity of the victim was noted in only 15% of cases, but there was some tendency for White victims to have non-White offenders. The age of the victim was almost always recorded, and younger victims tended to have younger offenders, female offenders, non-White offenders and smaller offenders. Regarding victim activities at the time of the crime, the victim drinking or in a place of entertainment was associated with male, older and White offenders, while victims who were out shopping tended to have female, younger and non-White offenders.

The victim's address was known in most cases (87%). Victims living in Central and Suburban Nottingham were disproportionately likely to have female, non-White and younger offenders. In addition, victims tended to live in the same areas as offenders. The distance between the victim's residence and the scene of the crime was one mile or less in nearly half (47%) of cases, and two-three miles in a further 20%. Hence, most victims lived close to the scene of the crime. Victims who lived far from the scene of the crime were more likely to have male and older offenders, while victims who lived near to the crime were more likely to have younger offenders.

We also investigated how far address-age-sex violence victim profiles predicted address-age-sex-ethnicity offender profiles for violence in construction and validation samples. For example, when the victim was a young city female, the offender was most commonly a young non-White city female. When the victim was an older county male, the offender was most commonly an older White county male. Overall, 51% of predicted victim profiles in the validation sample were correct.

How Far Do Offenders Repeat Similar Types of Offences and Victims?

An important issue is how far offenders are specialised as opposed to versatile. In principle, offender profiling is likely to be more useful with specialised offenders. Farrington and Lambert (1994) investigated specialisation in the present data by searching the previous criminal records of all 655 offenders. They found that 89% of burglars and 79% of violence offenders had a previous criminal record. (This refers to the criminal record at the time of the first arrest recorded in the period of our research.) Since only 11% of burglars and 21% of violent offenders would not have been found in existing records, this suggests that offender profiling is potentially useful as a technique for assisting in the detection of offenders. Burglars were significantly more likely than violence offenders to have previous recorded offences. As many as 36% of burglars and 24% of violence offenders had 10 or more previous recorded offences.

Just over half of the burglars had one or more previous burglaries, in comparison with about a quarter of the violence offenders. Similarly, nearly half of the violence offenders had at least one previous violence offence (wounding, grievous bodily harm, actual bodily harm, affray, threatening behaviour or robbery), in comparison with about a third of the burglars. Hence, restricting offender profiling to offenders with a recorded offence of the same type (eg. searching for burglars only among recorded burglars) would make it impossible to identify about half of the offenders. This suggests that characteristics of all offenders should be stored in an offender profiling system. More of the violence offenders also had a previously recorded offence of Breach of the Peace or public disorder. These figures agree with criminological research (eg. Stander et al., 1989) showing that there is some specialisation in burglary and violence superimposed on a fair degree of versatility in offending.

The 655 offenders committed a total of 1017 recorded offences leading to conviction during the time period of the research. These figures exclude offences 'taken into consideration'; the types of these offences were not specified in the records. For the 183 offenders with two or more recorded offences, it was possible to compare the characteristics of pairs of offences to see how far offenders repeated similar types of offences (Farrington and Lambert, 1997a). In total, 753 pairs of offences could be compared. However, in 46 cases, the offences in a pair were different (one was burglary and the other was violence). The main comparisons in this section are of 638 pairs of burglary offences and of 69 pairs of violence offences. The preponderance of burglary comparisons shows that the multiple offenders in this research tended to be repeat burglars.

As before, Kappa was used as the main measure of agreement between two offences in a pair. Two burglary offences tended to be committed in similar locations (Central Nottingham, Suburban Nottingham, Mansfield area, Newark area, Worksop/Retford area, etc.: Kappa = 0.72) and in similar sites (residences, businesses, shops, etc.: Kappa = 0.33). However, there was no marked tendency for burglars to commit their offences at similar times (0.18) or on similar days (0.08). Judging from the values of Kappa, there was only weak agreement between burglaries on the place of entry (front, back, rear, roof), the method (smash window, force entrance, other), instruments used (tools, blunt instruments, etc.) and going pre-equipped. However, there was perfect agreement on the method of escape (on foot, car, motorcycle/ bicycle, public transport).

Violence offenders were much more consistent in their locations of offences (0.77), sites (0.90), time of the day (0.67) and day of the week (0.71). Violence offenders were also consistent in their types of weapons used, whether they made their intentions clear from the start, whether they went pre-equipped, and whether they made any effort to disguise their identity. Generally, violence offences were more similar than burglaries, suggesting that offender profiling might be more useful with violence than with burglary in linking a series of similar offences to the same offender.

The location-site-time-day offence profiles were compared with each other, to see how similar they were. Since all four constituent variables were dichotomised, these were in principle 16-category variables, although the violence variable only had 8 categories in practice. In the case of burglary, the profiles of each offence in a pair agreed on 29% of occasions, and Kappa = 0.21. In the case of violence, the profiles of each offence in a pair agreed on 84% of occasions, and Kappa = 0.80. Hence, there was good agreement between offence profiles for violence, showing that violence offenders tended to commit similar types of offences.

The 655 recorded offenders had a total of 1084 recorded victims. For the 204 offenders with two or more victims, it was possible to compare the characteristics of victims in a pair to see how far offenders repeatedly chose similar types of victims (Farrington and Lambert, 1997a). Altogether, 952 pairs of victims could be compared. However, in 43 cases, the victims in a pair were different (one was of burglary and the other was of violence). The main comparisons in this section are of 684 pairs of burglary victims and 225 pairs of violence victims.

There was little tendency for offenders to choose burglary victims of similar ages (Kappa = 0.10) or sexes (0.07), but that could be because burglary is essentially a household crime and who is counted as the victim is somewhat arbitrary (as explained earlier). There was a marked tendency for offenders to choose violence victims of the same sex (0.57) but not particularly of the same age (0.22).

Successive victims of burglary and violence offenders tended to live in the same area (Kappa = 0.61 and 0.60). There was also a marked tendency for burglary victims to have similar occupations (coded as unemployed, employed, in education or housewife/ retired) and a lesser tendency for violence victims to have similar occupations. Successive violence victims tended to be engaged in the same activity (coded as walking/cycling, waiting for transport, driving, working, drinking/ entertainment, at home, out shopping; most were involved in drinking/entertainment). Similarly, there was some tendency for successive burglary victims to be engaged in the same activity (coded as working/school, away/holiday, asleep, at home, moving home, out shopping, out for evening entertainment, in another part of the building; most were at home).

The sex-age-address victim profiles were also compared with each other, to see how similar they were. Since all three constituent variables were dichotomised, these were in principle 8-category variables, although the burglary variable only had 6 categories in practice. In the case of burglary, the profiles of each victim in a pair agreed on 45% of occasions, and Kappa = 0.23. In the case of violence, the victim profiles agreed 47% of the time and Kappa = 0.24. These are rather low levels of agreement, showing little tendency for burglary and violence offenders to choose similar types of victims on successive offences.

Many offences were not committed alone but in groups of co-offenders. There were 83 co-offending pairs, 28 groups of three, 11 groups of four, and three groups of five co-offenders in our data. Comparing every offender with all possible co-offenders, there were 298 different co-offending pairs. (Because each offender could commit more than one offence, the number of co-offenders was not necessarily symmetrical. For example, person A could have two co-offenders, including person B, and person B could have three co-offenders, including person A.)

Kappa was used as the main measure of similarity between co-offenders. Co-offenders were most similar in address (Kappa = 0.75), sex (0.69), occupation (0.60), ethnicity (0.44), age (0.44) and tattoos (0.33). Occupation was coded as employed, unemployed or in education. They were not particularly similar in height (0.07), build (0.21), hair length (0.22), hair colour (0.05), eye colour (0.12), facial hair (0.16) or marital status (0.23). When the sex (2 categories) - ethnicity (2 categories) - age (6 categories) profiles of co-offenders were compared, they agreed 50% of the time, and Kappa = 0.37. Hence, knowing key characteristics of one co-offender made it possible to predict key characteristics of another.

Conclusions

Our research has shown the existence of numerous relationships that could form the basis of an offender profiling system. The following features at least could and should be coded and computerised from existing record forms:

(i)   *Offender*: address, sex, age (date of birth), ethnicity, height, accent, build, hair length, hair colour, facial hair, tattoos, distinctive physical features.

(ii) *Offence*: location, site, time, day, date, method, instruments or weapons, method of escape, disguise, offender under influence of drink or drugs.

(iii)   *Victim*: address, sex age, ethnicity, marital status, occupation, activity at the time of the crime, victim under influence of drink or drugs.

(iv)   *Victim Report of Offender*: all offender variables except address.

(v)   *Witness Report of Offender*: all offender variables except address.

The distinctive physical features (eg. bulging eyes, teeth missing) are worth recording even though they do not apply to many cases, because they might help to identify the offender in these few cases.

We have made some progress in developing offender and offence typologies, but we are very conscious that further work requires more extensive and more complete data. It is important to develop offender and offence typologies based on far more variables and categories than we have used. However, there are a number of problems that our research has highlighted and that need to be overcome, in addition to the major problem that many detected offenders (especially juveniles) are given unrecorded warnings (Farrington, 1992).

At the time of this research in Nottinghamshire, there was unsystematic and incomplete coverage of many items of interest, for example those on the C10 (description and police antecedents) form. We think it is unlikely that the Nottinghamshire police are very different from other forces in this respect. The problem is that much of the information on the C10 form was never used again, so there was little incentive for police officers to spend a great deal of time completing the form. Indeed, the Nottinghamshire police did start completing these forms more carefully when they saw that we were making use of them. This problem might be overcome by redesigning the form into a series of checklists, making it easy to ring the appropriate alternative each time. Also, the police could be trained in completing the forms and encouraged to record all items (eg. height) as accurately as possible. It may be a mistake to rely too much on offender self-reports. Once offenders realise that the information on the C10 form might help to detect them in the future, they might be motivated to provide inaccurate information.

An obvious problem with the C10 (NIB74) form at present is that the information on it is difficult or impossible to retrieve. This problem could be overcome by routinely computerising the data on the revised form. We understand that this is being done in the Phoenix computerised criminal record system introduced in May 1995, but it is unclear how easily the computerised data can be retrieved and used. We recommend that CRO operators should type in variables from ringed checklists on the C10 form when they type in details of the offence for storage in the CRO system. Data on changeable variables (eg. height or address) would then be routinely up-dated. In the interests of completeness, the C10 form should be filled in and computerised for all detected offenders, including those dealt with by cautions or unrecorded warnings. Similarly, information about the offence, the victim, and the description of the offender by the victim and witness should be coded and computerised using systematically completed checklists of questions. This would ensure that every topic (eg. whether the offender was under the influence of alcohol or drugs) would be systematically covered.

Further research is needed on many topics connected with offender profiling. An important issue is the rate of change of variables such as address, height and build over age and time. A major problem is how offence data, victim data, and victim and witness information on the offender can best be combined to predict the profile of the offender. One of the greatest challenges is how best to cope with a variable number of victims, a variable number of witnesses, a variable number of offenders, and a variable number of separate incidents.

Research is also needed on how best to classify physical features of the offender, dress, tattoos, and so on. The classification systems currently in operation seem to be based on common sense rather than systematic research, but there could be relevant scientific literature on the measurement of physical characteristics that could be used. Research could also be carried out on improving questions to offenders, victims and witnesses; for example, questions about being under the influence of alcohol or drugs could be made more specific, and hence more reliable and valid.

More fundamental research should also be carried out, designed to develop theories about why there are correlations between certain offender characteristics, offence characteristics and victim characteristics. These theories need to explain how offences arise from interactions between offenders and victims in situations. Existing criminological theories are of limited relevance, because few criminologists have been interested in investigating correlations between physical characteristics of offenders and specific details of offences. This more fundamental research should include interviews with offenders and victims. The theories should help to guide research on offender profiling by specifying particular characteristics of offenders, offences and victims that should be measured. Research is also needed on developing typologies of offenders. Studies are also required on the prediction of recidivism by offenders, so that recidivism probabilities and rates of offending can be taken into account in an offender profiling system. More research is also needed on the prediction of criminal careers, and especially on predicting specialisation and escalation. For example, Farrington and Hawkins (1991) found that nearly 90% of London boys convicted before age 21 who were both unemployed and heavy drinkers were reconvicted after age 21.

To a considerable extent, our research on offender profiling has been exploratory, but we feel that the relationships between offender, offence and victim characteristics are sufficiently promising to justify a larger-scale data collection effort and an attempt to construct and use more complex offender, offence and victim profiles. From a certain date, information on the police antecedents form in a particular local area should be coded and computerised for all arrested offenders. This information should then be used for operational purposes in trying to solve serious crimes that are still undetected after 24 hours. It should help in selecting persons for surveillance and interviewing, and in selecting questions to ask during interviews. The success of this computerised offender profiling system should be evaluated by determining its effect on detection rates.

If the detection rates of serious offences could be improved by setting up an offender profiling system, that would be to the benefit of law-abiding members of society. If such a system had been in operation in the 1970s, it should have been possible to identify Peter Sutcliffe as the Yorkshire Ripper much earlier, and hence to prevent a number of deaths and serious injuries. We believe that a statistical approach to offender profiling has considerable merit.

Acknowledgements

We are very grateful to Gloria Laycock and the Home Office Police Research Group, and to Barrie Irving and the Police Foundation, for supporting and funding this research, and to the Nottinghamshire and West Yorkshire Police for their invaluable assistance.

References

Ainsworth, P. (1995), *Psychology and Policing in a Changing World*, Chichester: Wiley.

Aitken, C., Connolly, T., Gammerman, A., Zhang, G. and Oldfield, D. (1995), *Predicting on Offender's Characteristics: An Evaluation of Statistical Modelling*.

Beattie, J. (1981), *The Yorkshire Ripper Story*, London: Quartet Books.

Bland, L. (1984), 'The Case of the Yorkshire Ripper: Mad, Bad, Beast or Male?', in P. Scraton and P. Gordon (eds), *Causes for Concern*, pp.184-209, Harmondsworth, Middlesex: Penguin.

Byford, L. (1984), 'Lessons to be Learned', *Police Review*, **92**, 1870-1871.

Canter, D.V. (1994), *Criminal Shadows* London: Harper Collins.

Canter, D.V. (1995), 'Psychology of Offender Profiling', in R. Bull and D. Carson (eds), *Handbook of Psychology in Legal Contexts*, pp.343-355, Chichester: Wiley.

Cohen, J. (1960), 'A Coefficient of Agreement for Nominal Scales', *Educational and Psychological Measurement*, **20**, 37-46.

Copson, G. (1995), *Coals to Newcastle? Police use of Offender Profiling*, London: Home Office Police Department.

Copson, G., Badcock, R., Boon, J. and Britton, P. (1997), 'Articulating a Systematic Approach to Clinical Crime Profiling', *Criminal Behaviour and Mental Health*, **7**, in press.

Davies, A. and Dale, A. (1995), *Locating the Stranger Rapist*, London: Home Office Police Department.

Doney, R.H. (1990), 'The Aftermath of the Yorkshire Ripper: The Response of the United Kingdom Police Service', in S. Eggar (ed.), *Serial Murder*, pp.95-112, New York: Praeger.

Farrington, D.P. (1992), 'Trends in English Juvenile Delinquency and their Explanation', *International Journal of Comparative and Applied Criminal Justice*, **16**, 151-163.

Farrington, D.P. and Dowds, E.A. (1985), 'Disentangling Criminal Behaviour and Police Reaction', in D. P. Farrington and J. Gunn (eds), *Reactions to Crime*, pp.41-72, Chichester: Wiley.

Farrington, D.P. and Hawkins, J.D. (1991), 'Predicting Participation, Early onset and later Persistence in Officially Recorded Offending', *Criminal Behaviour and Mental Health*, **1**, 1-33.

Farrington, D.P. and Lambert, S. (1994), 'Differences between Burglars and Violent Offenders', *Psychology, Crime and Law*, **1**, 107-116.

Farrington, D.P. and Lambert, S. (1997a), 'Predicting Offender Profiles from Offence and Victim Profiles', in P-O. H. Wikström, L.W. Sherman and W.G. Skogan (eds), *Problem-Solving Policing as Crime Prevention*, Boulder, Colorado: Westview Press.

Farrington, D.P. and Lambert, S. (1997b), 'Predicting Offender Profiles from Victim and Witness Descriptions', in J. Jackson and D. Bekerian (eds) *Understanding Offender Profiling: A Guide for Forensic Practitioners*, Chichester: Wiley.

Farrington, D.P. and Tarling, R. (1985) (eds), *Prediction in Criminology*, Albany, N.Y.: State University of New York Press.

Fleiss, J. L. (1981), *Statistical Methods for Rates and Proportions*, 2nd edn., New York: Wiley.

Godwin, M. and Canter, D.V. (1997), 'Encounter and Death: The Spatial Behaviour of U.S. Serial Killers', *Policing*, in press.

Grubin, D. (1995), 'Offender Profiling', *Journal of Forensic Psychiatry*, **6**, 259-262.

Hazelwood, R.R. and Burgess, A.W. (1987) (eds), *Practical Aspects of Rape Investigation*, Amsterdam: Elsevier.

Home Office (1993), *Criminal Statistics, England and Wales, 1991*, London: Her Majesty's Stationery Office.

Kind, S.S. (1987), *The Scientific Investigation of Crime*, Harrogate: Forensic Science Services.

Meehl, P.E. (1954), *Clinical versus Statistical Prediction* Minneapolis: University of Minnesota Press.

Reiss, A.J. and Farrington, D.P. (1991), 'Advancing Knowledge about Co-Offending: Results from a Prospective Longitudinal Survey of London Males', *Journal of Criminal Law and Criminology*, **82**, 360-395.

Ressler, R.K., Burgess, A.W. and Douglas, J.E. (1988), *Sexual Homicide: Patterns and Motives*, Lexington, Mass: Lexington Books.

Sawyer, J. (1966), 'Measurement and Prediction, Clinical and Statistical', *Psychological Bulletin*, **66**, 178-200.

Stander, J., Farrington, D.P., Hill, G. and Altham, P.M.E. (1989), 'Markov Chain Analysis and Specialisation in Criminal Careers', *British Journal of Criminology*, **29**, 317-335.

Towl, G.J. and Crighton, D.A. (1996), *The Handbook of Psychology for Forensic Practitioners*, London: Routledge.

West, D.J. and Farrington, D.P. (1973), *Who Becomes Delinquent?*, London: Heinemann.

Wilson, P. and Soothill, K. (1996), 'Psychological Profiling: Red, Green or Amber?', *Police Journal*, **69**, 12-20.

Yallop, D.A. (1981), *Deliver Us from Evil*, London: Futura.

10 Using Corporate Data to Combat Crime against Organisations: A Review of the Issues

NICK J. DODD

Corporate crime data (CCD) is a valuable source of information about actual criminal activity committed against organisations. However, it has received scant attention from researchers and organisations when assessing the risk of criminal behaviour in this context. This chapter argues that CCD requires re-evaluation by organisations as a source of knowledge that can be utilised as business intelligence to combat crime committed against them. At the same time it argues that behavioural research of this 'noisy' source of data can be undertaken to increase our understanding of crime against organisations. This increased understanding can directly inform both investigative and preventative strategies at the corporate level and theories of crime at the academic level. However, such requirements are not without their methodological difficulties, and these are reviewed. A discussion of the advantages of integrating traditional research approaches to corporate crime and direct assessment of criminal activity conclude the article.

Nick J. Dodd was awarded a BA (Hons) Psychology from University College, Swansea, The University of Wales and a PhD from the University of Liverpool. A keen interest in the application of psychology to investigating and preventing crime led to him being awarded an MSc in Investigative Psychology by the University of Surrey. A specialised interest in the psychological aspects of fraud developed during this period.

Offender Profiling Series: IV- Profiling Property Crimes
Edited by D. Canter and L. Alison. © 2000, Ashgate Publishing, Aldershot. pp 275-296

This received support from the insurance industry in an examination of the behavioural aspects of insurance claim fraud. A more recent interest has been exploring the psychological aspects of pilfering and its relationship to organisational culture and employee variables. This attracted the support of the Economic and Social Research Council and an international parcel delivery company. Concurrently, advisory roles have been undertaken on projects exploring compliance, control and security issues in the working environment.

10 Using Corporate Data to Combat Crime against Organisations: A Review of the Issues

NICK J. DODD

Introduction

The cost of crime to organisations has been well documented. Whether committed by people internal (employees), or external (usually customers/clients) to the organisation, crime in the workplace appears to result in staggering losses to businesses every year. Briefly, the Association of British Insurers estimates its losses from fraud for 1994 at £600 million, (Wagstaff 1994). The Confederation of British Industry (1990) reported that crime against businesses cost over £5 billion a year in 1990 (no up to date figures available); and Narula (1993), a forensic accountant, reported that 'Mortgage fraud is costing lending institutions well in excess of £3 billion' back in 1993.

Because losses of this kind appear to be very costly, as are subsequent investigations, most organisations adopt strategies to reduce the opportunity for them to occur. Traditionally, such strategies have been drawn up and deployed by internal experts who have been mainly concerned with the physical aspects of security. Consequently, these strategies have been entrenched in the systems and physical blocks that can be employed to halt crime against the organisation. Though these approaches have had some beneficial effects in the reduction of crime, it is often the case that they merely shift the method of the offence from abusing one loophole in the organisational structure or process to abusing another. Strategies rarely rely on any systematic understanding of criminal behaviour and, if they claim to, it often depends on an investigator's, or security manager's, more memorable cases. Thus, rather than an objective assessment of criminal activity, myths are propagated about the motives that prompt criminal behaviour and the modus operandi that offenders adopt. Due to this reliance on memorable cases, misinformed briefings about the nature of crime against a specific organisation can subsequently lead to the implementation of ineffective security strategies. It would seem reasonable to conclude that such strategies have paid little attention to the human aspects of such deviant activity as well as the source of such intelligence, which they maintain in-house. In this sense, organisations are failing to fully harness the true potential of the corporate data that they collate about crime committed against them in any systematic and useful way.

Similarly, researchers have also paid little attention to this rich source of information about corporate crime. Research in this area has spanned the disciplines of psychology, sociology, criminology and anthropology. Such a breadth of interdisciplinary research reflects the various implications of such deviant behaviour as well as the various factors that correlate with it. However, in spite of this breadth of interest a thorough literature review, Dodd (PhD in prep.) reveals that virtually no research has employed actual corporate crime data as its sample. The likes of Mars (1974) and Ditton (1977) have successfully embroiled themselves in criminal cultures such as dockworkers in Newfoundland and bread salesmen in England respectively. Their research took a participant observer approach and resulted in a set of hypotheses which underwent no empirical, statistical analysis to establish their validity. Whilst these sorts of studies have provided valuable accounts of a 'fiddling culture' in action, they do not provide organisations with an easily accessible methodology for assessing the risk of crime as part of a strategic approach to its reduction.

Other researchers have gone a step further in assessing the frequency of, and beliefs about, crime and criminal activity against organisations by directly sampling employees. These interview and questionnaire approaches have been the choice of some of the more heavily cited researchers in this area such as (Cressey, 1953). His research involved the interviewing of embezzlers to discover that the common theme motivating their deviant behaviour was what he termed a 'non-shareable problem' (p.29). This focused on financial difficulty as being the main source problem. Subsequent research such as Hollinger and Clark (1983) has cast doubts on such a conclusion. In their own work these latter researchers also employed a methodology of interviewing (complemented by large scale questionnaire surveys) with employees but they did not draw upon a sample of offenders as Cressey had done claiming that it is 'usually considered to be an extremely skewed sample' (p.15). However, they offered no explanation as to why this was considered to be so. Hollinger and Clark's findings enabled them to produce generalisable findings about attitudes towards, and opinions on, the effects of such variables as external economic pressures, youth and work, opportunity, job dissatisfaction and social control in producing deviant workplace behaviour.

Hollinger and Clark's study is a very important landmark in the way it brings together and analyses the main factors thought to relate to workplace deviant behaviour. However, like Cressey's study it fails to acknowledge the importance of corporate crime data which organisations are likely to maintain about criminal activity committed against them. This neglect by researchers is likely to have a knock on effect for organisations in producing a belief that corporate crime data has little to offer in terms of assessment of the risk of criminal activity. On the contrary, it is the contention of this article that ignoring such a rich source of material limits the understanding of crime in this context. Simultaneously, it leaves organisations with very little intelligence that can be operationalised in terms of reducing and detecting crime committed against them. Such approaches as Hollinger and Clark's would be more applicable if they also included analysis of actual criminal activity and assessed the interrelationships between attitudinal cultures, organisational norms, and actual criminal behaviour.

Corporate Crime Data requires Revaluation as a Valuable Source of Intelligence

While most businesses have lots of data, most have only limited amounts of the valuable expertise required to feed a rule-based system.

Dhar and Stein (1997)

Nowhere is this more true than for data pertaining to offenders who have committed crime against the organisation. Invariably, this information is not treated as data which is crucial to the organisation's everyday functioning. Instead, it is treated as anomalous and is often handled by individuals who operate independently of focused business teams. In this context it is likely to be the case that the organisation has:

> ... *made considerable progress in understanding and applying knowledge to create value. It is simply that this knowledge is often in isolated pockets. The first main thrust of creating a knowledge based business is therefore to 'know what you know', and then to share and leverage it throughout the business. The second main thrust is that of innovation - of creating new knowledge.*

Shyrme and Amidon (1997)

Corporate crime data should be treated precisely in this way and the organisation should be making efforts to ensure that their crime prevention/investigation departments, at least, are functioning as knowledge based units. If losses are denting profits to the extent mentioned in the introduction to this article, then their reduction is crucial to the organisation's everyday functioning. Companies should assess the kind of intelligence that is available in-house. For this to occur organisations need to utilise individuals who are 'information literate'. According to Mutch (1997) information literacy includes such abilities as knowing when there is a need for information, finding the needed information and using the information effectively. Once this information literacy is established, experts should be establishing rule based systems around the information that organisations maintain about offences and their perpetrators i.e. creating the *new knowledge* referred to above.

An effective method for achieving such a goal is through the analysis of crime data recorded by the company. This focused use of knowledge, and derived intelligence, will facilitate the early identification of offenders from analysis of the behaviour patterns of previous offenders. This approach has already been illustrated by Robertson (1998), and Dodd (PhD in prep.), who both fully employed data held in-house by the companies in question. This demonstrated to these organisations the value of information which is currently stored by them as unused data.

Both of these studies facilitated the establishment and deployment of investigative strategies, which were utilised for more effective identification of offenders both external and internal to the organisation. Such an informed expert system made significant contributions to assessing the risk of criminal activity occurring within the organisation as well as making estimates of criminal losses somewhat more accurate. They also had the potential to directly inform crime prevention strategies implemented by the organisations in question.

These studies serve only too well to highlight that organisations are often unaware of the importance of this data. They do not possess the skills to either; (1) recognise the potential corporate value of such information (2) to effectively convert it into reliable and valid business intelligence via appropriate analytical procedures. Even if organisations are capable at (1) other difficulties often arise with data quality in terms of validity and reliability. These are issues with which most organisations' research and development functions or crime investigation units are ill equipped to deal and, consequently, render the organisation less capable at (2). These are precisely the kind of skills which organisations need to adopt and embrace in order to fully realise the potential of the information they possess in-house. Such an approach will provide companies with a reliable resource upon which they can base valid strategy decisions.

This failure to recognise the potential value of CCD is further highlighted by the fact that this material is rarely stored electronically in databases. The use of hard copy storage means that any attempts at information transfer will be very cumbersome. This situation will not facilitate ease of analysis and knowledge sharing. Indeed, analysis is unlikely to be a focus of the organisation in preparing these documents in the first place but if the value of this information is realised then holding it on computer would make its transfer and dissemination through databases, intranets and other groupware a more effective task. A contributory factor in the decision to hold CCD as hard copies is the effect of the UK's Data Protection Act 1984. It is likely that organisations do not store CCD electronically through fear of falling foul of this protective legislation. However, it would appear that appropriate registration with the Data Protection Registrar of the information held on computer about individuals who have committed crime against the holding organisation for crime prevention and detection purposes and research of such activities would alleviate this fear.

How Can CCD be Used to Indicate the Scale of Crime against Organisations?

The lack of appreciation of the value of CCD appears to occur even at the level of recording the occurrence of crime and its related costs. Developing an understanding of the contribution that the analysis of in-house CCD can make can only be achieved if there is a prerequisite understanding of the scale of crime in this context. Murphy (1993) makes the following point about the nature and frequency of workplace crime in the US:

> *After examining the figures themselves and the processes by which these estimates are obtained, it is clear that anyone who quotes a particular figure as an accurate picture of the amount lost to theft, the extent of white-collar crime, the effects of employee drug use on productivity, or the like simply doesn't know what he or she is talking about.*

Murphy criticises the method of collection of such figures in the US and the way they are reported but in the UK there appears to be a paucity of any such statistics in the first place. A recent call to the Confederation of British Industry indicated that they had no new figures since their 1990 report *Crime: Managing the Business Risk*. Whilst specific industries may have figures available they are inevitably based on estimates rather than actual figures. There is usually no indication upon what these estimates were based and as such any researcher must be sceptical about their accuracy. An estimate is a dangerous statistic to rely upon because it 'can lend an aura of precision to the inexact' (Huff, 1973). Such inaccuracy leaves organisations with no real understanding of the scale of their problems. In terms of the organisations that this author has worked with, some of their representatives are not even sure how much their own organisation's total losses are for the previous year. Ask the same people how much of their total loss is due to employee theft and estimates abound from 5% to 70% within the same organisation. Once again, these figures are usually based on the experience of investigations. They do not base their estimates on a total loss figure because they were unable to quote one in the first place. Thus, this vagueness of Measurement supports Murphy's argument that statistics are often quoted without any real knowledge of the base rate (Murphy, 1993).

Clearly, the conclusion to be drawn here is that organisations, collectively and individually, have only general ideas about the losses they suffer at the hands of criminals in the UK. This does not help them form an accurate representation of the scale of criminal activity in operation against them. Simple assessments of this kind of activity that is detected, whether locally or for the whole organisation, would provide a more accurate figure. With this kind of audit would come explicit knowledge about areas of vulnerability, such as poor control environments, which can be prioritised and targeted for remedial action. This sort of intelligence is of great corporate value and can be shared on an industry wide basis to stem the increase of crime in this context. Furthermore, a more reliable audit of criminal activity may surprise many organisations with how low its frequency of occurrence and cost actually is. Identifying these lower levels of crime serves to highlight other areas of the organisation that may be producing loss such as weak procedural activity and monitoring, management and working conditions. This has been the case with at least one organisation with which this author has collaborated (Dodd, PhD in prep.) revealing that loss through employee theft was lower than 5% of total loss. In this instance a simple audit of CCD files indicated that loss through employee theft was considerably less than the 30-40% continually estimated by internal investigators and security experts. A validation of this discovery was subsequently obtained through a detailed, internal audit, carried out by the organisation in question. Therefore, this indicates that some organisations do propagate myths about certain types of activity within their functioning. In this case, the myth served to shift the blame away from the organisation to its employees. If this is a common practice, it does mean that organisations are missing a lot of information which could save them considerable amounts of money. By simply carrying out a reliable audit of a perceived problem they will produce valid information which could be used to inform business strategies. This would remove their reliance on the experiential accounts of investigators and employees that often serve to mislead and misinform strategies under development to combat crime.

How is Corporate Crime Data Different to Other Sources of Data?

Corporate data cannot automatically be treated in the same way that traditional social science treats data. Social scientists, in particular psychologists, have traditionally derived their data from carefully planned experimental designs intended to produce the optimal amount of data for analysis. This process has always intended to be as objective as possible. Invariably, the experimenter will have had the ability to manipulate the conditions of independent variables in order to monitor their effects upon certain phenomenon/phenomena (dependent variable). However, the analysis of corporate data removes some of the research's objectivity and manipulative ability in this respect. When coming to a research domain such as crime committed against organisations it is not feasible to design research in this way. Documented accounts of the crimes and the offenders are usually already available. In other words, because of this availability, the research is designed around existing data rather than the data being generated by the design. This is one of the main differences between corporate data and more traditionally derived data analysed in social science research.

This difference does have implications for research and adopted methodologies for analysis. Firstly, some variables used in the analysis will only be identified after documents have been examined. Traditionally, these variables would have been identified before any data was produced. Secondly, corporate data will have been generated to record different information to that which the researcher may be wishing to explore. In this context, files pertaining to individuals offending against organisations have been prepared purely to gather information on that individual's criminal or counterproductive activities in order to secure a prosecution and/or a disciplinary warning, resignation or dismissal, if it is an employee of the organisation. Thus, they are likely to contain some information, which is irrelevant to the researcher, as well as lack other information that has been demonstrated to be particularly important in the analysis of other types of criminal activity. Thus, CCD would be considered to be a 'noisy' source of information. Missing information can range from previous convictions to personal details to work history to ways in which offences were undertaken. For example, Dodd (PhD in prep.) found that information about previous criminal history, as well as other personal details, was severely lacking in these files. This is understandable if it is recorded that the information was not available. However, if nothing is recorded it is impossible to know whether this information was available and just not recorded, or whether the recorders just had no knowledge in this area. All of these sources of information have important implications for risk assessment of potential future criminal activity yet there is rarely a systematic attempt to capture such data in corporate offender files. In this instance, because the information is not being recorded for risk assessment purposes, it is not seen to be that important.

Thirdly, individuals other than the researcher or the research team will have recorded the information. This is likely to have automatically introduced problems related to bias, unreliability and inconsistency into the data. This will be one element of what Hollinger and Clark referred to as 'an extremely skewed sample'. It is exceptionally unlikely that organisations have standardised recording procedures to the degree that they ensure reliability of the information recorded by different individuals. The effects of these issues would have been reduced as much as possible by the more traditional experimental design. They also need to be minimised as much as possible when examining corporate data or else they will negate the objectivity of the research.

The Problem of Recording

These three implications highlight that it is of paramount importance to address the possibility of inconsistency in the methods of recording by the organisation. Files are likely to have been prepared by a number of different individuals from the company. Because of this there are likely to be discrepancies between files in terms of the information that they contain, as previously mentioned. This begs the question that if there is no mention of an offender's previous convictions in a file; for example, does this mean that they had none? Alternatively, does it mean that investigators or the person preparing the report overlooked this? A second alternative is that this information may not be considered to be important by the investigator or the person preparing the file, and was therefore left out. This could produce problems for any subsequent analysis procedure in terms of whether this information should be taken to mean that the offender had no convictions or that the information is missing. Obviously, for reliable research purposes it must be coded as missing. However, if the only mention of previous convictions is when information is available to suggest the offender definitely has them, a lot of information is being lost about those with no mention of presence or absence. These individuals with missing scores are likely to be in the majority and as such are an important part of the population about whom it will be difficult to draw valid conclusions due to this data coded as missing. Quite simply, because the information was not being prepared for research purposes there will have been no requirement to ensure that such ambiguities do not creep into the data set. This is entirely understandable when the focus of the data capturing exercise is to secure a dismissal or disciplinary warning, but if an organisation is to utilise its own vast levels of information as intelligence then the reliability of information upon which it is based must be ensured.

This inconsistency in the way that information is recorded in files is likely to lead to confusion in the way that the files are analysed. Most files of this nature, whatever the holding organisation, are often based on memos about the nature of the investigation passed between one company representative and another. Very rarely is there a case summary outlining what happened in the case. Similarly, there is virtually never a cover page describing the offender with his name, address, occupation, age, marital status etc. recorded. The inclusion of such simple documentation in these files would not only help the researcher but the organisation. Easy access to information would save time and provide the organisation in question with the opportunity to collate their own information and carry out analysis tasks which would, at the very least, identify trends in the characteristics and behaviours of individuals committing crimes against them. This can only ever contribute to the formulation of strategies to improve security but organisations will be losing considerable intelligence if they have to rely on disorganised information. In particular, information will be difficult to disseminate which will consequently make it exceptionally difficult to utilise as reliable business intelligence.

How Can This Data Be Utilised in This Context?

To negotiate these potential problems of bias and inconsistency such data yielding procedures as content analysis (Krippendorf, 1980) can be employed. This approach, in particular, provides a methodology for extracting information from existing records. It can be carried out by a number of researchers with the use of a standardised pro forma. This will usually ask such questions as 'Does the offender have any previous convictions'? Carried out properly this approach ensures reliability in the way that this pro forma is interpreted by the researchers. All those using it have to understand the question in the same way. For example, in the above question does this include speeding convictions or not? Some people would consider these to be convictions whilst others would not. These issues have to be ironed out early on or else biases will occur in the data.

This approach to generating data allows for the development of content dictionaries. Such dictionaries contain questions about the presence and absence of certain behaviours and characteristics of the offender, which are relevant to the research. A good published example of such a dictionary can be found in Canter and Fritzon (1998) in an examination of firesetting behaviour in arsonists. A content dictionary documents all the variables that have been drawn from the existing records and how they. are coded for research (at its most simple present, absent or missing). An example of a content dictionary, shorter than Canter and Fritzon's because of space requirements, was generated by (Dodd, PhD in works). This was designed to test the hypothesis that insurance claim fraudsters could be reliably distinguished in terms of the level of sophistication they displayed during their offences. The dictionary contained the following eight items:

1)   Does the insured display a knowledge of the system?

2)   Is the loss in this claim completely bogus?

3)   Have there been frequent changes of insurer?

4)   Have false/stolen documents been supplied?

5)   Have genuine documents been altered?

6)   Is the loss genuine in spite of the suspicion of the claim?

7)   Were all or some of the items claimed for never owned?

8)   Was there a recent cover change/increase and/or claim circumstance enquiry and/or policy commencement/renewal?

Each of the items consisted of the presence or absence of more than just one variable. For example, item 1 was coded as present if there was a response of 'yes' to one or more of its constituent variables. Examples of these variables are:

a)   was there an unexpected knowledge of the claims handling procedure;
b)   were there frequent or previous claims especially if repudiated, and;
c)   was it a fire or other claim where evidence was completely unavailable?

It was hypothesised that the first four items in the content dictionary dealt with increased sophistication and items five to eight with lower sophistication. In a Partial Order Scalogram Analysis, Shye (1976), revealed that insurance claim fraudsters could be distinguished empirically on these items and this would have specific preventative and investigative implications. These implications are discussed in more detail in the next section. Critics may argue that eight items may be too few to distinguish offenders on this basis. However, this analysis depended on the reliability of the CCD utilised. These were the only items from the information available which it was hypothesised would distinguish offenders in terms of their offence sophistication. If organisations re-evaluated CCD they would realise that capturing a richer source of data would complement this procedure.

This method of extracting and recording data about actual criminal activity maintained by organisations allows for univariate, as well as multivariate analysis of interactions between these variables. Furthermore, such research can serve to validate the methodologies of researchers such as Hollinger and Clark who did not draw upon such ecologically valid data sources.

What Contribution Can the Analysis of Corporate Crime Data Make?

Once databases of offence behaviour and offender characteristics have been established from content dictionaries the way is open to directly test hypotheses about criminal activity in this context. Success has already been achieved in the understanding of workplace criminal behaviour Dodd (PhD in prep.), fraud Dodd (1999) and employee theft Robertson (1998) through behavioural analysis of CCD collated in this way. For example, Dodd's (PhD in prep.) study of insurance claim fraudsters identified four approaches of fraudsters to their offences ranging from the opportunist to the sophisticated. The identification of these allowed for direct feedback to the insurance industry on how to identify potentially fraudulent claimants soon after they entered the claims handling system and the most appropriate methods for dealing with them without immediate recourse to loss adjusters. This research not only made a contribution to crime prevention in the insurance industry, but also to academic knowledge. It clearly demonstrated that:

> *[Fraudulent insurance claimants] ... cannot be described as particularly young or out of work. With this in mind, [insurance] fraud is best thought of as an 'armchair crime' whereby the middle class, early middle aged, financially secure man breaks the law from the comfort of his own home, with minimal apparent harm to others and maximum financial gain to himself.*

Dodd (1998)

Robertson's (1998) research focused on theft by employees from the employer, which was a courier and distribution company. Using content analysis of existing records and subsequent multivariate analysis Shye (1985) was able to identify that criminal activity in this organisation centred on such behavioural facets as *criminality*, *responsibility* and *opportunity*. The *criminality* group were defined as such because their conduct was more criminal in focus. They targeted bank traffic and left no evidence opening items. The members of this sub-group were more likely to have criminal links outside the organisation, accomplices inside the organisation, false addresses, lying in their job applications and pre-convictions. Most of their offending was confined to the first six years of their service. The *opportunity* sub-group was characterised by the theft of small items so flow value and their approach was more opportunist. They displayed little sophistication in their methods leaving debris from opened items clearly visible. Robertson suggested that this indicated 'criminal naiveté'. These offenders had more stable lifestyles with wide service range of two to 14 years. The final sub-group known as the *responsibility* group did not see financial gain as a motivator but, instead, abandoned items or took them home and hoarded them. Robertson concluded that their 'offending style appears more linked to capability and coping under pressure'. All of the members of this group had less than four years' service, no pre-convictions and were unmarried. However, they did have the highest prevalence of conduct problems within the sample. They were very general in terms of the items they targeted.

Such facets as these identified by Robertson may seem academic and abstract, but the fact that they consist of variables about actual criminal behaviour meant that Robertson was able to make direct recommendations to the company in question about the likely antecedents of criminal activity against it:

Investigators need to look critically at the behavioural style that is likely to characterise the individual committing crimes. This can be done systematically by examining the archives of previous investigations, and should not depend on experience or intuition.

By evaluating the *criminality, responsibility* and *opportunity* facets Robertson was able to identify their constituent elements that would help inform corporate investigative and preventative strategies. He emphasised the importance of conduct history and how simple misdemeanours appearing early in an employment history may be the beginning of the development of a deviant/criminal career against the organisation. He was also quick to point out that organisational processes and informal work groups, in some instances, are likely to provide the opportunity for crime. His important conclusion here being that 'Some employees are more vulnerable or at risk to criminal socialisation than others, and that policies need to be designed to address this'.

These studies highlight that, although it has been argued that analysing a sample of apprehended offenders may be a skewed sample, such analyses validate the findings of previous research through examining actual criminal activity. Furthermore, the employment of such a sample enabled these researchers to pick up on particular organisational nuances and feed information and intelligence directly back into the organisation or industry with which they were dealing. This would not have been possible with the general survey methods adopted by Hollinger and Clark. As a result of generating such intelligence, recommendations have been made to organisations on how to reduce their crime problems using certain rule based systems for early identification of offenders; the placing of certain classes of employee in vulnerable working environments; job selection procedures; job appraisal; and monitoring employee conduct to name but a few. Such feedback would be of limited validity from large-scale survey studies. Likewise such large-scale research is less accessible to organisations than actually evaluating their own information recorded and maintained in-house.

The importance of the analysis of CCD has been highlighted during the course of this paper. In spite of the limitations of the findings of those researchers who have not utilised CCD these findings are still of major importance in this context. The analysis of CCD can validate these attitude and opinion survey findings derived from employee samples. Such factors as job dissatisfaction, procedural activities, recruitment policies, commitment to the organisation and criminal behaviour norms are all likely to contribute to a deviant workplace climate (Murphy, 1993). The effects of such factors on the socialisation of new employees have been explored by Ditton (1977) and discussed by Murphy (1993). Whilst these factors have been identified as having negative socialisation effects no researcher has actually explored their uni- or multivariate relationships with actual criminal behaviour committed against the organisation. Relating the security or ethical mood, culture, norms or expectations of an organisation to actual criminal activity against it is a very important measure of the effects of how organisations feel about crime; how seriously they take it; and, how it is to be dealt with. Cherrington and Cherrington (1985) have already pointed out that organisations taking crime seriously, both in investigative and preventative terms, usually have much lower levels of crime recorded against them. This is an area currently undergoing research. Dodd, Reddy and Canter (in press) have identified, from surveying employee's attitudes to compliance with security, that personal beliefs are much more central to the decision to breach security than any organisational factors (including morale and commitment). The examination of the relationship of such factors to actual criminal activity is ongoing. Although, at this stage, it is not possible to understand how much organisational factors contribute to such personal beliefs. Such a comprehensive review of an organisation's criminal norms and its actual criminal activity will provide a source of information and intelligence previously unmatched in this context.

What is Required to Realise the Value of CCD for Crime Prevention, Investigation and Research Purposes?

> *... there is an unhealthy scepticism ... often based on ignorance, concerning the possibilities of collecting quantitative data on criminal activities.*

Thomas (1993)

The first step in such an approach is the requirement that organisations realise that corporate crime data is a rich source of intelligence which can be harnessed to inform preventative and investigative strategies. In other words, if the 'unhealthy scepticism' referred to above does actually exist then it needs to be dispelled. Research has already been undertaken which demonstrates this potential admirably and illustrates the utility of methods that can be adopted for translating this data into intelligence (Robertson, [7]).[1]

This translation requires the expertise of individuals, or teams, who have the ability to recognise the potential value of raw data as intelligence. They also need to possess the skills to facilitate the translation of such data. This is not just an issue of information literacy as Mutch suggested but also one of analytical ability. Whilst information needs to be handled appropriately to ensure reliability it also needs to be analysed effectively to produce valid findings. It is rare to find these skills in individuals but social scientists, in particular psychologists, are trained to fulfil these requirements. This is highlighted by the fact that police forces are currently employing trained psychologists in their

---

[1] Numbers in [ ] refer to a chapter in the present volume.

implementation and expansion of crime analysis units to fulfil these particular roles. Such an expansion has come from a recognition of the importance of specific types of information; a necessity to capture it in a reliable way, and a need to analyse it to produce valid investigative and preventative intelligence. It would seem that organisations would be wise to adopt a similar approach by either employing such expertise full-time or for the completion of short term objectives.

If this expertise is employed then strategies can be implemented for guaranteeing the reliability of data upon which valid decisions can be based. This is absolutely crucial in this context and would involve a more systematic recording of information by trained individuals. It would also impart the knowledge that the information was being recorded for the purpose of analysis as well as prosecution or reprimand. This crucial building block would lead to reliability in producing a realistic picture of criminal activity against organisations. A sound knowledge of the Data Protection Act and its restrictions and exemptions would complement this and enable companies to have the confidence to fully utilise information that they may legally maintain for crime prevention, detection and research purposes. Furthermore, the skills required to carry out surveys of employee attitudes and norms and their subsequent relationships to criminal activity would be available. Overall, this would contribute to organisations recognising that they possess a rich source of intelligence and enabling them to utilise it appropriately and effectively.

Conclusion

The appropriate use of corporate data is a prerequisite to developing business strategies for crime prevention and detection. Currently, corporate crime data is likely to be gathering dust without its potential as intelligence being realised. In CCD, organisations have the beginnings of informed policies that can reduce losses through assessing criminal activity. If they fail to harness the potential benefit of such data then they cannot reap the rewards of a holistic approach to security and crime prevention. This will incorporate physical security barriers as well as being complemented by the knowledge of organisational norms relating to crime. If these strands are brought together they can provide the organisation with a rich understanding of the risk of presenting themselves as a soft target to the potential criminal (whether internal or external). Reduction of the probability of appearing as such a target is one element of crime prevention that can be easily adopted. In order to maximise the potential of corporate crime data as business intelligence it needs to be reliably recorded and analysed. Valid methodologies are required for this purpose. This paper has demonstrated that these are available and that empirical research drawing upon actual criminal activity as its data source can inform organisational and academic knowledge. This has a direct implication for companies optimising the value of corporate crime data in order to inform crime prevention and detection policies without breaching the terms of the Data Protection Act 1984. Organisations, themselves, now need to embrace this knowledge and expertise and effectively apply it to this area of crime.

References

Canter, D.V. and Fritzon, K. (1998), 'Differentiating Arsonists: A Model of Firesetting Actions and Characteristics', *Legal and Criminological Psychology*, **3**, 73-96.

Cherrington, D.J. and Cherrington, J.O. (1985), 'The Climate of Honesty in Retail Stores', in W. Terris (ed.), *Employee Theft*, pp.51-65, Chicago: London House Press.

Confederation of British Industry (1990), *Crime: Managing the Business Risk*, London: CBI.

Cressey, D.R. (1953), *Other People's Money*, Glencoe, Illinois: The Free Press.

Dhar, V. and Stein, R. (1997), *Transforming Corporate Data into Business Intelligence*, pp.ix, Englewood Cliffs, N.J.: Prentice-Hall.

Ditton, J. (1977), *Part-time Crime: An Ethnography of Fiddling and Pilferage*, London: MacMillan.

Dodd, N.J. (in preparation [a]), *A multivariate model of employee crime* (provisional title).

Dodd, N.J. (in preparation [b]), *Distinguishing Insurance Claim Fraudsters through their Levels of Sophistication in Offence Behaviour* (provisional title).

Dodd, N.J., *Using Corporate Crime Data (CCD) to Evaluate Criminal Activity against Organisations: A Behavioural Science Approach*, PhD Thesis: The University of Liverpool.

Dodd, N.J., Reddy, S.J. and Canter, D.V. (in preparation), *Employee Attitudes to Compliance and Control with Security Measures in the Workplace* (provisional title).

Dodd, N.J. (1998), 'Applying Psychology to the Reduction of Insurance Claim Fraud', *Insurance Trends*, **18**, London: Association of British Insurers.

Hollinger, R.C. and Clark, J.P. (1983), *Theft by Employees*, Lexington, MA: Heath.

Huff, D. (1973), *How to Lie with Statistics*, London: Pelican.

Krippendorf, K. (1980), *Content Analysis*, Beverly Hills: Sage.

Mars, G. (1974), 'Dock Pilferage', in P. Rock and M. McIntosh (eds), *Deviance and Social Control*, London: Tavistock.

Murphy, K. (1993), *Honesty in the Workplace*, pp.200-201, California: Brooks/Cole.

Mutch, A (1997), 'Information Literacy: An Exploration', *International Journal of Information Management*, **17 (5)**, 377-386.

Narula, S. (1993), 'Unwitting but still Implicated', *Accountancy Age*, 18th February.

Shye, S. (1976), *Partial Order Scalogram Analysis of Profiles and its Relationship to Smallest Space Analysis of the Variables* (technical monograph), Jerusalem: The Israel Institute of Applied Social Research.

Shye, S. (1985), 'Smallest Space Analysis (SSA)', in T. Husen and T.N. Postlethwaite (eds), *International Encyclopedia of Education*, pp.4602-4608, Elmsford, NY: Pergamon.

Skyrme, D. and Amidon, D.M. (1997), *Creating the Knowledge-Based Business,* London: Business Intelligence Ltd.

Thomas, J.J. (1993), 'Measuring the Underground Economy: A Suitable Case for Interdisciplinary Treatment?', in C.M. Renzetti and R.M. Lee (eds), *Researching Sensitive Topics*, pp.52-70, London: Sage.

Wagstaff, J. (1994), 'The Middle Man', *Police Review*, 12th January.

11 Crime Analysis: Principles for Analysing Everyday Serial Crime

SIMON MERRY

In pursuit of 'intelligence led policing' the paper brings together psychological principles underpinning the understanding of crime to present an operational system for analysing volume crime. The account commences with an abridged history of crime analysis chronicling the longevity of the Modus Operandi system and the pins-in-map approach of more recent times. Drawing from research on temporal, spatial and crime scene behaviour the system defines the disciplines of Comparative Case Analysis, Suspect Identification and Target Profiling. The system, which is operational in at least one British Police Force, is illustrated by studies of house burglary and can be applied to any serial crime ranging from murder to cycle theft. The system organises mental processes and is supported by data handling and mapping technology rather than being driven by the latest commercially developed software.

Simon Merry completed a BA degree in Social Science with the Open University before obtaining his MSc in Investigative Psychology at the University of Liverpool. He is a Superintendent with Dorset Police and is a part-time PhD student conducting further research into the crime of house burglary. He has been responsible for transferring academic research into the operational policing sphere.

*Offender Profiling Series: IV- **Profiling Property Crimes***
Edited by D. Canter and L. Alison. © 2000, Ashgate Publishing, Aldershot. pp 297-318

11 Crime Analysis: Principles for Analysing Everyday Serial Crime

SIMON MERRY

Commonplace Crime

'The more featureless and common place a crime is, the more difficult is it to bring it home'. (Sir Arthur Conan Doyle, *The Adventures of Sherlock Holmes*, 1898, p.76). Doyle's fictional character was making the point that 'singularity is almost invariably a clue'. In doing so he highlights the problem of investigating everyday crime. By definition it is 'commonplace' and it is routinely recorded as 'featureless'.

Crime Analysts - Data Detectives

The concept of 'Intelligence led Policing' has thrust the Crime Analyst to the forefront of detecting and reducing crime. The traditional detective, who observes, listens, interrogates and deduces, remains the prime investigator of serious crime, but the sheer volume of featureless and commonplace serial crime has overwhelmed this conventional activity. Emerging to lead 'intelligent' policing is the data detective or crime analyst. These new detectives have no formal training in law, they do not necessarily visit the crime scene and they don't interview witnesses or question suspects. Data detectives like traditional investigators do understand human and criminal behaviour. In simple terms, they pursue the criminal around the database and map.

The Crime Analyst demands three pre-requisites. Firstly, a methodology relevant to the domain to be analysed, secondly, good data and lastly, technology to support. Assuming valid data and relevant technology is available, I set out to define the most important ingredient - The Method.

Methodology is at the heart of the process for it defines what data must be accurate and what systems are appropriate. Fundamentally, a method grounded in an understanding of human behaviour will draw out the behavioural links between crime and criminal. Thus, to analyse house burglary the analyst must understand the crime - why and how it is commissioned by the house burglar. House burglary is arguably the most serious of everyday crime and I will use it to illustrate the process.

Analysis - A Modern Approach?

Around the time of Doyle's insightful fiction, detectives in Whitechapel were seeking to identify 'Jack the Ripper'. The case illustrated police attempts to compare at least five crimes. The detectives examined the times, the places, the broad behaviour, the specific behaviour, and the physical evidence and ultimately they found no reason not to link the murders. The last point is crucial, after all, how often were five prostitutes murdered in such a craftsman-like way in Whitechapel by two or more independent offenders at the same time!

Simultaneously, police began investing in the pretentiously titled 'modus operandi' (M.O.) system for recording all crime. But, the M.O. approach relied too much on traits and disregarded the influence of situation. For example, in a series of burglaries it would be assumed there is no link if the main feature or signature of the offender is not present. So if the offender does not enter as usual by forcing the door because a window was open or does not steal jewellery because there was none to take, the system will fail to link.

What the M.O. approach and the Whitechapel investigation does underline is the notion that human or criminal behaviour is sufficiently consistent from crime to crime to engender similar behaviour. In other words criminals like non-criminals are slaves to their habits, attitudes to others and their level of skill.

'Jack the Ripper' demonstrated consistency in when, where and how he committed those gruesome crimes. So the system that is beginning to unfold is based on expectations of human behaviour.

Pins in Maps

More recently, the police have complimented the M.O. system by sticking pins in maps to denote location of crime. This process, known as crime pattern analysis made little reference to sequence, time of day, type of premises and whilst the M.O. record was available the linking process was haphazard. The pins tended to identify clusters or 'hotspots' (Brantingham and Brantingham, 1981), and not the serial work of individual offenders for three main reasons. Firstly, the pins come out at the end of each month and there is no evidence to support the proposition that offenders commence criminal activity on the first of the month! Secondly, the pins tend to cover the same areas month after month, namely the 'hotspots'. Lastly, flaws in the geographical analysis are created because maps do not depict addresses, and the pin rarely locates the scene of the crime with accuracy. An inch out could be critical.

Another essential point relates to the need for the analyst to understand the environmental nuances that influence the way space is used in a specific area. The environmental backcloth (Brantingham and Brantingham, 1993) describes the context that shapes and is shaped by the way people live and the way in which some commit crime. So, aggregating pins in a map highlights 'hotspots', it does not discriminate between offenders and therefore action to detect is limited.

What is Crime Analysis?

Crime Analysis is not yet satisfactorily defined. Diverse interpretations result in diverse practices, thus, undermining the potential investigative value of relating one crime to another and to criminal information. The fact that criminals are responsible for crime is not always evident from the division of labour often demonstrated by a separation between Criminal Intelligence Analysts and Crime Pattern Analysts. For example, Criminal Intelligence Officers may collate, analyse and disseminate intelligence without reference to the occurrence of crimes being committed by their subjects, whilst Crime Pattern Analysts, are linking crimes without reference to the individuals who may be responsible. This scenario is understandable given that the two disciplines have developed separately. They must be married together because in reality the crime and criminal are inextricably linked.

The 'Trevi' group of Home Office representatives has provided the beginnings of a useful definition of crime analysis. This divides analysis into 'Strategic' and 'Operational' arenas (Oldfield and Read 1995). 'Strategic' analysis broadly relates to the demography and geography of crime for the purposes of understanding the nature of the problem, setting policing style and allocating resources. 'Operational' analysis is concerned with the development of crime information into intelligence to direct daily prevention and detection activity. Here we are exploring 'Operational' Crime Analysis.

Put simply, Crime Analysis concerns the analysis of every crime with every other crime and with criminals to identify links that are not evident from routine police enquiries. In psychological research terms this may be translated into the analysis of a set of behaviours with other sets of behaviours and the individuals who may be responsible.

The Applicability of Science - Psychology

The principles of applying psychology to the decision-making process in murder or rape investigations can be equally applied to 'everyday' crime. Accessing scientific research on criminal behaviour has utility for the Senior Investigating Officer and the Crime Analyst. Both ask similar questions about the crime; Why this victim? Why here? Why now? Why this method?

Criminal behaviour is simply 'behaviour', which has been labelled and outlawed by contemporary society (Young 1981). By recognising crime as a set of behaviours, it becomes entirely logical to invite the scientist who has studied behaviour to contribute to the investigation process. The Detective spends a career studying other peoples' behaviour, but not from a formal rule based position. Whilst the Detective develops intuition from experience, the Psychologist draws on a cumulative and systematic knowledge of the laws of behaviour (Canter and Alison 1997). Together the Detective and the Psychologist can apply rules from their separate spheres to inform the analytical process. Indeed, both can contribute to identifying a suspect and the cumulative process of understanding behaviour.

Accepting that all crimes demonstrate behaviour and all serial crimes have a geographic dimension, it is evident that there is a generic and specific element to doing analysis. The generic aspect requires the understanding of human behaviour, whilst the specific element requires a clear understanding of how people operate in a geographic and culturally specific area. The latter does not imply that criminal behaviour is significantly related to place, but rather the use of common travel routes, activity centres and the presence of physical and psychological barriers combine to create a very local 'theatre' of operation - the environmental backcloth.

A Model

Where does analysis start - with the crime or the criminal? The answer is either or both, depending on what information is available.   The implication here is that analysis can only start with data in the form of information about crime(s) or criminal(s). The data is then analysed in pursuance of principles of behaviour and in relation to local environmental conditions. The analysis produces intelligence that may be acted upon and the outcome provides further data. This cumulative process is depicted in the model set out in figure 11.1.

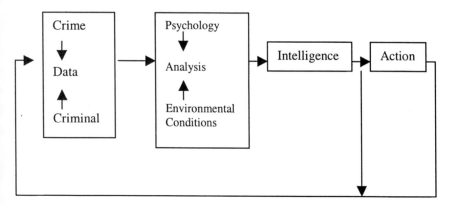

Comparative Case Analysis: Linking one crime to other crimes.
Suspect Identification: Inferring the offenders' identity.
Target Profiling: Predicting future temporal, spatial and crime scene behaviour of core
            offenders.

Figure 11.1: Model of Cumulative Crime Analysis

The model sets out the process of intelligence generation, however, some organisation of the analysis stage is required.

Organising Operational Crime Analysis

Three interrelated disciplines structure a holistic approach to the operational analysis of serial crime and these are detailed in table 11.1 below.

Table 11.1: Three Analytical Disciplines

Comparative Case Analysis	Linking on crime to other crimes
Suspect Identification	Inferring the offenders' identity
Target Profiling	Predicting future temporal, spatial and crime scene behaviour of core offenders

Thus, in figure 11.1 above, the analysis stage comprises the application of one or more of these three analytical disciplines. The system directs the operational analyst to pursue the disciplines through stages which first build towards an opinion that a number of crimes are linked to one offender. The analyst then proceeds to identify suspects from a database of past offenders. Independently or simultaneously, the analyst will compare emerging patterns with the temporal, spatial and crime scene behavioural profiles of known recidivist offenders.

The analyst translates findings into a report that is presented to a senior detective responsible for managing the police response to crime. A range of tactical options is then available to detect and/or prevent the developing series of crimes or 'hotspots'. Subsequently the analyst is responsible for measuring the impact of the policing intervention.

This system of Operational Crime Analysis and the theory underpinning the three disciplines is now illustrated.

Comparative Case Analysis

Linking crimes to a common offender, requires a systematic process in the same way that the investigation of the Whitechapel Murders linked all the cases to the unidentified Jack the Ripper. There are six stages.

(i)   *Temporal Behaviour* : Human behaviour is influenced by temporal schedules arising from a combination of biological, cultural, social and psychological drivers (McMurran, Hodge and Hollin 1997). At the basic level, sleeping and eating punctuate the day, but other psychological and physiological triggers encourage repetitive offending episodes. The analyst needs to identify the common cyclical behaviour of the serial criminal, however, the closer two crimes are the more likely they are to be linked to one offender. More research is required to elaborate this hypothesis.

(ii)   *Spatial Behaviour* : Studying the spatial behaviour of burglars indicates that their use of the environment is as constrained as any other individual and offending behaviour is frequently patterned and localised.   Brantingham and Brantingham (1981) suggest that individuals confine their excursions to their 'mental maps' of the local area and offending is likely to take place in familiar areas near to their home. Barker [3][1] explored this and indicated that burglars who had committed series of offences had done so not only close to home but also within a general circle around the home. Canter and Larkin (1993) applied these ideas to rapists and confirmed the 'circle hypothesis'. They described offenders as 'marauding' out from their base.

In another piece of unpublished research, a sample of 50 house burglaries committed in one town by different offenders revealed similar aggregate findings. These are set out in table 11.2.

Table 11.2: Distances Travelled from Base to Crime Scene

Distance to Crime	% of Sample
< ¼ mile	33%
< ½ mile	52%
< 1 mile	66%

---

[1] Numbers in [ ] refer to chapters in the present volume.

Although suburbs of neighbouring towns bordered the town, offenders living within the borough boundary committed 92% of crimes. This phenomenon suggests that the town boundary itself is a psychological barrier. These separate studies indicate that the home or base is related to the crime scene, that individuals are constrained in their travel by their home, activity centres, physical and psychological barriers. It is proposed that individuals become familiar with these centres of activity and offenders identify criminal opportunities when travelling the pathways in between. Offenders appear to trade off familiarity of area with the risk of being recognised and the taking of minimum risks for maximum reward.

Research tends to confirm the localness of house burglary and provides a rule base for analysing the geographic dimension of crime and particularly series crime.

The analyst must identify the common locally specific distances travelled by offenders. Spatial and temporal proximity are together good reasons to infer a link between two crimes. The analyst will then examine crime scene behaviour.

(iii)   *Broad Behaviour* : It is proposed that within a specific crime type there will be themes of behaviour as well as specific acts. The themes of behaviour are broader ranges of activity and in Merry and Harsent [2] it is argued that two themes operating within burglary are the facets of 'craft' and 'script'. Craft will represent an individual's level of skill based on experience, intelligence, manual dexterity and social contacts. Script demonstrates an individual interpersonal attitude and demonstrates how the offender relates to others. The behavioural themes can be utilised to measure or label a crime and consequently the criminal. For example a specific crime may be defined as high craft/low script.

The two facets represent characteristics that evolve slowly. Craft is something that develops through the experience of doing, in this case burglary. We can expect that an offender will learn and mature skills incrementally. An individual's interpersonal script is similarly consistent and degrees of disrespect and tolerance, for example, are likely to be similarly enacted across successive crime scenes.

The measure of skill and interpersonal attitude is detected from the collection of individual behaviours that go to make up the act of house burglary. In Merry and Harsent [2] the themes of 'pilferer', 'intruder', 'raider' and 'invader' are identified. This followed analysis of variables occurring within a sample of crimes. Figure 11.2 portrays the output of smallest space analysis and 35 variables located in accordance with their co-occurrence, thus, themes of behaviour can be teased out from the wider collection of activities present within the crime. The variables are defined in Appendix A.

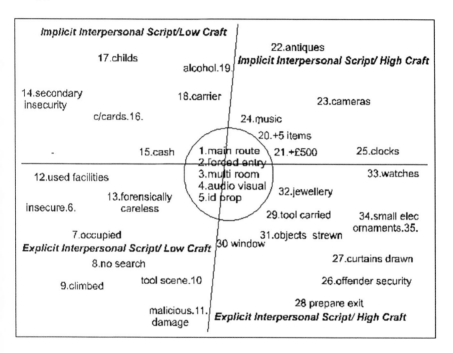

3 Dimensional SSA
Vector 1/Vector 2
Jaccard index similarity coefficient
Guttman-Lingoes coefficient of alienation = 0.18582
Numbers refer to list in Appendix A

Figure 11.2: SSA of House Burglary Behaviours (Interpersonal Script and Craft Facets)

The labelling process facilitates comparison of crimes in the expectation that one offender's theme will be repeated. It is hypothesised that two crimes occurring within a short time frame, within a similar locus and displaying similar broad behavioural themes will be linked. In figure 11.3, three crimes are depicted by reference to the intrinsic variables. The two on the left are similar ('intruders') and may be considered linked to the same offender, however, the variable set on the right ('invader') is significantly different and unlikely to be the work of the same person.

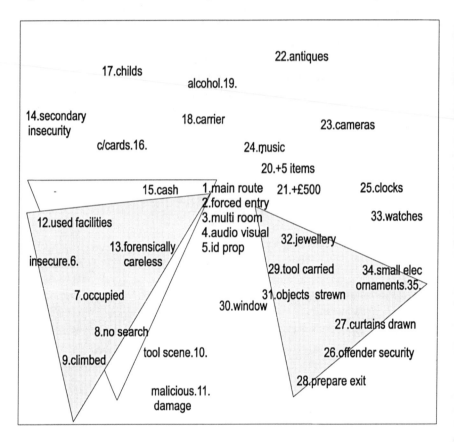

3 Dimensional SSA
Vector 1/Vector 2
Jaccard index similarity coefficient
Guttman-Lingoes coefficient of alienation = 0.18582

Figure 11.3: Smallest Space Analysis Depicting Similar and Dissimilar Behavioural Themes

(iv)   *Specific Behaviour* : Within the broader theme of behaviour an individual will repeat habits or idiosyncrasies that are both related to craft and interpersonal attitude. These acts have been referred to as crime scene signature and are central to the M.O. approach, for example, a search method, thing stolen or mess caused that may be specific to the individual. However, the signature or M.O. is the aspect that is most dependent on situation rather than individual and therefore it is the factor most susceptible to change. It will be noted in the examples, depicted in figure 11.3, that cash is stolen in only one of the linked crimes and the situation may be the explanation. That is, there was no cash to steal at one scene. The presence of the same specific behaviour tends to confirm a link, but absence does not prove there is no link.

(v)   *Physical Trace* : Physical traces are the variety of marks or deposits left behind by the offender, for example, clothing fibres, tool marks, fingerprints, glove marks, footprints or body fluids.

Whilst fibres and tool marks can tenuously contribute to a psychological profile of an offender the purpose of this stage is to step outside the behavioural analysis and make a comparison with physical evidence. Physical evidence is not always identified and therefore cannot be relied on, however, a fibre on its own may not be sufficient to link two crimes, but together with behavioural similarities the link may be made. The same applies to tool marks, footprints or a partial fingerprint. Of course, a full fingerprint or evidence of DNA at two crime scenes will provide a much stronger link.

(vi)   *Confirm Inference* : The final stage of the linking process only follows if the opinion so far is that two crimes are likely to be linked. It simply requires an assessment of any other factor that offers a substantive argument not to link.

The Principle of Parsimony (Reber, 1985) encourages a bias towards linking rather than assuming a more complicated explanation that more than one offender is committing the same type of crime, in a similar way in the same area and in the same time frame. This stage acts as a quality check on the inferences drawn from stages one to five.

Suspect Identification

The analysis of crime is aided by computerised mapping systems, which allow the sequence of crimes to be portrayed. The interval between activity and the direction or spread of crimes gives a clear indication of the movements of the offender during the period of the series. This data develops the profile of the offender and commences the process of identifying suspects. A hypothetical individual pattern of crime is illustrated in figure 11.4. The sequence of occurrence is detailed.

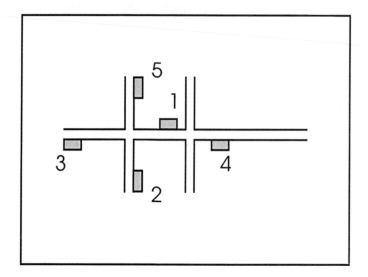

Figure 11.4: Hypothetical Individual Pattern of Crime

Advanced police crime and criminal intelligence systems store data, which may be systematically searched for suspects. The search is made on a geographical basis defined by the location and pattern of crimes. Therefore consecutive searches are made within concentric circles modulating out from the heart of the series as depicted in figure 11.5.

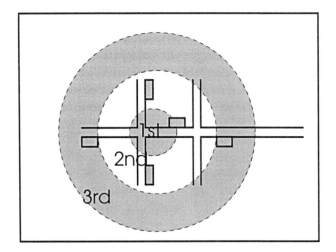

Figure 11.5: Sequential Search Pattern of Suspect Database

Suspects based within the search area may be identified from one or a combination of factors as follows.

(i)   *Background Characteristics* : Translating crime scene behaviours into offender background characteristics involves accurate interpretation of actions which facilitate inferences to be made about the person responsible. These may include predictions about the offender's base, personal circumstances and criminal history.

The patterning of a series of crimes can firstly benefit from the application of the circle hypothesis and the average distances usually travelled in a particular area. Secondly, the location will be part of a wider homogenous area defined by physical and/or psychological barriers, for example, an area to one side of a major road. These parameters can begin to focus a search for suspects within the criminal database. For example, an initial search within a 1/2-mile radius can be extended outwards. Similarly, the overlap of 1/2-mile radius circles around each linked crime will realise a priority area, which could form the centre of a search pattern for suspects.

Early unpublished research reveals some preliminary findings that present a basis for inferring background characteristics as detailed in table 11.3.

Table 11.3: Relationships between Offending Theme and Background Characteristics

Craft Theme	Script Theme	Age	Travel	Criminal History
Low craft	Low script	19 years	< ½ mile	Limited
Low craft	High script	19 years	< ½ mile	Limited
High craft	Low script	19 years	> ½ mile	Dishonesty/ Drugs
High craft	High script	19 years	> ½ mile	Dishonesty/ Disorder

As an example, from the actions at the crime scene indicating low craft it may be appropriate to infer that the offender would have travelled less than half a mile and would be less than 19 years of age with a limited criminal history. This hypothesis forms the basis of a search within a radius of half a mile for offenders with these background characteristics.

(ii) *Historical Offending Themes and Signature* : Comparing broad themes and specific actions at a crime scene with a suspect's past expressions of the same is more sophisticated than seeking out past convictions of crime types. Thus, an offender's record should reflect themes and signatures. The recording specification allows the offenders unfolding criminal career to be read and predictions or risk assessments made on future behaviour.

(iii) *Suspected Persons* : Searching within the same geographical area for convicted persons who are already suspected of current criminality.

All three processes will identify details of suspects, which are then subjected to further assessment by managers as described earlier.

Target Profiling

The converse of 'Suspect Identification' places the initial focus on the core criminal rather than the crime. A core or target offender is the recidivist who continues to be responsible for serial crime. The psychology of criminal behaviour has presented the concept of consistency and this encourages predictions about where and how an individual offender will behave. Target offenders can be assigned temporal, spatial and criminal theme profiles. By accumulating information about a target offender, an 'Awareness' or 'Action Space' profile can be established. The boundary will be inferred from the offender's base together with previous offending patterns (distance travelled and locations or type of locations), associates, sightings, pubs frequented and reference to the common use of the environment by local people. A hypothetical 'Action Space' or spatial profile is depicted in figure 11.6.

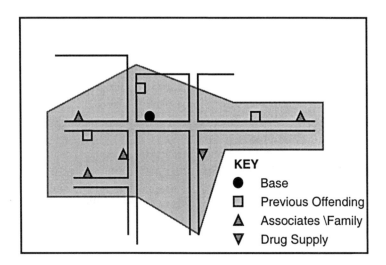

Figure 11.6: A Hypothetical 'Action Space'

The second aspect of the Target Profile is the prediction of criminal behaviour theme. This may be based on previous offending behaviour and/or the assimilation of more recent information of suspected activity. As previously stated, it is not to be expected that a criminal will behave in exactly the same way over prolonged periods, perhaps interspersed with spells of imprisonment.

However, skills, attitudes towards others and the individual's 'mental map' will evolve slowly and this dynamic must be accounted for when searching an offender's 'Action Space' for anticipated behaviours. This approach is applicable to local and travelling criminals - it is simply a matter of scale.

Figure 11.7 depicts the incidence of predicted criminal behaviour within a target's 'Action Space', which may indicate that the subject is active.

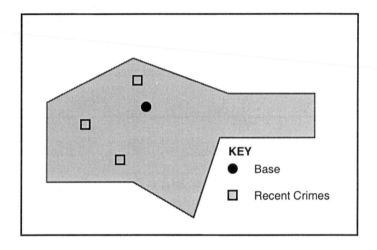

Figure 11.7: Indication of Target Activity within 'Action Space'

It will be recognised that the process of examining recent crimes from the perspective of the offender may add a bias towards inferring that two crimes are linked to that offender. This must be tested by exploring and ruling out other hypotheses.

Crime Analysis in Action

The rules of behaviour which are emerging from psychological research 'strike a chord' for the detective, who has worked a variety of cases without the opportunity to expose 'hunches' to scientific hypothesis testing. The 'rules' are a valuable heuristic device for the analyst who must formalise opinions about a developing series of crimes. The analyst must understand the crimeogenic and environmental backcloth of a specific area and appreciate the operation of criminal networks. This provides the context in which the three interrelated disciplines of Comparative Case Analysis, Suspect Identification and Target Profiling are applied.

Computerised relational databases and geographic information systems will assist these operations; however, it is the method rather than sophisticated tools which is paramount. Technology has been the focus of attention, but, unless valid and reliable algorithms for computing human behaviour can be developed, the computer will remain a tool for storing, retrieving and representing data. It is the application of thinking processes, which will provide the lead today and possibly the algorithm to detect crime tomorrow.

References

Brantingham, P. and Brantingham J. (1981), *Environmental Criminology*, Beverly Hills, CA.: Sage.

Brantingham, P. and Brantingham J. (1993), 'Nodes, Paths and Edges: Considerations on the Complexity of Crime and the Physical Environment', *Journal of Environmental Psychology*, **13**, 3-28.

Canter, D.V. and Alison, L. (1997), *Criminal Detection and the Psychology of Crime*, Aldershot: Dartmouth Press.

Canter, D.V. and Larkin, P. (1993), 'The Environmental Range of Serial Rapists', *Journal of Environmental Psychology*, **13**, 63-69.

Canter, D.V. (1994), *Criminal Shadows*, London: Harper Collins.

Doyle, A.C. (1898), *The Adventures of Sherlock Holmes*, Oxford: Oxford University Press.

Oldfield, R. and Read, T. (1995), 'Local Crime Analysis', *Police Research Group Crime Detection and Prevention Series: Paper 65*, London: Home Office Police Department.

McMurran, M., Hodge, J.E. and Hollin, C.R. (1997), *Addicted to Crime*, London: Wiley and Sons.

Reber, S.R. (1995), *Dictionary of Psychology*, London: Penguin.

Young, J. (1981), 'Thinking Seriously about Crime: Some Models of Criminology', in M. Fitzgerald, G. Mclennan and J. Pawson (eds), *Crime and Society*, London: Routledge.

Appendix A: Content Dictionary of the 35 Crime Scene Variables

1. *Main Thoroughfare*: Where the target premises are located on or within two turnings of a main thoroughfare.

2. *Forced Entry*: Where any form of physical force is employed to breach a secured premise.

3. *Multi-Rooms Searched*: Where more than one room has been entered and searched.

4. *Audio-Visual*: All valuable electrical equipment such as televisions, video recorders/cameras, hi-fi music systems and computer equipment.

5. *Identifiable Property Stolen*: Where the property stolen includes items that the thief is likely to perceive as identifiable by the loser. For example, electrical items with serial number or inscribed jewellery.

6. *Insecurity*: Entry gained by exploiting obvious insecurity. For example, a window or door left ajar. The weakness is essentially created by the householder not the burglar.

7. *Occupied*: Where the offender entered premises whilst one or more residents were present but unaware of the intrusion.

8. *No Search*: No broad search was carried out. Either i) property at specific sites within the premises was targeted (eg. cheque book and cards/cash removed from drawer, no other items or areas searched) or ii) burglar removing only property immediately available at point of entry.

9. *Climbed*: Where access to the premises was achieved by climbing to the entry point either using a ladder or existing fixtures. Usually indicated by entry point above ground level.

10. *Scene Tool*: Instrument used to gain entry was improvised from the burglary scene.

11. *Malicious Damage*: Overt acts of vandalism unnecessary for the commission of property theft such as; damage to property with or without extensive mess, written messages aimed at the householder or smearing the walls.

12. *Facility Use/Abuse*: Behaviours not directly concerned with execution of the burglary that are more comparable to the occupant's use of the

dwelling. Examples: drinking and eating the householder's food in situ; using the toilet.

13. *Forensically Careless*: Leaving any identifying evidence at the scene, typically finger or foot prints.

14. *Secondary Insecurity Exploited*: Where the householder has created an unobvious weakness in security. For example, by shutting but not locking a door or window, by concealing a key or leaving the key with an untrustworthy agent.

15. *Cash*: Theft of any value of currency, notes or coins.

16. *Credit Cards*: Theft of cash instruments such as credit/charge cards, benefit/pension books, cheque books and cheque/debit cards.

17. *Children's*: Theft of property obviously belonging to a child or any items removed from a child's room.

18. *Carrier Taken*: Removal of any low value item to carry stolen goods. For example, a bag, holdall or pillow-slip.

19. *Alcohol*: Removal of any alcoholic liquor.

20. *Over 5 Items Stolen*: Where total separate items stolen exceeds 5.

21. *Value Stolen Over 500 Pounds*: Where the victim's estimation of property stolen exceeds this total.

22. *Antiques/Furniture*: Anything classed as 'antique' except jewellery. All furniture and paintings.

23. *Camera*: Theft of camera equipment (not video cameras) including automatic cameras, lenses, camera cases. Also, theft of optical equipment such as binoculars.

24. *Music*: Theft of audio and video cassettes, compact discs and records.

25. *Clocks*: excluding wristwatches.

26. *Offender Security*: Premises secured by the offender to exclude occupants should they return, by wedging or locking internal/external doors closed.

27. *Curtains Drawn*: Curtains drawn by the burglar to conceal activity.

28. *Prepared Exit*: Point of escape prepared in advance.

29. *Tool Carried*: Where evidence suggested any use of a tool by the offender and that the implement was brought to the scene by the burglar. A 'tool' is defined as any instrument used, specialised or not. For example, glass-cutters to remove a window, a jemmy or plastic card are all 'tools'.

30. *Window*: Where access was gained via a window by force or insecurity.

31. *Objects Strewn*: Property within the dwelling scattered either in pursuance of a search or gratuitously. Despite scattering, property essentially intact and undamaged.

32. *Jewellery*: Removal of one or more items of jewellery, antique or modern.

33. *Watches*: Removal of one or more watches.

34. *Small Electrical*: Any low - medium value, small electrical equipment such as a shaver.

35. *Ornaments*: Removal of decorative or novelty ornaments not considered antique.